The Adventures of Philip vol. II

The Adventures of Philip
Vol. II

by

William Makepeace Thackeray

CAMBRIDGE
SCHOLARS
PUBLISHING

classic texts

The Adventures of Philip Vol. II, by William Makepeace Thackeray

This book in its current typographical format first published 2008 by

Cambridge Scholars Publishing

12 Back Chapman Street, Newcastle upon Tyne, NE6 2XX, UK

British Library Cataloguing in Publication Data
A catalogue record for this book is available from the British Library

ISBN (10): 1-4438-0200-X, ISBN (13): 978-1-4438-0200-0

CONTENTS

CHAPTER XXIV. NEC DULCES AMORES SPERNE, PUER, NEQUE TU CHOREAS

'MY dear,' Mrs. Baynes said to her daughter, 'you are going out a great deal in the world now. You will go to a great number of places where poor Philip cannot hope to be admitted.'

'Not admit Philip, mamma! then I'm sure I don't want to go,' cries the girl.

'Time enough to leave off going to parties when you can't afford it and marry him. When I was a lieutenant's wife, I didn't go to any parties out of the regiment, my dear!'

'Oh, then, I am sure I shall *never* want to go out!' Charlotte declares.

'You fancy he will always stop at home, I dare say. Men are not all so domestic as your papa. Very few love to stop at home like him. Indeed, I may say that I have made his home comfortable. But one thing is clear, my child. Philip can't always expect to go where we go. He is not in the position in life. Recollect, your father is a general officer, C.B., and may be K.C.B. soon, and your mother is a general officer's lady. *We* may go anywhere. I might have gone to the drawing-room at home if I chose. Lady Biggs would have been delighted to present me. Your aunt has been to the drawing-room, and she is only Mrs. Major MacWhirter; and most absurd it was of Mac to let her go. But she rules him in everything, and they have no children. I have, goodness knows! I sacrifice myself for my children. You little know what I deny myself for my children. I said to Lady Biggs, "No, Lady Biggs; my husband may go. He should go. He has his uniform, and it will cost him nothing except a fly and a bouquet for the man who drives; but *I* will not spend money on myself, for the hire of diamonds and feathers, and, though I yield in loyalty to *no* person, I dare say my Sovereign *won't miss* me." And I don't think her Majesty did. She has other things to think of besides Mrs. General Baynes, I suppose. She is a mother, and can appreciate a mother's sacrifices for her children.'

If I have not hitherto given you detailed reports of Mrs. General Baynes's conversation, I don't think, my esteemed reader, you will be very angry.

'Now, child,' the General's lady continued, 'let me warn you not to talk much to Philip about those places to which you go without him, and to which his position in life does not allow of his coming. Hide anything from him? Oh dear, no! Only for his own good, you understand. I don't tell everything to your papa. I should only worrit him and vex him. When anything will please him and make him happy, *then* I tell him. And about Philip? Philip, I must say it, my dear—I must as a mother say it—has his faults. He is an *envious* man. Don't look shocked. He thinks very well of himself; and having been a great deal spoiled, and made too much of in his unhappy father's time, he is so proud and haughty that he *forgets his position,* and thinks he ought to live with the highest society. Had Lord Ringwood left him a fortune, as Philip *led us to expect* when we gave our consent to this most unlucky match—for that my dear child should marry a beggar *is* most unlucky and most deplorable; I can't help saying so, Charlotte,—if I were on my deathbed I couldn't help saying so; and I wish with all my heart we had never seen or heard of him.— There! Don't go off in one of your tantrums! What was I saying, pray? I say that Philip is in no position, or rather in a very humble one, which—a mere newspaper-writer and a subaltern too—everybody acknowledges it to be. And if he hears us talking about our parties to which we have a right to go—to which you have a right to go with your mother, a general officer's lady—why, he'll be offended. He won't like to hear about them and think he can't be invited; and you had better not talk about them at all, or about the people you meet and dance with. At Mrs. Hely's you may dance with Lord Headbury, the ambassador's son. And if you tell Philip he will be offended. He will say that you boast about it. When I was only a lieutenant's wife at Barrackpore, Mrs. Captain Capers used to go to Calcutta to the Government House balls. I didn't go. But I was offended, and I used to say that Flora Capers gave herself airs, and was always boasting of her intimacy with the Marchioness of Hastings. We don't like our equals to be better off than ourselves. Mark my words. And if you talk to Philip about the people whom you meet in society, and whom he can't from his unfortunate station expect to know, you will offend him. That was why I nudged you to-day when you were going on about Mr. Hely. Anything so absurd! I saw Philip getting angry at once, and biting his moustaches, as he always does when he is angry—and swears quite out loud—so vulgar! There! you are going to be angry again, my love; I never saw anything like you! Is this my Charly who never was angry? I know the world, dear, and you don't. Look at me, how I manage your papa, and I tell you don't talk to Philip about things which offend him! Now, dearest, kiss your poor old mother who loves you. Go upstairs and bathe your eyes, and come down happy to dinner.' And at dinner Mrs. General Baynes was uncommonly gracious to Philip: and when gracious she was especially odious to Philip, whose magnanimous nature accommodated itself ill to the wheedling artifices of an ill-bred old woman.

Following this wretched mother's advice, my poor Charlotte spoke scarcely at all to Philip of the parties to which she went, and the amusements which she enjoyed without him. I dare say Mrs. Baynes was quite happy in thinking that she was 'guiding' her child rightly. As if a coarse woman, because she is mean, and greedy, and hypocritical, and fifty years old, has a right to lead a guileless nature into wrong! Ah! if some of us old folks were to go to school to our children, I am sure, madam, it would do us a great deal of good. There is a fund of good sense and honourable feeling about my great-grandson Tommy, which is more valuable than all his grandpapa's experience and knowledge of the world. Knowledge of the world forsooth! Compromise, selfishness modified, and double dealing. Tom disdains a lie: when he wants a peach, he roars for it. If his mother wishes to go to a party, she coaxes, and wheedles, and manages, and smirks, and curtseys for months, in order to get her end; takes twenty rebuffs, and comes up to the scratch again smiling;—and this woman is for ever lecturing her daughters, and preaching to her sons upon virtue, honesty, and moral behaviour!

Mrs. Hely's little party at the Hôtel de la Terrasse was very pleasant and bright; and Miss Charlotte enjoyed it, although her swain was not present. But Philip was pleased that his little Charlotte should be happy. She beheld with wonderment Parisian duchesses, American millionaires, dandies from the embassies, deputies and peers of France with large stars and wigs like papa. She gaily described her party to Philip; described, that is to say, everything but her own success, which was undoubted. There were many beauties at Mrs. Hely's, but nobody fresher or prettier. The Miss Blacklocks retired very early and in the worst possible temper. Prince Slyboots did not in the least heed their going away. His thoughts were all fixed upon little Charlotte. Charlotte's mamma saw the impression which the girl made, and was filled with a hungry joy. Good-natured Mrs. Hely complimented her on her daughter. 'Thank God, she is as good as she is pretty,' said the mother, I am sure speaking seriously this time, regarding her daughter. Prince Slyboots danced with scarce anybody else. He raised a perfect whirlwind of compliments round about Charlotte. She was quite a simple person, and did not understand one-tenth part of what he said to her. He strewed her path with roses of poesy: he scattered garlands of sentiment before her all the way from the antechamber downstairs, and so to the fly which was in waiting to take her and parents home to the boarding-house. 'By George, Charlotte, I think you have smitten that fellow,' cries the General, who was infinitely amused by young Hely—his raptures, his affectations, his long hair, and what Baynes called his low dress. A slight white tape and a ruby button confined Hely's neck. His hair waved over his shoulders. Baynes had never seen such a specimen. At the mess of the stout 120th, the lads talked of their dogs, horses, and sport. A young civilian, smattering in poetry, chattering in a dozen languages, scented, smiling, perfectly at ease with himself and the world, was a novelty to the old officer.

And now the Queen's birthday arrived—and that it may arrive for many scores of years yet to come is, I am sure, the prayer of all of us— and with the birthday his Excellency Lord Estridge's grand annual fête in honour of his sovereign. A card for their ball was left at Madame Smolensk's, for General, Mrs., and Miss Baynes; and no doubt Monsieur Slyboots Walsingham Hely was the artful agent by whom the invitation was forwarded. Once more the General's veteran uniform came out from the tin-box, with its dingy epaulets and little cross and ribbon. His wife urged on him strongly the necessity of having a new wig, wigs being very cheap and good at Paris; but Baynes said a new wig would make his old coat look very shabby, and a new uniform would cost more money than he would like to afford. So shabby he went *de cap à pied,* with a moulting feather, a threadbare suit, a tarnished wig, and a worn-out lace, *sibi constans*. Boots, trousers, sash, coat, were all old and worse for wear, and 'faith,' says he, 'my face follows suit.' A brave silent man was Baynes; with a twinkle of humour in his lean wrinkled face.

And if General Baynes was shabbily attired at the Embassy ball, I think I know a friend of mine who was shabby too. In the days of his prosperity, Mr. Philip was *parens cultor et infrequens* of balls, routs, and ladies' company. Perhaps because his father was angered at Philip's neglect of his social advantages and indifference as to success in the world, Philip was the more neglectful and indifferent. The elder's comedy-smiles, and solemn hypocritical politeness caused scorn and revolt on the part of the younger man. Philip despised the humbug, and the world to which such humbug could be welcome. He kept aloof from tea-parties then: his evening-dress clothes served him for a long time. I cannot say how old his dress-coat was at the time of which we are writing. But he had been in the habit of respecting that garment and considering it new and handsome for many years past. Meanwhile the coat had shrunk, or its wearer had grown stouter; and his grand embroidered, embossed, illuminated, carved and gilt velvet dress waistcoat, too, had narrowed, had become absurdly tight and short, and I dare say was the laughing-stock of many of Philip's acquaintances, whilst he himself, poor simple fellow, was fancying that it was a most splendid article of apparel. You know in the Palais Royal they hang out the most splendid reach-me-down dressing-gowns, waistcoats, and so forth. 'No,' thought Philip, coming out of his cheap dining-house, and swaggering along the arcades, and looking at the tailors' shops, with his hands in his pockets. 'My brown velvet dress waistcoat with the gold sprigs, which I had made at college, is a much more tasty thing than these gaudy ready-made articles. And my coat is old, certainly, but the brass buttons are still very bright and handsome, and, in fact, it is a most becoming and gentlemanlike thing.' And under this delusion the honest fellow dressed himself in his old clothes, lighted a pair of candles, and looked at himself with satisfaction in the looking-glass, drew on a pair of cheap gloves which he had bought, walked by the Quays, and over the Deputies' Bridge, across the Place Louis XV., and strutted up the Faubourg St. Honoré to the Hotel of the British Embassy. A half-mile *queue* of carriages was formed along the street, and of course the entrance to the hotel was magnificently illuminated.

A plague on those cheap gloves! Why had not Philip paid three francs for a pair of gloves, instead of twenty-nine sous? Mrs. Baynes had found a capital cheap glove shop, whither poor Phil had gone in the simplicity of his heart; and now as he went in under the grand illuminated *porte-cochère,* Philip saw that the gloves had given way at the thumbs, and that his hands appeared through the rents, as red as raw beefsteaks. It is wonderful how red hands will look through holes in white gloves. 'And there's that hole in my boot, too,' thought Phil; but he had put a little ink over the seam, and so the rent was imperceptible. The coat and waistcoat were tight, and of a past age. Never mind. The chest was broad, the arms were muscular and long, and Phil's face, in the midst of a halo of fair hair and flaming whiskers, looked brave, honest, and handsome. For a while his eyes wandered fiercely and restlessly all about the room from group to group; but now—ah! now—they were settled. They had met another pair of eyes, which lighted up with glad welcome when they beheld him. Two young cheeks mantled with a sweet blush. These were Charlotte's cheeks: and hard by them were mamma's, of a very different colour. But Mrs. General Baynes had a knowing turban on, and a set of garnets round her old neck, like gooseberries set in gold.

They admired the rooms: they heard the names of the great folks who arrived, and beheld many famous personages. They made their curtseys to the ambassadress. Confusion! With a great rip, the thumb of one of those cheap gloves of Philip's parts company from the rest of the glove, and he is obliged to wear it crumpled up in his hand: a dreadful mishap—for he is going to dance with Charlotte, and he will have to give his hand to the *vis-à-vis.*

Who comes up smiling, with a low neck, with waving curls and whiskers, pretty little hands exquisitely gloved, and tiny feet? 'Tis Hely Walsingham, lightest in the dance. Most affably does Mrs. General Baynes greet the young fellow. Very brightly and happily do Charlotte's eyes glance towards her favourite partner. It is certain that poor Phil can't hope at all to dance like Hely. 'And see what nice neat feet and hands he has got,' says Mrs. Baynes. 'Comme il est bien ganté! A gentleman ought to be always well gloved.'

'Why did you send me to the twenty-nine-sous shop?' says poor Phil, looking at his tattered hand-shoes and red obstrusive thumb.

'Oh, you!'—(here Mrs. Baynes shrugs her yellow old shoulders). *'Your* hands would burst through any gloves! How do you do, Mr. Hely? Is your mamma here? Of course she is! What a delightful party she gave us! The dear ambassadress looks quite unwell—most pleasing manners, I am sure; Lord Estridge, what a perfect gentleman!'

The Bayneses were just come. For what dance was Miss Baynes disengaged? ' As many as ever you like!' cries Charlotte, who, in fact, called Hely her little dancing-master, and never thought of him except as a partner. 'Oh, too much happiness! Oh, that this could last for ever!' sighed Hely, after a waltz, polka, mazurka, I know not what, and fixing on Charlotte the full blaze of his beauteous blue eyes. 'For ever?' cries Charlotte, laughing. 'I'm very fond of dancing, indeed; and you dance beautifully; but I don't know that I should like to dance for ever.' Ere the words are over, he is whirling her round the room again. His little feet fly with surprising agility. His hair floats behind him. He scatters odours as he spins. The handkerchief with which he fans his pale brow is like a cloudy film of muslin—and poor old Philip sees with terror that *his* pocket-handkerchief has got three great holes in it. His nose and one eye appeared through one of the holes while Phil was wiping his forehead. It was very hot. He was very hot. He was hotter, though standing still, than young Hely who was dancing. 'He! he! I compliment you on your gloves, and your handkerchief, I'm sure,' sniggers Mrs. Baynes, with a toss of her turban. Has it not been said that a bull is a strong, courageous, and noble animal, but a bull in a china-shop is not in his place? 'There you go. Thank you! I wish you'd go somewhere else,' cries Mrs. Baynes, in a fury. Poor Philip's foot has just gone through her flounce. How red is he! how much hotter than ever! There go Hely and Charlotte, whirling round like two opera-dancers! Philip grinds his teeth, he buttons his coat across his chest. How very tight it feels! How savagely his eyes glare! Do young men still look savage and solemn at balls? An ingenuous young Englishman ought to do that duty of dancing, of course. Society calls upon him. But I doubt whether he ought to look cheerful during the performance, or flippantly engage in so grave a matter.

As Charlotte's sweet round face beamed smiles upon Philip over Hely's shoulders, it looked so happy that he never thought of grudging her her pleasure: and happy he might have remained in this contemplation, regarding not the circle of dancers who were galloping and whirling on at their usual swift rate, but her, who was the centre of all joy and pleasure for him;—when suddenly a shrill voice was heard behind him, crying, 'Get out of the way, hang you!' and suddenly there bounced against him Ringwood Twysden, pulling Miss Flora Trotter round the room, one of the most powerful and intrepid dancers of that season at Paris. They hurtled past Philip; they shot him forward against a pillar. He heard a screech, an oath, and another loud laugh from Twysden, and beheld the scowls of Miss Trotter as that rapid creature bumped at length into a place of safety.

I told you about Philip's coat. It was very tight. The daylight had long been struggling to make an entry at the seams. As he staggered up against the wall, crack! went a great hole at his back; and crack! one of his gold buttons came off, leaving a rent in his chest. It was in those days when gold buttons still lingered on the breasts of some brave men, and we have said simple Philip still thought his coat a fine one.

There was not only a rent of the seam, there was not only a burst button, but there was also a rip in Philip's rich cut-velvet waistcoat, with the gold sprigs, which he thought so handsome—a great heartrending scar. What was to be done? Retreat was necessary. He told Miss Charlotte of the hurt he had received, whose face wore a very comical look of pity at his misadventure—he covered part of his wound with his gibus hat—and he thought he would try and make his way out by the garden of the hotel, which, of course, was illuminated, and bright, and crowded, but not so very bright and crowded as the saloons, galleries, supper-rooms, and halls of gilded light in which the company, for the most part, assembled.

So our poor wounded friend wandered into the garden, over which the moon was shining with the most blank indifference at the riddling, feasting, and particoloured lamps. He says that his mind was soothed by the aspect of yonder placid moon and twinkling stars, and that he had altogether forgotten his trumpery little accident and torn coat and waistcoat: but I doubt about the entire truth of this statement, for there have been some occasions when he, Mr. Philip, has mentioned the subject, and owned that he was mortified and in a rage.

Well. He went into the garden: and was calming himself by contemplating the stars, when, just by that fountain where there is Pradier's little statue of—Moses in the bulrushes, let us say—round which there was a beautiful row of illuminated lamps, lighting up a great coronal of flowers, which my dear readers are at liberty to select and arrange according to their own exquisite taste;—near this little fountain he found three gentlemen talking together.

The high voice of one Philip could hear, and knew from old days. Ringwood Twysden, Esquire, always liked to talk and to excite himself with other persons' liquor. He had been drinking the Sovereign's health with great assiduity, I suppose, and was exceedingly loud and happy. With Ringwood was Mr. Woolcomb, whose countenance the lamps lit up in a fine lurid manner, and whose eyeballs gleamed in the twilight: and the third of the group was our young friend Mr. Lowndes.

'I owed him one, you see, Lowndes,' said Mr. Ringwood Twysden. 'I hate the fellow! Hang him, always did! I saw the great hulkin' brute standin' there. Couldn't help myself. Give you my honour, couldn't help myself. I just drove Miss Trotter at him—sent her elbow well into him, and spun him up against the wall. The buttons cracked off the beggar's coat, begad! What business had he there, hang him? Gad, sir, he made a cannon off an old woman in blue, and went into—'

Here Mr. Ringwood's speech came to an end: for his cousin stood before him, grim and biting his moustache.

'Hullo!' piped the other. 'Who wants you to overhear my conversation? Dammy, I say! I—'

Philip put out that hand with the torn glove. The glove was in a dreadful state of disruption now. He worked the hand well into his kinsman's neck, and twisting Ringwood round into a proper position, brought that poor old broken boot so to bear upon the proper quarter, that Ringwood was discharged into the little font, and lighted amidst the flowers, and the water, and the oil-lamps, and made a dreadful mess and splutter amongst them. And as for Philip's coat, it was torn worse than ever.

I don't know how many of the brass buttons had revolted and parted company from the poor old cloth, which cracked and split, and tore under the agitation of that beating angry bosom. I blush as I think of Mr. Firmin in this ragged state, a great rent all across his back, and his prostrate enemy lying howling in the water, amidst the spluttering crashing oil-lamps at his feet. When Cinderella quitted her first ball, just after the clock struck twelve, we all know how shabby she looked. Philip was a still more disreputable object when he slunk away. I don't know by what side door Mr. Lowndes eliminated him. He also benevolently took charge of Philip's kinsman and antagonist Mr. Ringwood Twysden. Mr. Twysden's hands, coat-tails, etc., were very much singed and scalded by the oil, and cut by the broken glass, which was all extracted at the Beaujon Hospital, but not without much suffering on the part of the patient. But though young Lowndes spoke up for Philip, in describing the scene (I fear not without laughter), his Excellency caused Mr. Firmin's name to be erased from his party lists: and I am sure no sensible man will defend Philip's conduct for a moment.

Of this lamentable fracas which occurred in the hotel garden, Miss Baynes and her parents had no knowledge for a while. Charlotte was too much occupied with her dancing, which she pursued with all her might; papa was at cards with some sober male and female veterans, and mamma was looking with delight at her daughter, whom the young gentlemen of many embassies were charmed to choose for a partner. When Lord Headbury, Lord Estridge's son, was presented to Miss Baynes, her mother was so elated that she was ready to dance too. I do not envy Mrs. Major MacWhirter, at Tours, the perusal of that immense manuscript in which her sister recorded the events of the ball. Here was Charlotte, beautiful, elegant, accomplished, *admired everywhere,* with young men, young *noblemen* of immense property and expectations, *wild about her;* and engaged by a promise to a rude, ragged, *presumptuous,* ill-bred young man, *without a penny in the world*—wasn't it provoking? Ah, poor Philip! How that little sour yellow mother-in-law elect did scowl at him when he came with rather a shame-faced look to pay his duty to his sweetheart on the day after the ball. Mrs. Baynes had caused her daughter to dress with extra smartness, had forbidden the poor child to go out, and coaxed her, and wheedled her, and dressed her with I know not what ornaments of her own, with a fond expectation that Lord Headbury, that the yellow young Spanish *attaché,* that the sprightly Prussian secretary, and Walsingham Hely, Charlotte's partners at the ball, would certainly call; and the only equipage that appeared at Madame Smolensk's gate was a hack cab, which drove up at evening, and out of which poor Philip's well-known tattered boots came striding. Such a fond mother as Mrs. Baynes may well have been out of humour.

As for Philip, he was unusually shy and modest. He did not know in what light his friends would regard his escapade of the previous evening. He had been sitting at home all the morning in state, and in company with a Polish colonel, who lived in his hotel, and whom Philip had selected to be his second in case the battle of the previous night should have any suite. He had left that colonel in company with a bag of tobacco and an order for unlimited beer, whilst he himself ran up to catch a glimpse of his beloved. The Bayneses had not heard of the battle of the previous night. They were full of the ball, of Lord Estridge's affability, of the Golconda Ambassador's diamonds, of the appearance of the Royal princes who honoured the fête, of the most fashionable Paris talk in a word. Philip was scolded, snubbed, and coldly received by mamma; but he was used to that sort of treatment, and greatly relieved by finding that she was unacquainted with his own disorderly behaviour. He did not tell Charlotte about the quarrel: a knowledge of it might alarm the little maiden; and so for once our friend was discreet, and held his tongue.

But if he had any influence with the editor of *Galignani's Messenger,* why did he not entreat the conductors of that admirable journal to forego all mention of the fracas at the Embassy ball? Two days after the fête, I am sorry to say, there appeared a paragraph in the paper narrating the circumstances of the fight. And the guilty Philip found a copy of that paper on the table before Mrs. Baynes and the General when he came to the Champs Elysées according to his wont. Behind that paper sat Major-General Baynes, C.B., looking confused, and beside him his lady frowning like Rhadamanthus. But no Charlotte was in the room.

CHAPTER XXV. INFANDI DOLORES

PHILIP'S heart beat very quickly at seeing this grim pair, and the guilty newspaper before them, on which Mrs. Baynes's lean right hand was laid. 'So, sir,' she cried, 'you still honour us with your company: after distinguishing yourself as you did the night before last. Fighting and boxing like a porter at his Excellency's ball. It's disgusting! I have no other word for it: disgusting!' And here I suppose she nudged the General, or gave him some look or signal by which he knew he was to come into action; for Baynes straightway advanced and delivered his fire.

'Faith, sir, more bub-ub-blackguard conduct I never heard of in my life! That's the only word for it: the only word for it,' cries Baynes,

'The General knows what blackguard conduct is, and yours is that conduct, Mr. Firmin! It is all over the town: is talked of everywhere: will be in all the newspapers. When his Lordship heard of it, he was furious. Never, never, will you be admitted into the Embassy again, after disgracing yourself as you have done,' cries the lady.

'Disgracing yourself, that's the word. And disgraceful your conduct was, begad!' cries the officer second in command.

'You don't know my provocation,' pleaded poor Philip. 'As I came up to him Twysden was boasting that he had struck me—and—and laughing at me.'

'And a pretty figure you were to come to a ball. Who could help laughing, sir?'

'He bragged of having insulted me, and I lost my temper, and struck him in return. The thing is done and can't be helped,' growled Philip.

'Strike a little man before ladies! Very brave indeed!' cries the lady.

'Mrs. Baynes!'

'I call it cowardly. In the army we consider it cowardly to quarrel before ladies,' continues Mrs. General B.

'I have waited at home for two days, to see if he wanted any more,' groaned Philip.

'Oh, yes! After insulting and knocking a little man down, you want to murder him! And you call that the conduct of a Christian— the conduct of a gentleman!'

'The conduct of a ruffian, by George!' says General Baynes.

'It was prudent of you to choose a very little man, and to have the ladies within hearing!' continues Mrs. Baynes. 'Why, I wonder you haven't beaten my dear children next. Don't you, General, wonder he has not knocked down our poor boys? They are quite small. And it is evident that ladies being present is no hindrance to Mr. Firmin's *boxing-matches.*'

'The conduct is gross and unworthy of a gentleman,' reiterates the General.

'You hear what that man says—that old man, who never says an unkind word? That veteran, who has been in twenty battles, and never struck a man before women yet? Did you, Charles? *He* has given you his opinion. He has called you a name which I won't soil my lips with repeating, but which you deserve. And do you suppose, sir, that I will give my blessed child to a man who has acted as you have acted, and been called a—? Charles! General! I will go to my grave rather than see my daughter given up to such a man!'

'Good Heavens!' said Philip, his knees trembling under him. 'You don't mean to say that you intend to go from your word, and—'

'Oh! you threaten about money, do you? Because your father was a cheat, you intend to try and make us suffer, do you?' shrieks the lady. 'A man who strikes a little man before ladies will commit any act of cowardice, I dare say. And if you wish to beggar my family, because your father was a rogue—'

'My dear!' interposes the General.

'Wasn't he a rogue, Baynes? Is there any denying it? Haven't you said so a hundred and a hundred times? A nice family to marry into! No, Mr. Firmin! You may insult me as you please. You may strike little men before ladies. You may lift your groat wicked hand against that poor old man, in one of your tipsy fits: but I know a mother's love, a mother's duty—and I desire that we see you no more.'

'Great Powers!' cries Philip, aghast. 'You don't mean to—to separate me from Charlotte, General? I have your word. You encouraged me. I shall break my heart. I'll go down on my knees to that fellow. I'll—oh!—you don't mean what you say!' And, scared and sobbing, the poor fellow clasped his strong hands together, and appealed to the General.

Baynes was under his wife's eye. 'I think,' he said, 'your conduct has been confoundedly bad, disorderly, and ungentlemanlike. You can't support my child, if you marry her. And if you have the least spark of honour in you, as you say you have, it is you, Mr. Firmin, who will break off the match, and release the poor child from certain misery. By George, sir, how is a man who fights and quarrels in a nobleman's ball-room to get on in the world? How is a man, who can't afford a decent coat to his back, to keep a wife? The more I have known you, the more I have felt that the engagement would bring misery upon my child! Is that what you want? A man of honour—' ('*Honour!*' in italics, from Mrs. Baynes.)

'Hush, my dear!—A man of spirit would give her up, sir. What have you to offer but beggary, by George? Do you want my girl to come home to your lodgings, and mend your clothes?'

'I think I put that point pretty well, Bunch my boy,' said the General, talking of the matter afterwards. 'I hit him there, sir.'

The old soldier did indeed strike his adversary there with a vital stab. Philip's coat, no doubt, was ragged, and his purse but light. He had sent money to his father out of his small stock. There wore one or two servants in the old house in Parr Street who had been left without their wages, and a part of these debts Philip had paid. He knew his own violence of temper, and his unruly independence. He thought very humbly of his talents, and often doubted of his capacity to get on in the world. In his less hopeful moods, he trembled to think that he might be bringing poverty and unhappiness upon his dearest little maiden, for whom he would joyfully have sacrificed his blood, his life. Poor Philip sank back sickening and fainting almost under Baynes's words.

'You'll let me—you'll let me see her?' he gasped out.

'She's unwell. She is in her bed. She can't appear to-day!' cried the mother.

'Oh, Mrs. Baynes! I must—I must see her,' Philip said; and fairly broke out in a sob of pain.

'This is the man that strikes men before women!' said Mrs. Barnes. 'Very courageous, certainly!'

'By George, Eliza!' the General cried out, starting up, 'it's too bad—'

'Infirm of purpose, give me the daggers!' Philip yelled out, whilst describing the scene to his biographer in after days. 'Macbeth would never have done the murders but for that little quiet woman at his side. When the Indian prisoners are killed, the squaws always invent the worst tortures. You should have seen that fiend and her livid smile, as she was drilling her gimlets into my heart. I don't know how I offended her, I tried to like her, sir. I had humbled myself before her, I went on her errands. I played cards with her. I sat and listened to her dreadful stories about Barrackpore and the Governor-General. I wallowed in the dust before her, and she hated me, I can see her face now: her cruel yellow face, and her sharp teeth and her grey eyes. It was the end of August, and pouring a storm that day, I suppose my poor child was cold and suffering upstairs, for I heard the poking of a fire in her little room. When I hear a fire poked overhead now—twenty years after—the whole thing comes back to me; and I suffer over again that infernal agony. Were I to live a thousand years, I could not forgive her. I never did her a wrong, but I can't forgive her. Ah, my Heaven, how that woman tortured me!'

'I think I know one or two similar instances,' said Mr. Firmin's biographer.

'You are always speaking ill of women,' said Mr. Firmin's biographer's wife.

'No, thank Heaven!' said the gentleman. 'I think I know some of whom I never thought or spoke a word of evil. My dear, will yon give Philip some more tea?' and with this the gentleman's narrative is resumed.

The rain was beating down the avenue as Philip went into the street He looked up at Charlotte's window: but there was no sign. There was a flicker of a fire there. The poor girl had the fever, and was shuddering in her little room, weeping and sobbing on Madame Smolensk's shoulder. 'Que c'était pitié à voir,' Madame said. Her mother had told her she must break from Philip; had invented and spoken a hundred calumnies against him; declared that he never cared for her; that he had loose principles, and was for ever haunting theatre* and bad company, 'It's not true, mother, it's not true!' the little girl had cried, flaming up in revolt for a moment: but she soon subsided in tears and misery, utterly broken by the thought of her calamity. Then her father had been brought to her, who had been made to belief some of the stories against poor Philip, and who was commanded his wife to impress them upon the girl. And Baynes tried to obey orders; but he was scared and cruelly pained by the sight of his little maiden's grief and suffering. He attempted a weak expostulation, and began a speech or two. But his heart failed him. He retreated behind his wife. *She* never hesitated in speech or resolution, and her language became more bitter as her ally faltered. Philip was a drunkard; Philip was a prodigal; Philip was a frequenter of dissolute haunts and loose companions. She had the best authority for what she said. Was not a mother anxious for the welfare of her own child? ('Begad, you don't suppose your own mother would do anything that was not for your welfare, now?' broke in the General feebly.) 'Do you think if he had not been drunk he would have ventured to commit such an atrocious outrage as that at the Embassy? And do you suppose I want a drunkard and a beggar to marry my daughter? Your ingratitude, Charlotte, is horrible!' cries mamma. And poor Philip, charged with drunkenness, had dined for seventeen sous, with a carafon of beer, and had counted on a supper that night by little Charlotte's side: so, while the child lay sobbing on her bed, the mother stood over her, and lashed her. For General Baynes,—a brave man, a kind-hearted man,—to have to look on whilst this torture was inflicted, must have been a hard duty. He could not eat the boarding-house dinner, though he took his place at the table at the sound of the dismal bell. Madame herself was not present at the meal; and you know poor Charlotte's place was vacant. Her father went upstairs, and paused by her bedroom door, and listened. He heard murmurs within, and Madame's voice, as he stumbled at the door, cried harshly, 'Qui est là?' He entered, Madame was sitting on the bed, with Charlotte's head on her lap. The thick brown tresses were falling over the child's white night-dress, and she lay almost motionless, and sobbing freely. 'Ah, it is you, General!' said Madame. 'You have done a pretty work, sir!' 'Mamma says, won't you take something, Charlotte dear?' faltered the old man. 'Will you leave her tranquil?' said Madame, with her deep voice. The father retreated. When Madame went out presently to get that panacea, *une tasse de thé,* for her poor little friend, she found the old gentleman seated on a portmanteau at his door. 'Is she—is she a little better now?' he sobbed out. Madame shrugged her shoulders, and looked down on the veteran with superb scorn. 'Vous n'êtes qu'un poltron, Général!' she said, and swept downstairs. Baynes was beaten indeed. He was suffering horrible pain. He was quite unmanned, and tears were trickling down his old cheeks as he sat wretchedly there in the dark. His wife did not leave the table as long as dinner and dessert lasted. She read *Galignani* resolutely afterwards. She told the children not to make a noise, as their sister was upstairs with a bad headache. But she revoked that statement as it were (as she revoked at cards presently), by asking the Miss Bolderos to play one of their duets.

I wonder whether Philip walked up and down before the house that night? Ah! it was a dismal night for all of them: a racking pain, a cruel sense of shame, throbbed under Baynes's cotton tassel; and as for Mrs. Baynes, I hope there was not much rest or comfort under *her* old nightcap. Madame passed the greater part of the night in a great chair in Charlotte's bedroom, where the poor child heard the hours toll one after the other, and found no comfort in the dreary rising of the dawn.

At a very early hour of the dismal rainy morning, what made poor little Charlotte fling her arms round Madame, and cry out, 'Ah, que je vous aime! ah, que vous êtes bonne, Madame!' and smile almost happily through her tears? In the first place, Madame went to Charlotte's dressing-table, whence she took a pair of scissors. Then the little maid sat up on her bed, with her brown hair clustering over her shoulders; and Madame took a lock of it, and cut a thick curl; and kissed poor little Charlotte's red eyes; and laid her pale cheek on the pillow, and carefully covered her; and bade her, with many tender words, to go to sleep. 'If you are very good, and will go to sleep, he shall have it in half-an-hour,' Madame said. 'And as I go downstairs, I will tell Françoise to have some tea ready for you when you ring.' And this promise, and the thought of what Madame was going to do, comforted Charlotte in her misery. And with many fond fond prayers for Philip, and consoled by thinking, 'Now she must have gone the greater part of the way; now she must be with him; now he knows I will never never love any but him,' she fell asleep at length on her moistened pillow: and was smiling in her sleep, and I dare say dreaming of Philip, when the noise of the fall of a piece of furniture roused her, and she awoke out of her dream to see the grim old mother, in her white nightcap and white dressing-gown, standing by her side.

Never mind. 'She has seen him now. She has told him now,' was the child's very first thought as her eyes fairly opened. 'He knows that I never never will think of any but him.' She felt as if she was actually there in Philip's room, speaking herself to him; murmuring vows which her fond lips had whispered many and many a time to her lover. And now he knew she would never break them, she was consoled and felt more courage.

'You have had some sleep, Charlotte?' asks Mrs. Baynes. 'Yes, I have been asleep, mamma.' As she speaks, she feels under the pillow a little locket containing— what? I suppose a scrap of Mr. Philip's lank hair.

'I hope you are in a less wicked frame of mind than when I left you last night,' continues the matron. ,

'Was I wicked for loving Philip? Then I am wicked still, mamma!' cries the child, sitting up in her bed. And she clutches that little lock of hair which nestles under her pillow.

'What nonsense, child! This is what you get out of your stupid novels. I tell you he does not think about you. He is quite a reckless careless libertine.'

'Yes, so reckless and careless that we owe him the bread we eat. He doesn't think of me! Doesn't he? Ah—' Here she paused as a clock in a neighbouring chamber began to strike. 'Now,' she thought, 'he has got my message!' A smile dawned over her face. She sank back on her pillow, turning her head from her mother. She kissed the locket and murmured: 'Not think of me! Don't you, don't you, my dear!' She did not heed the woman by her side, hear her voice, or for a moment seem aware of her presence. Charlotte was away in Philip's room; she saw him talking with her messenger; heard his voice so deep and so sweet; knew that the promises he had spoken he never would break. With gleaming eyes and flushing cheeks she looked at her mother, her enemy. She held her talisman locket and pressed it to her heart. No, she would never be untrue to him! No, he would never never desert her! And as Mrs. Baynes looked at the honest indignation beaming in the child's face, she read Charlotte's revolt, defiance, perhaps victory. The meek child who never before had questioned an order, or formed a wish which she would not sacrifice at her mother's order, was now in arms asserting independence. But I should think mamma is not going to give up the command after a single act of revolt; and that she will try more attempts than one to cajole or coerce her rebel.

Meanwhile let Fancy leave the talisman locket nestling on Charlotte's little heart (in which soft shelter methinks it were pleasant to linger). Let her wrap a shawl round her, and affix to her feet a pair of stout goloshes; let her walk rapidly through the muddy Champs Elysées, where, in this inclement season, only a few policemen and artisans are to be found moving. Let her pay a halfpenny at the Pont des Invalides, and so march stoutly along the quays, by the Chamber of Deputies, where as yet deputies assemble: and trudge along the river side, until she reaches Seine Street, into which, as you all know, the Rue Poussin debouches. This was the road brave Madame Smolensk took on a gusty, rainy, autumn morning, and on foot, for five-franc pieces were scarce with the good woman. Before the Hôtel Poussin *(ah, qu'on y était bien à vingt ans!)* is a little painted wicket which opens, ringing, and then there is the passage, you know, with the stair leading to the upper regions, to Monsieur Philippe's room, which is on the first floor, as is that of Bouchard, the painter, who has his atelier over the way. A bad painter is Bouchard, but a worthy friend, a cheery companion, a modest amiable gentleman. And a rare good fellow is Laberge of the second floor, the poet from Carcassonne, who pretends to be studying law, but whose heart is with the Muses, and whose talk is of Victor Hugo and Alfred de Musset, whose verses he will repeat to all comers.

Near Laberge (I think I have heard Philip say) lived Escasse, a Southern man too—a capitalist—a clerk in a bank, *quoi!*—whose apartment was decorated sumptuously with his own furniture, who had Spanish wine and sausages in cupboards, and a bag of dollars for a friend in need. Is Escasse alive still? Philip Firmin wonders, and that old Colonel, who lived on the same floor, and who had been a prisoner in England? What wonderful descriptions that Colonel Dujarret had of *les Meess Anglaises* and their singularities of dress and behaviour! Though conquered and a prisoner, what a conqueror and enslaver he was, when in our country! You see, in his rough way, Philip used to imitate these people to his friends, and we almost fancied we could see the hotel before us. It was very clean; it was very cheap; it was very dark; it was very cheerful;—capital coffee and bread-and-butter for breakfast for fifteen sous; capital bedroom *au premier* for thirty francs a month—dinner if you would for I forget how little, and a merry talk round the pipes and the grog afterwards—the grog, or the modest *eau sucrée*. Here Colonel Dujarrot recorded his victories over both sexes. Here Colonel Tymowski sighed over his enslaved Poland. Tymowski was the second who was to act for Philip, in case the Ringwood Twysden affair should have come to any violent conclusion. Here Laberge bawled poetry to Philip, who no doubt in his turn confided to the young Frenchman his own hopes and passion; Deep into the night he would sit talking of his love, of her goodness, of her beauty, of her innocence, of her dreadful mother, of her good old father. *Que sais-je?* Have we not said that when this man had anything on his mind, straightway he bellowed forth his opinions to the universe? Philip, away from his love, would roar out her praises for hours and hours to Laberge, until the candles burned down, until the hour for rest was come and could be delayed no longer. Then he would hie to bed with a prayer for her; and the very instant ho awoke begin to think of her and bless her, and thank God for her love. Poor as Mr. Philip was, yet as the possessor of health, content, honour, and that priceless pure jewel the girl's love, *I* think we will not pity him much; though, on the night when he received his dismissal from Mrs. Baynes, he must have passed an awful time, to be sure. Toss, Philip, on your bed of pain, and doubt, and fear. Toll, heavy hours, from night till dawn. Ah! 'twas a weary night through which two sad young hearts heard you tolling.

At a pretty early hour the various occupants of the crib at the Rue Poussin used to appear in the dingy little *salle-à-manger,* and partake of the breakfast there provided. Monsieur Menou, in his shirt-sleeves, shared and distributed the meal. Madame Menou, with a Madras handkerchief round her grizzling head, laid down the smoking coffee on the shining oilcloth, whilst each guest helped himself out of a little museum of napkins to his own particular towel. The room was small: the breakfast was not fine: the guests who partook of it were certainly not remarkable for the luxury of clean linen; but Philip—who is many years older now than when he dwelt in this hotel, and is not pinched for money at all you will be pleased to hear (and between ourselves has become rather a gourmand)—declares he was a very happy youth at this humble Hôtel Poussin, and sighs for the days whoa he was sighing for Miss Charlotte

Well, he has passed a dreadful night of gloom and terror. I doubt that he has bored Laberge very much with Iris tears and despondency. And now morning has come, and, as he is having his breakfast with one or more of the before-named worthies, the little boy-of-all-work enters, grinning, his *plumeau* under his arm, and cries, 'Une dame pour M. Philippe!'

'Une dame!' says the French colonel, looking up from his paper. 'Allez, mauvais sujet!'

'Grand Dieu! what has happened?' cries Philip, running forward, as he recognises Madame's tall figure in the passage. They go up to his room, I suppose, regardless of the grins and sneers of the little hoy with the *plumeau,* who aids the maid-servant to make the beds; and who thinks Monsieur Philippe has a very elderly acquaintance.

Philip closes the door upon his visitor, who looks at him with so much hope, kindness, confidence in her eyes, that the poor follow is encouraged almost ere she begins to speak. 'Yes, you have reason; I come from the little person,' Madame Smolensk said. 'The means of resisting that poor dear angel! She has passed a sad night! What? You, too, have not been to bed, poor young man!' Indeed Philip had only thrown himself on his bed, and had kicked there, and had groaned there, and had tossed there; and had tried to read, and, I dare say, remembered afterwards, with a strange interest, the book he read, and that other thought which was throbbing in his brain all the time whilst he was reading, and whilst the wakeful hours went wearily tolling by.

'No, in effect,' says poor Philip, rolling a dismal cigarette; 'the night has not been too fine. And she has suffered too? Heaven bless her!' And then Madame Smolensk told how the little dear angel had cried all the night long, and how the Smolensk had not succeeded in comforting her, until she promised she would go to Philip, and tell him that his Charlotte would be his for ever and ever; that she never could think of any man but him; that he was the best, and the dearest, and the bravest, and the truest Philip, and that she did not believe one word of those wicked stories told against him by—'Hold, Monsieur Philippe, I suppose Madame la Générale has been talking about you, and loves you no more,' cried Madame Smolensk. 'We other women are assassins—assassins, see you! But Madame la Générale went too far with the little maid. She is an obedient little maid, the dear Miss!—trembling before her mother, and always ready to yield—only now her spirit is roused: and she is yours and yours only. The little dear gentle child! Ah, how pretty she was, leaning on my shoulder. I held her there—yes, there, my poor garçon, and I cut this from her neck, and brought it to thee. Come, embrace me. Weep; that does good, Philip. I love thee well. Go—and thy little—it is an angel!' And so, in the hour of their pain, myriads of manly hearts have found woman's love ready to soothe their anguish.

Leaving to Philip that thick curling lock of brown hair (from a head where now, mayhap, there is a line or two of matron silver), this Samaritan plods her way back to her own house, where her own cares await her. But though the way is long, Madame's step is lighter now, as she thinks how Charlotte at the journey's end is waiting for news of Philip; and I suppose there are more kisses and embraces, when the good soul meets with the little suffering girl, and tells her how Philip will remain for ever true and faithful; and how true love must come to a happy ending; and how she, Smolensk, will do all in her power to aid, comfort, and console her young friends. As for the writer of Mr. Philip's memoirs, you see I never try to make any concealments. I have told you, all along, that Charlotte and Philip are married, and I believe they are happy. But it is certain that they suffered dreadfully at this time of their lives; and my wife says that Charlotte, if she alludes to the period and the trial, speaks as though they had both undergone some hideous operation, the remembrance of which for ever causes a pang to the memory. So, my young lady, will you have your trial one day, to be borne, pray Heaven, with a meek spirit. Ah, how surely the turn comes to all of us! Look at Madame Smolensk at her luncheon-table, this day after her visit to Philip at his lodging, after comforting little Charlotte in her pain. How brisk she is! How good-natured! How she smiles! How she speaks to all her company, and carves for her guests! You do not suppose she has no griefs and cares of her own? You know better. I dare say she is thinking of her creditors; of her poverty; of that accepted bill which will come due next week, and so forth. The Samaritan who rescues you, most likely, has been robbed and has bled in his day, and it is a wounded arm that bandages yours when bleeding.

If Anatole, the boy who scoured the plain at the Hôtel Poussin, with his *plumeau* in his jacket-pocket, and his slippers soled with scrubbing brushes, saw the embrace between Philip and his good friend, I believe, in his experience at that hotel, he never witnessed a transaction more honourable, generous, and blameless. Put what construction you will on the business, Anatole, you little imp of mischief! your mother never gave you a kiss more tender than that which Madame Smolensk bestowed on Philip—than that which she gave Philip—than that which she carried back from him and faithfully placed on poor little Charlotte's pale round cheek. The world is full of love and pity, I say. Had there been less suffering, there would have been less kindness. I, for one, almost wish to be ill again, so that the friends who succoured me might once more come to my rescue.

To poor little wounded Charlotte in her bed, our friend the mistress of the boarding-house brought back inexpressible comfort. Whatever might betide, Philip would never desert her! 'Think you I would ever have gone on such an embassy for a French girl, or interfered between her and her parents?' Madame asked. Never, never! But you and Monsieur Philippe are already betrothed before Heaven; and I should despise you, Charlotte, I should despise him, were either to draw back. This little point being settled in Miss Charlotte's mind, I can fancy she is immensely soothed and comforted; that hope and courage settle in her heart; that the colour comes back to her young cheeks; that she can come and join her family as she did yesterday. 'I told you she never cared about him,' says Mrs. Baynes to her husband. 'Faith, no: she can't have cared for him much,' says Baynes, with something of a sorrow that his girl should be so light-minded. But you and I, who have been behind the scenes, who have peeped into Philip's bedroom and behind poor Charlotte's modest curtains, know that the girl had revolted from her parents; and so children will if the authority exercised over them is too tyrannical or unjust. Gentle Charlotte, who scarce ever resisted, was aroused and in rebellion: honest Charlotte, who used to speak all her thoughts, now hid them, and deceived father and mother:—yes, deceived:—what a confession to make regarding a young lady, the *prima donna* of our opera! Mrs. Baynes is, as usual, writing her lengthy scrawls to sister MacWhirter at Tours, and informs the Major's lady that she has very great satisfaction in at last being able to announce 'that that most imprudent and in all respects ineligible engagement between her Charlotte and *a certain young man,* son of a bankrupt London physician, is come to an end. Mr. F.'s conduct has been so wild, so *gross,* so *disorderly* and *ungentlemanlike,* that the General (and you know, Maria, how soft and *tweet a tempered* man Baynes is) has told Mr. Firmin his opinion in unmistakable words, and forbidden him to continue his visits. After seeing him every day for six months, during which time she has accustomed herself to his peculiarities, and his often coarse and odious expressions and conduct, no wonder the separation has been a shock to dear Char, though I believe the young man feels nothing who has been *the cause of all this grief.* That he cares but little for *her,* has been my opinion *all along,* though she, artless child, gave him her whole affection. He has been accustomed to throw over women; and the brother of a young lady whom Mr. F. *had courted and left* (and who has made a most excellent match since) showed his indignation at Mr. F.'s conduct at the Embassy ball the other night, on which the young man took advantage of his greatly superior size and strength to begin a *vulgar boxing-match,* in which both parties were severely wounded. Of course you saw the paragraph in *Galignani* about the whole affair. I sent our dresses, but it did not print them, though our names appeared as amongst the company. Anything more singular than the appearance of Mr. F. you cannot well imagine. I wore my garnets; Charlotte (who attracted universal admiration) was in etc. etc. Of course, the separation has occasioned her a good deal of pain; for Mr. F. certainly behaved with much kindness and forbearance on a previous occasion. But the General will *not hear* of the continuance of the connection. He says the young man's conduct has been too gross and shameful; and when once roused, you know, I might as well attempt to chain a tiger as Baynes. Our poor Char will suffer no doubt in consequence of the behaviour of this brute, but she has ever been an obedient child, who knows how to honour her father and mother. *She bears up wonderfully,* though, of course, the dear child suffers at the parting. I think if *she were to go to you and MacWhirter at*

Tours for a month or two, she would be all the better for *change of air,* too, dear Mac. Come and fetch her, and we will pay the *dawk.* She would go to certain poverty and wretchedness did she marry this most violent and disreputable young man. The General sends regards to Mac, and I am,' etc.

That these were the actual words of Mrs. Baynes's letter I cannot, as a veracious biographer, take upon myself to say. I never saw the document, though I have had the good fortune to peruse others from the same hand. Charlotte saw the letter some time after, upon one of those not unfrequent occasions, when a quarrel occurred between the two sisters—Mrs. Major and Mrs. General—and Charlotte mentioned the contents of the letter to a friend of mine who has talked to me about his affairs, and especially his love affairs, for many and many a long hour. And shrewd old woman as Mrs. Baynes may be, you may see how utterly she was mistaken in fancying that her daughter's obedience was still secure. The little maid had left father and mother, at first with their eager sanction; her love had been given to Firmin; and an inmate—a prisoner if you will—under her father's roof, her heart remained with Philip, however time or distance might separate them.

And now, as we have the command of Philip's desk, and are free to open and read the private letters which relate to his history, I take leave to put in a document which was penned in his place of exile by his worthy father, upon receiving the news of the quarrel described in the last chapter of these memoirs:—

'Astor House, New York: *September*27.

'DEAR PHILIP,—I received the news in your last kind and affectionate letter with not unmingled pleasure: but ah, what pleasure in life does not carry its *amari aliquid* along with it! That you are hearty, cheerful, and industrious, earning a small competence, I am pleased indeed to think: that you talk about being married to a penniless girl I can't say gives me a very sincere pleasure. "With your good looks, good manners, attainments, you might have hoped for a better match than a half-pay officer's daughter. But 'tis useless speculating on what might have been. We are puppets in the hands of fate, most of us. We are carried along by a power stronger than ourselves. It has driven me, at sixty years of age, from competence, general respect, high position, to poverty and exile. So be it! *laudo manentem,* as my delightful old friend and philosopher teaches me—*si celeres quatit pennas*—you know the rest. Whatever our fortune may be, I hope that my Philip and his father will bear it with the courage of gentlemen.

'Our papers have announced the death of your poor mother's uncle, Lord Ringwood, and I had a fond lingering hope that he might have left some token of remembrance to his brother's grandson. He has not. You have *probam pauperiem sine dote.* You have courage, health, strength, and talent. I was in greater straits than you are at your age. *My* father was not as indulgent as yours, I hope and trust, has been. From debt and dependence I worked myself up to a proud position by my own efforts. That the storm overtook me and engulphed me afterwards, is true. But

I am like the merchant of my favourite poet: I still hope—ay, at sixty-three!—to mend my shattered ships, *indocilis pauperiem pati.* I still hope to pay back to my dear boy that fortune which ought to have been his, and which went down in my own shipwreck. Something tells me I must!—I will!

'I agree with you that your escape from Agnes Twysden has been *a piece of good fortune for you,* and am much diverted by your account of her *dusky innamorato*! Between ourselves, the fondness of the Twysdens for money amounted to meanness. And though I always received Twysden in dear old Parr Street, as I trust a gentleman should, his company was insufferably tedious to me, and his vulgar loquacity odious. His son also was little to my taste. Indeed I was *heartily relieved* when I found your connection with that family was over, knowing their rapacity about money, and that it was your fortune, not you, they were anxious to secure for Agnes.

'You will be glad to hear that I am in not inconsiderable practice already. My reputation as a physician had preceded me to this country. My work on Gout was favourably noticed here, and in Philadelphia, and in Boston, by the scientific journals of those great cities. People are more generous and compassionate towards misfortune here than in our cold-hearted island. I could mention several gentlemen of New York who have suffered shipwreck like myself, and are now prosperous and respected. I had the good fortune to be of considerable professional service to Colonel J. B. Fogle, of New York, on our voyage out; and the Colonel, who is a leading personage here, has shown himself not at all ungrateful. Those who fancy that at New York people cannot appreciate and understand the manners of a gentleman, are *not a little mistaken*; and a man who, like myself, has lived with the best society in London, has, I flatter myself, not lived in that society *quite in vain.* The Colonel is proprietor and editor of one of the most brilliant and influential journals of the city. You know that arms and the toga are often worn here by the same individual, and—

'I had actually written thus far when I read in the Colonel's paper —the *New York Emerald*—an account of your battle with your cousin at the Embassy ball! Oh, you pugnacious Philip! Well, young Twysden was very vulgar, very rude and overbearing, and, I have no doubt, deserved the chastisement you gave him. By the way, the correspondent of the *Emerald* makes some droll blunders regarding you in his letter. We are all fair game for publicity in this country, where the press is free *with a vengeance*; and your private affairs, or mine, or the President's, or our gracious Queen's, for the matter of that, are discussed with a freedom which certainly *amounts to licence.* The Colonel's lady is passing the winter in Paris, where I should wish you to pay your respects to her. Her husband has been most kind to me. I am told that Mrs. F. lives in the very choicest French society, and the friendship of this family may be useful to you as to your affectionate father,

G. B. F.

'Address as usual, until you hear further from me, as Dr. Brandon, New York. I wonder whether Lord Estridge has asked you after his old college friend? When he was Headbury and at Trinity, he and a certain pensioner whom men used to nickname Brummell Firmin were said to be the best dressed men in the University. Estridge has advanced to rank, to honours! You may rely on it, that he will have one of the *very next* vacant garters. What a different, what an unfortunate career, has been his quondam friend's!—an exile, an inhabitant of a small room in a great hotel, where I sit at a scrambling public table with all sorts of coarse people! The way in which they bolt their dinner, often *with a knife,* shocks me. Your remittance was most welcome, small as it was. It shows my Philip has *a kind heart.* Ah! why, why are you thinking of marriage, who are so poor? By the way, your encouraging account of your circumstances has induced me to draw upon you for 100 dollars. The bill will go to Europe by the packet which carries this letter, and has kindly been cashed for me by my friends, Messrs. Plaster and Shinman, of Wall Street, respected bankers of this city. Leave your card with Mrs. Fogle. Her husband himself may be useful to you and your ever attached Father.'

We take the *New York Emerald* at Bays's, and in it I had read a very amusing account of our friend Philip, in an ingenious correspondence entitled 'Letters from an Attaché,' which appeared in that journal. I even copied the paragraph to show to my wife, and perhaps to forward to our friend.

'I promise you,' wrote the attaché, 'the new country did not disgrace the old at the British Embassy ball on Queen Vic's birthday. Colonel Z. B. Hoggins's lady, of Albany, and the peerless bride of Elijah J. Dibbs, of Twenty-ninth Street in your city, were the observed of all observers for splendour, for elegance, for refined native beauty. The Royal Dukes danced with nobody else; and at the attention of one of the Princes to the lovely Miss Dibbs, I observed his Royal Duchess looked as black as thunder. Supper handsome. Back Delmonico to beat it. Champagne so-so. By the way, the young fellow who writes here for the *Pall Mall Gazette* got too much of the champagne on board—as usual, I am told. The Honourable R. Twysden, of London, was rude to my young chap's partner, or winked at him offensively, or trod on his toe, or I don't know what—but young F. followed him into the garden; hit out at him; sent him flying like a spread eagle into the midst of an illumination, and left him there sprawling. Wild rampageous fellow this young F.; has already spent his own fortune, and ruined his poor old father, who has been forced to cross the water. Old Louis Philippe went away early. He talked long with our Minister about his travels in our country. I was standing by, but in course ain't so ill-bred as to say what passed between them.'

In this way history is written. I dare say about others besides Philip, in English papers as well as American, have fables been narrated.

CHAPTER XXVI. CONTAINS A TUG OF WAR

WHO was the first to spread the report that Philip was a prodigal, who had ruined his poor confiding father? I thought I knew a person who might be interested in getting under any shelter, and sacrificing even his own son for his own advantage. I thought I knew a man who had done as much already, and surely might do so again; but my wife flew into one of her tempests of indignation, when I hinted something of this, clutched her own children to her heart, according to her maternal wont, asked me was there any power would cause me to belie *them?* and sternly rebuked me for daring to be so wicked, heartless, and cynical. My dear creature, wrath is no answer. You call me heartless and cynic, for saying men are false and wicked. Have you never heard to what lengths some bankrupts will go? To appease the wolves who chase them in the winter forest, have you not read how some travellers will cast all their provisions out of the sledge? then, when all the provisions are gone, don't you know that they will fling out perhaps the sister, perhaps the mother, perhaps the baby, the little dear tender innocent? Don't you see him tumbling among the howling pack, and the wolves gnashing, gnawing, crashing, gobbling him up in the snow? O horror—horror! My wife draws all the young ones to her breast as I utter these fiendish remarks. She hugs them in her embrace, and says, 'For shame!' and that I am a monster, and so on. Go to! Go down on your knees, woman, and acknowledge the sinfulness of our humankind. How long had our race existed ere murder and violence began? and how old was the world ere brother slew brother?

Well, my wife and I came to a compromise. I might have my opinion, but was there any need to communicate it to poor Philip? No, surely. So I never sent him the extract from the *New York Emerald;* though, of course, some other good-natured friend did, and I don't think my magnanimous friend cared much. As for supposing that his own father, to cover his own character, would lie away his son's —such a piece of artifice was quite beyond Philip's comprehension, who has been all his life slow in appreciating roguery, or recognising that there is meanness and double-dealing in the world. When he once comes to understand the fact; when he once comprehends that Tartuffe is a humbug and swelling Bufo is a toady; then my friend becomes as absurdly indignant and mistrustful as before he was admiring and confiding. Ah, Philip! Tartuffe has a number of good respectable qualities; and Bufo, though an underground odious animal, may have a precious jewel in his head. 'Tis you are cynical. *I* see the good qualities in these rascals whom you spurn. I see. I shrug my shoulders. I smile: and you call me cynic.

It was long before Philip could comprehend why Charlotte's mother turned upon him, and tried to force her daughter to forsake him. 'I have offended the old woman in a hundred ways,' he would say. 'My tobacco annoys her; my old clothes offend her; the very English I speak is often Greek to her, and she can no more construe my sentences than I can the Hindostanee jargon she talks to her husband at dinner.' 'My dear fellow, if you had ten thousand a year she would try and construe your sentences, or accept them even if not understood,' I would reply. And some men, whom you and I know to be mean, and to be false, and to be flatterers and parasites, and to be inexorably hard and cruel in their own private circles, will surely pull a long face to-morrow, and say, 'Oh! the man's so cynical.'

I acquit Baynes of what ensued. I hold Mrs. B. to have been the criminal—the stupid criminal. The husband, like many other men extremely brave in active life, was at home timid and irresolute. Of two heads that lie side by side on the same pillow for thirty years, one must contain the stronger power, the more enduring resolution. Baynes, away from his wife, was shrewd, courageous, gay at times; when with her he was fascinated, torpid under the power of this baleful superior creature. 'Ah, when we were subs together in camp in 1803, what a lively fellow Charley Baynes was!' his comrade, Colonel Bunch, would say. 'That was before he ever saw his wife's yellow face; and what a slave she has made of him!'

After that fatal conversation which ensued on the day succeeding the ball, Philip did not come to dinner at Madame's according to his custom. Mrs. Baynes told no family stories, and Colonel Bunch, who had no special liking for the young gentleman, did not trouble himself to make any inquiries about him. One, two, three days passed, and no Philip. At last the Colonel says to the General, with a sly look at Charlotte, 'Baynes, where is our young friend with the moustache? We have not seen him these three days.' And he gives an arch look at poor Charlotte. A burning blush flamed up in little Charlotte's pale face, as she looked at her parents and then at their old friend. 'Mr; Firmin does not come, because papa and mamma have forbidden him,' says Charlotte. 'I suppose he only comes where he is welcome.' .And, having made this audacious speech, I suppose the little maid tossed her little head up; and wondered, in the silence which ensued, whether au the company could hear her heart thumping.

Madame, from her central place, where she is carving, sees, from the looks of her guests, the indignant flushes on Charlotte's face, the confusion on her father's, the wrath on Mrs. Baynes's, that some dreadful words are passing; and in vain endeavours to turn the angry current of talk. 'Un petit canard délicieux, goutez-en, madame!' she cries. Honest Colonel Bunch sees the little maid with eyes flashing with anger, and trembling in every limb. The offered duck having failed to create a diversion, he, too, tries a feeble commonplace. 'A little difference, my dear,' he says, in an under voice. 'There will be such in the best-regulated families. Canard sauvage très bong, Madame, avec—' but he is allowed to speak no more, for—

'What would you do, Colonel Bunch,' little Charlotte breaks out with her poor little ringing trembling voice—'that is, if you were a young man, if another young man struck you and insulted you?' I say she utters this in such a clear voice, that Françoise, the *femme-de-chambre,* that Auguste, the footman, that all the guests hear, that all the knives and forks stop their clatter.

'Faith, my dear, I'd knock him down if I could,' says Bunch; and he catches hold of the little maid's sleeve, and would stop her speaking if he could.

'And that is what Philip did,' cries Charlotte aloud; 'and mamma has turned him out of the house—yes, out of the house, for acting like a man of honour!'

'Go to your room this instant, Miss!' shrieks mamma. As for old Baynes, his stained old uniform is not more dingy-red than his wrinkled face and his throbbing temples. He blushes under his wig, no doubt, could we see beneath that ancient artifice.

'What is it? Madame your mother dismisses you of my table? I will come with you, my dear Miss Charlotte!' says Madame, with much dignity. 'Serve the sugared plate, Auguste! My ladies, you will excuse me! I go to attend the dear Miss, who seems to me ill.' And she rises up, and she follows poor little blushing, burning, weeping Charlotte: and again, I have no doubt, takes her in her arms and kisses, and cheers, and caresses her—at the threshold of the door—there by the staircase, among the cold dishes of the dinner, where Moira and Macgrigor had one moment before been marauding.

'Courage, ma fille, courage, mon enfant! Tenez! Behold something to console thee!' and Madame takes out of her pocket a little letter, and gives it to the girl, who at sight of it kisses the superscription, and then, in an anguish of love, and joy, and grief, falls on the neck of the kind woman, who consoles her in her misery. Whose writing is it Charlotte kisses? Can you guess by any means? Upon my word, Madame Smolensk, I never recommend ladies to take daughters to *your* boarding-house., And I like you so much, I would not tell of you, but you know the house is shut up this many a long day. Oh! the years slip away fugacious; and the grass has grown over graves; and many and many joys and sorrows have been born and have died since then for Charlotte and Philip: but that grief aches still in their bosoms at times; and that sorrow throbs at Charlotte's heart again whenever she looks at a little yellow letter in her trinket-box: and she says to her children, 'Papa wrote that to me before we were married, my dears,' There are scarcely half-a-dozen words in the little letter, I believe; and two of them are 'for ever.'

I could draw a ground-plan of Madame's house in the Champs Elysées if I liked, for has not Philip shown me the place and described it to me many times? In front, and facing the road and garden, were Madame's room and the salon; to the back was the salle-à-manger; and a stair ran up the house (where the dishes used to be laid during dinner-time, and where Moira and Macgrigor fingered the meats and puddings). Mrs. General Baynes's rooms were on the first floor, looking on the

Champs Elysées, and into the garden-court of the house below. And on this day, as the dinner was necessarily short (owing to unhappy circumstances), and the gentlemen were left alone glumly drinking their wine or grog, and Mrs. Baynes had gone upstairs to her own apartment, had slapped her boys and was looking out of window—was it not provoking that of all days in the world young Hely should ride up to the house on his capering mare, with his flower in his button-hole, with his little varnished toe-tips just touching his stirrups, and after performing various caracolades and gambadoes in the garden, kiss his yellow-kidded hand to Mrs. General Baynes at the window, hope Miss Baynes was quite well, and ask if he might come in and take a cup of tea? Charlotte, lying on Madame's bed in the ground-floor room, heard Mr. Hely's sweet voice asking after her health, and the crunching of his horse's hoofs on the gravel, and she could even catch glimpses of that little form as the horse capered about in the court, though of course he could not see her where she was lying on the bed with her letter in her hand. Mrs. Baynes at her window had to wag her withered head from the casement, to groan out, 'My daughter is lying down, and has a bad headache, I am sorry to say,' and then she must have had the mortification to see Hely caper off, after waving her a genteel adieu. The ladies in the front salon, who assembled after dinner, witnessed the transaction, and Mrs. Bunch, I dare say, had a grim pleasure at seeing Eliza Baynes's young sprig of fashion, of whom Eliza was for ever bragging, come at last, and obliged to ride away, not bootless, certainly (for where were feet more beautifully *chaussés*?), but after a bootless errand.

Meanwhile the gentlemen sat a while in the dining-room, after the British custom which such veterans liked too well to give up. Other two gentlemen boarders went away, rather alarmed by that storm and outbreak in which Charlotte had quitted the dinner-table, and left the old soldiers together, to enjoy, as was their after-dinner custom, a sober glass of 'something hot,' as the saying is. In truth, Madame's wine was of the poorest; but what better could you expect for the money?

Baynes was not eager to be alone with Bunch, and I have no doubt began to blush again when he found himself *tête-à-tête* with his old friend. But what was to be done? The General did not dare to go upstairs to his own quarters, where poor Charlotte was probably crying, and her mother in one of her tantrums. Then in the salon there were the ladies of the boarding-house party, and there Mrs. Bunch would be sure to be at him. Indeed, since the Byneses were launched in the great world, Mrs. Bunch was untiringly sarcastic in her remarks about lords, ladies, attachés, ambassadors, and fine people in general. So Baynes sat with his friend, in the falling evening, in much silence, dipping his old nose in the brandy-and-water.

Little square-faced, red-faced, whisker-dyed Colonel Bunch sat opposite his old companion, regarding him not without scorn. Bunch had a wife. Bunch had feelings. Do you suppose those feelings had not been worked upon by that wife in private colloquies? Do you suppose —when two old women have lived together in pretty much the same rank of life—if one suddenly gets promotion, is carried off to higher spheres, and talks of her new friends, the countesses, duchesses, ambassadresses, as of course she will—do you suppose, I say, that the unsuccessful woman will be pleased at the successful woman's success? Your knowledge of your own heart, my dear lady, must tell you the truth in this matter. I don't want you to acknowledge that you are angry because your sister has been staying with the Duchess of Fitzbattleaxe, but you are, you know. You have made sneering remarks to your husband on the subject, and such remarks, I have no doubt, were made by Mrs. Colonel Bunch to *her* husband, regarding her poor friend Mrs. General Baynes.

During this parenthesis we have left the General dipping his nose in the brandy-and-water. He can't keep it there for ever. He must come up for air presently. His face must come out of the drink, and sigh over the table.

'What's this business, Baynes?' says the Colonel. 'What's the matter with poor Charly?'

'Family affairs—differences will happen,' says the General.

'I do hope and trust nothing has gone wrong with her and young Firmin, Baynes?'

The General does not like those fixed eyes staring at him under those bushy eyebrows, between those bushy blackened whiskers.

'Well, then, yes, Bunch, something *has* gone wrong; and given me and—and Mrs. Baynes—a deuced deal of pain, too. The young fellow has acted like a blackguard, brawling and fighting at an ambassador's ball, bringing us all to ridicule. He's not a gentleman; that's the long and short of it, Bunch; and so let's change the subject.'

'Why, consider the provocation he had!' cries the other, disregarding entirely his friend's prayer. 'I heard them talking about the business at Galignani's this very day. A fellow swears at Firmin; runs at him; brags that he has pitched him over; and is knocked down for his pains. By George! I think Firmin was quite right. Were any man to do as much to me or you, what should we do, even at our age?'

'We are military men. I said I didn't wish to talk about the subject, Bunch,' says the General in rather a lofty manner.

'You mean that Tom Bunch has no need to put his oar in?'

'Precisely so,' says the other curtly.

'Mum's the word! Let us talk about the dukes and duchesses at the ball. *That*'s more in your line, now,' says the Colonel, with rather a sneer.

'What do you mean by duchesses and dukes? What do you know about them, or what the deuce do I care?' asks the General.

'Oh, they are tabooed too! Hang it, there's no satisfying you,' growls the Colonel.

'Look here, Bunch,' the General broke out; 'I must speak, since you won't leave me alone. I am unhappy. You can see that well enough. For two or three nights past I have had no rest. This engagement of my child and Mr. Firmin can't come to any good. You see what he is—an overbearing, ill-conditioned, quarrelsome fellow. What chance has Charly of being happy with such a fellow?'

'I hold my tongue, Baynes. You told me not to put my oar in,' growls the Colonel.

'Oh, if that's the way you take it, Bunch, of course there's no need for me to go on any more,' cries General Baynes. 'If an old friend won't give an old friend advice, by George, or help him in a strait, or say a kind word when he's unhappy, I have done. I have known you for forty years, and I am mistaken in you—that's all.'

'There's no contenting you. You say, "Hold your tongue," and I shut my mouth. I hold my tongue, and you say, "Why don't you speak?" Why don't I? Because you won't like what I say, Charles Baynes: and so what's the good of more talking?'

'Confound it!' cries Baynes, with a thump of his glass on the table, 'but what *do* you say?'

'I say, then, as you will have it,' cries the other, clenching his fiats in his pockets, —'I say you are wanting a pretext for breaking off this match, Baynes. I don't say it is a good one, mind; but your word is passed, and your honour engaged to a young fellow to whom you are under deep obligation.'

'What obligation? Who has talked to you about my private affairs? cries the General, reddening. 'Has Philip Firmin been bragging about his—?'

'You have yourself, Baynes. When you arrived here, you told me over and over again what the young fellow had done: and you certainly thought he acted like a gentleman *then*. If you choose to break your word to him now—'

'Break my word! Great Powers, do you know what you are saying, Bunch?'

'Yes, and what you are doing, Baynes.'

'Doing? and what?'

'A damned shabby action; that's what you are doing, if you want to know. Don't tell *me*. Why, do you suppose Sarah—do you suppose everybody doesn't see what you are at? You think you can get a better , match for the girl, and you and Eliza are going to throw the young fellow over: and the fellow who held his hand, and might have ruined you, if he liked. I say it is a cowardly action!'

'Colonel Bunch, do you dare to use such a word to me!' calls out the^General, starting to his feet.

'Dare be hanged! I say it's a shabby action!' roars the other, rising too.

'Hush! unless you wish to disturb the ladies! Of course you know what your expression means, Colonel Bunch?' and the General drops his voice and sinks back to his chair.

'I know what my words mean, and I stick to 'em, Baynes,' growls the other; 'which is more than you can say of yours.'

'I am dee'd if any man alive shall use this language to me,' says the General, in the softest whisper, 'without accounting to me for it.'

'Did you ever find me backward, Baynes, at that kind of thing?' growls the Colonel, with a face like a lobster and eyes starting from his head.

'Very good, sir. To-morrow, at your earliest convenience. I shall be at Galignani's from eleven till one. With a friend, if possible.—What is it, my love? A game at whist? Well, no, thank you; I think I won't play cards to-night.'

It was Mrs. Baynes who entered the room when the two gentlemen were quarrelling; and the bloodthirsty hypocrites instantly smoothed their ruffled brows and smiled on her with perfect courtesy.

'Whist—no! I was thinking should we send out to meet him? He has never been in Paris.'

'Never been in Paris?' said the General, puzzled.

'He will be here to-night, you know. Madame has a room ready for him.'

'The very thing, the very thing!' cries General Baynes, with great glee. And Mrs. Baynes, all unsuspicious of the quarrel between the old friends, proceeds to inform Colonel Bunch that Major MacWhirter was expected that evening. And then that tough old Colonel Bunch knew the cause of Baynes's delight. A second was provided for the General—the very thing Baynes wanted.

We have seen how Mrs. Baynes, after taking counsel with her General, had privily sent for MacWhirter. Her plan was that Charlotte's uncle should take her for a while to Tours, and .make her hear reason. Then Charly's foolish passion for Philip would pass away. Then, if he dared to follow her so far, her aunt and uncle, two dragons of virtue and circumspection, would watch and guard her. Then, if Mrs. Hely was still of the same mind, she and her son might easily take the post to Tours, where, Philip being absent, young Walsingham might plead his passion. The best part of the plan, perhaps, was the separation of our young couple. Charlotte would recover. Mrs. Baynes wag sure of that. The little girl had made no outbreak until that sudden insurrection at dinner which we have witnessed; and her mother, who had domineered over the child all her life, thought she was still in her power. She did not know that she had passed the bounds of authority, and that with her behaviour to Philip her child's allegiance had revolted.

Bunch then, from Baynes's look and expression, perfectly understood what his adversary meant, and that the General's second was found. His own he had in his eye—a tough little old army surgeon of Peninsular and Indian times, who lived hard by, who would aid as second and doctor too, if need were—and so kill two birds with one stone, as they say. The Colonel would go forth that very instant and seek for Dr. Martin, and be hanged to Baynes, and a plague on the whole transaction and the folly of two old friends burning powder in such a quarrel. But he knew what a bloodthirsty little fellow that henpecked silent Baynes was when roused; and as for himself—a fellow use that kind of language to *me*! By George, Tom Bunch was not going to baulk him!

Whose was that tall figure prowling about Madame's house in the Champs Elyse'es when Colonel Bunch issued forth in quest of his friend; who had been watched by the police and mistaken for a suspicious character; who had been looking up at Madame's windows now that the evening shades had fallen> Oh, you goose of a Philip! (for of course, my dears, you guess that the spy was P. F., Esq.) you look up at the *premier,* and there is the Beloved in Madame's room on the ground-floor;— in yonder room, where a lamp is burning and casting a faint light across the bars of the *jalousie.* If Philip knew she was there he would be transformed into a clematis, and climb up the bars of the window, and twine round them all night. But you see he thinks she is on the first-floor; and the glances of his passionate eyes are taking aim at the wrong windows. And now Colonel Bunch comes forth in his stout strutting way, in his little military cape—quick march—and Philip is startled like a guilty thing surprised, and dodges behind a tree in the avenue.

The Colonel departed on his murderous errand Philip still continues to ogle the window of his heart (the wrong window), defiant of the policeman, who tells him to *circuler.* He has not watched here many minutes more, ere a hackney-coach drives up with portmanteaus on the roof and a lady and gentleman within.

You see Mrs. MacWhirter thought she, as well as her husband, might have a peep at Paris. As Mac's coach-hire was paid, Mrs. Mac could afford a little outlay of money. And if they were to bring Charlotte back—Charlotte in grief and agitation, poor child—a matron, an aunt, would be a much fitter companion for her than a major, however gentle-So the pair of MacWhirters journeyed from Tours—a long journey it was before railways were invented—and after four-and-twenty hours of squeeze in the diligence, presented themselves at nightfall at Madame Smolensk's.

The Baynes boys dashed into the garden at the sound of wheels. 'Mamma— mamma! it's Uncle Mac!' these innocents cried, as they ran to the railings. 'Uncle Mac! what could bring him? Oh! they are going to send me to him! they are going to send me to him!' thought Charlotte, starting on her bed. And on this, I dare say, a certain locket was kissed more vehemently than ever.

'I say, ma!' cries the ingenious Moira, jumping back to the house: 'it's Uncle Mac, and Aunt Mac, too!'

'What?' cries mamma, with anything but pleasure in her voice; and then, turning to the dining-room, where her husband still sat, she called out, 'General! here's MacWhirter and Emily!'

Mrs. Baynes gave her sister a very grim kiss.

'Dearest Eliza, I thought it was such a good opportunity of coming, and that I might be so useful, you know!' pleads Emily.

'Thank you. How do you do, MacWhirter?' says the grim Générale.

'Glad to see you, Baynes my boy!'

'How d' ye do, Emily? Boys, bring your uncle's traps. Didn't know Emily was coming, Mac. Hope there's room for her!' sighs the General, coming forth from his parlour.

The Major was struck by the sad looks and pallor of his brother-in-law. 'By George, Baynes, you look as yellow as a guinea. How's Tom Bunch?'

'Come into this room along with me. Have some brandy-and-water, Mac? Auguste! Odevie O sho!' calls the General; and Auguste, who out of the new-comers' six packages has daintily taken one very small mackintosh cushion, says, 'Comment? encore du grog, General?' and, shrugging his shoulders, disappears to procure the refreshment at his leisure.

The sisters disappear to their embraces; the brothers-in-law retreat to the salle-à-manger, where General Baynes has been sitting, gloomy and lonely, for half-an-hour past, thinking of his quarrel with his old comrade, Bunch. He and Bunch have been chums for more than forty years. They have been in action together, and honourably mentioned in the same report. They have had a great regard for each other; and each knows the other is an obstinate old mule, and, in a quarrel, will die rather than give way. They have had a dispute out of which there is only one issue. Words have passed which no man, however old, by George! can brook from any friend, however intimate, by Jove! No wonder Baynes is grave. His family is large; his means are small. To-morrow he may be under fire of an old friend's pistol. In such an extremity he knows how each will behave. No wonder, I say, the General is solemn.

'What's in the wind now, Baynes?' asks the Major, after a little drink and a long silence. 'How is poor little Char?'

'Infernally ill—I mean behaved infernally ill,' says the General, biting his lips.

'Bad business! Bad business! Poor little child!' cries the Major.

'Insubordinate little devil!' says the pale General, grinding his teeth. 'We'll see which shall be master!'

'What! you have had words?'

'At this table, this very day. She sat here and defied her mother and me, by George! and flung out of the room like a tragedy queen. She must be tamed, Mac, or my name's not Baynes.'

MacWhirter knew his relative of old, and that this quiet submissive man, when angry, worked up to a white heat as it were. 'Sad affair; hope you'll both come round, Baynes,' sighs the Major, trying bootless commonplaces; and seeing this last remark had no effect, he bethought him of recurring to their mutual friend. 'How's Tom Bunch?'the Major asked cheerily.

At this question Baynes grinned in such a ghastly way that MacWhirter eyed him with wonder. 'Colonel Bunch is very well,' the General said, in a dismal voice; at least, he was half-an-hour ago. He was sitting there;' and he pointed to an empty spoon lying in an empty beaker, whence the spirit and water had departed.

'What has been the matter, Baynes?' asked the Major. 'Has anything happened between you and Tom?'

'I mean that, half-an-hour ago, Colonel Bunch used words to me which I'll bear from no man alive; and you have arrived just in the nick of time, MacWhirter, to take my message to him. Hush! here's the drink.'

' oici, messieurs!' Auguste at length has brought up a second supply of brandy-and-water. The veterans mingled their jorums; and whilst his brother-in-law spoke, the alarmed MacWhirter sipped occasionally *intentusque ora tenebat.*

CHAPTER XXVII. I CHARGE YOU, DROP YOUR DAGGERS!

GENERAL BAYNES began the story which you and I have heard at length. He told it in his own way. He grew very angry with himself whilst defending himself. He had to abuse Philip very fiercely, in order to excuse his own act of treason. He had to show that his act was not his act; that, after all, he never had promised; and that, if he had promised, Philip's atrocious conduct ought to absolve him from any previous promise. I do not wonder that the General was abusive, and out of temper. Such a crime as he was committing can't be performed cheerfully by a man who is habitually gentle, generous, and honest. I do not say that men cannot cheat, cannot lie, cannot inflict torture, cannot commit rascally actions, without in the least losing their equanimity; hut these are men habitually false, knavish, and cruel. They are accustomed to break their promises, to cheat their neighbours in bargains, and what not. A roguish word or action more or less is of little matter to them: their remorse only awakens after detection, and they don't begin to repent till they come sentenced out of the dock. But here was an ordinarily just man withdrawing from his promise, turning his back on his benefactor, and justifying himself to himself by maligning the man whom he injured. It is not an uncommon event, my dearly beloved brethren and esteemed miserable sister sinners; but you like to say a preacher is 'cynical' who admits this sad truth—and, perhaps, don't care to hear about the subject on more than one day in the week.

So, in order to make out some sort of case for himself, our poor good old General Baynes chose to think and declare that Philip was so violent, ill-conditioned, and abandoned a fellow, that no faith ought to be kept with him; and that Colonel Bunch had behaved with such brutal insolence that Baynes must call him to account. As for the fact that there was another, a richer, and a much more eligible suitor, who was likely to offer for his daughter, Baynes did not happen to touch on this point at all; preferring to speak of Philip's hopeless poverty, disreputable conduct, and gross and careless behaviour.

Now MacWhirter, having, I suppose, little to do at Tours, had read Mrs. Baynes's letters to her sister Emily, and remembered them. Indeed, it was but very few months since Eliza Baynes's letters had been full of praise of Philip, of his love for Charlotte, and of his noble generosity in foregoing the great claim which he had upon the General his mother's careless trustee. Philip was the first suitor Charlotte had had: in her first glow of pleasure, Charlotte's mother had covered yards of paper with compliments, interjections, and those *scratches* or *dashes* under her words, by which some ladies are accustomed to point their satire or emphasise their delight. He was an admirable young man—wild, but generous, handsome, noble! He had forgiven his father thousands and thousands of pounds which the Doctor owed him—all his mother's fortune; and he had acted *most nobly* by her trustees— that she must say, though poor dear weak Baynes was one of them! Baynes who was as simple as a child. Major Mac and his wife had agreed that Philip's forbearance was very generous and kind, but after all that there was no special cause for rapture at the notion of their niece marrying a struggling young fellow without a penny in the world; and they had been not a little amused with the change of tone in Eliza's later letters, when she began to go out in the great world, and to look coldly upon poor penniless Firmin, her hero of a few months since. Then Emily remembered how Eliza had always been fond of great people; how her head was turned by going to a few parties at Government House; how absurdly she went on with that little creature Fitzrickets (because he was an Honourable, forsooth) at Dumdum. Eliza was a good wife to Baynes; a good mother to the children; and made both ends of a narrow income meet with surprising dexterity; but Emily was bound to say of her sister Eliza, that a more, etc. etc. etc. And when the news came at length that Philip was to be thrown overboard, Emily clapped her hands together, and said to her husband, 'Now, Mac, didn't I always tell you so? If she could get a fashionable husband for Charlotte, I *knew* my sister would put the Doctor's son to the door!' That the poor child would Buffer considerably, her aunt was assured. Indeed, before her own union with Mac, Emily had undergone heartbreakings and pangs of separation on her own account. The poor child would want comfort and companionship. *She* would go to fetch her niece. And though the Major said, 'My dear, you want to go to Paris, and buy a new bonnet,' Mrs. MacWhirter spurned the insinuation, and came to Paris from a mere sense of duty.

So Baynes poured out his history of wrongs to his brother-in-law, who marvelled to hear a man, ordinarily chary of words and cool of demeanour, so angry and so voluble. If he had done a bad action, at least, after doing it, Baynes had the grace to be very much out of humour. If I ever, for my part, do anything wrong in my family, or to them, I accompany that action with a furious rage and blustering passion. I won't have wife or children question it. No querulous Nathan of a family friend (or an incommodious conscience, may be) shall come and lecture *me* about my ill-doings. No—no. Out of the house with him! Away, you preaching bugbear, don't try to frighten *me*! Baynes, I suspect, to browbeat, bully, and out-talk the Nathan pleading in his heart—Baynes will out-bawl that prating monitor, and thrust that inconvenient preacher out of sight, out of hearing, drive him with angry words from our gate. Ah! in vain we expel him; and bid John say, not at home! There he is when we wake, sitting at our bed-foot. We throw him overboard for daring to put an oar in our boat. Whose ghastly head is that looking up from the water and swimming alongside us, row we never so swiftly? Fire at him. Brain him with an oar, one of you, and pull on! Flash goes the pistol. Surely that oar has stove the old skull in? See! there comes the awful companion popping up out of water again, and crying, 'Remember, remember, I am here, I am here!' Baynes had thought to bully away one monitor by the threat of a pistol, and here was another swimming alongside of his boat. And would you have it otherwise, my dear reader, for you, for me? That you and I shall commit sins, in this, and ensuing years, is certain; but I hope—I hope they won't be past praying for. Here is Baynes, having just done a bad action, in a dreadfully wicked, murderous, and dissatisfied state of mind. His chafing, bleeding temper is one raw; his whole soul one rage, and wrath, and fever. Charles Baynes, thou old sinner, I pray that Heaven may turn thee to a better state of mind. I will kneel down by thy side, scatter ashes on my own bald pate, and we will quaver out *Peccavimus* together.

'In one word, the young man's conduct has been so outrageous and disreputable that I can't, Mac, as a father of a family, consent to my girl's marrying him. Out of a regard for her happiness, it is my duty to break off the engagement,' cries the General, finishing the story.

'Has he formally released you from that trust business?' asked the Major.

'Good heavens, Mac!' cries the General, turning very red. 'You know I am as innocent of all wrong towards him as you are!'

'Innocent—only you did not look to your trust—'

'I think ill of him, sir. I think he is a wild, reckless, overbearing young fellow,' calls out the General, very quickly, 'who would make my child miserable; but I don't think he is such a blackguard as to come down on a retired elderly man with a poor family—a numerous family; a man who has bled and fought for his Sovereign in the Peninsula, and in India, as the "Army List" will show you, by George! I don't think Firmin will be such a scoundrel as to come down on me, I say; and I must say, MacWhirter, I think it is most unhandsome of you to allude to it—most unhandsome, by George!'

'Why, you are going to break off your bargain with him; why should he keep his compact with you?' asks the gruff Major.

'Because,' shouted the General, 'it would be a sin and a shame that an old man with seven children, and broken health, who has served in every place—yes, in the West and East Indies, by George!—in Canada—in the Peninsula, and at New Orleans;—because he has been deceived and humbugged by a miserable scoundrel of a doctor into signing a sham paper, by George! should be ruined, and his poor children and wife driven to beggary, by Jove! as you seem to recommend young Firmin to do, Jack MacWhirter; and I'll tell you what, Major MacWhirter, I take it dee'd unfriendly of you; and I'll trouble you not to put your oar into *my boat* and meddle with *my affairs,* that's all, and I'll know who's at the bottom of it, by Jove! It's the grey mare, Mac—it's your *better half,* MacWhirter—it's that confounded, meddling, sneaking, backbiting, domineering—'

'What next?' roared the Major. 'Ha, ha, ha! Do you think I don't know, Baynes, who has put you on doing what I have no hesitation in calling a most sneaking and rascally action—yes, a rascally action, by George! I am not going to mince matters! Don't come your Major-General or your Mrs. Major-General over me! It's Eliza that has set you on. And if Tom Bunch has been telling you that you have been breaking from your word, and are acting shabbily, Tom is right; and you may get somebody else to go out with you, General Baynes, for, by George, I won't!'

'Have you come all the way from Tours, Mac, in order to insult me?' asks the General.

'I came to do you a friendly turn; to take charge of your poor girl, upon whom you are being very hard, Baynes. And this is the reward I get! Thank you. No more grog! What I have had is rather *too strong* for me already.' And the Major looks down with an expression of scorn at the emptied beaker, the idle spoon before him.

As the warriors were quarrelling over their cups, there came to them a noise as of brawling and of female voices without. 'Mais, madame!' pleads Madame Smolensk, in her grave way. 'Taisez-vous, madame; laissez-moi tranquille, s'il vous plait!' exclaims the well-known voice of Mrs. General Baynes, which I own was never very pleasant to me, either in anger or good-humour. 'And your Little,— who tries to sleep in my chamber!' again pleads the mistress of the boarding-house. 'Vous n'avez pas droit d'appeler Mademoiselle Baynes petite!' calls out the General's lady. And Baynes, who was fighting and quarrelling himself just now, trembled when he heard her. His angry face assumed an alarmed expression. He looked for means of escape. He appealed for protection to MacWhirter, whose nose he had been ready to pull anon. Samson was a mighty man, but he was a fool in the hands of a woman. Hercules was a brave man and a strong, but Omphale twisted him round her spindle. Even so Baynes, who had fought in India, Spain, America, trembled before the partner of his bed and name.

It was an unlucky afternoon. Whilst the husbands had been quarrelling in the dining-room over brandy-and-water, the wives, the sisters, had been fighting over their tea in the salon. I don't know what the other boarders were about. Philip never told me. Perhaps they had left the room to give the sisters a free opportunity for embraces and confidential communication. Perhaps there were no lady-boarders left. Howbeit, Emily and Eliza had tea; and before that refreshing meal was concluded, those dear women were fighting as hard as their husbands in the adjacent chamber.

Eliza, in the first place, was very angry at Emily's coming without invitation. Emily, on her part, was angry with Eliza for being angry. 'I am sure, Eliza,' said the spirited and injured MacWhirter, 'that is the third time you have alluded to it since we have been here. Had you and all your family come to Tours, Mac and I would have made them welcome—children and all; and I am sure yours make trouble enough in a house.'

'A private house is not like a boarding-house, Emily. Here Madame makes us pay frightfully for extras,' remarks Mrs. Baynes.

'I am sorry I came, Eliza. Let us say no more about it. I can't go away to-night,' says the other.

'And most unkind it is that speech to make, Emily. Any more tea?'

'Most unpleasant to have to make that speech, Eliza. To travel a whole day and night;—and I never able to sleep in a diligence—to hasten to my sister because I thought she was in trouble, because I thought a sister might comfort her; and to be received as you re—as you—oh, oh, oh—boh! How stoopid I am!' A handkerchief dries the tears: a smelling-bottle restores a little composure. 'When you came to us at Dumdum, with two—o—o children in the whooping-cough, I am sure Mac and I gave you a very different welcome.'

The other was smitten with remorse. She remembered her sister's kindness in former days. 'I did not mean, sister, to give you pain,' she said. 'But I am very unhappy myself, Emily. My child's conduct is making me most unhappy.'

'And very good reason you have to be unhappy, Eliza, if woman ever had,' says the other.

'Oh, indeed, yes!' gasps the General's lady.

'If any woman ought to feel remorse, Ebza Baynes, I am sure it's you. Sleepless nights! What was mine in the diligence, compared to the nights you must have? I said so to myself. "I am wretched," I said, "but what must *she* be?"'

'Of course, as a feeling mother, I feel that poor Charlotte is unhappy, my dear.'

'But what makes her so, my dear?' cries Mrs. MacWhirter, who presently showed that she was mistress of the whole controversy. 'No wonder Charlotte is unhappy, dear love! Can a girl be engaged to a young man, a most interesting young man, a clever, accomplished, highly-educated young man—'

'What?' cries Mrs. Baynes.

'Haven't I your letters? I have them all in my desk. They are in that hall now. Didn't you tell me so over and over again; and rave about him, till I thought you were in love with him yourself almost?' cries Mrs. Mac.

'A most indecent observation!' cries out Eliza Baynes, in her deep awful voice. 'No woman, no sister, shall say that to me!'

'Shall I go and get the letters? It used to be, "Dear Philip has just left us. Dear Philip has been more than a son to me. He is our preserver!" Didn't you write all that to me over and over again? And because you have found a richer husband for Charlotte, you are going to turn your preserver out of doors!'

'Emily MacWhirter, am I to sit here and be accused of crimes, *uninvited*, mind— *uninvited*, mind, by my sister? Is a general officer's lady to be treated in this way by a brevet-major's wife? Though you are my senior in age, Emily, I am yours in rank. Out of any room in England, but this, I go before you! And if you have come *uninvited* all the way from Tours to insult me in my own house—'

'House, indeed! pretty house! Everybody else's house as well as yours!'

'Such as it is, I never asked you to come into it, Emily!'

'Oh, yes! You wish me to go out in the night. Mac! I say!'

'Emily!' cries the Generaless.

'Mac, I say!' screams the Majoress, flinging open the door of the salon, 'my sister wishes me to go. Do you hear me?'

'Au nom de Dieu, madame, pensez à cette pauvre petite, qui souffre à côté,' cries the mistress of the house, pointing to her own, adjoining chamber, in which, we have said, our poor little Charlotte was lying.

'Nappley pas Madamaselle Baynes petite, sivoplay!' booms out Mrs. Baynes's contralto.

'MacWhirter, I say, Major MacWhirter!' cries Emily, flinging open the door of the dining-room where the two gentlemen were knocking their own heads together. 'MacWhirter! My sister chooses to insult me, and say that a brevet-major's wife—'

'By George! are you fighting, too?' asks the General.

'Baynes, Emily MacWhirter has insulted me!' cries Mrs. Baynes.

'It seems to have been a settled thing beforehand,' yells the General 'Major MacWhirter has done the same thing by me! He has forgotten that he is a gentleman, and that I am.'

'He only insults you because he thinks you are his relative, and must bear everything from him,' says the General's wife.

'By George! I will not bear everything from him!' shouts the General. The two gentlemen and their two wives are squabbling in the hall. Madame and the servants are peering up from the kitchen regions. I dare say the boys from the topmost banisters are saying to each other, 'Row between ma and Aunt Mac!' I dare say scared little Charlotte, in her temporary apartment, is, for a while, almost forgetful of her own grief; and wondering what quarrel is agitating her aunt and mother, her father and uncle? Place the remaining male and female boarders about in the corridors and on the landings, in various attitudes expressive of interest, of satiric commentary, wrath at being disturbed by unseemly domestic quarrel:—in what posture you will. As for Mrs. Colonel Bunch, she, poor thing, does not know that the General and her own Colonel have entered on a mortal quarrel. She imagines the dispute is only between Mrs. Baynes and her sister as yet; and she has known this pair quarrelling for a score of years past. 'Toujours comme ça, fighting vous savez, et puis make it up again. Oui,' she explains to a French friend on the landing.

In the very midst of this storm Colonel Bunch returns, his friend and second, Dr. Martin, on his arm. He does not know that two battles have been fought since his own combat. His, we will say, was Ligny. Then came Quatre-Bras, in which Baynes and MacWhirter were engaged. Then came the general action of Waterloo. And here enters Colonel Bunch, quite unconscious of the great engagements which have taken place since his temporary retreat in search of reinforcements.

'How are you, MacWhirter?' cries the Colonel of the purple whiskers. 'My friend, Dr. Martin!' And as he addresses himself to the General, his eyes almost start out of his head, as if they would shoot themselves into the breast of that officer.

'My dear, hush! Emily MacWhirter, had we not better defer this most painful dispute? The whole house is listening to us!' whispers the General, in a rapid low voice. 'Doctor—Colonel Bunch—Major MacWhirter, had we not better go into the dining-room?'

The General and the Doctor go first, Major MacWhirter and Colonel Bunch pause at the door. Says Bunch to MacWhirter: 'Major, you act as the General's friend in this affair? It's most awkward, but, by George! Baynes has said things to me that I won't bear, were he my own flesh and blood, by George! And I know him a deuced deal too well to think he will ever apologise!'

'He has said things to me, Bunch, that I won't bear from fifty brothers-in-law, by George!' growls MacWhirter.

'What? Don't you bring me any message from him?'

'I tell you, Tom Bunch, I want to send a message to him. Invite me to his house, and insult me and Emily when we come! By George, it makes my blood boil! Insult us after travelling twenty-four hours in a confounded diligence, and say we're not invited! He and his little catamaran.'

'Hush!' interposed Bunch.

'I say catamaran, sir! don't tell *me*! They came and stayed with us four months at Dumdum—the children ill with the pip, or some confounded thing—went to Europe, and left me to pay the doctor's bill; and now, by—'

Was the Major going to invoke George, the Cappadocian champion, or Olympian Jove? At this moment a door, by which they stood, opens. You may remember there were three doors, all on that landing; if you doubt me, go and see the house (Avenue de Valmy, Champs Elysées, Paris). A third door opens, and a young lady comes out, looking very pale and sad, and her hair hanging over her shoulders!—her hair, which hung in rich clusters generally, but I suppose tears have put it all out of curl.

'Is it you, Uncle Mac? I thought I knew your voice, and I heard Aunt Emily's,' says the little person.

'Yes, it is I, Charly,' says Uncle Mac. And he looks into the round face, which looks so wild and is so full of grief unutterable that Uncle Mac is quite melted, and takes the child to his arms, and says, 'What is it, my dear?' And he quite forgets that he proposes to blow her father's brains out in the morning. 'How hot your little hands are!'

'Uncle, uncle!' she says, in a swift febrile whisper, 'you 're come to take me away, I know. I heard you and papa, I heard mamma and Aunt Emily speaking quite loud! But if I go—I'll—I'll never love any but him!'

'But whom, dear?'

'But Philip, uncle.'

'By George, Char, no more you shall!' says the Major. And herewith the poor child, who had been sitting up on her bed whilst this quarrelling of sisters,—whilst this brawling of majors, generals, colonels,—whilst this coming of hackney-coaches,— whilst this arrival and departure of visitors on horseback,—had been taking place, gave a fine hysterical scream, and fell into her uncle's arms laughing and crying wildly.

This outcry, of course, brought the gentlemen from their adjacent room, and the ladies from theirs.

'What are you making a fool of yourself about?' growls Mrs. Baynes, in her deepest bark.

'By George, Eliza, you are too bad!' says the General, quite white.

'Eliza, you are a brute!' cries Mrs. MacWhirter.

'So she is!' shrieks Mrs. Bunch from the landing-place overhead, where other lady-boarders were assembled looking down on this awful family battle.

Eliza Baynes knew she had gone too far. Poor Charly was scarce conscious by this time, and wildly screaming, 'Never, never!'...When, as I live, who should burst into the premises but a young man with fair hair, with flaming whiskers, with flaming eyes, who calls out, 'What is it? I am here, Charlotte, Charlotte!'

Who is that young man? We had a glimpse of him, prowling about the Champs Elysées just now, and dodging behind a tree when Colonel Bunch went out in search of his second. Then the young man saw the MacWhirter hackney-coach approach the house. Then he waited and waited, looking to that upper window behind which we know his beloved was *not* reposing. Then he beheld Bunch and Dr. Martin arrive. Then he passed through the wicket into the garden, and heard Mrs. Mac and Mrs. Baynes fighting. Then there came from the passage—where, you see, this battle was going on—that ringing dreadful laugh and scream of poor Charlotte; and Philip Firmin burst like a bombshell into the midst of the hall where the battle was raging, and of the family circle who were fighting and screaming.

Here is a picture I protest. We have—first, the boarders on the first landing, whither, too, the Baynes children have crept in their nightgowns. Secondly, we have Auguste, Francoise the cook, and the assistant coming up from the basement. And, third, we have Colonel Bunch, Dr. Martin, Major MacWhirter, with Charlotte in his arms; Madame, General B., Mrs. Mac, Mrs. General B., all in the passage, when our friend the bombshell bursts in amongst them.

'What is it? Charlotte, I am here!' cries Philip, with his great voice; at hearing which, little Char gives one final scream, and, at the next moment, she has fainted quite dead—but this time she is on Philip's shoulder.

'You brute, how dare you do this?' asks Mrs. Baynes, glaring at the young man.

'It is *you* who have done it, Eliza!' says Aunt Emily.

'And so she has, Mrs. MacWhirter!' calls out Mrs. Colonel Bunch, from the landing above.

And Charles Baynes felt he had acted like a traitor, and hung down his head. He had encouraged his daughter to give her heart away, and she had obeyed him. When he saw Philip I think he was glad: so was the Major, though Firmin, to be sure, pushed him quite roughly up against the wall.

'Is this vulgar scandal to go on in the passage before the whole house?' gasped Mrs. Baynes.

'Bunch brought me here to prescribe for this young lady,' says little Dr. Martin, in a very courtly way. 'Madame, will you get a little sal-volatile from Anjubeau's in the Faubourg; and let her be kept very quiet!'

'Come, Monsieur Philippe, it is enough like that!' cries Madame, who can't repress a smile. 'Come to your chamber, dear little!'

'Madame!' cries Mrs. Baynes, ' une mère—'

Madame shrugs her shoulders. 'Une mère, une belle mère, ma foi!' she says. 'Come, mademoiselle!'

There were only very few people in the boarding-house: if they knew, if they saw, what happened, how can we help ourselves? But that they had all been sitting over a powder-magazine, which might have blown up and destroyed one, two, three, five people, even Philip did not know, until afterwards, when, laughing, Major MacWhirter told him how that meek but most savage Baynes had first challenged Bunch, had then challenged his brother-in-law, and how all sorts of battle, murder, sudden death might have ensued had the quarrel not come to an end.

Were your humble servant anxious to harrow his reader's feelings, or display his own graphical powers, you understand that I never would have allowed those two gallant officers to quarrel and threaten each other's very noses, without having the insult wiped out in blood. The Bois de Boulogne is hard by the Avenue de Valmy, with plenty of cool fighting ground. The *octroi* officers never stop gentlemen going out at the neighbouring barrier upon duelling business, or prevent the return of the slain victim in the hackney-coach when the dreadful combat is over. From my knowledge of Mrs. Baynes's character, I have not the slightest doubt that she would have encouraged her husband to fight; and, the General down, would have put pistols into the hands of her boys, and bidden them carry on the *vendetta*; but as I do not, for my part, love to see brethren at war, or Moses and Aaron tugging white handfuls out of each other's beards, I am glad there is going to be no fight between the veterans, and that either's stout old breast is secure from the fratricidal bullet.

Major MacWhirter forgot all about bullets and battles when poor little Charlotte kissed him, and was not in the least jealous when he saw the little maiden clinging on Philip's arm. He was melted at the sight of that grief and innocence, when Mrs. Baynes still continued to bark out her private rage, and said: 'If the General won't protect me from insult, I think I had better go.'

'By Jove, I think you had!' exclaimed MacWhirter, to which remark the eyes of the Doctor and Colonel Bunch gleamed an approval.

'*Allons,* Monsieur Philippe. Enough like that—let me take her to bed again,' Madame resumed. 'Come, dear miss!'

What a pity that the bedroom was but a yard from where they stood!

Philip felt strong enough to carry his little Charlotte to the Tuileries. The thick brown locks, which had fallen over his shoulders, are lifted away. The little wounded heart that had lain against his own, parts from him with a reviving throb. Madame and her mother carry away little Charlotte. The door of the neighbouring chamber closes on her. The sad little vision has disappeared. The men, quarrelling anon in the passage, stand there silent.

'I heard her voice outside,' said Philip, after a little pause (with love, with grief, with excitement, I suppose his head was in a whirl). 'I heard her voice outside, and I couldn't help coming in.'

'By George, I should think not, young fellow!' says Major MacWhirter, stoutly shaking the young man by the hand.

'Hush, hush!' whispers the Doctor; 'she must be kept quite quiet. She has had quite excitement enough for to-night. There must be no more scenes, my young fellow.'

And Philip says, when in this his agony of grief and doubt he found a friendly hand put out to him, he himself was so exceedingly moved that he was compelled to fly out of the company of the old men, into the night, where the rain was pouring—the gentle rain.

While Philip, without Madame Smolensk's premises, is saying his tenderest prayers, offering up his tears, heart-throbs, and most passionate vows of love for little Charlotte's benefit, the warriors assembled within once more retreat to a colloquy in the salle-à-manger; and, in consequence of the rainy state of the night, the astonished Auguste has to bring a third supply of hot water for the four gentlemen attending the Congress. The Colonel, the Major, the Doctor, ranged themselves on one side the table, defended, as it were, by a line of armed tumblers, flanked by a strong brandy bottle and a stout earthwork, from an embrasure in which scalding water could be discharged. Behind these fortifications the veterans awaited their enemy, who, after marching up and down the room for a while, takes position finally in their front and prepares to attack. The General remounts his *cheval de bataille,* but cannot bring the animal to charge as fiercely as before. Charlottes white apparition has come amongst them, and flung her fair arms between the men of war. In vain Baynes tries to get up a bluster, and to enforce his passion with by Georges, by Joves, and words naughtier still. That weak, meek, quiet, henpecked, but most bloodthirsty old General found himself forming his own minority, and against him bis old comrade Bunch, whom he had insulted and nose-pulled; his brother-in-law MacWhirter, whom he had nose-pulled and insulted; and the Doctor, who had been called in as the friend of the former. As they faced him, shoulder to shoulder, each of those three acquired fresh courage from his neighbour. Each, taking his aim, deliberately poured his fire into Baynes. To yield to such odds, on the other hand, was not so distasteful to the veteran, as to have to give up his sword to any single adversary. Before he would own himself in the wrong to any individual, he would eat that individual's ears and nose: but to surrounded by three enemies, and strike your flag before such odds, was no disgrace; and Baynes could take the circumbendibus way of apology to which some proud spirits will submit. Thus he could say to the Doctor, 'Well, Doctor, perhaps I was hasty in accusing Bunch of employing bad language to me. A bystander can see these things sometimes when a principal is too angry; and as you go against me— well—there, then, I ask Bunch's pardon.' That business over, the MacWhirter reconciliation was very speedily brought about. 'Fact was, was in a confounded ill-temper—very much disturbed by events of the day—didn't mean anything but this, that, and so forth.' If this old chief had to eat humble pie, his brave adversaries were anxious that he should gobble up his portion as quickly as possible, and turned away their honest old heads as he swallowed it. One of the party told his wife of the quarrel which had arisen, but Baynes never did. 'I declare, sir,' Philip used to say, 'had she known anything about the quarrel that night, Mrs. Baynes would have made her husband turn out of bed at midnight, and challenge his old friends over again!' But then there was no love between Philip and Mrs. Baynes, and in those whom he hates he is accustomed to see little good.

Thus, any gentle reader who expected to be treated to an account of the breakage of the sixth commandment will close this chapter disappointed. Those stout old rusty swords which were fetched off their hooks by the warriors, their owners, were returned undrawn to their flannel cases. Hands were shaken after a fashion—at least no blood was shed. But, though the words spoken between the old boys were civil enough, Bunch, MacWhirter, and the Doctor could not alter their opinion that

Philip had been hardly used, and that the benefactor of his family merited a better treatment from General Baynes.

Meanwhile, that benefactor strode home through the rain in a state of perfect rapture. The rain refreshed him, as did his own tears. The dearest little maiden had sunk for a moment on his heart, and, as she lay there, a thrill of hope vibrated through his whole frame. Her father's old friends had held out a hand to him, and bid him not despair. Blow wind, fall autumn rains! In the midnight, under the gusty trees, amidst which the lamps of the *réverbères* are tossing, the young fellow strides back to his lodgings. He is poor and unhappy, but he has Hope along with him. He looks at a certain breast-button of his old coat ere he takes it off to sleep. 'Her cheek was lying there,' he thinks—'just there.' My poor little Charlotte! what could she have done to the breast-button of the old coat?

CHAPTER XXVIII. IN WHICH MRS. MACWHIRTER HAS A NEW BONNET

NOW though the unhappy Philip slept quite soundly, so that his boots, those tramp-worn sentries, remained *en faction* at his door until quite a late hour next morning; and though little Charlotte, after a prayer or two, sank into the sweetest and most refreshing girlish slumber, Charlotte's father and mother had a had night; and, for my part, I maintain that they did not deserve a good one. It was very well for Mrs. Baynes to declare that it was Mac-Whirter's snoring which kept them awake (Mr. and Mrs. Mac being lodged in the bedroom over their relatives)—I don't say a snoring neighbour is pleasant—but what a bedfellow is a bad conscience! Under Mrs. Baynes's night-cap the grim eyes lie open all night; on Baynes's pillow is a silent wakeful head that hears the hours toll. 'A plague upon the young man!' thinks the female *bonnet de nuit;* 'how dare he come in and disturb everything? How pale Charlotte will look to-morrow when Mrs. Hely calls with her son! When she has been crying she looks hideous, and her eyelids and nose are quite red. She may fly out and say something wicked and absurd, as she did to-day. I wish I had never seen that insolent young man, with his carroty beard and vulgar blucher boots! If my boys were grown up, he should not come hectoring about the house as he does; *they* would soon find a way of punishing his impudence!' Baulked revenge and a hungry disappointment, I think, are keeping that old woman awake; and,if she hears the hours tolling, it is because wicked thoughts make her sleepless.

As for Baynes, I believe that old man is awake, because he is awake to the shabbiness of his own conduct. His conscience has got the better of him, which he has been trying to bully out of doors. Do what he will, that reflection forces itself upon him. Mae, Bunch, and the Doctor all saw the thing at once, and went dead against him. He wanted to break his word to a young fellow, who, whatever his faults might be, had acted most nobly and generously by the Baynes family. He might have been ruined but for Philip's forbearance; and showed his gratitude by breaking his promise to the young fellow. He was a henpecked man—that was the fact. He allowed his wife to govern him: that little old plain cantankerous woman asleep yonder. Asleep was she? No. He knew she wasn't. Both were lying quite still, wide awake, pursuing their dismal thoughts. Only Charles was owning that he was a sinner, whilst Eliza his wife, in a rage at her last defeat, was meditating how she could continue and still win her battle.

Then Baynes reflects how persevering his wife is; how, all through life, she has come back and back and back to her point, until he has ended by an almost utter subjugation. He will resist for a day: she will fight for a year, for a life. If once she hates people, the sentiment always remains with her fresh and lively. Her jealousy never dies; nor her desire to rule. What a life she will lead poor Charlotte now she has declared against Philip. The poor child will be subject to a dreadful tyranny: the father knows it. As soon as he leaves the house on his daily walks the girl's torture will begin. Baynes knows how his wife can torture a woman. As she groans out a hollow cough from her bed in the midnight, the guilty man lies quite mum under his own counterpane. If she fancies him awake, it will be *his* turn to receive the torture. Ah, Othello, *mon ami*! when you look round at married life, and know what you know, don't you wonder that the bolster is not used a great deal more freely on both sides? Horrible cynicism! Yes—I know. These propositions served raw are savage, and shock your sensibility; cooked with a little piquant sauce, they are welcome at quite polite tables.

'Poor child! Yes, by George! What a life her mother will lead her!' thinks the General, rolling uneasy on the midnight pillow. 'No rest for her, day or night, until she marries the man of her mother's choosing. And she has a delicate chest— Martin says she has; and she wants coaxing and soothing, and pretty coaxing she will have from mamma!' Then, I dare say, the past rises up in that wakeful old man's uncomfortable memory. His little Charlotte is a child again, laughing on his knee, and playing with his accoutrements as he comes home from parade. He remembers the fever which she had, when she would take medicine from no other hand; and how, though silent with her mother, with him she would never tire of prattling, prattling. Guilt-stricken old man! are those tears trickling down thy old nose? It is midnight. We cannot see. When you brought her to the river, and parted with her to send her to Europe, how the little maid clung to you, and cried, 'Papa, papa!' Staggering up the steps of the ghaut, how you wept yourself—yes, wept tears of passionate tender grief at parting with the darling of your soul. And now, deliberately, and for the sake of money, you stab her to the heart, and break your plighted honour to your child. 'And it is yonder cruel, shrivelled, bilious, plain old woman who makes me do all this, and trample on my darling and torture her!' he thinks. In Zoffany's famous picture of Garrick and Mrs. Pritchard as Macbeth and Lady Macbeth, Macbeth stands in an attitude hideously contorted and constrained, while Lady Mac is firm and easy. Was this the actor's art, or the poet's device? Baynes is wretched, then. He is wrung with remorse, and shame and pity. Well, I am glad of it. Old man, old man! how darest thou to cause that child's tender little bosom to bleed? How bilious he looks the next morning! I declare as yellow as his grim old wife. When Mrs. General B. hears the children their lessons, how she will scold them! It is my belief she will bark through the morning chapter, and scarce understand a word of its meaning. As for Charlotte, when she appears with red eyes, and ever so little colour in her round cheek, there is that in her look and demeanour which warns her mother to refrain from too familiar abuse or scolding. The girl is in rebellion. All day Char was in a feverish state, her eyes flashing war. There was a song which Philip loved in those days: the song of Ruth. Char sat down to the piano, and sang it with a strange energy. 'Thy people shall be my people'—she sang with all her heart—'and thy God my God!' The slave had risen. The little heart was in arms and mutiny. The mother was scared by her defiance.

As for the guilty old father: pursued by the fiend remorse, he fled early from his house, and read all the papers at Galignani's without comprehending them. Madly regardless of expense, he then plunged into one of those luxurious restaurants in the Palais Royal, where you get soup, three dishes, a sweet, and a pint of delicious wine for two frongs, by George! But all the luxuries there presented to him could not drive away care, or create appetite. Then the poor old wretch went off, and saw a ballet at the Grand Opera. In vain. The pink nymphs had not the slightest fascination for him. He hardly was aware of their ogles, bounds, and capers. He saw a little maid with round sad eyes—his Iphigenia whom he was stabbing. He took more brandy-and-water at cafés on his way home. In vain, in vain, I tell you! The old wife was sitting up for him, scared at the unusual absence of her lord. She dared not remonstrate with him when he returned. His face was pale. His eyes were fierce and bloodshot. When the General had a particular look, Eliza Baynes cowered in silence. Mac, the two sisters, and, I think, Colonel Bunch (but on this point my informant, Philip, cannot be sure) were having a dreary rubber when the General came in. Mrs. B. knew by the General's face that he had been having recourse to alcoholic stimulus. But she dared not speak. A tiger in a jungle was not more savage than Baynes sometimes. 'Where's Char?' he asked in his dreadful, his Bluebeard voice. 'Char was gone to bed,' said mamma, sorting her trumps. 'Hm! Augoost, Odevee, Osho!' Did Eliza Baynes interfere, though she knew he had had enough? As soon interfere with a tiger, and tell him he had eaten enough Sepoy. After Lady Macbeth had induced Mac to go through that business with Duncan, depend upon it, she was very deferential and respectful to her general. No groans, prayers, remorses could avail to bring his late Majesty back to life again. As for you, old man, though your deed is done, it is not past recalling. Though you have withdrawn from your word on a sordid money pretext; made two hearts miserable, stabbed cruelly that one which you love best in the world; acted with wicked ingratitude towards a young man, who has been nobly forgiving towards you and yours; and are suffering with rage and remorse, as you own your crime to yourself; —your dee is not past recalling as yet. You may soothe that anguish and dry those tears. It is but an act of resolution on your part, and a firm resumption of your marital authority. Mrs. Baynes, after her crime, is quite humble and gentle. She has half murdered her child, and stretched Philip on an infernal rack of torture; but she is quite civil to everybody at Madame's house. Not one word does she say respecting Mrs. Colonel Bunch's outbreak of the night before. She talks to sister Emily about Paris, the fashions, and Emily's walks on the Boulevard and the Palais Royal with her Major. She bestows ghastly smiles upon sundry lodgers at table. She thanks Augoost when he serves her at dinner—and says, 'Ah, madame, que le boof est bong aujourd'hui, rien que j'aime comme le potofou.' Oh, you old hypocrite! But you know I, for my part, always disliked the woman, and said her good-humour was more detestable than her anger. You hypocrite! I say again:—ay, and avow that there were other hypocrites at the table, as you shall presently hear.

When Baynes got an opportunity of speaking unobserved, as he thought, to Madame, you may be sure the guilty wretch asked her how his little Charlotte was. Mrs. Baynes trumped her partner's best heart at that moment, but pretended to observe or overhear nothing. 'She goes better—she sleeps,' Madame said. 'Mr. the Doctor Martin has commanded her a calming potion.' And what if I were to tell you that somebody had taken a little letter from Charlotte, and actually had given fifteen sous to a Savoyard youth to convey that letter to somebody else? What if I were to tell you that the party to whom that letter was addressed, straightway wrote an answer—directed to Madame de Smolensk, of course? I know it was very wrong; but I suspect Philip's prescription did quite as much good as Dr. Martin's, and don't intend to be very angry with Madame for consulting the unlicensed practitioner. Don't preach to me, madam, about morality, and dangerous examples set to young people. Even at your present mature age, and with your dear daughters around you, if your ladyship goes to hear the 'Barber of Seville,' on which side are your sympathies—on Dr. Bartolo's, or Miss Rosina's?

Although, then, Mrs. Baynes was most respectful to her husband, and by many grim blandishments, humble appeals, and forced humiliations, strove to conciliate and soothe him, the General turned a dark lowering face upon the partner of his existence: her dismal smiles were no longer pleasing to him: he returned curt 'Ohs!' and 'Ahs!' to her remarks. When Mrs. Hely and her son and her daughter drove up in their family coach to pay yet a second visit to the Baynes family, the General flew in a passion, and cried, 'Bless my soul, Eliza, you can't think of receiving visitors, with our poor child sick in the next room? It's inhuman!' The scared woman ventured on no remonstrances. She was so frightened that she did not attempt to scold the younger children. She took a piece of work, and sat amongst them, furtively weeping. Their artless queries and unseasonable laughter stabbed and punished the matron. You see people do wrong, though they are long past fifty years of age. It is not only the scholars, but the ushers, and the head-master himself, who sometimes deserves a chastisement. I, for my part, hope to remember this sweet truth, though I live into the year 1900.

To those other ladies boarding at Madame's establishment, to Mrs. Mac and Mrs. Colonel Bunch, though they had declared against him, and expressed their opinions in the frankest way on the night of the battle royal, the General was provokingly polite and amiable. They had said, but twenty-four hours since, that the General was a brute; and Lord Chesterfield could not have been more polite to a lovely young duchess than was Baynes to these matrons next day. You have heard how Mrs. Mac had a strong desire to possess a new Paris bonnet, so that she might appear with proper lustre among the ladies on the promenade at Tours? Major and Mrs. Mac and Mrs. Bunch talked of going to the Palais Royal (where MacWhirter said he had remarked some uncommonly neat things, by George! at the corner shop under the glass gallery). On this, Baynes started up, and said he would accompany his friends, adding, 'You know, Emily, I promised you a hat ever so long ago!' And those four went away together, and not one offer did Baynes make to his wife to join the party; though her best bonnet, poor thing, was a dreadfully old performance, with moulting feathers, rumpled ribbons, tarnished flowers and lace, bought in St. Martin's Alley months and months before. Emily, to be sure, said to her sister, 'Eliza, won't *you* be of the party? We can take the omnibus at the corner, which will land us at the very gate.' But as Emily gave this unlucky invitation, the General's face wore an expression of ill-will so savage and terrific, that Eliza Baynes said, 'No, thank you, Emily; Charlotte is still unwell, and I—I may be wanted at home.' And the party went away without Mrs. Baynes; and they were absent I don't know how long: and Emily MacWhirter came back to the boarding-house in a bonnet—the sweetest thing you ever saw!—green piqué velvet, with a *ruche* full of rosebuds, and a bird of paradise perched on the top, pecking at a bunch of the most magnificent grapes, poppies, ears of corn, barley, etc., all indicative of the bounteous autumn season. Mrs. General Baynes had to see her sister return home in this elegant bonnet; to welcome her; to acquiesce in Emily's remark that the General had done the genteel thing; to hear how the party had further been to Tortoni's and had ices; and then to go upstairs to her own room, and look at her own battered blowsy old *chapeau,* with its limp streamers, hanging from its peg. This humiliation, I say, Eliza Baynes had to bear in silence, without wincing, and, if possible, with a smile on her face.

In consequence of circumstances before indicated, Miss Charlotte was pronounced to be very much better when her papa returned from his Palais Royal trip. He found her seated on Madame's sofa, pale, but with the wonted sweetness in her smile. He kissed and caressed her with many tender words. I dare say he told her there was nothing in the world he loved so much as his Charlotte. He would never willingly do anything to give her pain, never! She had been his good girl, an his blessing, all his life! Ah! that is a prettier little picture to imagine—that repentant man, and his child clinging to him—than the tableau overhead, viz., Mrs. Baynes looking at her old bonnet. Not one word was said about Philip in the talk between Baynes and his daughter, but those tender paternal looks and caresses carried hope into Charlotte's heart; and when her papa went away (she said afterwards to a female friend), 'I got up and followed him, intending to show him Philip's letter. But at the door I saw mamma coming down the stairs; and she looked so dreadful, and frightened me so, that I went back.' There are some mothers I have heard of, who won't allow their daughters to read the works of this humble homilist, lest they should imbibe 'dangerous' notions, etc. etc. My good ladies, give them 'Goody Two-shoes' if you like, or whatever work, combining instruction and amusement, you think most appropriate to their juvenile understandings; but I beseech you to be gentle with them. I never saw people on better terms with each other, more frank, affectionate, and cordial, than the parents and the grown-up young folks in the United States. And why? Because the children were spoiled, to be sure! I say to you, get the confidence of yours—before the day comes of revolt and independence, after which love returneth not.

Now, when Mrs. Baynes went in to her daughter, who had been sitting pretty comfortably kissing her father on the sofa in Madame's chamber, all those soft tremulous smiles and twinkling dew-drops of compassion and forgiveness which anon had come to soothe the little maid, fled from cheek and eyes. They began to flash again with their febrile brightness, and her heart to throb with dangerous rapidity. 'How are you now?' asks mamma, with her deep voice. 'I am much the same,' says the girl, beginning to tremble. 'Leave the child; you agitate her, madam,' cries the mistress of the house, coming in after Mrs. Baynes. That sad, humiliated, deserted mother goes out from her daughter's presence, hanging her head. She put on the poor old bonnet, and had a walk that evening on the Champs Elysées with her little ones, and showed them Guignol: she gave a penny to Guignol's man. It is my belief that she saw no more of the performance than her husband had seen of the ballet the night previous, when Taglioni, and Noblet, and Duvernay danced before his hot eyes. But then, you see, the hot eyes had been washed with a refreshing water since, which enabled them to view the world much more cheerfully and brightly. Ah, gracious Heaven gives us eyes to see our own wrong, however dim age may make them; and knees not too stiff to kneel, in spite of years, cramp, and rheumatism! That stricken old woman, then, treated her children to the trivial comedy of Guignol. She did not cry out when the two boys climbed up the trees of the Elysian Fields, though the guardians bade them descend. She bought pink sticks of barley-sugar for the young ones. Withdrawing the glistening sweetmeats from their lips, they pointed to Mrs. Hely's splendid barouche as it rolled citywards from the Bois de Boulogne. The grey shades were falling, andAuguste was in the act of ringing the first dinner-bell at Madame Smolensk's establishment, when Mrs. General Baynes returned to her lodgings.

Meanwhile, Aunt MacWhirter had been to pay a visit to little Miss Charlotte, in the new bonnet which the General, Charlotte's papa, had bought for her. This elegant article had furnished a subject of pleasing conversation between niece and aunt, who held each other in very kindly regard, and all the details of the bonnet, the blue flowers, scarlet flowers, grapes, sheaves of corn, lace, etc., were examined and admired in detail. Charlotte remembered the dowdy old English thing which Aunt Mac wore when she went out? Charlotte did remember the bonnet, and laughed when Mrs. Mac described how papa, in the hackney coach on their return home, insisted upon taking the old wretch of a bonnet, and flinging it out of the coach-window into the road, where an old chiffonnier passing picked it up with his iron hook, put it on his own head, and walked away grinning. I declare, at the recital of this narrative, Charlotte laughed as pleasantly and happily as in former days; and, no doubt, there were more kisses between this poor little maid and her aunt.

Now, you will remark, that the General and his party, though they returned from the Palais Royal in a hackney coach, went thither on foot, two and two—viz., Major MacWhirter leading, and giving his arm to Mrs. Bunch (who, I promise you, knew the shops in the Palais Royal well), and the General following at some distance, with his sister-in-law for a partner.

In that walk a conversation very important to Charlotte's interests took place between her aunt and her father.

'Ah, Baynes! this is a sad business about dearest Char,' Mrs. Mac broke out with a sigh.

'It is, indeed, Emily,' says the General, with a very sad groan on his part.

'It goes to my heart to see you, Baynes; it goes to Mac's heart. We talked about it ever so late last night. You were suffering dreadfully; and all the brandy-pawnee in the world won't cure you, Charles.'

'No, faith,' says the General, with a dismal screw of the mouth. ' ou see, Emily, to see that child suffer tears my heart out—by George, it does. She has been the best child, and the most gentle, and the merriest, and the most obedient, and I never had a word of fault to find with her; and—poo-ooh!' Here the General's eyes, which have been winking with extreme rapidity, give way; and at the signal pooh! there issue out from them two streams of that eye-water which we have said is sometimes so good for the sight.

'My dear kind Charles, you were always a good creature,' says Emily, patting the arm on which hers rests. Meanwhile Major-General Baynes, C.B., puts his bamboo cane under his disengaged arm, extracts from his hind pocket a fine large yellow bandanna pocket-handkerchief, and performs a prodigious loud obbligato—just under the spray of the Rond-point fountain, opposite the Bridge of the Invalides, over which poor Philip has tramped many and many a day and night to see his little maid.

'Have a care with your cane, then, old imbecile!' cries an approaching foot-passenger, whom the General meets and charges with his iron ferule.

'Mille pardong, mosoo; je vous demande mille pardong,' says the old man, quite meekly.

'You are a good soul, Charles,' the lady continues; 'and my little Char is a darling. You never would have done this of your own accord. Mercy! And see what it was coming to! Mac only told me last night. You horrid bloodthirsty creature! Two challenges—and dearest Mac as hot as pepper! Oh, Charles Baynes, I tremble when I think of the danger from which you have all been rescued! Suppose you brought home to Eliza—suppose dearest Mac brought home to me killed by this arm on which I am leaning. Oh, it is dreadful, dreadful! We are sinners all, that we are, Baynes!'

'I humbly ask pardon for having thought of a great crime. I ask pardon,' says the General, very pale and solemn.

'If you had killed dear Mac, would you ever have had rest again, Charles?'

'No; I think not. I should not deserve it,' answers the contrite Baynes.

'*You* have a good heart. It was not *you* who did this. I know who it was. She always had a dreadful temper. The way in which she used to torture our poor dear Louisa who is dead, I can hardly forgive now, Baynes. Poor suffering angel! Eliza was at her bedside nagging and torturing her up to the very last day. Did you ever see her with her nurses and servants in India? The way in which she treated them was—'

'Don't say any more. I am aware of my wife's faults of temper. Heaven knows it has made me suffer enough!' says the General, hanging his head down.

'Why, man—do you intend to give way to her altogether? I said to Mac last night, "Mac, does he intend to give way to her altogether? The 'Army List' doesn't contain the name of a braver man than Charles Baynes, and is my sister Eliza to rule him entirely, Mac?" I said. No, if you stand up to Eliza, I know from experience she will give way. We have had quarrels, scores and hundreds, as you know, Baynes.'

'Faith, I do,' owns the General, with a sad smile on his countenance.

'And sometimes she has had the best and sometimes I have had the best, Baynes! But I never yielded, as you do, without a fight for my own. No, never, Baynes! And me and Mac are shocked, I tell you fairly, when we see the way in which you give up to her!'

'Come, come! I think you have told me often enough that I am henpecked,' says the General.

'And you give up not yourself only, Charles, but your dear dear child —poor little suffering love!'

'The young man's a beggar!' cries the General, biting his lips.

'What were you, what was Mac and me when we married? We hadn't much beside our pay, had we? we rubbed on through bad weather and good, managing as best we could, loving each other, God be praised! And here we are, owing nobody anything, and me going to have a new bonnet!' and she tossed up her head, and gave her companion a good-natured look through her twinkling eyes.

'Emily, you have a good heart! that's the truth,' says the General.

'And *you* have a good heart, Charles, as sure as my name's MacWhirter; and I want you to act upon it, and I propose—'

'What?'

'Well, I propose that—' But now they have reached the Tuileries garden gates, and pass through, and continue their conversation in the midst of such a hubbub that we cannot overhear them. They cross the garden, and so make their way into the Palais Royal, and the purchase of the bonnet takes place; and in the midst of the excitement occasioned by *that* event, of course, all discussion of domestic affairs becomes uninteresting.

But the gist of Baynes's talk with his sister-in-law may be divined from the conversation which presently occurred between Charlotte and her aunt. Charlotte did not come in to the public dinner. She was too weak for that; and '*un bon bouillon*' and a wing of fowl were served to her in the private apartment where she had been reclining all day. At dessert, however, Mrs. MacWhirter took a fine bunch of grapes and a plump rosy peach from the table, and carried them to the little maid, and their interview may be described with sufficient accuracy, though it passed without other witnesses.

From the outbreak on the night of quarrels, Charlotte knew that her aunt was her friend. The glances of Mrs. MacWhirter's eyes, and the expression of her bonny homely face, told her sympathy to the girl. There were no pallors now, no angry glances, no heart-beating. Miss Char could even make a little joke when her aunt appeared, and say, 'What beautiful grapes! Why, aunt, you must have taken them out of the new bonnet.'

'You should have had the bird of paradise, too, dear, only I see you have not eaten your chicken. She is a kind woman, Madame Smolensk I like her. She gives very nice dinners. I can't think how she does it for the money, I am sure!'

'She has been very very kind to me'; and I love her with all my heart!' cries Charlotte.

'Poor darling! We have all our trials, and yours have begun, my love!'

'Yes, indeed, aunt!' whimpers the young person; upon which osculation possibly takes place.

'My dear! when your papa took me to buy the bonnet, we had a long talk, and it was about you.'

'About me, aunt?' warbles Miss Charlotte.

'He would not take mamma; he would only go with me, alone. I knew he wanted to say something about you; and what do you think it was? My dear, you have been very much agitated here. You and your poor mamma are likely to disagree for some time. She will drag you to those balls and fine parties, and bring you those *fme partners.*'

'Oh, I hate them!' cries Charlotte. Poor little Walsingham Hely, what had he done to be hated?

'Well. It is not for me to speak of a mother to her own daughter. But you know mamma has *a way* with her. She expects to be obeyed. She will give you no peace. She will come back to her point again and again. You know how she speaks of some one—a certain gentleman? If ever she sees him, she will be rude to him. Mamma can be rude at times—that I must say of my own sister. As long as you remain here—'

'Oh, aunt, aunt! Don't take me away, don't take me away!' cries Charlotte.

'My dearest, are you afraid of your old aunt, and your Uncle Mac, who is so kind, and has always loved you? Major MacWhirter has a will of his own, too, though of course I make no allusions. *We* know how admirably somebody has behaved to your family. Somebody who has been most *ungratefully* treated, though of course I make no allusions. If you have given away your heart to your father's *greatest benefactor,* do you suppose I and Uncle Mac will quarrel with you? When Eliza married Baynes (your father was a penniless subaltern, then, my dear,—and my sister was certainly neither a fortune nor a beauty), didn't she go dead against the wishes of *our* father? Certainly she did! But she said she was of age—that she was, and a great deal more, too—and she would do as she liked, and she made Baynes marry her. Why should you be afraid of coming to us, love? You are nearer somebody here, but can you see him? Your mamma will never let you go out, but she will follow you like a shadow. You may write to him. Don't tell *me,* child. Haven't I been young myself? and when there was a difficulty between Mac and poor papa, didn't Mac write to me, though he hates letters, poor dear, and certainly is a *stick* at them? And, though we were forbidden, had we not twenty ways of telegraphing to each other? Law! your poor dear grandfather was in such a rage with me once, when he found one, that he took down his great buggy whip to me, a grown girl!'

Charlotte, who has plenty of humour, would have laughed at this confession some other time, but now she was too much agitated by that invitation to quit Paris, which her aunt had just given her. Quit Paris? Lose the chance of seeing her dearest friend, her protector! If he was not with her, was he not near her? Yes, near her always! On that horrible night, when all was so desperate, did not her champion burst forward to her rescue? Oh, the dearest and bravest! Oh, the tender and true!

'You are not listening, you poor child!' said Aunt Mac, surveying her niece with looks of kindness. 'Now listen to me once more. Whisper!' And sitting down on the settee by Charlotte's side, Aunt Emily first kissed the girl's round cheek, and then whispered into her ear.

Never, I declare, was medicine so efficacious, or rapid of effect, as that wondrous distilment which Aunt Emily poured into her niece's ear! 'Oh, you goose!' she began by saying, and the rest of the charm she whispered into that pearly little pink shell round which Miss Charlotte's soft brown ringlets clustered. Such a sweet blush rose straightway to the cheek! Such sweet lips began to cry, 'Oh, you dear dear aunt,' and then began to kiss aunt's kind face, that, I declare, if I knew the spell, I would like to pronounce it right off, with such a sweet young patient to practise on.

'When do we go? To-morrow, aunt, n'est-ce pas? Oh, I am quite strong! never felt so well in my life! I'll go and pack up *this instant,'* cries the young person.

'Doucement! Papa knows of the plan. Indeed, it was he who proposed it.'

'Dearest, best father!' ejaculates Miss Charlotte.

'But mamma does not; and if you show yourself very eager, Charlotte, she may object, you know. Heaven forbid that *I* should counsel dissimulation to a child! but under the circumstances, my love. At least I own what happened between Mac and me. Law! *I* didn't care for papa's buggy whip! I knew it would not hurt; and as for Baynes, I am sure he would not hurt a fly. Never was man more sorry for what he has done. He told me so whilst we walked away from the bonnet-shop, whilst he was carrying my old yellow. We met somebody near the Bourse. How sad he looked, and how handsome, too! *I* bowed to him, and kissed my hand to him, that is, the knob of my parasol. Papa couldn't shake hands with him, because of my bonnet, you know, in the brown paper bag. He has a grand beard, indeed! He looked like a wounded lion. I said so to papa. And I said, "It is you who wound him, Charles Baynes!" "I know that," papa said. "I have been thinking of it. I can't sleep at night for thinking about it: and it makes me dee'd unhappy." You know what papa sometimes says? Dear me! You should have heard them, when Eliza and I joined the army, years and years ago!'

For once, Charlotte Baynes was happy at her father's being unhappy. The little maiden's heart had been wounded to think that her father could do his Charlotte a wrong. Ah! take warning by him, ye greybeards! And however old and toothless, if you have done wrong, own that you have done so; and sit down and say grace, and mumble your humble pie!

The General, then, did not shake hands with Philip; but Major MacWhirter went up in the most marked way, and gave the wounded lion his own paw, and said, 'Mr. Firmin, glad to see you! If ever yon come to Tours, mind, don't forget my wife and me. Fine day. Little patient much better! Bon courage, as they say!'

I wonder what sort of a bungle Philip made of his correspondence with the *Pall Mall Gazette* that night? Every man who lives by his pen, if by chance he looks back at his writings of former years, lives in the past again. Our griefs, our pleasures, our youth, our sorrows, our dear dear friends, resuscitate. How we tingle with shame over some of those fine passages! How dreary are those disinterred jokes! It was Wednesday night. Philip was writing off at home, in his inn, one of his grand tirades, dated 'Paris, Thursday'—so as to be in time, you understand, for the post of Saturday, when the little waiter comes and says, winking, 'Again that lady, Monsieur Philippe!'

'What lady?' asks our own intelligent correspondent.

'That old lady who came the other day, you know.'

'C'est moi, mon ami!' cries Madame Smolensk's well-known grave voice. 'Here is a letter, d'abord. But that says nothing. It was written before the grande nouvelle— the great news—the good news!'

'What good news?' asks the gentleman.

'In two days Miss goes to Tours with her aunt and uncle—this good Macvirterre. They have taken their places by the diligence of Lafitte and Caillard. They are thy friends. Papa encourages her going. Here is their card of visit. Go thou also; they will receive thee with open arms. What hast thou, my son?'

Philip looked dreadfully sad. An injured and unfortunate gentleman at New York had drawn upon him, and he had paid away everything he had but four francs, and he was living on credit until his next remittance arrived.

'Thou hast no money! I have thought of it. Behold of it! Let him wait—the proprietor!' And she takes out a bank-note, which she puts in the young man's hand.

'Tiens, il l'embrasse encor, c'te vieille!' says the little knife-boy. 'J'aimerais pas ça, moi, par exemp'!'

CHAPTER XXIX. IN THE DEPARTMENTS OF SEINE, LOIRE, AND STYX (INFÉRIEUR)

OUR dear friend Mrs. Baynes was suffering under the influence of one of those panics which sometimes seized her, and during which she remained her husband's most obedient Eliza and vassal. When Baynes wore a certain expression of countenance, we have said that his wife knew resistance to be useless. That expression, I suppose, he assumed, when he announced Charlotte's departure to her mother, and ordered Mrs. General Baynes to make the necessary preparations for the girl. 'She might stay some time with her aunt,' Baynes stated. 'A change of air would do the child a great deal of good. Let everything necessary in the shape of hats, bonnets, winter clothes, and so forth, be got ready.' 'Was Char, then, to stay away so long?' asked Mrs. B. 'She has been so happy here that you want to keep her, and fancy she can't be happy without you!' I can fancy the General grimly replying to the partner of his existence. Hanging down her withered head, with a tear mayhap trickling down her cheek, I can fancy the old woman silently departing to do the bidding of her lord. She selects a trunk out of the store of Baynes's baggage. A young lady's trunk was a trunk in those days. Now it is a two or three storied edifice of wood, in which two or three full-grown bodies of young ladies (without crinoline) might be packed. I saw a little old countrywoman at the Folkestone station last year with her travelling baggage contained in a band-box tied up in an old cotton handkerchief hanging on her arm; and she surveyed Lady Knightsbridge's twenty-three black trunks, each well-nigh as large as her Ladyship's opera-box. Before these great edifices that old woman stood wondering dumbly. That old lady and I had lived in a time when crinoline was not; and yet, I think, women looked even prettier in that time than they do now. Well, a trunk and a band-box were fetched out of the baggage heap for little Charlotte, and I dare say her little brothers jumped and danced on the box with much energy to make the lid shut, and the General brought out his hammer and nails, and nailed a card on the box with 'Mademoiselle Baynes' thereon printed. And mamma had to look on and witness those preparations. And Walsingham Hely had called; and he wouldn't call again, she knew; and that fair chance for the establishment of her child was lost by the obstinacy of her self-willed reckless husband. That woman had to water her soup with her furtive tears, to sit of nights behind hearts and spades, and brood over her crushed hopes. If I contemplate that wretched old Niobe much longer, I shall begin to pity her. Away softness! Take out thy arrows, the poisoned, the barbed, the rankling, and prod me the old creature well, god of the silver bow! Eliza Baynes had to look on, then, and see the trunks packed; to see her own authority over her own daughter wrested away from her; to see the undutiful girl prepare with perfect delight and alacrity to go away, without feeling a pang at leaving a mother who had nursed her through adverse illnesses, who had scolded her for seventeen years.

The General accompanied the party to the diligence office. Little Char was very pale and melancholy indeed when she took her place in the coupé. 'She should have a corner: she had been ill, and ought to have a corner,' Uncle Mac said, and cheerfully consented to be bodkin. Our three special friends are seated. The other passengers clamber into their places. Away goes the clattering team, as the General waves an adieu to his friends. 'Monstrous fine horses those grey Normans; famous breed, indeed,' he remarks to his wife on his return.

'Indeed,' she echoes. 'Pray, in what part of the carriage was Mr. Firmin?' she presently asks.

'In no part of the carriage at all!' Baynes answers fiercely, turning beetroot red. And thus, though she had been silent, obedient, hanging her head, the woman showed that she was aware of her master's schemes, and why her girl had been taken away. She knew; but she was beaten. It remained for her but to be silent and bow her head. I dare say she did not sleep one wink that night. She followed the diligence in its journey. 'Char is gone,' she thought. 'Yes; in due time he will take from me the obedience of my other children, and tear them out of my lap.' He—that is, the General—was sleeping meanwhile. He had had in the last few days four awful battles—with his child, with his friends, with his wife—in which latter combat he had been conqueror. No wonder Baynes was tired, and needed rest. Any one of those engagements was enough to weary the veteran.

If we take the liberty of looking into double-bedded rooms, and peering into the thoughts which are passing under private nightcaps, may we not examine the coupé of a jingling diligence with an open window, in which a young lady sits wide awake by the side of her uncle and aunt? These perhaps are asleep; but she is not. Ah! she is thinking of another journey! that blissful one from Boulogne, when *he* was there yonder in the imperial, by the side of the conductor. When the MacWhirter party had come to the diligence office, how her little heart had beat! How she had looked under the lamps at all the people lounging about the court! How she had listened when the clerk called out the names of the passengers; and, mercy, what a fright she had been in, lest he should be there after all, while she stood yet leaning on her father's arm! But there was no-well, names, I think, need scarcely be mentioned. There was no sign of the individual in question. Papa kissed her, and sadly said good-bye. Good Madame Smolensk came with an adieu and an embrace for her dear Miss, and whispered, 'Courage, mon enfant,' and then said, 'Hold, I have brought you some bonbons.' There they were in a little packet. Little Charlotte put the packet into her little basket. Away goes the diligence, but the individual had made no sign.

Away goes the diligence; and every now and then Charlotte feels the little packet in her little basket. What does it contain—oh, what?

If Charlotte could but read with her heart, she would see in that little packet—the sweetest bonbon of all perhaps it might be, or, ah me! the bitterest almond! Through the night goes the diligence, passing relay after relay. Uncle Mac sleeps. I think I have said he snored. Aunt Mac is quite silent, and Char sits plaintively with her lonely thoughts and her bonbons, as miles, hours, relays pass.

'These ladies will they descend and take a cup of coffee, a cup of bouillon?' at last cries a waiter at the coupé door, as the carriage stops in Orleans. 'By all means a cup of coffee,' says Aunt Mac. 'The little Orleans wine is good,' cries Uncle Mac. 'Descendons!'

'This way, madame,' says the waiter. 'Charlotte my love, some coffee?'

'I will—I will stay in the carriage. I don't want anything, thank you,' says Miss Charlotte. And the instant her relations are gone, entering the gate of the Lion Noir, where, you know, are the Bureaux des Messageries Lafitte, Caillard et Cie—I say, on the very instant when her relations have disappeared, what do you think Miss Charlotte does?

She opens that packet of bonbons with fingers that tremble—tremble so, I wonder how she could undo the knot of the string (or do you think she had untied that knot under her shawl in the dark? I can't say. We never shall know). Well; she opens the packet. She does not care one fig for the lollipops, almonds, and so forth. She pounces on a little scrap of paper, and is going to read it by the light of the steaming stable lanterns, when-oh, what made her start so?-

In those old days there used to be two diligences which travelled nightly to Tours, setting out at the same hour, and stopping at almost the same relays. The diligence of Lafitte and Caillard supped at the Lion Noir at Orleans—the diligence of the Messageries Royales stopped at the Ecu de France, hard by.

Well, as the Messageries Royales are supping at the Ecu de France, a passenger strolls over from that coach, and strolls and strolls until he comes to the coach of Lafitte, Caillard, and Company, and to the coupé window where Miss Baynes is trying to decipher her bonbon.

He comes up—and as the night-lamps fall on his face and beard—his rosy face, his yellow beard—oh! What means that scream of the young lady in the coupé of Lafitte, Caillard et Compagnie! I declare she has dropped the letter which she was about to read. It has dropped into a pool of mud under the diligence off fore-wheel. And he with the yellow beard, and a sweet happy laugh, and a tremble in his deep voice, says, 'You need not read it. It was only to tell you what you know.'

Then the coupé window says, 'Oh, Philip! Oh, my—'

My what? You cannot hear the words, because the grey Norman horses come squealing and clattering up to their coach-pole with such accompanying cries and imprecations from the horse-keepers and postillions, that no wonder the little warble is lost. It was not intended for you and me to hear; but perhaps you can guess the purport of the words. Perhaps in quite old old days, you may remember having heard such little whispers, in a time when the song-birds in your grove carolled that kind of song very pleasantly and freely. But this, my good madam, is written in February. The birds are gone: the branches are bare: the gardener has actually swept the leaves off the walks: and the whole affair is an affair of a past year, you understand. Well! *carpe diem, fugit hora,* etc. etc. There, for one minute, for two minutes, stands Philip over the diligence off fore-wheel, talking to Charlotte at the window, and their heads are quite close—quite close. What are those two pairs of lips warbling, whispering? 'Hi! Gare! Ohé!' The horsekeepers, I say, quite prevent you from hearing; an here come the passengers out of the Lion Noir, Aunt Mac still munching a great slice of bread-and-butter. Charlotte is quite comfortable, and does not want anything, dear aunt, thank you. I hope she nestles in her corner, and has a sweet slumber. On the journey the twin diligences pass and repass each other. Perhaps Charlotte looks out of her window sometimes and towards the other carriage. I don't know. It is a long time ago. What used you to do in old days, ere railroads were, and when diligences ran? They were slow enough; but they have got to their journey's end somehow. They were tight, hot, dusty, dear, stuffy, and uncomfortable; but, for all that, travelling was good sport sometimes. And if the world would have the kindness to go back for five-and-twenty or thirty years, some of us who have travelled on the Tours and Orleans Railway very comfortably would like to take the diligence journey now.

Having myself seen the city of Tours only last year, of course I don't remember much about it. A man remembers boyhood, and the first sight of Calais, and so forth. But after much travel or converse with the world, to see a new town is to be introduced to Jones. He is like Brown; he is not unlike Smith. In a little while you hash him up with Thompson. I dare not be particular, then, regarding Mr. Firmin's life at Tours, lest I should make topographical errors, for which the critical schoolmaster would justly inflict chastisement. In the last novel I read about Tours, there were blunders from the effect of which you know the wretched author never recovered. It was by one Scott, and had young Quentin Durward for a hero, and Isabel de Croye for a heroine; and she sat in her hostel, and sang, 'Ah, County Guy, the hour is nigh.' A pretty ballad enough: but what ignorance, my dear sir! What descriptions of Tours, of Liège, are in that fallacious story! Yes, so fallacious and misleading, that I remember I was sorry, not because the description was unlike Tours, but because Tours was unlike the description.

So Quentin Firmin went and put up at the snug little hostel of the Faisan; and Isabel de Baynes took up her abode with her uncle the Sire de MacWhirter; and I believe Master Firmin had no more money in his pocket than the Master Durward whose story the Scottish novelist told some forty years since. And I cannot promise you that our young English adventurer shall marry a noble heiress of vast property, and engage the Boar of Ardennes in a hand-to-hand combat; that sort of Boar, madam, does not appear in our modern drawing-room histories. Of others, not wild, there be plenty. They gore you in clubs. They seize you by the doublet, and pin you against posts in public streets. They run at you in parks. I have seen them sit at bay after dinner, ripping, gashing, tossing a whole company. These our young adventurer had in good sooth to encounter, as is the case with most knights. Who escapes them? I remember an eminent person talking to me about bores for two hours once. Oh, you stupid eminent person! You never knew that you yourself had tusks, little eyes in your *hure*; a bristly mane to cut into tooth-brushes; and a curly tail! I have a notion that the multitude of bores is enormous in the world. If a man is a bore himself, when he is bored—and you can't deny this statement—then what am I, what are you, what your father, grandfather, son—all your amiable acquaintance, in a word? Of this I am sure. Major and Mrs. MacWhirter were not brilliant in conversation. What would you and I do, or say, if we listen to the tittle-tattle of Tours? How the clergyman was certainly too fond of cards, and going to the café; how the dinners those Popjoys gave were too absurdly ostentatious; and Popjoy, we know, in the Bench last year. How Mrs. Flights, going on with that Major of French Carabiniers, was really too etc. etc. 'How could I endure those people?' Philip would ask himself, when talking of that personage in after days, as he loved and loves to do. 'How could I endure them, I say? Mac was a good man; but I knew secretly in my heart, sir, that he was a bore. Well: I loved him. I liked his old stories. I liked his bad old dinners: there is a very comfortable Touraine wine, by the way—a very warming little wine, sir. Mrs. Mac you never saw, my good Mrs. Pendennis. Be sure of this, you never would have liked her. Well, I did. I liked her house, though it was damp, in a damp garden, frequented by dull people. I should like to go and see that old house now. I am perfectly happy with my wife, but I sometimes go away from her to enjoy the luxury of living over our old days again. With nothing in the world but an allowance which was precarious, and had been spent in advance; with no particular plans for the future, and a few five-franc pieces for the present,—by Jove, sir, how did I dare to be so happy? What idiots we were, my love, to be happy at all! We were mad to marry. Don't tell me: with a purse which didn't contain three months' consumption, would we dare to marry now? We should be put into the mad ward of the workhouse: that would be the only place for us. Talk about trusting in Heaven. Stuff and nonsense, ma'am! I have as good a right to go and buy a house in Belgrave Square, and trust to Heaven for the payment, as I had to marry when I did. We were paupers, Mrs. Char, and you know that very well!'

'Oh, yes. We were very wrong: very!' says Mrs. Charlotte, looking up to her chandelier of her ceiling (which, by the way, is of very handsome Venetian old glass). 'We were very wrong, were not we, my dearest?' And herewith she will begin to kiss and fondle two or more babies that disport in her room, as if two or more babies had anything to do with Philip's argument, that a man has no right to marry who has no pretty well-assured means of keeping a wife.

Here, then, by the banks of Loire, although Philip had but a very few francs in his pocket, and was obliged to keep a sharp look-out on his expenses at the Hotel of the Golden Pheasant, he passed a fortnight of such happiness as I, for my part, wish to all young folks who read his veracious history. Though he was so poor, and ate and drank so modestly in the house, the maids, waiters, the landlady of the Pheasant were as civil to him—yes, as civil as they were to the gouty old Marchioness of Carabas herself, who stayed here on her way to the south, occupied the grand apartments, quarrelled with her lodging, dinner, breakfast, bread-and-butter in general, insulted the landlady in bad French, and only paid her bill under compulsion. Philip's was a little bill, but he paid it cheerfully. He gave only a small gratuity to the servants, but he was kind and hearty, and they knew he was poor. He was kind and hearty, I suppose, because he was so happy. I have known the gentleman to be by no means civil; and have heard him storm, and hector, and browbeat landlord and waiters, as fiercely as the Marquis of Carabas himself. But now Philip the Bear was the most gentle of bears, because his little Charlotte was leading him.

Away with trouble and doubt, with squeamish pride and gloomy care! Philip had enough money for a fortnight, during which Tom Glazier, of the *Monitor,* promised to supply Philip's letters for the *Pall Mall Gazette.* All the designs of France, Spain, Russia, gave that idle 'own correspondent' not the slightest anxiety. In the morning it was Miss Baynes; in the afternoon it was Miss Baynes. At six it was dinner and Charlotte; at nine it was Charlotte and tea. 'Anyhow, love-making does not spoil his appetite,' Major MacWhirter correctly remarked. Indeed, Philip had a glorious appetite; and health bloomed in Miss Charlotte's cheek, and beamed in her happy little heart. Dr. Firmin, in the height of his practice, never completed a cure more skilfully than that which was performed by Dr. Firmin, junior.

'I ran the thing so close, sir,' I remember Philip bawling out, in his usual energetic way, whilst describing this period of his life's greatest happiness to his biographer, 'that I came back to Paris outside the diligence, and had not money enough to dine on the road. But I bought a sausage, sir, and a bit of bread—and a brutal sausage it was, sir—and I reached my lodgings with exactly two sous in my pocket.' Roger Bontemps himself was not more content than our easy philosopher.

So Philip and Charlotte ratified and sealed a treaty of Tours, which they determined should never be broken by either party. Marry without papa's consent? Oh, never! Marry anybody but Philip? Oh, never—never! Not if she lived to be a hundred, when Philip would in consequence be in his hundred and ninth or tenth year, would this young Joan have any but her present Darby. Aunt Mac, though she may not have been the most accomplished or highly-bred of ladies, was a warm-hearted and affectionate Aunt Mac. She caught in a mild form the fever from these young people. She had not much to leave, and Mac's relations would want all *he* could spare when he was gone. But Charlotte should have her garnets, and her teapot, and her India shawl—that she should.[i] And with many blessings this enthusiastic old lady took leave of her future nephew-in-law when he returned to Paris and duty. Crack your whip, and scream your *hi*! and be off quick, postillion and diligence! I am glad we have taken Mr. Firrnin out of that dangerous, lazy, love-making place. Nothing is to me so sweet as sentimental writing. I could have written hundreds of pages describing Philip and Charlotte, Charlotte and Philip. But a stern sense of duty intervenes. My modest Muse puts a finger on her lip, and says, 'Hush about that business!' Ah, my worthy friends, you little know what soft-hearted people those cynics are! If you could have come on Diogenes by surprise, I dare say you might have found him reading sentimental novels and whimpering in his tub. Philip shall leave his sweetheart and go back to his business, and we will not have one word about tears, promises, raptures, parting. Never mind about these sentimentalities, but please rather to depict to yourself our young fellow so poor that when the coach stops for dinner at Orleans he can only afford to purchase a penny loaf and a sausage for his own hungry cheek. When he reached the Hotel Poussin with his meagre carpet-bag, they served him a supper which he ate to the admiration of all beholders in the little coffee-room. He was in great spirits and gaiety. He did not care to make any secret of his poverty, and how he had been unable to afford to pay for dinner. Most of the guests at Hôtel Poussin knew what it was to be poor. Often and often they had dined on credit when they put back their napkins into their respective pigeon-holes. But my landlord knew his guests. They were poor men—honest men. They paid him in the end, and each could help his neighbour in a strait.

After Mr. Firmin's return to Paris, he did not care for a while to go to the Elysian Fields. They were not Elysian for him, except in Miss Charlotte's company He resumed his newspaper correspondence, which occupied but a day in each week, and he had. the other six—nay, he scribbled on the seventh day likewise, and covered immense sheets of letter-paper with remarks upon all manner of subjects, addressed to a certain Mademoiselle, Mademoiselle Baynes, chez M. le Major Mac, etc. On these sheets of paper Mr. Firmin could talk so long, so loudly, so fervently, so eloquently to Miss Baynes, that she was never tired of hearing, or he of holding forth. He began imparting his dreams and his earliest sensations to his beloved before breakfast. At noon-day he gave her his opinion of the contents of the morning papers. His packet was ordinarily full and brimming over by post time, so that his expressions of love and fidelity leaked from under the cover, or were squeezed into the queerest corners, where, no doubt, it was a delightful task for Miss Baynes to trace out and detect those little Cupids which a faithful lover dispatched to her. It would be, 'I have found this little corner unoccupied. Do you know what I have to say in it? Oh, Charlotte, I,' etc. etc. My sweet young lady, you can guess, or will one day guess, the rest; and will receive such dear, delightful, nonsensical double letters, and will answer them with that elegant propriety which I have no doubt Miss Baynes showed in her replies. Ah! if who are writing and receiving such letters, or who have written and received such, or who remember writing and receiving such letters, would order a copy of this novel from the publishers, what reams, and piles, and pyramids of paper our ink would have to blacken! Since Charlotte and Philip had been engaged to each other, he had scarcely, except in those dreadful ghastly days of quarrel, enjoyed the luxury of absence from his soul's blessing—the exquisite delights of writing to her. He could do few things in moderation, this man—and of this delightful privilege of writing to Charlotte he now enjoyed his heart's fill.

After brief enjoyment of the weeks of this rapture, when winter was come on Paris, and icicles hung on the bough, how did it happen that one day, two days, three days passed, and the postman brought no little letter in the well-known little handwriting for Monsieur, Monsieur Philip Firmin, à Paris? Three days, four days, and no letter. O torture, could she be ill? Could her aunt and uncle have turned against her, and forbidden her to write, as her father and mother had done before? O grief, and sorrow, and rage! As for jealousy, our leonine friend never knew such a passion. It never entered into his lordly heart to doubt of his little maiden's love. But still four, five days have passed, and not one word has come from Tours. The little Hôtel Poussin was in a commotion. I have said that when our friend felt any passion very strongly he was sure to speak of it. Did Don Quixote lose any opportunity of declaring to the world that Dulcinea del Toboso was peerless among women? Did not Antar bawl out in battle, 'I am the lover of Ibla'? Our knight had taken all the people of the hotel into his confidence somehow. They all knew of his condition—all, the painter, the poet, the half-pay Polish officer, the landlord, the hostess, down to the little knife-boy who used to come in with, 'The factor comes of to pass—no letter this morning.'

No doubt Philip's political letters became, under this outward pressure, very desponding and gloomy. One day, as he sat gnawing his moustaches at his desk, the little Anatole enters his apartment and cries, 'Tenez, M. Philippe. That lady again!' And the faithful, the watchful, the active Madame Smolensk once more made her appearance in his chamber.

Philip blushed and hung his head for shame. 'Ungrateful brute that I am,' he thought; 'I have been back more than a week, and never thought a bit about that good kind soul who came to my succour. I am an awful egotist. Love is always so.'

As he rose up to greet his friend, she looked so grave, and pale, and sad, that he could not but note her demeanour. 'Bon Dieu! had anything happened?'

'Ce pauvre Général is ill, very ill, Philip,' Smolensk said, in her grave voice.

He was so gravely ill, Madame said, that his daughter had been sent for.

'Had she come?' asked Philip, with a start.

'You think but of her—you care not for the poor old man. You are all the same, you men. All egotists—all. Go! I know you! I never knew one that was not,' said Madame.

Philip has his little faults: perhaps egotism *is* one of his defects. Perhaps it is yours, or even mine.

'You have been here a week since Thursday last, and you have never written or sent to a woman who loves you well. Go! It was not well, Monsieur Philippe.'

As soon as he saw her, Philip felt that he had been neglectful and ungrateful. We have owned so much already. But how should Madame know that he had returned on Thursday week? When they looked up after her reproof, his eager eyes seemed to ask this question.

'Could she not write to me and tell me that you were come back? Perhaps she knew that you would not do so yourself. A woman's heart teaches her these experiences early,' continued the lady sadly. Then she added: 'I tell you, you are good-for-nothings, all of you! And I repent me, see you, of having had the bêtise to pity you!'

'I shall have my quarter's pay on Saturday. I was coming to you then,' said Philip.

'Was it that I was speaking of? What! you are all cowards, men all! Oh, that I have been beast, beast, to think at last I had found a man of heart!'

How much or how often this poor Ariadne had trusted and been forsaken, I have no means of knowing, or desire of inquiring. Perhaps it is as well for the polite reader, who is taken into my entire confidence, that we should not know Madame de Smolensk's history from the first page to the last. Granted that Ariadne was deceived by Theseus: but then she consoled herself, as we may all read in 'Smith's Dictionary'; and then she must have deceived her father in order to run away with Theseus. I suspect;—I suspect, I say, that these women who are so *very* much betrayed, are—but we are speculating on this French lady's antecedents, when Charlotte, her lover, and her family are the persons with whom we have mainly to do.

These two, I suppose, forgot self, about which each for a moment had been busy, and Madame resumed:—'Yes, you have reason; Miss is here. It was time. Hold! Here is a note from her.' And Philip's kind messenger once more put a paper into his hands.

'My dearest father is very very ill. Oh, Philip! I am so unhappy; and he is so good, and gentle, and kind, and loves me so!'

'It is true,' Madame resumed. 'Before Charlotte came, he thought only of her. When his wife comes up to him, he turns from her. I have not loved her much, that lady, that is true. But to see her now, it is *navrant*. He will take no medicine from her. He pushes her away. Before Charlotte came, he sent for me, and spoke as well as his poor throat would let him, this poor General! His daughter's arrival seemed to comfort him. But he says, " Not my wife! not my wife.

And the poor thing has to go away and cry in the chamber at the side. He says—in his French, you know—he has never been well since Charlotte went away. He has often been out. He has dined but rarely at our table, and there has always been a silence between him and Madame la Générale. Last week he had a great inflammation of the chest. Then he took to bed, and Monsieur the Docteur came— the little doctor whom you know. Then a quinsy has declared itself, and he now is scarce able to speak. His condition is most grave. He lies suffering, dying, perhaps —yes, dying, do you hear? And you are thinking of your little schoolgirl! Men are all the same. Monsters! Go!'

Philip, who, I have said, is very fond of talking about Philip, surveys his own faults with great magnanimity and good-humour, and acknowledges them without the least intention to correct them. 'How selfish we are!' I can hear him say, looking at himself in the glass. 'By George! sir, when I heard simultaneously the news of that poor old man's illness, and of Charlotte's return, I felt that I wanted to see *her* that instant. I must go to her, and speak to her. The old man and his suffering did not seem to affect me. It is humiliating to have to own that we are selfish beasts. But we are, sir—we are brutes, by George! and nothing else.'—And he gives a finishing twist to the ends of his flaming moustaches as he surveys them in the glass.

Poor little Charlotte was in such affliction that of course she must have Philip to console her at once. No time was to be lost. Quick! a cab this moment: and, coachman, you shall have an extra for drink if you go quick to the Avenue de Valmy! Madame puts herself into the carriage, and as they go along, tells Philip more at length of the gloomy occurrences of the last few days. Four days since the poor General was so bad with his quinsy that he thought he should not recover, and Charlotte was sent for. He was a little better on the day of her arrival; but yesterday the inflammation had increased; he could not swallow; he could not speak audibly; he was in very great suffering and danger. He turned away from his wife. The unhappy Generaless had been to Madame Bunch, in her tears and grief, complaining that after twenty years' fidelity and attachment her husband had withdrawn his regard from her. Baynes attributed even his illness to his wife; and at other times said it was a just punishment for his wicked conduct in breaking his word to Philip and Charlotte. If he did not see his dear child again he must beg her forgiveness for having made her suffer so. He had acted wickedly and ungratefully, and his wife had forced him to do what he did. He prayed that Heaven might pardon him. And he had behaved with wicked injustice towards Philip, who had acted most generously towards his family. And he had been a scoundrel—he knew he had—and Bunch, and MacWhirter, and the Doctor all said so—and it was that woman's doing. And he pointed to the scared wife as he painfully hissed out these words of anger and contrition:—'When I saw that child ill, and almost made mad, because I broke my word, I felt I was a scoundrel, Martin; and I was; and that woman made me so; and I deserve to be shot; and I shan't recover; I tell you I shan't.' Dr. Martin, who attended the General, thus described his patient's last talk and behaviour to Philip.

It was the Doctor who sent Madame in quest of the young man. He found poor Mrs. Baynes with hot tearless eyes and livid face, a wretched sentinel outside the sick chamber. 'You will find General Baynes very ill, sir,' she said to Philip with a ghastly calmness, and a gaze he could scarcely face. 'My daughter is in the room with him. It appears I have offended him, and he refuses to see me.' And she squeezed a dry handkerchief which she held, and put on her spectacles again, and tried again to read the Bible in her lap.

Philip hardly knew the meaning of Mrs. Baynes's words as yet. He was agitated by the thought of the General's illness, perhaps by the notion that the beloved was so near. Her hand was in his a moment afterwards; and, even in that sad chamber, each could give the other a soft pressure, a fond silent signal of mutual love and faith.

The poor man laid the hands of the young people together, and his own upon them. The suffering to which he had put his daughter seemed to be the crime which specially affected him. He thanked Heaven he was able to see he was wrong. He whispered to his little maid a prayer for pardon in one or two words, which caused poor Charlotte to sink on her knees and cover his fevered hand with tears and kisses. Out of all her heart she forgave him. She had felt that the parent she loved and was accustomed to honour had been mercenary and cruel. It had wounded her pure heart to be obliged to think that her father could be other than generous, and just, and good. That he should humble himself before her, smote her with the keenest pang of tender commiseration. I do not care to pursue this last scene. Let us close the door as the children kneel by the sufferer's bedside, and to the old man's petition for forgiveness, and to the young girl's sobbing vows of love and fondness, say a reverent Amen.

By the following letter, which he wrote a few days before the fatal termination of his illness, the worthy General, it would appear, had already despaired of his recovery:—

'MY DEAR MAC,—I speak and breathe with such difficulty as I write this from my bed, that I doubt whether I shall ever leave it I do not wish to vex poor Eliza, and in my state cannot *enter into disputes* which I know would ensue regarding settlement of property. When I left England there was a claim hanging over me (young Firmin's) at which I was needlessly frightened, as having to satisfy it would swallow up *much more than everything I possessed in the world.* Hence made arrangements for leaving everything in Eliza's name and the children after. Will with Smith and Thompson, Raymond Buddings, Gray's Inn. Think Char *won't be happy for a long time with her mother.* To break from F., who has been most generous to us, will break her heart. Will you and Emily keep her for a little? I gave *F. my promise.* As you told me, I have acted ill by him, which I own and deeply lament. If Char marries, *she ought to have her share.* May God bless her, her father prays, in case he should not see her again. And with best love to Emily, am yours, dear Mac, sincerely,   CHARLES BAYNES.'

On the receipt of this letter, Charlotte disobeyed her father's wish, and set forth from Tours instantly, under her worthy uncle's guardianship. The old soldier was in his comrade's room when the General put the hands of Charlotte and her lover together. He confessed his fault, though it is hard for those who expect love and reverence to have to own to wrong and to ask pardon. Old knees are stiff to bend: brother reader, young or old, when our last hour comes, may ours have grace to do as much.

CHAPTER XXX. RETURNS TO OLD FRIENDS

THE three old comrades and Philip formed the little mourning procession which followed the General to his place of rest at Montmartre. When the service has been read, and the last volley has been fired over the buried soldier, the troops march to quarters with a quick step, and to a lively tune. Our veteran has been laid in the grave with brief ceremonies. We do not even prolong his obsequies with a sermon. His place knows him no longer. There are a few who remember him: a very very few who grieve for him—so few that to think of them is a humiliation almost. The sun sets on the earth, and our dear brother has departed off its face. Stars twinkle; dews fall; children go to sleep in awe and, maybe, tears; the sun rises on a new day, which he has never seen, and children wake hungry. They are interested about their new black clothes, perhaps. They are presently at their work, plays, quarrels. They are looking, forward to the day when the holidays will be over, and the eyes which shone here yesterday so kindly are gone, gone, gone. A drive to the cemetery, followed by a coach with four acquaintances dressed in decorous black, who separate and go to their homes or clubs, and wear your crape for a few days after— can most of us expect much more? The thought is not ennobling or exhilarating, worthy sir. And, pray, why should we be proud of ourselves? Is it because we have been so good, or are so wise and great, that we expect to be beloved, lamented, remembered? Why, great Xerxes or blustering Bobadil must know in that last hour and resting-place how abject, how small, how low, how lonely they are, and what a little dust will cover them. Quick, drums and fifes, a lively tune! Whip the black team, coachman, and trot back to town again—to the world, and to business, and duty! I am for saying no single unkindness of General Baynes which is not forced upon me by my story-teller's office. We know from Marlborough's story that the bravest man and greatest military genius is not always brave or successful in his battles with his wife; that some of the greatest warriors have committed errors in accounts and the distribution of *meum* and *tuum*. We can't disguise from ourselves the fact that Baynes permitted himself to be misled, and had weaknesses not quite consistent with the highest virtue.

When he became aware that his carelessness in the matter of Mrs. Firmin's trust money had placed him in her son's power, we have seen how the old Geueral, in order to avoid being called to account, fled across the water with his family and all his little fortune, and how terrified he was on landing on a foreign shore to find himself face to face with this dreadful creditor. Philip's renunciation of all claims against Baynes soothed and pleased the old man wonderfully. But Philip might change his mind, an adviser at Baynes's side repeatedly urged. To live abroad was cheaper and safer than to live at home. Accordingly Baynes, his wife, family, and money, all went into exile, and remained there.

What savings the old man had I don't accurately know. He and his wife were very dark upon this subject with Philip: and when the General died, his widow declared herself to be almost a pauper! It was impossible that Baynes should have left much money; but that Charlotte's share should have amounted to—that sum which may or may not presently be stated—was a little *too* absurd! You see Mr. and Mrs. Firmin are travelling abroad just now. When I wrote to Firmin, to ask if I might mention the amount of his wife's fortune, he gave me no answer; nor do I like to enter upon these matters of calculation without his explicit permission. He is of a hot temper; he might, on his return, grow angry with the friend of his youth, and say, 'Sir, how dare you to talk about my private affairs? and what has the public to do with Mrs. Firmin's private fortune?'

When, the last rites over, good-natured Uncle Mac proposed to take Charlotte back to Tours, her mother made no objection. The widow had tried to do the girl such an injury, that perhaps the latter felt forgiveness was impossible. Little Char loved Philip with all her heart and strength; had been authorised and encouraged to do so, as we have seen. To give him up now, because a richer suitor presented himself, was an act of treason from which her faithful heart revolted, and she never could pardon the instigator. You see, in this simple story, I scarcely care even to have reticence or secrets. I don't want you to understand for a moment that Walsingham Hely was still crying his eyes out about Charlotte. Goodness bless you! It was two or three weeks ago—four or five weeks ago, that he was in love with *her.* He had not seen the Duchesse d'Ivry then, about whom you may remember he had the quarrel with Podichon, at the club in the Rue de Grammont. (He and the Duchesse wrote poems to each other, each in the other's native language.) The Charlotte had long passed out of the young fellow's mind. That butterfly had fluttered off from our English rosebud, and had settled on the other elderly flower! I don't know that Mrs. Baynes was aware of young Hely's fickleness at this present time of which we are writing; but his visits had ceased, and she was angry and disappointed; and not the less angry because her labour had been in vain. On her part, Charlotte could also be resolutely unforgiving. Take her Philip from her! Never, never! Her mother force her to give up the man whom she had been encouraged to love? Mamma should have defended Philip, not betrayed him! If I command my son to steal a spoon, shall he obey me? And if he do obey and steal, and be transported, will he love me afterwards? I think I can hardly ask for so much filial affection.

So there was strife between mother and daughter; and anger not the less bitter, on Mrs. Baynes's part, because her husband, whose cupidity or fear had, at first, induced him to take her side, had deserted her and gone over to her daughter. In the anger of that controversy Baynes died, leaving the victory and right with Charlotte. He shrank from his wife: would not speak to her in his last moments. The widow had these injuries against her daughter and Philip: and thus neither side forgave the other. She was not averse to the child's going away to her uncle: put a lean hungry face against Charlotte's lip, and received a kiss which I fear had but little love in it. I don't envy those children who remain under the widow's lonely command; or poor Madame Smolensk, who has to endure the arrogance, the grief, the avarice of that grim woman. Nor did Madame suffer under this tyranny long. *Galignani's Messenger* very soon announced that she had lodgings to let, and I remember being edified by reading one day in the *Pall Mall Gazette* that elegant apartments, select society, and an excellent table were to be found in one of the most airy and fashionable quarters of Paris. Inquire of Madame la Baronne de S-sk, Avenue de Valmy, Champs Elysées.

We guessed without difficulty how this advertisement found its way to the *Pall Mall Gazette*; and very soon after its appearance Madame de Smolensk's friend, Mr. Philip, made his appearance at our tea-table in London. He was always welcome amongst us elders and children. He wore a crape on his hat. As soon as the young ones were gone, you may be sure he poured his story out; and enlarged upon the death, the burial, the quarrels, the loves, the partings we have narrated. How could he be put in a way to earn three or four hundred a year? That was the present question. Ere he came to see us, he had already been totting up ways and means. He had been with our friend Mrs. Brandon: was staying with her. The Little Sister thought three hundred would be sufficient. They could have her second floor —not for nothing; no, no, but at a moderate price, which would pay her. They could have attics, if more rooms were needed. They could have her kitchen fire, and one maid, for the present, would do all their work. Poor little thing! She was very young. She would be past eighteen by the time she could marry; the Little Sister was for early marriages, against long courtships. 'Heaven helps those as helps themselves,' she said. And Mr. Philip thought this excellent advice, and Mr. Philip's friend, when asked for *his* opinion—'Candidly now, what's your opinion?'—said, 'Is she in the next room? Of course you mean you are married already.'

Philip roared one of his great laughs. No, he was not married already. Had he not said that Miss Baynes was gone away to Tours to her aunt and uncle? But that he wanted to be married; but that he could never settle down to work till he married; but that he could have no rest, peace, health till he married that angel, he was ready to confess. Ready? All the street might hear him calling out the name and expatiating on the angelic charms and goodness of his Charlotte. He spoke so loud and long on this subject that my wife grew a little tired; and my wife *always* likes to hear other women praised, that (she says) I know she does. But when a man goes on roaring for an hour about Dulcinea? You know such talk becomes fulsome at last; and, in fine, when he was gone, my wife said, 'Well, he is very much in love; so were you—I mean long before my time, sir; but does love pay the housekeeping bills, pray?'

'No, my dear. And love is always controlled by other people's advice:—always,' says Philip's friend; who, I hope, you will perceive was speaking ironically.

Philip's friends had listened not impatiently to Philip's talk about Philip. Almost all women will give a sympathising hearing to men who are in love. Be they ever so old, they grow young again with that conversation, and renew their own early times. Men are not quite so generous: Tityrus tires of hearing Corydon discourse endlessly on the charms of his shepherdess. And yet egotism is good talk. Even dull autobiographies are pleasant to read: and if to read, why not to hear? Had Master Philip not been such an egotist, he would not have been so pleasant a companion. Can't you like a man at whom you laugh a little? I had rather such an open-mouthed conversationist than your cautious jaws that never unlock without a careful application of the key. As for the entrance to Mr. Philip's mind, that door was always open when he was awake, or not hungry, or in a friend's company. Besides his love, and his prospects in life, his poverty, etc., Philip had other favourite topics of conversation. His friend the Little Sister was a great theme with him; his father was another favourite subject of his talk. By the way, his father had written to the Little Sister. The Doctor said he was sure to prosper in his newly-adopted country. He and another physician had invented a new medicine, which was to effect wonders, and in a few years would assuredly make the fortune of both of them. He was never without one scheme or another for making that fortune which never came. Whenever he drew upon poor Philip for little sums, his letters were sure to be especially magniloquent and hopeful. 'Whenever the Doctor says he has invented the philosopher's stone,' said poor Philip, 'I am sure there will be a postscript to say that a little bill will be presented for so much, at so many days' date.'

Had he drawn on Philip lately? Philip told us when, and how often. We gave him all the benefit of our virtuous indignation. As for my wife's eyes, they gleamed with anger. What a man: what a father! Oh, he was incorrigible! 'Yes, I am afraid he is,' says poor Phil comically, with his hands roaming at ease in his pockets. They contained little else than those big hands. 'My father is of a hopeful turn. His views regarding property are peculiar. It is a comfort to have such a distinguished parent, isn't it? I am always surprised to hear that he is not married again. I sigh for a mother-in-law,' Philip continued.

'Oh, *don't,* Philip!' cried Mrs. Laura, in a pet. 'Be generous: be forgiving: be noble: be Christian! Don't be cynical, and imitating—you know whom!'

Whom could she possibly mean, I wonder? After flashes, there came showers in this lady's eyes. Prom long habit I can understand her thoughts, although she does not utter them. She was thinking of those poor, noble, simple, friendless young people; and asking Heaven's protection for them. I am not in the habit of over-praising my friends, goodness knows. The foibles of this one I have described honestly enough. But if I write down here that he was courageous, cheerful in adversity, generous, simple, truth-loving, above a scheme—after having said that he was a noble young fellow—*dixi;* and I won't cancel the words.

Ardent lover as he was, our friend was glad to be back in the midst of the London smoke, and wealth, and bustle. The fog agreed with his lungs, he said. He breathed more freely in our great city than in that little English village in the centre of Paris which he had been inhabiting. In his hotel, and at his café (where he composed his eloquent 'own correspondence'), he had occasion to speak a little French, but it never came very trippingly from his stout English tongue. 'You don't suppose I would like to be taken for a Frenchman,' he would say, with much gravity. I wonder who ever thought of mistaking friend Philip for a Frenchman?

As for that faithful Little Sister, her house and heart were still at the young man's service. We have not visited Thornhaugh Street for some time. Mr. Philip, whom we have been bound to attend, has been too much occupied with his love-making to bestow much thought on his affectionate little friend. She has been trudging meanwhile on her humble course of life, cheerful, modest, laborious, doing her duty, with a helping little hand ready to relieve many a fallen wayfarer on her road. She had a room vacant in her house when Philip came:—a room, indeed! Would she not have had a house vacant, if Philip wanted it? But in the interval since we saw her last, the Little Sister, too, has had to assume black robes. Her father, the old Captain, has gone to his rest. His place is vacant in the little parlour: his bedroom is ready for Philip, as long as Philip will stay. She did not profess to feel much affliction for the loss of the Captain. She talked of him constantly as though he were present; and made a supper for Philip and seated him in her pa's chair. How she bustled about on the night when Philip arrived! what a beaming welcome there was in her kind eyes! Her modest hair was touched with silver now; but her cheeks were like apples; her little figure was neat, and light, and active: and her voice, with its gentle laugh, and little sweet bad grammar, has always seemed one of the sweetest of voices to me.

Very soon after Philip's arrival in London, Mrs. Brandon paid a visit to the wife of Mr. Firmin's humble servant and biographer, and the two women had a fine sentimental consultation. All good women, you know, are sentimental. The idea of young lovers, of match-making, of amiable poverty, tenderly excites and interests them. My wife, at this time, began to pour off fine long letters to Miss Baynes, to which the latter modestly and dutifully replied, with many expressions of fervour and gratitude for the interest which her friend in London was pleased to take in the little maid. I saw by these answers that Charlotte's union with Philip was taken as a received point by these two ladies. They discussed the ways and means. They did not talk about broughams, settlements, town and country houses, pin-moneys, trousseaux: and my wife, in computing their sources of income, always pointed out that Miss Charlotte's fortune, though certainly small, would give a very useful addition to the young couple's income. 'Fifty pounds a year not much! Let me tell you, sir, that fifty pounds a year is a very pretty little sum: if Philip can but make three hundred a year himself, Mrs. Brandon says they ought to be able to live quite nicely.' You ask, my genteel friend, is it possible that people can live for four hundred a year? How do they manage, *ces pauvres gens*? They eat, they drink, they are clothed, they are warmed, they have roofs over their heads, and glass in their windows; and some of them are as good, happy, and well-bred as their neighbours who are ten times as rich. Then, besides this calculation of money, there is the fond woman's firm belief that the day will bring its daily bread for those who work for it and ask for it in the proper quarter; against which reasoning many a man knows it is in vain to argue. As to my own little objections and doubts, my wife met them by reference to Philip's former love-affair with his cousin, Miss Twysden. 'You had no objection in that case, sir,' this logician would say. 'You would have had him take a creature without a heart. *You* would cheerfully have seen him made miserable for life, because you thought there was money enough and a genteel connection. Money indeed! Very happy Mrs. Woolcomb is with her money. Very creditably to all sides has *that* marriage turned out!' I need scarcely remind my readers of the unfortunate result of that marriage. Woolcomb's behaviour to his wife was the agreeable talk of London society and of the London clubs very soon after the pair were joined together in holy matrimony. Do we not all remember how Woolcomb was accused of striking his wife, of starving his wife, and how she took refuge at home and came to her father's house with a black eye? The two Twysdens were so ashamed of this transaction, that father and son left off coming to Bays's, where I never heard their absence regretted but by one man, who said that Talbot owed him money for losses at whist for which he could get no settlement.

Should Mr. Firmin go and see his aunt in her misfortune? Bygones might be bygones, some of Philip's advisers thought. Now Mrs. Twysden was unhappy, her heart might relent to Philip, whom she certainly had loved as a boy. Philip had the magnanimity to call upon her; and found her carriage waiting at the door. But a servant, after keeping the gentleman waiting in the dreary well-remembered hall, brought him word that his mistress was out, smiled in his face with an engaging insolence, and proceeded to put cloaks, court-guides, and other female gear into the carriage in the presence of this poor deserted nephew. This visit it must be owned was one of Mrs. Laura's romantic efforts at reconciling enemies: as if, my good creature, the Twysdens ever let a man into their house who was poor or out of fashion! They lived in a constant dread lest Philip should call to borrow money of them. As if they ever lent money to a man who was in need! If they ask the respected reader to their house, depend upon it they think he is well-to-do. On the other hand, the Twysdens made a very handsome entertainment for the new Lord of Whipham and Ringwood who now reigned after his kinsman's death. They affably went and passed Christmas with him in the country; and they cringed and bowed before Sir John Ringwood as they had bowed and cringed before the Earl in his time. The old Earl had been a Tory in his latter days when Talbot Twysden's views were also very conservative. The present Lord of Ringwood was a Whig. It is surprising how liberal the Twysdens grew in the course of a fortnight's after-dinner conversation and pheasant-shooting talk at Ringwood. 'Hang it! you know,' young Twysden said, in his office afterwards, 'a fellow must go with the politics of his family, you know!' and he bragged about the dinners, wines, splendours, cooks, and preserves of Ringwood as freely as in the time of his noble grand-uncle. Any one who has kept a house-dog in London, which licks your boots and your platter, and fawns for the bones in your dish, knows how the animal barks and flies at the poor who come to the door. The Twysdens, father and son, were of this canine species: and there are vast packs of such dogs here and elsewhere.

If Philip opened his heart to us, and talked unreservedly regarding his hopes and his plans, you may be sure he had his little friend, Mrs. Brandon, also in his confidence, and that no person in the world was more eager to serve him. Whilst we were talking about what was to be done, this little lady was also at work in her favourite's behalf. She had a firm ally in Mrs. Mugford, the proprietor's lady of the *Pall Mall Gazette.* Mrs. Mugford had long been interested in Philip, his misfortunes and his love affairs. These two good women had made a sentimental hero of him. Ah! that they could devise some feasible scheme to help him! And such a chance actually did very soon present itself to these delighted women.

In almost all the papers of the new year appeared a brilliant advertisement, announcing the speedy appearance in Dublin of a new paper. It was to be called THE SHAMROCK, and its first number was to be issued on the ensuing St. Patrick's day. I need not quote at length the advertisement which heralded the advent of this new periodical. The most famous pens of the national party in Ireland were, of course, engaged to contribute to its columns. Those pens would be hammered into steel of a different shape when the opportunity should offer. Beloved prelates, authors of world-wide fame, bards, the bold strings of whose lyres had rung through the isle already, and made millions of noble hearts to beat, and, by consequence, double the number of eyes to fill; philosophers, renowned for science; and illustrious advocates, whose manly voices had ever spoken the language of hope and freedom to an etc. etc., would be found rallying round the journal, and proud to wear the symbol of THE SHAMROCK. Finally, Michael Cassidy, Esquire, was chosen to be the editor of this new journal.

This was the M. Cassidy, Esquire, who appeared, I think, at Mr. Firmin's call-supper; and who had long been the sub-editor of the *Pall Mall Gazette.* If Michael went to Dame Street, why should not Philip be sub-editor at Pall Mall? Mrs. Brandon argued. Of course there would be a score of candidates for Michael's office. The editor would like the patronage. Barnet, Mugford's partner in the *Gazette,* would wish to appoint his man. Cassidy, before retiring, would assuredly intimate his approaching resignation to scores of gentlemen of his nation, who would not object to take the Saxon's pay until they finally shook his yoke off, and would eat his bread until the happy moment arrived when they could knock out his brains in fair battle. As soon as Mrs. Brandon heard of the vacant place, that moment she determined that Philip should have it. It was surprising what a quantity of information our little friend possessed about artists, and pressmen, and their lives, families, ways and means. Many gentlemen of both professions came to Mr. Ridley's chambers and called on the Little Sister on their way to and fro. How Tom Smith had left the *Herald,* and gone to the *Post;* what price Jack Jones had for his picture, and who sat for the principal figures—I promise you Madam Brandon had all these interesting details by heart; and I think I have described this little person very inadequately if I have not made you understand that she was as intrepid a little jobber as ever lived, and never scrupled to go any length to serve a friend. To be Archbishop of Canterbury, to be professor of Hebrew, to be teacher of a dancing-school, to be organist for a church: for any conceivable place or function this little person would have asserted Philip's capability. 'Don't tell me! He can dance or preach (as the case may be), or write beautiful! And as for being unfit to be a sub-editor, I want to know, has he not as good a head and as good an education as that Cassidy, indeed? And is not Cambridge College the best college in the world? It is, I say. And he went there ever so long. And he might have taken the very best prize, only money was no object to him then, dear fellow, and he did not like to keep the poor out of what he didn't want!'

Mrs. Mugford had always considered the young man as very haughty, but quite the gentleman, and speedily was infected by her gossip's enthusiasm about him. My wife hired a fly, packed several of the children into it, called upon Mrs. Mugford, and chose to be delighted with that lady's garden, with that lady's nursery—with everything that bore the name of Mugford. It was a curiosity to remark in what a flurry of excitement these women plunged, and how they schemed, and coaxed, and caballed, in order to get this place for their protégé. My wife thought—she merely happened to surmise: nothing more, of course—that Mrs. Mugford's fond desire was to shine in the world. 'Could we not ask some people—with—with what you call handles to their names,—I think I before heard you use some such term, sir,—to meet the Mugfords? Some of Philip's old friends, who I am sure would be very happy to serve him.' Some such artifice was, I own, practised. We coaxed, cajoled, fondled the Mugfords for Philip's sake, and Heaven forgive Mrs. Laura her hypocrisy. We had an entertainment then, I own. We asked our finest company, and Mr. and Mrs. Mugford to meet them: and we prayed that unlucky Philip to be on his best behaviour to all persons who were invited to the feast.

Before my wife this lion of a Firmin was as a lamb. Rough, captious, and overbearing in general society, with those whom he loved and esteemed Philip was of all men the most modest and humble. He would never tire of playing with our children, joining in their games, laughing and roaring at their little sports. I have never had such a laugher at my jokes as Philip Firmin. I think my wife liked him for that noble guffaw with which he used to salute those pieces of wit. He arrived a little late sometimes with his laughing chorus, but ten people at table were not so loud as this faithful friend. On the contrary, when those people for whom he has no liking venture on a pun or other pleasantry, I am bound to own that Philip's acknowledgment of their waggery must be anything but pleasant or flattering to them. Now, on occasion of this important dinner, I enjoined him to be very kind, and very civil, and very much pleased with everybody, and to stamp upon nobody's corns, as, indeed, why should he, in life? Who was he to be *censor morum*? And it has been said that no man could admit his own faults with a more engaging candour than our friend.

We invited, then, Mugford, the proprietor of the *Pall Mall Gazette,* and his wife; and Bickerton, the editor of that periodical; Lord Ascot, Philip's old College friend; and one or two more gentlemen. Our invitations to the ladies were not so fortunate. Some were engaged, others away in the country keeping Christmas. In fine, we considered ourselves rather lucky in securing old Lady Hixie, who lives hard by in Westminster, and who will pass for a lady of fashion when no person of greater note is present. My wife told her that the object of the dinner was to make our friend Firmin acquainted with the editor and proprietor of the *Pall Mall Gazette,* with whom it was important that he should be on the most amicable footing. Oh! very well. Lady Hixie promised to be quite gracious to the newspaper gentleman and his wife; and kept her promise most graciously during the evening. Our good friend Mrs. Mugford was the first of our guests to arrive. She drove 'in her trap' from her villa in the suburbs; and after putting up his carriage at a neighbouring livery-stable, her groom volunteered to help our servants in waiting at dinner. His zeal and activity were remarkable. China smashed, and dish-covers clanged in the passage. Mrs. Mugford said that 'Sam was at his old tricks'; and I hope the hostess showed she was mistress of herself amidst that fall of china. Mrs. Mugford came before the appointed hour, she said, in order to see our children. 'With our late London dinner hours,' she remarked, 'children was never seen now.' At Hampstead, hers always appeared at the dessert, and enlivened the table with their innocent outcries for oranges and struggles for sweetmeats. In the nursery, where one little maid, in her crisp long night-gown, was saying her prayers; where another Uttle person, in the most airy costume, was standing before the great barred fire; where a third Lilliputian was sitting up in its night-cap and surplice, surveying the scene below from its crib;—the ladies found our dear Little Sister installed. She had come to see her little pets (she had known two or three of them from the very earliest times). She was a great favourite amongst them all; and, I believe, conspired with the cook down below in preparing certain delicacies for the table. A fine conversation then ensued about our children, about the Mugford children, about babies in general. And then the artful women (the house-mistress and the Little Sister) brought Philip on the *tapis,* and discoursed, *à qui mieux,* about his virtues, his misfortunes, his engagement, and that dear little creature to whom he was betrothed. This conversation went on until carriage-wheels were heard in the square, and the knocker (there were actually knockers in that old-fashioned place and time) began to peal. 'Oh, bother! There's the company a-comin',' Mrs. Mugford said; and, arranging her cap and flounces, with neat-handed Mrs. Brandon's aid, came downstairs, after taking a tender leave of the little people, to whom she sent a present next day of a pile of fine Christmas books, which had come to the *Pall*

Mall Gazette for review. The kind woman had been coaxed, wheedled, and won over to our side, to Philip's side. He had *her* vote for the sub-editorship, whatever might ensue.

Most of our guests had already arrived, when at length Mrs. Mugford was announced. I am bound to say that she presented a remarkable appearance, and that the splendour of her attire was such as is seldom beheld.

Bickerton and Philip were presented to one another, and had a talk about French politics before dinner, during which conversation Philip behaved with perfect discretion and politeness. Bickerton had happened to hear Philip's letters well spoken of—in a good quarter, mind; and his cordiality increased when Lord Ascot entered, called Philip by his surname, and entered into a perfectly free conversation with him. Old Lady Hixie went into perfectly good society, Bickerton condescended to acknowledge. 'As for Mrs. Mugford,' says he, with a glance of wondering compassion at that lady, 'of course, I need not tell you that *she* is seen nowhere—nowhere.' This said, Mr. Bickerton stepped forward, and calmly patronised my wife, gave me a good-natured nod for my own part; reminded Lord Ascot that he had had the pleasure of meeting him at Egham; and then fixed on Tom Page, of the Bread-and-Butter Office (who I own is one of our most genteel guests), with whom he entered into a discussion of some political matter of that day—I forget what: but the main point was that he named two or three leading public men with whom he had discussed the question, whatever it might be. He named very great names, and led us to understand that with the proprietors of those very great names he was on the most intimate and confidential footing. With his owners—with the proprietor of the *Pall Mall Gazette,* he was on the most distant terms, and indeed I am afraid that his behaviour to myself and my wife was scarcely respectful. I fancied I saw Philip's brow gathering wrinkles as his eye followed this man strutting from one person to another, and patronising each. The dinner was a little late, from some reason best known in the lower regions. 'I take it,' says Bickerton, winking at Philip, in a pause of the conversation, 'that our good friend and host is not much used to giving dinners. The mistress of the house is evidently in a state of perturbation.' Philip gave such a horrible grimace that the other at first thought he was in pain.

'You, who have lived a great deal with old Ringwood, know what a good dinner is,' Bickerton continued, giving Firmin a knowing look.

'Any dinner is good which is accompanied with such a welcome as I get here,' said Philip.

'Oh! very good people, very good people, of course!' cries Bickerton.

I need not say he thinks he has perfectly succeeded in adopting the air of a man of the world. He went off to Lady Hixie and talked with her about the last great party at which he had met her; and then he turned to the host, and remarked that my friend, the Doctor's son, was a fierce-looking fellow. In five minutes he had the good fortune to make himself hated by Mr. Firmin. He walks through the world patronising his betters. 'Our good friend is not much used to giving dinners,'—isn't he? I say, what do we mean by continuing to endure this man? Tom Page, of the Bread-and-Butter Office, is a well-known diner-out; Lord Ascot is an earl's son. Bickerton, in a pretty loud voice, talked to one or other of these during dinner and across the table. He sat next to Mrs. Mugford, but he turned his back on that bewildered woman, and never condescended to address a word to her personally. 'Of course, I understand you, my dear fellow,' he said to me when, on the retreat of the ladies, we approached within whispering distance. 'You have these people at dinner for reasons of state. You have a book coming out, and want to have it noticed in the paper! I make a point of keeping these people at a distance—the only way of dealing with them, I give you my word.'

Not one offensive word had Philip said to the chief writer of the *Pall Mall Gazette*; and I began to congratulate myself that our dinner would pass without any mishap, when some one unluckily happening to praise the wine, a fresh supply was ordered. 'Very good claret. Who is your wine-merchant? Upon my word, I get better claret here than I do in Paris—don't you think so, Mr. Pernor? Where do you generally dine at Paris?'

'I generally dine for thirty sous, and three francs on grand days, Mr. Beckerton,' growls Philip.

'My name is Bickerton.' ('What a vulgar thing for a fellow to talk about his thirty-sous dinners!' murmured my neighbour to me.) 'Well, there is no accounting for tastes! When I go to Paris, I dine at the Trois Frères. Give me the Burgundy at the Trois Frères.'

'That is because you great leader-writers are paid better than poor correspondents. I shall be delighted to be able to dine better.' And with this Mr. Firmin smiles at Mr. Mugford, his master and owner.

'Nothing so vulgar as talking shop,' says Bickerton, rather loud.

'I am not ashamed of the shop I keep. Are you of yours, Mr. Bickerton?' growls Philip.

'F. had him there,' says Mr. Mugford.

Mr. Bickerton got up from table, turning quite pale. 'Do you mean to be offensive, sir?' he asked.

'Offensive, sir? No, sir. Some men are offensive without meaning it. *You* have been several times to-night!' says Lord Philip.

'I don't see that I am called upon to bear this kind of thing at any man's table!' cried Mr. Bickerton. 'Lord Ascot, I wish you goodnight!'

'I say, old boy, what's the row about?' asked his Lordship. And we were all astonished as my guest rose and left the table in great wrath.

'Serve him right, Firmin, I say!' said Mr. Mugford, again drinking off a glass.

'Why, don't you know?' says Tom Page. 'His father keeps a haberdasher's shop at Cambridge, and sent him to Oxford, where he took a good degree.'

And this had come of a dinner of conciliation—a dinner which was to advance Philip's interest in life!

'Hit him again, I say,' cried Mugford, whom wine had rendered eloquent. 'He's a supercilious beast, that Bickerton is, and I hate him, and so does Mrs. M.'

CHAPTER XXXI. NARRATES THAT FAMOUS JOKE ABOUT MISS GRIGSBY

FOR once Philip found that he had offended without giving general offence. In the confidence of female intercourse, Mrs. Mugford had already, in her own artless but powerful language, confirmed her husband's statement regarding Mr. Bickerton, and declared that B. was a beast, and she was only sorry that Mr. F. had. not hit him a little harder. So different are the opinions which different individuals entertain of the same event 1 I happen to know that Bickerton, on his side, went away, averring that we were quarrelsome under-bred people; and that a man of any refinement had best avoid that kind of society. He does really and seriously believe himself our superior, and will lecture almost any gentleman on the art of being one. This assurance is not at all uncommon with your *parvenu*. Proud of his newly-acquired knowledge of the art of exhausting the contents of an egg, the well-known little boy of the apologue rushed to impart his knowledge to his grandmother, who had been for many years familiar with the process which the child had just discovered. Which of us has not met with some such instructors? I know men who would be ready to step forward and teach Taglioni how to dance, Tom Sayers how to box, or the Chevalier Bayard how to be a gentleman. We most of us know such men, and undergo, from time to time, the ineffable benefit of their patronage.

Mugford went away from our little entertainment vowing, by George, that Philip shouldn't want for a friend at the proper season; and this proper season very speedily arrived. I laughed one day, on going to the *Pall Mall Gazette* office, to find Philip installed in the sub-editor's room, with a provision of scissors, wafers, and paste-pots, snipping paragraphs from this paper and that, altering, condensing, giving titles, and so forth; and, in a word, in regular harness. The three-headed calves, the great prize gooseberries, the old maiden ladies of wonderful ages who at length died in country places—it was wonderful (considering his little experience) how Firmin hunted out these. He entered into all the spirit of his business. He prided himself on the clever titles which he found for his paragraphs. When his paper was completed at the week's end, he surveyed it fondly—not the leading articles, or those profound and yet brilliant literary essays which appeared in the *Gazette* —but the births, deaths, marriages, markets, trials, and what not. As a shop-boy having decorated his master's window, goes into the street, and pleased surveys his work; so the fair face of the *Pall Mall Gazette* rejoiced Mr. Firmin, and Mr. Bince, the printer of the paper. They looked with an honest pride upon the result of their joint labours. Nor did Firmin relish pleasantry on the subject. Did his friends allude to it, and ask if he had shot any especially fine *canard* that week?

Mr. Philip's brow would corrugate and his cheeks redden. He did not like jokes to be made at his expense: was not his a singular antipathy?

In his capacity of sub-editor, the good fellow had the privilege of taking and giving away countless theatre orders, and panorama and diorama tickets: the *Pall Mall Gazette* was not above accepting such little bribes in those days, and Mrs. Mugford's familiarity with the names of opera singers, and splendid appearance in an opera-box, were quite remarkable. Friend Philip would bear away a heap of these cards of admission, delighted to carry off our young folks to one exhibition or another. But once at the Diorama, where our young people sat in the darkness, very much frightened as usual, a voice from out the midnight gloom cried out: '*Who has come in with orders from the Pall Mall Gazette?*' A lady, two scared children, and Mr. Sub-editor Philip, all trembled at this dreadful summons. I think I should not dare to print the story even now, did I not know that Mr. Finnin was travelling abroad. It was a blessing the place was dark, so that none could see the poor sub-editor's blushes. Rather than cause any mortification to this lady, I am sure Philip would have submitted to rack and torture. But, indeed, her annoyance was very slight, except in seeing her friend annoyed. The humour of the scene surpassed the annoyance in the lady's mind, and caused her to laugh at the mishap; but I own our little boy (who is of an aristocratic turn, and rather too sensitive to ridicule from his schoolfellows) was not at all anxious to talk upon the subject, or to let the world know that he went to a place of public amusement 'with an order.'

As for Philip's landlady, the Little Sister, she, you know, had been familiar with the press, and pressmen, and orders for the play for years past. She looked quite young and pretty with her kind smiling face and neat tight black dress, as she came to the theatre—it was to an Easter piece—on Philip's arm, one evening. Our children saw her from their cab, as they, too, were driving to the same performance. It was, 'Look, mamma! There's Philip and the Little Sister!' And then came such smiles, and nods, and delighted recognitions from the cab to the two friends on foot! Of course I have forgotten what was the piece which we all saw on that Easter evening. But those children will never forget; no, though they live to be a hundred years old, and though their attention was distracted from the piece by constant observation of Philip and his companion in the public boxes opposite.

Mr. Firmin's work and pay were both light, and he accepted both very cheerfully. He saved money out of his little stipend. It was surprising how economically he could live with his little landlady's aid and counsel. He would come to us, recounting his feats of parsimony with a childish delight: he loved to contemplate his sovereigns, as week by week the little pile accumulated. He kept a noble eye upon sales and purchased now and again articles of furniture. In this way he brought home a piano to his lodgings, on which he could no more play than he could dance on the tight-rope; but he was given to understand that it was a very fine instrument; and my wife played on it one day when we went to visit him, and he sat listening, with his great hands on his knees, in ecstasies. He was thinking how one day, please Heaven, he should see other hands touching the keys—and player and instrument disappeared in a mist before his happy eyes. His purchases were not always lucky. For example, he was sadly taken in at an auction about a little pearl ornament. Some artful Hebrews at the sale conspired and 'ran him up,' as the phrase is, to a price more than equal to the value of the trinket. 'But you know who it was for, ma'am,' one of Philip's apologists said. 'If she would like to wear his ten fingers he would cut 'em off and send 'em to her. But he keeps 'em to write her letters and verses—and most beautiful they are, too.'

'And the dear fellow, who was bred up in splendour and luxury, Mrs. Mugford, as you, ma'am, know too well—he won't drink no wine now. A little whisky and a glass of beer is all he takes. And his clothes—he who used to be so grand—you see how he is now, ma'am. Always the gentleman—and, indeed, a finer or grander looking gentleman never entered a room; but he is saving—you know for what, ma'am.'

And, indeed, Mrs. Mugford *did* know; and so did Mrs. Pendennis and Mrs. Brandon. And these three women worked themselves into a perfect fever, interesting themselves for Mr. Firmin. And Mugford, in his rough funny way, used to say, 'Mr. P., a certain Mr. Heff has come and put our noses out of joint. He has, as sure as my name is Hem. And I am getting quite jealous of our sub-editor, and that is the long and short of it. But it's good to see him haw-haw Bickerton if ever they meet in the office, that it is! Bickerton won't bully *him* any more, I promise you!'

The conclaves and conspiracies of these women were endless in Philip's behalf. One day, I let the Little Sister out of my house with a handkerchief to her eyes, and in a great state of flurry and excitement, which perhaps communicates itself to the gentleman who passes her at his own door. The gentleman's wife is, on her part, not a little moved and excited. 'What do you think Mrs. Brandon says? Philip is learning shorthand. He says he does not think he is clever enough to be a writer of any mark;—but he can be a reporter, and with this, and his place at Mr. Mugford's, he thinks he can earn enough to—. Oh, he is a fine fellow!' I suppose feminine emotion stopped the completion of this speech. But when Mr. Philip slouched in to dinner that day, his hostess did homage before him; she loved him; she treated him with a tender respect and sympathy which her like are ever wont to bestow upon brave and honest men in misfortune.

Why should not Mr. Philip Firmin, barrister-at-law, bethink him that he belonged to a profession which has helped very many men to competence, and not a few to wealth and honours? A barrister might surely hope for as good earnings as could be made by a newspaper reporter. We all know instances of men who, having commenced their careers as writers for the press, had carried on the legal profession simultaneously, and attained the greatest honours of the bar and the bench. 'Can I sit in a Pump Court garret waiting for attorneys'?' asked poor Phil; 'I shall break my heart before they come. My brains are not worth much; I should addle them altogether in poring over law-books. I am not at all a clever fellow, you see; and I haven't the ambition and obstinate will to succeed which carry on many a man with no greater capacity than my own. I may have as good brains as Bickerton, for example: but I am not so *bumptious* as he is. By claiming the first place wherever he goes, he gets it very often. My dear friends, don't you see how modest I am1? There never was a man less likely to get on than myself—you must own that; and I tell you that Charlotte and I must look forward to a life of poverty, of cheese-parings, and second-floor lodgings at Pentonville or Islington. That's about my mark. I would let her off, only I know she would not take me at my word —the dear little thing! She has set her heart upon a hulking pauper; that's the truth. And I tell you what I am going to do. I am going seriously to learn the profession of poverty, and make myself master of it. What's the price of cow-heel and tripe? You don't know. I do; and the right place to buy 'em. I am as good a judge of sprats as any man in London. My tap in life is to be small beer henceforth, and I am growing quite to like it, and think it is brisk, and pleasant, and wholesome.' There was not a little truth in Philip's account of himself, and his capacities and incapacities. Doubtless he was not born to make a great name for himself in the world. But do we like those only who are famous? As well say we will only give our regard to men who have ten thousand a year, or are more than six feet high.

While of his three female friends and advisers, my wife admired Philip's humility, Mrs. Brandon and Mrs. Mugford were rather disappointed at his want of spirit, and to think that he aimed so low. I shall not say which side Firmin's biographer took in this matter. Was it my business to applaud or rebuke him for being humble-minded, or was I called upon to advise at all? My amiable reader, acknowledge that you and I in life pretty much go our own way. We eat the dishes we like because we like them, not because our neighbour relishes them. We rise early, or sit up late; we work, idle, smoke, or what not, because we choose so to do, not because the doctor orders. Philip, then, was like you and me, who will have our own way when we can. Will we not? If you won't, you do not deserve it. Instead of hungering after a stalled ox, he was accustoming himself to be content with a dinner of herbs. Instead of braving the tempest, he chose to take in sail, creep along shore, and wait for calmer weather.

So, on Tuesday of every week let us say, it was this modest sub editor's duty to begin snipping and pasting paragraphs for the ensuing Saturday's issue. He cut down the parliamentary speeches, giving due favouritism to the orators of the *Pall Mall Gazette* party, and meagre outlines of their opponent's discourses. If the leading public men on the side of the *Pall Mall Gazette* gave entertainments, you may be sure they were duly chronicled in the fashionable intelligence; if one of their party wrote a book it was pretty sure to get praise from the critic. I am speaking of simple old days, you understand. Of course there is *no* puffing, or jobbing, or false praise, or unfair censure now. Every critic knows what he is writing about, and writes with no aim but to tell truth.

Thus Philip, the dandy of two years back, was content to wear the shabbiest old coat; Philip, the Philippus of one-and-twenty, who rode showy horses, and rejoiced to display his horse and person in the park, now humbly took his place in an omnibus, and only on occasions indulged in a cab. From the roof of the larger vehicle he would salute his friends with perfect affability, and stare down on his aunt as she passed in her barouche. He never could be quite made to acknowledge that she purposely would not see him; or he would attribute her blindness to the quarrel which they had had, not to his poverty and present position. As for his cousin Ringwood, 'That fellow would commit any baseness,' Philip acknowledged; 'and it is I who have cut *him,*' our friend averred.

A real danger was lest our friend should in his poverty become more haughty and insolent than he had been in his days of better fortune, and that he should make companions of men who were not his equals. Whether was it better for him to be slighted in a fashionable club, or to swagger at the head of the company in a tavern parlour? This was the danger we might fear for Firmin. It was impossible not to confess that he was choosing to take a lower place in the world than that to which he had been born.

'Do you mean that Philip is lowered, because he is poor?' asked an angry lady, to whom this remark was made by her husband—man and wife being both very good friends to Mr. Firmin.

'My dear,' replies the worldling of a husband, 'suppose Philip were to take a fancy to buy a donkey and sell cabbages? He would be doing no harm; but there is no doubt he would lower himself in the world's estimation.'

'Lower himself!' says the lady, with a toss of her head. 'No man lowers himself by pursuing an honest calling. No man!'

'Very good. There is Grundsell, the greengrocer, out of Tuthill Street, who waits at our dinners. Instead of asking him to wait, we should beg him to sit down at table; or perhaps *we* should wait, and stand with a napkin behind Grundsell.'

'Nonsense!'

'Grundsell's calling is strictly honest, unless he abuses his opportunities, and smuggles away—'

'—smuggles away stuff and nonsense!'

'Very good: Grundsell is *not* a fitting companion, then, for us, or the nine little Grundsells for our children. Then why should Philip give up the friends of his youth, and forsake a club for a tavern parlour? You can't say our little friend, Mrs. Brandon, good as she is, is a fitting companion for him?'

'If he had a good little wife, he would have a companion of his own degree; and he would be twice as happy; and he would be out of all danger and temptation—and the best thing he can do is to marry directly!' cries the lady. 'And, my dear, I think I shall write to Charlotte and ask her to come and stay with us.'

There was no withstanding this argument. As long as Charlotte was with us we were sure that Philip would be out of harm's way, and seek for no other company. There was a snug little bedroom close by the quarters inhabited by our own children. My wife pleased herself by adorning this chamber, and Uncle Mac happening to come to London on business about this time, the young lady came over to us under his convoy, and I should like to describe the meeting between her and Mr. Philip in our parlour. No doubt it was very edifying. But my wife and I were not present, *vous concevez*. We only heard one shout of surprise and delight from Philip as he went into the room where the young lady was waiting. We had but said, 'Go into the parlour, Philip. You will find your old friend Major Mac there. He has come to Londonon business, and has news of—' There was no need to speak, for here Philip straightway bounced into the room.

And then came the shout. And then out came Major Mac, with such a droll twinkle in his eyes! What artifices and hypocrisies had we not to practise previously, so as to keep our secret from our children, who assuredly would have discovered it! I must tell you that the *paterfamilias* had guarded against the innocent prattle and inquiries of the children regarding the preparation of the little bedroom, by informing them that it was intended for Miss Grigsby, the governess with whose advent they had long been threatened. And one of our girls when the unconscious Philip arrived, said, 'Philip, if you go into the parlour,you will find *Miss Grigsby, the governess, there.'* And then Philip entered into that parlour, and then arose that shout, and then out came Uncle Mac, and then, etc. etc. And we called Charlotte Miss Grigsby all dinner-time; and we called her Miss Grigsby next day, and the more we called her Miss Grigsby the more we all laughed. And the baby, who could not speak plain yet, called her Miss Gibby, and laughed loudest of all; and it was such fun. But I think Philip and Charlotte had the best of the fun, my dears, though they may not have laughed quite so loud as we did.

As for Mrs. Brandon, who, you may be sure, speedily came to pay us a visit, Charlotte blushed, and looked quite beautiful when she went up and kissed the Little Sister. 'He *have* told you about me, then!' she said, in her soft little voice, smoothing the young lady's brown hair. 'Should I have known him at all but for you, and did you not save his life for me when he was ill?' asked Miss Baynes. 'And mayn't I love everybody who loves him?' she asked. And we left these women alone for a quarter of an. hour, during which they became the most intimate friends in the world. And all our household, great and small, including the nurse (a woman of a most jealous, domineering, and uncomfortable fidelity), thought well of our gentle young guest, and welcomed Miss Grigsby.

Charlotte, you see, is not so exceedingly handsome as to cause other women to perjure themselves by protesting that she is no great things after all. At the period with which we are concerned, she certainly had a lovely complexion, which her black dress set off, perhaps. And when Philip used to come into the room, she had always a fine garland of roses ready to offer him, and growing upon her cheeks, the moment he appeared. Her manners are so entirely unaffected and simple that they can't be otherwise than good: for is she not grateful, truthful, unconscious of self, easily pleased and interested in others *1* Is she very witty? I never said so—though that she appreciated *some* men's wit (whose names need not be mentioned) I cannot doubt. 'I say,' cries Philip, on that memorable first night of her arrival, and when she and other ladies had gone to bed, 'by George! isn't she glorious, I say! What can I have done to win such a pure little heart as that? *Non sum dignus.* It is too much happiness—too much, by George!' And his voice breaks behind his pipe, and he squeezes two fists into eyes that are brimful of joy and thanks. Where Fortune bestows such a bounty as this, I think we need not pity a man for what she withdraws. As Philip walks away at midnight (walks away? is turned out of doors; or surely he would have gone on talking till dawn), with the rain beating in his face, and fifty or a hundred pounds for all his fortune in his pocket, I think there goes one of the happiest of men—the happiest and richest. For is he not possessor of a treasure which he could not buy, or would not sell, for all the wealth of the world?

My wife may say what she will, but she assuredly is answerable for the invitation to Miss Baynes, and for all that ensued in consequence. At a hint that she would be a welcome guest in our house, in London, where all her heart and treasure lay, Charlotte Baynes gave up straightway her dear aunt at Tours, who had been kind to her; her dear uncle, her dear mamma, and all her dear brothers—following that natural law which ordains that a woman, under certain circumstances, shall resign home, parents, brothers, sisters, for the sake of that one individual who is henceforth to be dearer to her than all. Mrs. Baynes, the widow, growled a complaint at her daughter's ingratitude, but did not refuse her consent. She may have known that little Hely, Charlotte's volatile admirer, had fluttered off to another flower by this time, and that a pursuit of that butterfly was in vain: or she may have heard that he was going to pass the spring—the butterfly season—in London, and hoped that he perchance might again light on her girl. Howbeit, she was glad enough that her daughter should accept an invitation to our house, and owned that as yet the poor child's share of this life's pleasures had been but small. Charlotte's modest little trunks were again packed, then, and the poor child was sent off, I won't say with how small a provision of pocket-money, by her mother. But the thrifty woman had but little, and of it was determined to give as little as she could. 'Heaven will provide for my child,' she would piously say; and hence interfered very little with those agents whom Heaven sent to befriend her children. 'Her mother told Charlotte that she would send her some money next Tuesday,' the Major told us; 'but, between ourselves, I doubt whether she will. Between ourselves, my sister-in-law is always going to give money next Tuesday: but somehow Wednesday comes, and the money has not arrived. I could not let the little maid be without a few guineas, and have provided her out of a half-pay purse;

but mark me, that pay-day Tuesday will never come.' Shall I deny or confirm the worthy Major's statement? Thus far I will say, that Tuesday most certainly came; and a letter from her mamma to Charlotte, which said that one of her brothers and a younger sister were going to stay with Aunt Mac; and that as Char was so happy with her most hospitable and kind friends, a fond widowed mother, who had given up all pleasures for herself, would not interfere to prevent a darling child's happiness.

It has been said that three women, whose names have been given up, were conspiring in the behalf of this young person and the young man her sweetheart. Three days after Charlotte's arrival at our house, my wife persists in thinking that a drive into the country would do the child good, orders a brougham, dresses Charlotte in her best, and trots away to see Mrs. Mugford at Hampstead. Mrs. Brandon is at Mrs. Mugford's, of course quite by chance: and I feel sure that Charlotte's friend compliments Mrs. Mugford upon her garden, upon her nursery, upon her luncheon, upon everything that is hers. 'Why, dear me,' says Mrs. Mugford (as the ladies discourse upon a certain subject), 'what does it matter? Me and Mugford married on two pound a week; and on two pound a week my dear eldest children were born. It was a hard struggle sometimes, but we were all the happier for it; and I'm sure if a man won't risk a little he don't deserve much. I know *I* would risk, if I were a man, to marry such a pretty young dear. And I should take a young man to be but a mean-spirited fellow who waited and went shilly-shallying when he had but to say the word and be happy. I thought Mr. F. was a brave courageous gentleman, I did, Mrs. Brandon. Do you want me for to have a bad opinion of him? My dear, a little of that cream. It's very good. We 'ad a dinner yesterday, and a cook down from town, on purpose.' This speech, with appropriate imitations of voice and gesture, was repeated to the present biographer by the present biographer's wife, and he now began to see in what webs and meshes of conspiracy these artful women had enveloped the subject of the present biography.

Like Mrs. Brandon, and the other matron, Charlotte's friend, Mrs. Mugford became interested in the gentle young creature, and kissed her kindly, and made her a present on going away. It was a brooch in the shape of a thistle, if I remember aright, set with amethysts and a lovely Scottish stone called, I believe, a cairngorm. 'She ain't no style about her; and I confess, from a general's daughter, brought up on the Continent, I should have expected better. But we'll show her a little of the world and the opera, Brandon, and she'll do very well, of that I make no doubt.' And Mrs. Mugford took Miss Baynes to the opera, and pointed out the other people of fashion there assembled. And delighted Charlotte was. I make no doubt there was a young gentleman of our acquaintance at the back of the box who was very happy too. And this year, Philip's kinsman's wife, Lady Ringwood, had a box, in which Philip saw her and her daughters, and little Ringwood Twysden paying assiduous court to her Ladyship. They met in the crush-room by chance again, and Lady Ringwood looked hard at Philip and the blushing young lady on his arm. And it happened that Mrs. Mugford's carriage—the little one-horse trap which opens and shuts so conveniently—and Lady Ringwood's tall emblazoned chariot of state, stopped the way together. And from the tall emblazoned chariot the ladies looked not unkindly at the trap which contained the beloved of Philip's heart: and the carriages departed each on its way; and Ringwood Twysden, seeing his cousin advancing towards him, turned very pale, and dodged at a double quick down an arcade. But he need not have been afraid of Philip. Mr. Firmin's heart was all softness and benevolence at that time. He was thinking of those sweet sweet eyes that had just glanced to him a tender good-night; of that little hand which a moment since had hung with fond pressure on his arm. Do you suppose in such a frame of mind he had leisure to think of a nauseous little reptile crawling behind him? He was so happy that night, that Philip was King Philip again. And he went to the Haunt, and sang his song of 'Garryowen na Gloria,' and greeted the boys assembled, and spent at least three shillings over his supper and drinks. But the next day being Sunday, Mr. Firmin was at Westminster Abbey, listening to the sweet church chants, by the side of the very same young person whom he had escorted to the opera on the night before. They sat together so close that one must have heard exactly as well as the other. I dare say it is edifying to listen to anthems *à deux*. And how complimentary to the clergyman to have to wish that the sermon was longer! Through the vast cathedral aisles the organ notes peal gloriously. Ruby and topaz and amethyst blaze from the great church windows. Under the tall arcades the young people went together. Hand in hand they passed, and thought no ill.

Do gentle readers begin to tire of this spectacle of billing and cooing? I have tried to describe Mr. Philip's love affairs with as few words and in as modest phrases as may be—omitting the raptures, the passionate vows, the reams of correspondence, and the usual commonplaces of his situation. And yet, my dear madam, though you and I may be past the age of billing and cooing, though your ringlets, which I remember a lovely auburn, are now—well—are now a rich purple and green black, and my brow may be as bald as a cannon-ball;—I say, though we are old, we are not too old to forget. We may not care about the pantomime much now, but we like to take the young folks, and see them rejoicing. From the window where I write, I can look down into the garden of a certain square. In that garden I can at this moment see a young gentleman and lady of my acquaintance pacing up and down. They are talking some such talk as Milton imagines our first parents engaged in; and yonder garden is a paradise to my young friends. Did they choose to look outside the railings of the square, or at any other objects than each other's noses, they might see—the tax-gatherer we will say—with his book, knocking at one door, the doctor's brougham at a second, a hatchment over the windows of a third mansion, the baker's boy discoursing with the housemaid over the railings of a fourth. But what to them are these phenomena of life? Arm in arm my young folks go pacing up and down their Eden, and discoursing about that happy time which I suppose is now drawing near, about that charming little snuggery for which the furniture is ordered, and to which, Miss, your old friend and very humble servant will take the liberty of forwarding his best regards and a neat silver teapot. I dare say, with these young people, as with Mr. Philip and Miss Charlotte, all occurrences of life seem to have reference to that event which forms the subject of their perpetual longing and contemplation. There is the doctor's brougham driving away, and Imogene says to Alonzo, 'What anguish I shall have if you are ill!' Then there is the carpenter putting up the hatchment. 'Ah, my love, if you were to die, I think they might put up a hatchment for both of us,' says Alonzo, with a killing sigh. Both sympathise with Mary and the baker's boy whispering over the railings. Go to, gentle baker's boy, we also know what it is to love!

The whole soul and strength of Charlotte and Philip being bent upon marriage, I take leave to put in a document which Philip received at this time; and can imagine that it occasioned no little sensation:—

'Astor House, New York.

'AND so you are returned to the great city—to the *fumum,* the *strepitum,* and I sincerely hope the *opes,* of our Borne! Your own letters are but brief; but I have an occasional correspondent (there are few, alas! who remember *the exile!*) who keeps me *au courant* of my Philip's history, and tells me that you are industrious, that you are cheerful, that you prosper. Cheerfulness is the companion of Industry, Prosperity their offspring. That that prosperity may attain *the fullest growth,* is an absent father's fondest prayer! Perhaps ere long I shall be able to announce to you that I too am prospering. I am engaged in pursuing a scientific discovery here (it is medical, and connected with my own profession), of which the results *ought* to lead to Fortune, unless the jade has for ever deserted George Brand Firmin! So you have embarked in the drudgery of the press, and have become a member of *the fourth estate.* It has been despised, and press-man and poverty were for a long time supposed to be synonymous. But the power, the wealth of the press are daily developing, and they will increase yet further. I confess I should have liked to hear that my Philip was pursuing his profession of the bar, at which honour, splendid competence, nay, aristocratic rank, are the prizes of *the bold, the industrious, and the deserving.* Why should you not?—should I not still hope that you may gain legal eminence and position? A father who has had much to suffer, who is descending the vale of years alone and in a distant land, would be soothed in his exile if he thought his son would one day be able to repair the shattered fortunes of his race. But it is not yet, I fondly think, too late. You may yet qualify for the bar, and one of its prizes may fall to you. I confess that it was not without a pang of grief I heard from our kind little friend Mrs. B., you were studying shorthand in order to become a newspaper reporter. And has Fortune, then, been so relentless to me that my son is to be compelled to follow such a calling? I shall try and be resigned. I had hoped higher things for you—for me.

'My dear boy, with regard to your romantic attachment for Miss Baynes, which our good little Brandon narrates to me, in her *peculiar orthography,* but with much *touching simplicity*—I make it a rule not to say a word of comment, of warning, or remonstrance. As sure as you are your father's son, you will take your own line in any matter of attachment to a woman, and all the fathers in the world won't stop you. In Philip of four-and-twenty I recognise his father thirty years ago. My father scolded, entreated, quarrelled with me, never forgave me. I will learn to be more generous towards my son. I may grieve, but I bear you no malice. If ever I achieve wealth again, you shall not be deprived of it. I suffered so myself from a harsh father, that I will never be one to my son!

'As you have put on the livery of the Muses, and regularly entered yourself of the Fraternity of the Press, what say you to a little addition to your income by letters addressed to my friend, the editor of the new journal, called here the *Gazette of the Upper Ten Thousands* It is *the* fashionable journal published here; and your qualifications are precisely those which would make your services valuable as a contributor. Doctor Geraldine, the editor, is not, I believe, a relative of the Leinster family, but a self-made man, who arrived in this country some years since, poor, and an exile from his native country. He advocates Repeal politics in Ireland; but with these of course you need have nothing to do. And he is much too liberal to expect these from his contributors. I have been of service professionally to Mrs. Geraldine and himself. My friend of the *Emerald* introduced me to the Doctor. Terrible enemies in print, in private they are perfectly good friends, and the little passages of arms between the two journalists serve rather to amuse than to irritate. "The grocer's boy from Ormond Quay" (Geraldine once, it appears, engaged in that useful but humble calling), and the "miscreant from Cork"—the editor of the *Emerald* comes from that city—assail each other in public, but drink whisky-and-water *galore* in private. If you write for Geraldine, of course you will say nothing disrespectful about *grocers' boys. His dollars are good silver,* of that you may be sure. Dr. G. knows a part of your history: he knows that you are now fairly engaged in literary pursuits; that you are a man of education, a gentleman, a man of the world, a man of courage. I have answered for your possessing all these qualities. (The Doctor, in his droll humorous way, said that if you were a chip of the old block you would be just what he called " the grit.") Political treatises are not so much wanted as personal news regarding the notabilities of London, and these, I assured him, you were the very man to be able to furnish. You, who know everybody; who have lived, with the great world—the world of lawyers, the world of artists, the world of the University-have already had an experience which few gentlemen of the press can boast of, and may turn that experience to profit. Suppose you were to trust a little to your imagination in composing these letters? there can be no harm in being *poetical.* Suppose an *intelligent correspondent* writes that he has met the D-ke of W-ll-ngt-n, had a private interview with the Pr-m-r, and so forth, who is to say him nay? And this is the kind of talk our *gobemouches* of New York delight in. My worthy friend, Doctor Geraldine, for example—between ourselves his name is Finnigan, but his private history is *strictly entre nous*—when he first came to New York astonished the people by the copiousness of his anecdotes regarding the *English aristocracy,* of whom he knows as much as he does of the Court of Pekin. He was smart, ready, sarcastic, amusing; he found readers: from one success he advanced to another, and the *Gazette of the Upper Ten Thousand* is likely to make *this worthy man's fortune.* You really may be serviceable to him, and may justly earn the *liberal remuneration* which he offers for a weekly letter. Anecdotes of men and women of fashion—the more gay and lively the more welcome—the *quicquid agunt homines,* in a word,—should be the *farrago libelli.* Who are the reigning beauties of London? and Beauty, you know, has a rank and fashion of its own. Has any one lately won or lost on the turf or at play? What are the clubs talking about? Are there any duels'? What is the last scandal? Does the good old Duke keep his health? Is that affair over between the Duchess of This and Captain That?

'Such is the information which our *badauds* here like to have, and for which my friend the Doctor will pay at the rate of — dollars per letter. Your name need not appear at all. The remuneration is certain. *C'est à prendre ou à laisser,* as our lively neighbours say. Write in the first place in confidence to me; and in whom can you confide more safely than in your father?

'You will, of course, pay your respects to your relative the new Lord of Ringwood. For a young man whose family is so powerful as yours, there can surely be no derogation in entertaining some feudal respect, and who knows whether and how soon Sir John Ringwood may be able to help his cousin? By the way, Sir John is a Whig, and your paper is a Conservative. But you are, above all, *homme du monde.* In such a subordinate place as you occupy with the *Pall Mall Gazette,* a man's private politics do not surely count at all. If Sir John Ringwood, your kinsman, sees any way of helping you, so much the better, and of course your politics will be those of your family. I have no knowledge of him. He was a very quiet man at college, where, I regret to say, your father's friends were not of the quiet sort at all. I trust I have repented. I have sown my wild oats. And ah! how pleased I shall be to hear that my Philip has bent *his* proud head a little, and is ready to submit more than he used of old to the customs of the world. Call upon Sir John, then. As a Whig gentleman of large estate, I need not tell you that he will expect *respect* from you. He is your kinsman; the representative of your grandfather's gallant and noble race. He bears the name your mother bore. To *her* my Philip was always gentle, and for her sake you will comply with the wishes of your affectionate father,

G. B. F.

'I have not said a word of compliment to Mademoiselle. I wish her so well that I own I wish she were about to marry a richer suitor than my dear son. Will fortune ever permit me to embrace my daughter-in-law, and take your children on my knee? You will speak kindly to them of their grandfather, will you not? Poor General Baynes, I have heard, used violent and unseemly language regarding me, which I most heartily pardon. I am grateful when I think *that I never did General B. an injury*: grateful and proud to accept benefits from my own son. These I treasure up in my heart; and still hope I shall be able to repay with something more substantial than my fondest prayers. Give my best wishes, then, to Miss Charlotte, and try and teach her to think kindly of her Philip's father.'

Miss Charlotte Baynes, who kept the name of Miss Grigsby, the governess, amongst all the roguish children of a facetious father, was with us one month, and her mamma expressed great cheerfulness at her absence, and at the thought that she had found such good friends. After two months, her uncle, Major MacWhirter, returned from visiting his relations in the North, and offered to take his niece back to France again. He made this proposition with the jolliest air in the world, and as if his niece would jump for joy to go back to her mother. But to the Major's astonishment, Miss Baynes turned quite pale, ran to her hostess, flung herself into that lady's arms, and then there began an osculatory performance which perfectly astonished the good Major. Charlotte's friend, holding Miss Baynes tight in her embrace, looked fiercely at the Major over the girl's shoulder, and defied him to take her away from that sanctuary.

'Oh, you dear good dear friend!' Charlotte gurgled out, and sobbed I know not what more expressions of fondness and gratitude.

But the truth is, that two sisters, or mother and daughter, could not love each other more heartily than these two personages. Mother and daughter forsooth! You should have seen Charlotte's piteous look when sometimes the conviction would come on her that she ought at length to go home to mamma; such a look as I can fancy Iphigenia casting on Agamemnon, when, in obedience to a painful sense of duty, he was about to—to use the sacrificial knife. No, we all loved her. The children would howl at the idea of parting with their Miss Grigsby. Charlotte, in return, helped them to very pretty lessons in music and French—served hot, as it were, from her own recent studies at Tours—and a good daily governess operated on the rest of their education to everybody's satisfaction.

And so months rolled on and our young favourite still remained with us. Mamma fed the little maid's purse with occasional remittances; and begged her hostess to supply her with all necessary articles from the milliner. Afterwards, it is true, Mrs. General Baynes...But why enter upon these painful family disputes in a chapter which has been devoted to sentiment?

As soon as Mr. Firmin received the letter above faithfully copied (with the exception of the pecuniary offer, which I do not consider myself at liberty to divulge), he hurried down from Thornhaugh Street to Westminster. He dashed by Buttons, the page; he took no notice of my wondering wife at the drawing-room door; he rushed to the second-floor, bursting open the schoolroom door, where Charlotte was teaching our dear third daughter to play 'In my Cottage near a Wood.' 'Charlotte! Charlotte!' he cried out.

'La, Philip! don't you see Miss Grigsby is giving us lessons?' said the children.

But he would not listen to those wags, and still beckoned Charlotte to him. That young woman rose up and followed him out of the door, as, indeed, she would have followed him out of the window; and there, on the stairs, they read Dr. Firmin's letter, with their heads quite close together, you understand.

'Two hundred a year more,' said Philip, his heart throbbing so that he could hardly speak; 'and your fifty—and two hundred the *Gazette* —and—'

'Oh, Philip!' was all Charlotte could say, and then—There was a pretty group for the children to see, and for an artist to draw!

CHAPTER XXXII. WAYS AND MEANS

OF course any man of the world, who is possessed of decent prudence, will perceive that the idea of marrying on four hundred and fifty pounds a year, so secured as was Master Philip's income, was preposterous and absurd. In the first place, you can't live on four hundred and fifty pounds a year, that is a certainty. People do live on less, I believe. But a life without a brougham, without a decent house, without claret for dinner, and a footman to wait, can hardly be called existence. Philip's income might fail any day. He might not please the American paper. He might quarrel with the *Pall Mall Gazette.* And then what would remain to him? Only poor little Charlotte's fifty pounds a year! So Philip's most intimate male friend—a man of the world, and with a good deal of experience—argued. Of course I was not surprised that Philip did not choose to take my advice; though I did not expect he would become so violently angry, call names almost, and use most rude expressions, when, *at his express desire,* this advice was tendered to him. If he did not want it, why did he ask for it? The advice might be unwelcome to him, but why did he choose to tell me at my own table, over my own claret, that it was the advice of a sneak and a worldling? 'My good fellow, that claret, though it is a second growth, and I can afford no better, cost seventy-two shillings a dozen. How much is six times three hundred and sixty-five? A bottle a day is the least you can calculate' (the fellow would come to my house and drink two bottles to himself, with the utmost nonchalance). ' A bottle per diem of that light claret—of that second-growth stuff—costs one hundred and four guineas a year, do you understand? or, to speak plainly with you, *one hundred and nine pounds four shillings*!'

'Well,' says Philip, 'après? We'll do without. Meantime I will take what I can get!' and he tosses off about a pint as he speaks (these *mousseline* glasses are not only enormous, but they break by dozens). He tosses off a pint of my Larose, and gives a great roar of laughter, as if he had said a good thing!

Philip Firmin *is* coarse and offensive at times, and Bickerton in holding this opinion is not altogether wrong.

'I'll drink claret when I come to you, old boy,' he says, grinning; 'and at home I will have whisky-and-water.'

'But suppose Charlotte is ordered claret!'

'Well, she can have it,' says this liberal lover; 'a bottle will last her a week.'

'Don't you see,' I shriek out, 'that even a bottle a week costs something like—six by fifty-two—eighteen pounds a year!' (I own it is really only fifteen twelve; but, in the hurry of argument, a man *may* stretch a figure or so.) 'Eighteen pounds for Charlotte's claret; as much, at least, you great boozy toper, for your whisky and beer. Why, you actually want a tenth part of your income for the liquor you consume! And then clothes; and then lodging; and then coals; and then doctor's bills; and then pocket-money; and then seaside for the little dears. Just have the kindness to add these things up, and you will find that you have about two-and-ninepence left to pay the grocer and the butcher.'

'What you call prudence,' says Philip, thumping the table and, of course, breaking a glass, I call cowardice—I call blasphemy! Do you mean, as a Christian man, to tell me that two young people and a family, if it should please Heaven to send them one, cannot subsist upon five hundred pounds a year? Look round, sir, at the myriads of God's creatures who live, love, are happy and poor, and be ashamed of the wicked doubt which you utter!' And he starts up, and strides up and down the dining-room, curling his flaming moustache, and rings the bell fiercely, and says, 'Johnson, I've broke a glass. Get me another.'

In the drawing-room, my wife asks what we two were fighting about? And, as Charlotte is upstairs, telling the children stories as they are put to bed, or writing to her dear mamma, or what not, our friend bursts out with more rude and violent expressions than he had used in the dining-room over my glasses which he was smashing, tells my own wife that I am an atheist, or at best a miserable sceptic and Sadducee: that I doubt of the goodness of Heaven, and am not thankful for my daily bread. And, with one of her kindling looks directed towards the young man, of course my wife sides with him. Miss Char presently came down from the young folks, and went to the piano and played us Beethoven's 'Dream of Saint Jerome,' which always soothes me, and charms me, so that I fancy it is a poem of Tennyson in music. And our children, as they sink off to sleep overhead, like to hear soft music, which soothes them into slumber, Miss Baynes says. And Miss Charlotte looks very pretty at her piano: and Philip lies gazing at her; with his great feet and hands tumbled over one of our arm-chairs And the music, with its solemn cheer, makes us all very happy and kind-hearted, and ennobles us somehow as we listen. And my wife wears her *benedictory* look whenever she turns towards these young people. She has worked herself up to the opinion that yonder couple ought to marry. She can give chapter and verse for her belief. To doubt about the matter at all is wicked according to her notions. And there are certain points upon which, I humbly own, that I don't dare to argue with her.

When the women of the house have settled a matter, is there much use in man's resistance? If my harem orders that I shall wear a yellow coat and pink trousers, I know that, before three months are over, I shall be walking about in *rose-tendre* and canary-coloured garments. It is the perseverance which conquers, the daily return to the object desired. Take my advice, my dear sir, when you see your womankind resolute about a matter, give up at once, and have a quiet life. Perhaps to one of these evening entertainments, where Miss Baynes played the piano, as she did very pleasantly, and Mr. Philip's great clumsy fist turned the leaves, little Mrs. Brandon would come tripping in, and as she surveyed the young couple, her remark would be, 'Did you ever see a better suited couple?' When I came home from chambers, and passed the dining-room door, my eldest daughter with a knowing face would bar the way and say, 'You mustn't go in there, papa! Miss Grigsby is there, and Master Philip is *not to be disturbed at his lessons*!' Mrs. Mugford had begun to arrange marriages between her young people and ours from the very first day she saw us; and Mrs. M.'s ch. filly Toddles, rising two years, and our three-year-old colt Billyboy, were rehearsing in the nursery the endless little comedy which the grown-up young persons were performing in the drawing-room.

With the greatest frankness Mrs. Mugford gave her opinion that Philip, with four or five hundred a year, would be no better than a sneak if he delayed to marry. How much had she and Mugford when *they* married, she would like to know? 'Emily Street, Pentonville, was where *we* had apartments,' she remarked; 'we were pinched sometimes; but we owed nothing: and our house-keeping books I can show you.' I believe Mrs. M. actually brought these dingy relics of her honeymoon for my wife's inspection. I tell you, my house was peopled with these friends of matrimony. Flies were for ever in requisition, and our boys were very sulky at having to sit for an hour at Shoolbred's, while certain ladies lingered there over blankets, tablecloths, and what not. Once I found my wife and Charlotte flitting about Wardour Street, the former lady much interested in a great Dutch cabinet, with a glass cupboard and corpulent drawers. And that cabinet was, ere long, carted off to Mrs. Brandon's, Thornhaugh Street; and in that glass cupboard there was presently to be seen a neat set of china for tea and breakfast. The end was approaching. That event, with which the third volume of the old novels used to close, was at hand. I am afraid our young people can't drive off from St. George's in a chaise and four, and that no noble relative will lend them his castle for the honeymoon. Well: some people cannot drive to happiness, even with four horses; and other folks can reach the goal on foot My venerable Muse stoops down, unlooses her *cothurnus* with some difficulty, and prepares to fling that old shoe after the pair.

Tell, venerable Muse! what were the marriage gifts which friendship provided for Philip and Charlotte? Philip's cousin, Ringwood Twysden, came simpering up to me at 'Bays's Club' one afternoon, and said: 'I hear my precious cousin is going to marry. I think I shall send him a broom to sweep a crossin'.' I was nearly going to say, 'This was a piece of generosity to be expected from your father's son'; but the fact is, that I did not think of this withering repartee until I was crossing

St. James's Park on my way home, when Twysden of course was out of ear-shot. A great number of my best witticisms have been a little late in making their appearance in the world. If we could but hear the unspoken jokes, how we should all laugh; if we could but speak them, how witty we should be! When you have left the room, you have no notion what clever things I was going to say when you baulked me by going away. Well, then, the fact is, the Twysden family gave Philip nothing on his marriage, being the exact sum of regard which they professed to have for him.

MRS. MAJOR MACWHIRTER gave the bride an Indian brooch, representing the Taj Mahal at Agra, which General Baynes had given to his sister-in-law in old days. At a later period, it is true, Mrs. Mac asked Charlotte for the brooch back again; but this was when many family quarrels had raged between the relatives—quarrels which to describe at length would be to tax too much the writer and the readers of this history.

MRS. MUGFORD presented an elegant plated coffee-pot, six drawing-room almanacs (spoils of the *Pall Mall Gazette),* and fourteen richly cut jelly-glasses, most useful for negus if the young couple gave evening parties; for dinners they would not be able to afford.

MRS. BRANDON made an offering of two tablecloths and twelve dinner napkins, most beautifully worked, and I don't know how much house linen.

THE LADY OF THE PRESENT WRITER—Twelve tea-spoons in bullion, and a pair of sugar-tongs. Mrs. Baynes, Philip's mother-in-law, sent him also a pair of sugar-tongs, of a light manufacture, easily broken. He keeps a tong to the present day, and speaks very satirically regarding that relic.

PHILIP'S INN OF COURT—A bill for commons and Inn taxes, with the Treasurer's compliments.

And these, I think, formed the items of poor little Charlotte's meagre trousseau. Before Cinderella went to the ball she was almost as rich as our little maid. Charlotte's mother sent a grim consent to the child's marriage, but declined herself to attend it. She was ailing and poor. Her year's widowhood was just over. She had her other children to look after. My impression is that Mrs. Baynes thought she would be out of Philip's power so long as she remained abroad, and that the General's savings would be secure for him. So she delegated her authority to Philip's friends in London, and sent her daughter a moderate wish for her happiness, which may or may not have profited the young people.

'Well, my dear, you are rich, compared to what I was when I married,' little Mrs. Brandon said to her young friend. 'You will have a good husband. That is more than I had. You will have good friends; and I was almost alone for a time, until it pleased God to befriend me.' It was not without a feeling of awe that we saw these young people commence that voyage of life on which henceforth they were to journey together; and I am sure that of. the small company who accompanied them to the silent little chapel where they were joined in marriage there was not one who did not follow them with tender good wishes and heartfelt prayers. They had a little purse provided for a month's holiday. They had health, hope, good spirits, good friends. I have never learned that life's trials were over after marriage; only lucky is he who has a loving companion to share them. As for the lady with whom Charlotte had stayed before her marriage, she was in a state of the most lachrymose sentimentality. She sat on the bed in the chamber which the little maid had vacated. Her tears flowed copiously. She knew not why, she could not tell how the girl had wound herself round her maternal heart. And I think if Heaven had decreed this young creature should be poor, it had sent her many blessings and treasures in compensation.

Every respectable man and woman in London will, of course, pity these young people, and reprobate the mad risk which they were running, and yet, by the influence and example of a sentimental wife probably, so madly sentimental have I become, that I own sometimes I almost fancy these misguided wretches were to be envied.

A melancholy little chapel it is where they were married, and stands hard by our house. We did not decorate the church with flowers, or adorn the beadles with white ribbons. We had, I must confess, a dreary little breakfast, not in the least enlivened by Mugford's jokes, who would make a speech *de circonstance,* which was not, I am thankful to say, reported in the *Pall Mall Gazette.* 'We shan't charge you for advertising the marriage *there,* my dear,' Mrs. Mugford said. 'And I've already took it myself to Mr. Burjoyce.' Mrs. Mugford had insisted upon pinning a large white favour upon John, who drove her from Hampstead: but that was the only ornament present at the nuptial ceremony, much to the disappointment of the good lady. There was a very pretty cake, with two doves in sugar on the top, which the Little Sister made and sent, and no other hymeneal emblem. Our little girls as bridesmaids appeared, to be sure, in new bonnets and dresses, but everybody else looked so quiet and demure, that when we went into the church, three or four street urchins knocking about the gate, said, 'Look at 'em. They're going to be 'ung.' And so the words are spoken, and the indissoluble knot is tied. Amen. For better, for worse, for good days or evil, love each other, cling to each other, dear friends. Fulfil your course, and accomplish your life's toil. In sorrow, soothe each other; in illness, watch and tend. Cheer, fond wife, the husband's struggle; lighten his gloomy hours with your tender smiles, and gladden his home with your love. Husband, father, whatsoever your lot, be your heart pure, your life honest. For the sake of those who bear your name, let no bad action sully it. As you look at those innocent faces, which ever tenderly greet you, be yours, too, innocent, and your conscience without reproach. As the young people kneel before the altar railing, some such thoughts as these pass through a friend's mind who witnesses the ceremony of their marriage. Is not all we hear in that place meant to apply to ourselves, and to be carried away for everyday cogitation?

After the ceremony we sign the book, and walk back demurely to breakfast. And Mrs. Mugford does not conceal her disappointment at the small preparations made for the reception of the marriage party. 'I call it shabby, Brandon; and I speak my mind. No favours. Only your cake. No speeches to speak of. No lobster-salad: and wine on the sideboard. I thought your Queen Square friends knew how to do the thing better! When one of *my* gurls is married, I promise you we shan't let her go out of the backdoor; and at least we shall have the best four greys that Newman's can furnish. It's my belief your young friend is getting too fond of money, Brandon, and so I have told Mugford.' But these, you see, were only questions of taste. Good Mrs. Mugford's led her to a green satin dress and a pink turban, when other ladies were in grey or quiet colours. The intimacy between our two families dwindled immediately after Philip's marriage; Mrs. M., I am sorry to say, setting us down as shabby-genteel people, and she couldn't bear screwing—never could!

Well: the speeches were spoken. The bride was kissed, and departed with her bridegroom: they had not even a valet and lady's-maid to bear them company. The route of the happy pair was to be Canterbury, Folkestone, Boulogne, Amiens, Paris, and Italy perhaps, if their little stock of pocket-money would serve them so far. But the very instant when half was spent, it was agreed that these young people should turn their faces homeward again; and meanwhile the printer and Mugford himself agreed that they would do Mr. Sub-editor's duty. How much had they in the little purse for their pleasure-journey? That is no business of ours, surely; but with youth, health, happiness, love, amongst their possessions, I don't think our young friends had need to be discontented. Away then they drive in their cab to the railway station. Farewell, and Heaven bless you, Charlotte and Philip! I have said how I found my wife crying in her favourite's vacant bedroom. The marriage table did coldly furnish forth a funeral kind of dinner. The cold chicken choked us all, and the jelly was but a sickly compound to my taste, though it was the Little Sister's most artful manufacture. I own for one I was quite miserable. I found no comfort at clubs, nor could the last new novel fix my attention. I saw Philip's eyes, and heard the warble of Charlotte's sweet voice. I walked off from Bays's,' and through Old Parr Street, where Philip had lived, and his parents entertained me as a boy; and then tramped to Thornhaugh Street, rather ashamed of myself. The maid said mistress was in Mr. Philip's rooms, the two pair,—and what was that I heard on the piano as I entered the apartment? Mrs. Brandon sat there hemming some chintz window-curtains, or bed-curtains, or what not: by her side sat my own eldest girl stitching away very resolutely; and at the piano—the piano which Philip had bought—there sat my own wife picking out that 'Dream of Saint Jerome,' of Beethoven, which Charlotte used to play so delicately. We had tea out of Philip's tea-things, and a nice hot cake, which consoled some of us. But I have known few evenings more melancholy than that. It felt like the first night at school after the holidays, when we all used to try and appear cheerful, you know. But ah! how dismal the gaiety was; and how dreary that lying awake in the night, and thinking of the happy days just over!

The way in which we looked forward for letters from our bride and bridegroom was quite a curiosity. At length a letter arrived from these personages: and as it contains no secret, I take the liberty to print it *in extenso*.

'Amiens: *Friday*. Paris: *Saturday*.

'DEAREST FRIENDS,—(For the dearest friends you *are* to us, and will continue to be *as long as we live*),—We perform our promise of writing to you to say that we are *well*, and *safe*, and *happy*! Philip says I mustn't use *dashes*, but I can't *help it*. He says, he supposes I am *dashing* off a letter. You know his joking way. Oh, what a blessing it is to see him so happy. And if he is happy, I am. I tremble to think *how* happy. He sits opposite me, smoking his cigar, looking so noble! *I like it*, and I went to our room and *brought him this one*. He says, " Char, if I were to say bring me your head, you would order a waiter to cut it off." Pray, did I not promise three days ago to love, honour, and obey him, and am I going to break my promise already? I hope not. I pray not. All my life I hope I shall be trying to keep that promise of mine. We like Canterbury almost as much as dear Westminster. We had an open carriage and took *a glorious drive* to Folkestone, and in the crossing Philip was ill, and I wasn't. And he looked very droll; and he was in a dreadful bad humour; and that was my first appearance as nurse. I think I should like him to be *a little* ill sometimes, so that I may sit up and take care of him. We went through the cords at the custom-house at Boulogne; and I remembered how, two years ago, I passed through those very cords with my poor papa, and *he* stood outside, and saw us! We went to the Hôtel des Bains. We walked about the town. We went to the Tintelleries, where we used to live, and to your house in the Haute Ville, where I remember *everything as if it was yesterday*. Don't you remember, as we were walking one day, you said, "Charlotte, there is the steamer coming; there is the smoke of his funnel"; and I said, "What steamer?" and you said, "The Philip, to be sure." And he came up, smoking his pipe! We passed over and over the old ground where we used to walk. We went to the pier, and gave money to the poor little hunchback who plays the guitar, and he said, *"Merci, madame."* How droll it sounded! And that good kind Marie at the Hôtel des Bains remembered us, and called us *"mes enfans."* And if you were not the most good-natured woman *in the world,* I think I should be ashamed to write such nonsense.

'Think of Mrs.. Brandon having knitted me a purse, which she gave me as we went away from *dear dear* Queen Square; and when I opened it, there were five sovereigns in it! When we found what the purse contained, Philip used one of his great *jurons* (as he always does when he is most tender-hearted), and he said that woman was an angel, and that we would keep those five sovereigns, and never change them. Ah! I am thankful my husband has such friends! I will love all who love him—you most of all. For were not you the means of bringing this noble heart to me? I fancy I have known *bigger people,* since I have known you, and some of your friends. Their talk is simpler, their thoughts are greater than—those with whom I used to live. P. says, Heaven has given Mrs. Brandon such a great heart, that she must have a good intellect. If loving my Philip be wisdom, I know some one who will be very wise!

'If I was not in a very great hurry to see mamma, Philip said we might stop a day at Amiens. And we went to the Cathedral, and to whom do you think it is dedicated? To *my* saint: to Saint Firmin! And oh! I prayed to Heaven to give me strength to devote my life to *my saint's service,* to love him always, as a pure true wife: in sickness to guard him, in sorrow to soothe him. I will try and *learn* and *study,* not to make my intellect equal to his—very few women can hope for that—but that I may better comprehend him, and give him a companion more worthy of him. I wonder whether there are many men in the world as clever as our husbands? Though Philip is so modest. He says he is not clever *at all.* Yet I know he is, and grander somehow than other men. I said nothing, but I used to listen at Queen Square; and some who came who thought best of themselves, seemed to me pert, and worldly, and small; and some were like princes somehow. My Philip is one of the princes. Ah, dear friend! may I not give thanks where thanks are due, that I am chosen to be the wife of a true gentleman? Kind, and brave, and loyal Philip! Honest and generous,—above deceit or selfish scheme. Oh! I hope it is not wrong to be so happy!

'We wrote to mamma and dear Madame Smolensk to say we were coming. Mamma finds Madame de Valentinois's boarding-house even dearer than dear Madame Smolensk's. I *don't mean* a pun! She says she has found out that Madame de Valentinois's real name is Cornichon; that she was a person of the worst character, and that cheating at *écarté* was practised at her house. She took up her own two francs and another two-franc piece from the card-table, saying that Colonel Boulotte was cheating, and by rights the money was hers. She is going to leave Madame de Valentinois at the end of her month, or as soon as our children, who have the measles, can move. She desired that on no account I would come to see her at Madame V.'s; and she brought Philip £12, 10s. in five-franc pieces, which she laid down on the table before him, and said it was my first quarter's payment. It is not due yet, I know. "But do you think I will be beholden," says she, "to a man like you?" And P. shrugged his shoulders, and put the *rouleau* of silver pieces into a drawer. He did not say a word, but, of course, I saw he was ill-pleased. "What shall we do with your fortune, Char?" he said, when mamma went away. And a part we spent at the opera and at Véry's restaurant, where we took our dear kind Madame Smolensk. Ah, how good that woman was to me! Ah, how I suffered in that house when mamma wanted to part me from Philip! We walked by and saw the windows of the room where that horrible horrible tragedy was performed, and Philip shook his fist at the green *jalousies.* "Good heavens!" he said: "how, my darling, how I was made to suffer there!" I bear no malice. I will do no injury. But I can never forgive: never! I can forgive mamma, who made my husband so unhappy; but can I love her again? Indeed and indeed I have tried. Often and often in my dreams that horrid tragedy is acted over again; and they are taking him from me, and I feel as if I should die. When I was with you I used often to be afraid to go to sleep for fear of that dreadful dream, and I kept one of his letters under my pillow so that I might hold it in the night. And now! No one can part us!—oh, no one!—until the end comes!

'He took me about to all his old *bachelor haunts;* to the Hôtel Poussin, where he used to live, which is very dingy but comfortable. And he introduced me to the landlady, in a Madras handkerchief, and to the landlord (in earrings and with no coat on), and to the little boy who *frottes* the floors. And he said, "*Tiens*" and "*Merci, madame!*" as we gave him a five-franc piece *out of my fortune.* And then we went to the café opposite the Bourse, where Philip used to write his letters; and then we went to the Palais Royal, where Madame de Smolensk was in waiting for us. And then we went to the play. And then we went to Tortoni's to take ices. And then we walked a part of the way home with Madame Smolensk under a hundred million blazing stars; and then we walked down the Champs Elysées avenues, by which Philip used to come to me, and beside the plashing fountains shining under the silver moon. And, oh, Laura! I wonder under the silver moon was anybody so happy as your *loving and grateful*   C. F.

'*P.S.*' [In the handwriting of Philip Firmin, Esq.]—'My dear Friends,—I'm so jolly that it seems like a dream. I have been watching Charlotte scribble scribble for an hour past; and wondered and thought is it actually true? and gone and convinced myself of the truth by looking at the paper and the dashes which she will put under the words. My dear friends, what have I done in life that I am to be made a present of a little angel? Once there was so much wrong in me, and my heart was so black and revengeful, that I knew not what might happen to me. She came and rescued me. The love of this creature purifies me—and—and I think that is all. I think I only want to say that I am the happiest man in Europe. That Saint Firmin at Amiens! Didn't it seem like a good omen? By St. George! I never heard of St. F. until I lighted on him in the Cathedral. When shall we write next? Where shall we tell you to direct? We don't know where we are going. We don't want letters. But we are not the less grateful to dear kind friends; and our names are   P. and C. P.'

CHAPTER XXXIII. DESCRIBES A SITUATION INTERESTING BUT NOT UNEXPECTED

ONLY very wilful and silly children cry after the moon. Sensible people who have shed their sweet tooth can't be expected to be very much interested about honey. We may hope Mr. and Mrs. Philip Firmin enjoyed a pleasant wedding tour and that sort of thing: but as for chronicling its delights or adventures, Miss Sowerby and I vote that the task is altogether needless and immoral. Young people are already much too sentimental, and inclined to idle maudlin reading. Life is earnest, Miss Sowerby remarks (with a strong inclination to spell 'earnest' with a large E). Life is labour. Life is duty. Life is rent. Life is taxes. Life brings its ills, bills, doctor's pills. Life is not a mere calendar of honey and moonshine. Very good. But without love, Miss Sowerby, life is just death, and I know, my dear, you would no more care to go on with it, than with a new chapter of—of our dear friend Boreham's new story.

Between ourselves, Philip's humour is not much more lightsome than that of the ingenious contemporary above named; but if it served to amuse Philip himself, why baulk him of a little sport? Well, then: he wrote us a great ream of lumbering pleasantries, dated Paris, Thursday; Geneva, Saturday. Summit of Mont Blanc, Monday; Timbuctoo, Wednesday. Pekin, Friday—with facetious descriptions of those spots and cities. He said that in the last-named place Charlotte's shoes being worn out, those which she purchased were rather tight for her, and the high heels annoyed her. He stated that the beef at Timbuctoo was not cooked enough for Charlotte's taste, and that the Emperor's attentions were becoming rather marked, and so forth; whereas poor little Char's simple postscripts mentioned no travelling at all; but averred that they were staying at Saint Germain, and as happy as the day was long. As happy as the day was long? As it was short, alas! Their little purse was very slenderly furnished; and in a very very brief holiday, poor Philip's few napoleons had almost all rolled away. Luckily, it was payday when the young people came back to London. They were almost reduced to the Little Sister's wedding present: and surely they would rather work than purchase a few hours' more ease with that poor widow's mite.

Who talked and was afraid of poverty? Philip, with his two newspapers, averred that he had enough; more than enough; could save; could put by. It was at this time that Ridley, the Academician, painted that sweet picture, No. 1976—of course you remember it—'Portrait of a Lady.' He became romantically attached to the second-floor lodger; would have no noisy parties in his rooms, or smoking, lest it should annoy her. Would Mrs. Firmin desire to give entertainments of her own? His studio and sitting-room were at her orders. He fetched and carried. He brought presents, and theatre-boxes; and would have cut off his head had she demanded, and laid it at the little bride's feet, so tenderly did he regard her. And she gave him back in return for all this romantic adoration a condescending shake of a soft little hand, and a kind look from a pair of soft eyes, with which the painter was fain to be content. Low of stature, and of misshapen form, J. J. thought himself naturally outcast from marriage and love, and looked in with longing eyes at the paradise which he was forbidden to enter. And Mr. Philip sat within this Palace of Delight; and lolled at his ease, and took his pleasure, and Charlotte ministered to him. And once in a way, my lord sent out a crumb of kindness, or a little cup of comfort, to the outcast at the gate who blessed his benefactress, and my lord his benefactor, and was thankful. Charlotte had not twopence: but she had a little court. It was the fashion for Philip's friends to come and bow before her. Very fine gentlemen who had known him at college, and forgot him, or, sooth to say, thought him rough and overbearing, now suddenly remembered him, and his young wife had quite fashionable assemblies at her five o'clock tea-table. All men liked her, and Miss Sowerby of course says Mrs. Firmin was a good-natured, quite harmless little woman, rather pretty, and—you know, my dear—such as men like. Look you, if I like cold veal, dear Sowerby, it is that my tastes are simple. A fine tough old dry camel, no doubt, is a much nobler, and more sagacious animal—and perhaps you think a double hump is quite a delicacy.

Yes: Mrs. Philip was a success. She had scarce any female friends as yet, being too poor to go into the world: but she had Mrs. Pendennis, and dear little Mrs. Brandon, and Mrs. Mugford, whose celebrated trap repeatedly brought delicacies for the bride from Hampstead, whose chaise was once or twice a week at Philip's door, and who was very much exercised and impressed by the fine company whom she met in Mrs. Firmin's apartments. 'Lord Thingamburys card! what next, Brandon, upon my word? Lady Slowby at home? well, I never, Mrs. B.!' In such artless phrases Mrs. Mugford would express her admiration and astonishment during the early time, and when Charlotte still retained the good lady's favour. That a state of things far less agreeable ensued, I must own. But though there is ever so small a cloud in the sky even now, let us not heed it for a while, and bask and be content and happy in the sunshine. 'Oh, Laura, I tremble when I think how happy I am!' was our little bird's perpetual warble. 'How did I live when I was at home with mamma?' she would say. 'Do you know that Philip never even scolds me? If he were to say a rough word I think I should die; whereas mamma was barking barking from morning till night, and I didn't care a pin.' This is what comes of injudicious scolding, as of any other drug. The wholesome medicine loses its effect. The inured patient calmly takes a dose that would frighten or kill a stranger. Poor Mrs. Baynes's crossed letters came still, and I am not prepared to pledge my word that Charlotte read them all. Mrs. B. offered to come and superintend and take care of dear Philip when an interesting event should take place. But Mrs. Brandon was already engaged for this important occasion, and Charlotte became so alarmed lest her mother should invade her, that Philip wrote curtly, and positively forbade Mrs. Baynes. You remember the picture 'A Cradle,' by J. J.? the two little rosy feet brought I don't know how many hundred guineas apiece to Mr. Ridley. The mother herself did not study babydom more fondly and devotedly than Ridley did in the ways, looks, features, anatomies, attitudes, baby-clothes, etc., of this first-born infant of Charlotte and Philip Firmin. My wife is very angry because I have forgotten whether the first of the young Firmin brood was a boy or a girl, and says I shall forget the names of my own children next. Well? 'At this distance of time, I *think* it was a boy,—for their boy is very tall, you know—a great deal taller—*Not* a boy? Then, between ourselves, I have no doubt it was a—' 'A goose,' says the lady, which is not even reasonable.

This is certain: we all thought the young mother looked very pretty, with her pink cheeks and beaming eyes, as she bent over the little infant. J. J. says he thinks there is something *heavenly* in the looks of young mothers at that time. Nay, he goes so far as to declare that a tigress at the Zoological Gardens looks beautiful and gentle as she bends her black nozzle over her cubs. And if a tigress, why not Mrs. Philip? O ye powers of sentiment, in what a state J. J. was about this young woman! There is a brightness in a young mother's eye: there are pearl and rose tints on her cheek, which are sure to fascinate a painter. This artist used to hang about Mrs. Brandon's rooms, till it was droll to see him. I believe he took off his shoes in his own studio, so as not to disturb by his creaking the lady overhead. He purchased the most preposterous mug, and other presents for the infant. Philip went out to his club or his newspaper as he was ordered to do. But Mr. J. J. could not be got away from Thornhaugh Street, so that little Mrs. Brandon laughed at him—absolutely laughed at him.

During all this while Philip and his wife continued in the very greatest favour with Mr. and Mrs. Mugford, and were invited by that worthy couple to go with their infant to Mugford's villa at Hampstead, where a change of air might do good to dear baby and dear mamma. Philip went to this village retreat. Streets and terraces now cover over the house and grounds which worthy Mugford inhabited, and which people say he used to call his Russian Irby. He had amassed in a small space a heap of country pleasures. He had a little garden; a little paddock; a little greenhouse; a little cucumber-frame; a little stable for his little trap; a little Guernsey cow; a little dairy; a little pigsty; and with this little treasure the good man was not a little content. He loved and praised everything that was his. No man admired his own port more than Mugford, or paid more compliments to his own butter and home-baked bread. He enjoyed his own happiness. He appreciated his own worth. He loved to talk of the days when he was a poor boy on London streets, and now—'now try that glass of port, my boy, and say whether the Lord Mayor has got any better,' he would say, winking at his glass and his company. To be virtuous, to be lucky, and constantly to think and own that you are so—is not this true happiness? To sing hymns in praise of himself is a charming amusement; —at least to the performer; and anybody who dined at Mugford's table was pretty sure to hear some of this music after dinner. I am sorry to say Philip did not care for this trumpet-blowing. He was frightfully bored at Haverstock Hill; and when bored, Mr. Philip is not altogether an agreeable companion. He will yawn in a man's face. He will contradict you freely. He will say the mutton is tough, or the wine not fit to drink; that such and such an orator is overrated, and such and such a politician is a fool. Mugford and his guest had battles after dinner, had actually high words. 'What-hever is it, Mugford? and what were you quarrelling about in the dining-room?' asks Mrs. Mugford. 'Quarrelling? It's only the sub-editor snoring,' said the gentleman, with a flushed face. 'My wine ain't good enough for him; and now my gentleman must put his boots upon a chair and go to sleep under my nose. He *is* a cool hand, and no mistake, Mrs. M.' At this juncture poor little Char would gently glide down from a visit to her baby: and would play something on the piano, and soothe the rising anger; and then Philip would come in from a little walk in the shrubberies, where he had been blowing a little cloud. Ah! there was a little cloud rising indeed:—quite a little one—nay, not so little. When you consider that Philip's bread depended on the goodwill of these people, you will allow that his friends might be anxious regarding the future. A word from Mugford, and Philip and Charlotte and the child were adrift on the world. And these points Mr. Firmin would freely admit, while he stood discoursing of his own affairs (as he loved to do), his hands in his pockets, and his back warming at our fire.

'My dear fellow,' says the candid bridegroom, 'these things are constantly in my head. I used to talk about 'em to Char, but I don't now. They disturb her, the poor thing; and she clutches hold of the baby; and—and it tears my heart out to think that any grief should come to her. I try and do my best, my good people—but when I'm bored I can't help showing I'm bored, don't you see? I can't be a hypocrite. No, not for two hundred a year, or for twenty thousand. You can't make a silk purse out of that sow's-ear of a Mugford. A very good man. I don't say no. A good father, a good husband, a generous host, and a most tremendous bore, and cad. Be agreeable to him? How can I be agreeable when I am being killed? He has a story about Leigh Hunt being put into Newgate, where Mugford, bringing him proofs, saw Lord Byron. I cannot keep awake during that story any longer; or, if awake, I grind my teeth, and swear inwardly, so that I know I'm dreadful to hear and see. Well, Mugford has yellow satin sofas in the droaring-room"—'

'Oh, Philip!' says a lady; and two or three circumjacent children set up an insane giggle, which is speedily and sternly silenced.

'I tell you she calls it "droaring-room." You know she does, as well as I do. She is a good woman: a kind woman: a hot-tempered woman. I hear her scolding the servants in the kitchen with immense vehemence, and at prodigious length. But how can Char frankly be the friend of a woman who calls a drawing-room a droaring-room? With our dear little friend in Thornhaugh Street, it is different. She makes no pretence even at equality. Here is a patron and patroness, don't you see?

When Mugford walks me round his paddock and gardens, and says, "Look year, Firmin"; or scratches one of his pigs on the back, and says, "We'll 'ave a cut of this fellow on Saturday'"—(explosive attempts at insubordination and derision on the part of the children again are severely checked by the parental authorities)—"we'll 'ave a cut of this fellow on Saturday," I feel inclined to throw him or myself into the trough over the palings. Do you know that that man put that hand into his pocket and offered me some filberts?'

Here I own the lady to whom Philip was addressing himself turned pale and shuddered.

'I can no more be that man's friend que celui du domestique qui vient d'apporter le what-d' you-call-'em? le coal-scuttle'—(John entered the room with that useful article during Philip's oration—and we allowed the elder children to laugh this time, for the fact is, none of us knew the French for coal-scuttle, and I will wager there is no such word in Chambaud). 'This holding back is not arrogance,' Philip went on. 'This reticence is not want of humility. To serve that man honestly is one thing; to make friends with him, to laugh at his dull jokes, is to make friends with the mammon of unrighteousness, is subserviency and hypocrisy on my part. I ought to say to him, Mr. Mugford, I will give you my work for your wage; I will compile your paper, I will produce an agreeable miscellany containing proper proportions of news, politics, and scandal, put titles to your paragraphs, see the *Pall Mall Gazette* ship-shape through the press, and go home to my wife and dinner. You are my employer, but you are not my friend, and-bless my soul! there is five o'clock striking!' (The time-piece in our drawing-room gave that announcement as he was speaking.) 'We have what Mugford calls a white-choker dinner to-day, in honour of the pig!' And with this Philip plunges out of the house, and I hope reached Hampstead in time for the entertainment.

Philip's friends in Westminster felt no little doubt about his prospects, and the Little Sister shared their alarm. 'They are not fit to be with those folks,' Mrs. Brandon said, 'though as for Mrs. Philip, dear thing, I am sure nobody can ever quarrel with *her*. With me it's different. I never had no education, you know—no more than the Mugfords, but I don't like to see my Philip sittin' down as if he was the guest and equal of that fellar.' Nor indeed did it ever enter 'that fellar's' head that Mr. Frederick Mugford could be Mr. Philip Firmin's equal. With our knowledge of the two men, then, we all dismally looked forward to a rupture between Firmin and his patron.

As for the New York journal, we were more easy in respect to Philip's success in that quarter. Several of his friends made a vow to help him. We clubbed club-stories; we begged from our polite friends anecdotes (that would bear sea-transport) of the fashionable world. We happened to overhear the most remarkable conversations between the most influential public characters who had no secrets from us. We had astonishing intelligence at most European courts; exclusive reports of the Emperor of Russia's last joke—his last? his next, very likely. We knew the most secret designs of the Austrian Privy Council; the views which the Pope had in his eye; who was the latest favourite of the Grand Turk, and so on. The Upper Ten Thousand at New York were supplied with a quantity of information which I trust profited them. It was 'Palmerston remarked yesterday at dinner,' or, 'The good old Duke said last night at Apsley House to the French Ambassador,' and the rest. The letters were signed 'Philalethes'; and, as nobody was wounded by the shafts of our long-bow, I trust Mr. Philip and his friends may be pardoned for twanging it. By information procured from learned female personages, we even managed to give accounts, more or less correct, of the latest ladies' fashions. We were members of all the clubs; we were present at the routs and assemblies of the political leaders of both sides. We had little doubt that Philalethes would be successful at New York, and looked forward to an increased payment for his labours. At the end of the first year of Philip Firmin's married life, we made a calculation by which it was clear that he had actually saved money. His expenses, to be sure, were increased. There was a baby in the nursery: but there was a little bag of sovereigns in the cupboard, and the thrifty young fellow hoped to add still more to his store.

We were relieved at finding that Firmin and his wife were not invited to repeat their visit to their employer's house at Hampstead. An occasional invitation to dinner was still sent to the young people; but Mugford, a haughty man in his way, with a proper spirit of his own, had the good sense to see that much intimacy could not arise between him and his sub-editor, and magnanimously declined to be angry at the young fellow's easy superciliousness. I think that indefatigable Little Sister was the peacemaker between the houses of Mugford and Firmin junior, and that she kept both Philip and his master on their good behaviour. At all events, and when a quarrel did arise between them, I grieve to have to own it was poor Philip who was in the wrong.

You know in the old old days the young king and queen never gave any christening entertainment without neglecting to invite some old fairy, who was furious at the omission. I am sorry to say Charlotte's mother was so angry at not being appointed godmother to the new baby, that she omitted to make her little quarterly payment of £12, 10s.; and has altogether discontinued that payment from that remote period up to the present time; so that Philip says his wife has brought him a fortune of £35, paid in three instalments. There was the first quarter paid when the old lady 'would not be beholden to a man like him.' Then there came a second quarter—and then—but I dare say I shall be able to tell when and how Philip's mamma-in-law paid the rest of her poor little daughter's fortune.

Well, Regent's Park is a fine healthy place for infantine diversion, and I don't think Philip at all demeaned himself in walking there with his wife, her little maid, and his baby on his arm. 'He is as rude as a bear, and his manners are dreadful; but he has a good heart, that I will say for him,' Mugford said to me. In his drive from London to Hampstead Mugford once or twice met the little family group, of which his sub-editor formed the principal figure; and for the sake of Philip's young wife and child Mr. M. pardoned the young man's vulgarity, and treated him with long-suffering.

Poor as he was, this was his happiest time, my friend is disposed to think. A young child, a young wife, whose whole life was a tender caress of love for child and husband, a young husband watching both:—I recall the group, as we used often to see it in those days, and see a something sacred in the homely figures. On the wife's bright face what a radiant happiness there is, and what a rapturous smile! Over the sleeping infant and the happy mother the father looks with pride and thanks in his eyes. Happiness and gratitude fill his simple heart, and prayer involuntary to the Giver of good, that he may have strength to do his duty as father, husband; that he may be enabled to keep want and care from those dear innocent beings; that he may defend them, befriend them, leave them a good name. I am bound to say that Philip became thrifty and saving for the sake of Char and the child; that he came home early of nights; that he thought his child a wonder; that he never tired of speaking about that infant in our house, about its fatness, its strength, its weight, its wonderful early talents and humour. He felt himself a man now for the first time, he said. Life had been play and folly until now. And now especially he regretted that he had been idle, and had neglected his opportunities as a lad. Had he studied for the bar, he might have made that profession now profit able, and a source of honour and competence to his family. Our friend estimated his own powers very humbly; I am sure he was not the less amiable on account of that humility. O fortunate he, of whom Love is the teacher, the guide and master, the reformer and chastener! Where was our friend's former arrogance, self-confidence, and boisterous profusion'? He was at the feet of his wife and child. He was quite humbled about himself; or gratified himself in fondling and caressing these. They taught him, he said; and as he thought of them, his heart turned in awful thanks to the gracious Heaven which had given them to him. As the tiny infant hand closes round his fingers, I can see the father bending over mother and child, and interpret those maybe unspoken blessings which he asks and bestows. Happy wife, happy husband! However poor his little home may be, it holds treasures and wealth inestimable; whatever storms may threaten without, the home fireside is brightened with the welcome of the dearest eyes.

CHAPTER XXXIV. IN WHICH I OWN THAT PHILIP TELLS AN UNTRUTH

CHARLOTTE (and the usual little procession of nurse, baby, etc.) once made their appearance at our house in Queen Square, where they were ever welcomed by the lady of the mansion. The young woman was in a great state of elation, and when we came to hear the cause of her delight, her friends too opened the eyes of wonder. She actually announced that Dr. Firmin had sent over a bill of forty pounds (I may be incorrect as to the sum) from New York. It had arrived that morning, and she had seen the bill, and Philip had told her that his father had sent it; and was it not a comfort to think that poor Dr. Firmin was endeavouring to repair some of the evil which he had done; and that he was repenting, and, perhaps, was going to become quite honest and good? This was indeed an astounding piece of intelligence; and the two women felt joy at the thought of that sinner repenting, and some one else was accused of cynicism, scepticism, and so forth, for doubting the correctness of the information. 'You believe in no one, sir. You are always incredulous about good,' etc. etc. etc., was the accusation brought against the reader's very humble servant. Well, about the contrition of this sinner I confess I still continued to have doubts; and thought a present of forty pounds to a son, to whom he owed thousands, was no great proof of the Doctor's amendment.

And oh! how vexed some people were when the real story came out at last! Not for the money's sake—not because they were wrong in argument, and I turned out to be right. Oh no! But because it was proved that this unhappy Doctor had no present intention of repenting at all. This brand would not come out of the burning, whatever we might hope, and the Doctor's supporters were obliged to admit as much when they came to know the real story. 'Oh, Philip,' cries Mrs. Laura, when next she saw Mr. Firmin. 'How pleased I was to hear of that letter!'

'What letter?' asks the gentleman.

'That letter from your father at New York,' says the lady.

'Oh,' says the gentleman addressed, with a red face.

'What then? Is it not—is it not all true?' we ask.

'Poor Charlotte does not understand about business,' says Philip; 'I did not read the letter to her. Here it is.' And he hands over the *document to* me, and I hare the liberty to publish it.

New York —

'AND so, my dear Philip, I may congratulate myself on having achieved *ancestral* honour, and may add grandfather to my titles? How quickly this one has come! I feel myself a young man still, *in spite of the blows of misfortune*—at least I know I was a young man but yesterday, when I may say with our dear old poet, "Non sine gloriâ militavi." Suppose I too were to tire of solitary widowhood and re-enter the married state? There are one or two ladies here who would still condescend to look not unfavourably *on the retired English gentleman*. Without vanity I may say it, a man of birth and position in England acquires a polish and refinement of manner which dollars cannot purchase, and many a *Wall Street millionary* might envy!

'Your wife has been pronounced to be an angel by a *little correspondent* of mine, who gives me much fuller intelligence of my family than my son condescends to furnish. Mrs. Philip I hear is gentle; Mrs. Brandon says she is beautiful,—she is all good-humoured. I hope you have taught her to think not *very* badly of her husband's fatter? I was the dupe of villains who lured me into their schemes; who robbed me of a life's earnings; who induced me by their *false representations* to have such confidence in them, that I embarked all my own property, and yours, my poor boy, alas! in their undertakings. Your Charlotte will take the liberal, the wise, the *just* view of the case, and pity rather than blame my misfortune. Such is the view, I am happy to say, generally adopted in this city: where there are men of the world who know the vicissitudes of a mercantile career, and can make allowances for misfortune. What made Borne at first great and prosperous? Were its first colonists all wealthy patricians? Nothing can be more satisfactory than the disregard shown here *to mere pecuniary difficulty*. At the same time to be a gentleman is to possess no trifling privilege in this society, where the advantages of birth, respected name, and early education *always* tell in the possessor's favour. Many persons whom I visit here have certainly not these advantages—and in the highest society of the city I could point out individuals who have had pecuniary misfortunes like myself, who have gallantly renewed the combat after their fall, and are *now fully* restored to competence, to wealth, and the respect of the world! I was in a house in Fifth Avenue last night. Is Washington White shunned by his fellow-men because he has been a bankrupt three times? Anything more elegant or profuse than his entertainment I have not witnessed on this continent. His lady had diamonds which a duchess might envy. The most costly wines, the most magnificent supper, and myriads of canvas-backed ducks covered his board. Dear Charlotte, my friend Captain Colpoys brings you over three brace of these from your father-in-law, who hopes they will furnish your little inner-table. We eat currant jelly with them here, but I like an old English lemon and *cayenne sauce better.*

'By the way, dear Philip, I trust you will not be inconvenienced by a little financial operation, which necessity (aha!) has compelled me to perform. Knowing that your quarter with the *Upper Ten, Thousand Gazette* was now due, I have made so bold as to request Colonel to pay it over to me. Promises to pay must be met here as with us—an obdurate holder of an unlucky acceptance of mine (I am happy to say there are very few such) would admit of *no delay,* and I have been compelled to appropriate my poor Philip's earnings. I have only put you off for ninety days: with your credit and wealthy friends yon can *easily negotiate the bill enclosed,* and I *promise you* than when presented it shall be honoured by my Philip's ever affectionate father,   G. B F.

'By the way, your Philalethes' letters are not *quite spicy* enough, my worthy friend the Colonel says. They are *elegant and gay,* but the public here desires to have more *personal news; a little scandal about Queen Elizabeth,* you understand? Can't you attack somebody? Look at the letters and articles published by my respected friend of the *New York Emerald*! The readers here like a *high-spiced article*: and I recommend P. F. to put a little more pepper in his dishes. What a comfort to me it is to think, that I have procured this place for you, and have been enabled to help my son and his young family!   G. B. F.'

Enclosed in this letter was a slip of paper which poor Philip supposed to be a cheque when he first beheld it, but which turned out to be his papa's promissory note, payable at New York four months after date. And this document was to represent the money which the elder Firmin had received in his son's name! Philip's eyes met his friend's when they talked about this matter. Firmin looked almost as much ashamed as if he himself had done the wrong.

'Does the loss of this money annoy you?' asked Philip's friend.

'The manner of the loss does,' said poor Philip. 'I don't care about the money. But he should not have taken this. He should not have taken this. Think of poor Charlotte and the child being in want possibly! Oh, friend, it's hard to bear, isn't it? I'm an honest fellow, ain't I? I think I am. I pray Heaven I am. In any extremity of poverty could I have done this? Well. It was my father who introduced me to these people. I suppose he thinks he has a right to my earnings: and if he is in want, you know, so he has.'

'Had you not better write to the New York publishers and beg them henceforth to remit to you directly?' asks Philip's friend.

'That would be to tell them that he has disposed of the money,' groans Philip. 'I can't tell them that my father is a—'

'No; but you can thank them for having handed over such a sum on your account to the Doctor: and warn them that you will draw on them from this country henceforth. They won't in this case pay the next quarter to the Doctor.'

'Suppose he is in want, ought I not to supply him?' Firmin said. 'As long as there are four crusts in the house, the Doctor ought to have one. Ought I to be angry with him for helping himself, old boy?' and he drinks a glass of wine, poor fellow, with a rueful smile. By the way, it is my duty to mention here, that the elder Firmin was in the habit of giving very elegant little dinner parties at New York, where little dinner parties are much more costly than in Europe—'in order,' he said, 'to establish and keep up his connection as a physician.' As a *bon-vivant,* I am informed, the Doctor began to be celebrated in his new dwelling-place, where his anecdotes of the British aristocracy were received with pleasure in certain circles.

But it would be as well henceforth that Philip should deal directly with his American correspondents, and not employ the services of so very expensive a broker. To this suggestion he could not but agree. Meanwhile,—and let this be a warning to men never to deceive their wives in any the slightest circumstances; to tell them *everything* they wish to know, to keep nothing hidden from those dear and excellent beings—you must know, ladies, that when Philip's famous ship of dollars arrived from America, Firmin had promised his wife that baby should have a dear delightful white cloak trimmed with the most lovely tape, on which poor Charlotte had often cast a longing eye as she passed by the milliner and curiosity shops in Hanway Yard, which, I own, she loved to frequent. Well; when Philip told her that his father had sent home forty pounds, or what not, thereby deceiving his fond wife, the little lady went away straight to her darling shop in the Yard— (Hanway Yard has become a street now, but ah! it is always delightful)—Charlotte, I say, went off, ran off to Hanway Yard, pavid with fear lest the darling cloak should be gone, found it—oh, joy!—still in Miss Isaacson's window; put it on baby straightway then and there; kissed the dear infant, and was delighted with the effect of the garment, which all the young ladies at Miss Isaacson's pronounced to be perfect; and took the cloak away on baby's shoulders, promising to send the money, five pounds, if you please, next day. And in this cloak baby and Charlotte went to meet papa when he came home; and I don't know which of them, mamma or baby, was the most pleased and absurd and happy baby of the two. On his way home from his newspaper, Mr. Philip had orders to pursue a certain line of streets, and when his accustomed hour for returning from his business drew nigh, Mrs. Char went down Thornhaugh Street, down Charlotte Street, down Rathbone Place, with Betsy the nursekin and baby in the new cloak. Behold, he comes at last:— papa—striding down the street. He sees the figures: he sees the child, which laughs, and holds out its little pink hands, and crows a recognition. And 'Look— look, papa,' cries the happy mother. (Away! I cannot keep up the mystery about the baby any longer, and though I had forgotten for a moment the child's sex, remembered it the instant after, and that it was a girl, to be sure, and that its name was Laura Caroline.) 'Look, look, papa!' cries the happy mother. 'She has got another little tooth since the morning, such a beautiful little tooth—and look here, sir, don't you observe anything?'

'Any what?' asks Philip.

'La! sir,' says Betsy, giving Laura Caroline a great toss, so that her white cloak floats in the air.

'Isn't it a dear cloak?' cries mamma; 'and doesn't baby look like an angel in it?' I bought it at Miss Isaacson's to-day, as you got your money from New York; and oh, my dear, it only cost five guineas.'

'Well, it's a week's work,' sighs poor Philip; 'and I think I need not grudge that to give Charlotte pleasure.' And he feels his empty pockets rather ruefully.

'God bless you, Philip,' says my wife, with her eyes full. 'They came here this morning, Charlotte and the nurse and the baby in the new—the new—' Here the lady seized hold of Philip's hand, and fairly broke out into tears. Had she embraced Mr. Firmin before her husband's own eyes, I should not have been surprised. Indeed she confessed that she was on the point of giving way to this most sentimental outbreak.

And now, my brethren, see how one crime is the parent of many, and one act of duplicity leads to a whole career of deceit. In the first place, you see, Philip had deceived his wife—with a pious desire, it is true, of screening his father's little peculiarities—but, *ruat cœlum,* we must tell no lies. No: and from this day forth I order John never to say Not at home to the greatest bore, dun, dawdle of my acquaintance. If Philip's father had not deceived him, Philip would not have deceived his wife; if he had not deceived his wife, she would not have given five guineas for that cloak for the baby. If she had not given five guineas for the cloak, my wife would never have entered into a secret correspondence with Mr. Firmin, which might, but for my own sweetness of temper, have bred jealousy, mistrust, and the most awful quarrels—nay duels—between the heads of the two families. Fancy Philip's body lying stark upon Hampstead Heath with a bullet through it, dispatched by the hand of his friend! Fancy a cab driving up to my own house, and from it—under the eyes of the children at the parlour-windows—their father's bleeding corpse ejected!—Enough of this dreadful pleasantry! Two days after the affair of the cloak, I found a letter in Philip's handwriting addressed to my wife, and thinking that the note had reference to a matter of dinner then pending between our families, I broke open the envelope and read as follows:—

'Thornhaugh Street: *Thursday.*

'MY DEAR KIND GODMAMMA,—As soon as ever I can write and speak, I will thank you for being so kind to me. My mamma says she is very jealous, and as she bought my cloak she can't think of allowing you to pay for it. But she desires me never to forget your kindness to us, and though I don't know anything about it now she promises to tell me when I am old enough. Meanwhile I am your grateful and affectionate little goddaughter,   L.C. F.'

Philip was persuaded by his friends at home to send out the request to his New York employers to pay his salary henceforth to himself; and I remember a dignified letter came from his parent, in which the matter was spoken of in sorrow rather than in anger; in which the Doctor pointed out that this precautionary measure seemed to imply a doubt on Philip's side of his father's honour; and surely,

surely, he was unhappy enough and unfortunate enough already without meriting this mistrust from his son. The duty of a son to honour his father and mother was feelingly pointed out, and the Doctor meekly trusted that Philip's children would give *him* more confidence than he seemed to be inclined to award to his unfortunate father. Never mind. He should bear no malice. If Fortune ever smiled on him again, and something told him she would, he would show Philip that he could forgive; although he might not perhaps be able to forget that in his exile, his solitude, his declining years, his misfortune, his own child had mistrusted him. This he said was the most cruel blow of all for his susceptible heart to bear.

This letter of paternal remonstrance was enclosed in one from the Doctor to his old friend the Little Sister, in which he vaunted a discovery which he and some other scientific gentlemen were engaged in perfecting—of a medicine which was to be extraordinarily efficacious in cases in which Mrs. Brandon herself was often specially and professionally engaged, and he felt sure that the sale of this medicine would go far to retrieve his shattered fortune. He pointed out the complaints in which this medicine was most efficacious. He would send some of it, and details regarding its use, to Mrs. Brandon, who might try its efficacy upon her patients. He was advancing slowly, but steadily, in his medical profession, he said; though, of course, he had to suffer from the jealousy of his professional brethren. Never mind. Better times, he was sure, were in store for all; when his son should see that a wretched matter of forty pounds more should not deter him from paying all just claims upon him. Amen! We all heartily wished for the day when Philip's father should be able to settle his little accounts. Meanwhile, the proprietors of the *Gazette of the Upper Ten Thousand* were instructed to write directly to their London correspondent.

Although Mr. Firmin prided himself, as we have seen, upon his taste and dexterity as sub-editor of the *Pall Mall Gazette,* I must own that he was a very insubordinate officer, with whom his superiors often had cause to be angry. Certain people were praised in the *Gazette*—certain others were attacked. Very dull books were admired, and very lively works attacked. Some men were praised for everything they did; some others were satirised, no matter what their works were. 'I find,' poor Philip used to say with a groan, 'that in matters of criticism especially there are so often private reasons for the praise and the blame administered, that I am glad, for my part, my only duty is to see the paper through the press. For instance, there is Harrocks, the tragedian, of Drury Lane: every piece in which he appears is a masterpiece, and his performance the greatest triumph ever witnessed. Very good. Harrocks and my excellent employer are good friends, and dine with each other; and it is natural that Mugford should like to have his friend praised, and to help him in every way. But Balderson, of Covent Garden, is also a very fine actor. Why can't our critic see his merit as well as Harrocks'? Poor Balderson is never allowed any merit at all. He is passed over with a sneer, or a curt word of cold commendation, while columns of flattery are not enough for his rival.'

'Why, Mr. F., what a flat you must be, askin' your pardon,' remarked Mugford, in reply to his sub-editor's simple remonstrance. 'How can we praise Balderson, when Harrocks is our friend? Me and Harrocks are thick. Our wives are close friends. If I was to let Balderson be praised, I should drive Harrocks mad. I *can't* praise Balderson, don't you see, out of justice to Harrocks!'

Then there was a certain author whom Bickerton was for ever attacking. They had had a private quarrel, and Bickerton revenged himself in this way. In reply to Philip's outcries and remonstrances, Mr. Mugford only laughed: 'The two men are enemies, and Bickerton hits him whenever he can. Why, that's only human nature, Mr. F.,' says Philip's employer.

'Great heavens!' bawls out Firmin, ' do you mean to say that the man is base enough to strike at his private enemies through the press?'

'Private enemies! private gammon, Mr. Firmin!' cries Philip's employer. 'If I have enemies—and I have, there's no doubt about that—I serve them out whenever and wherever I can. And let me tell you I don't half relish having my conduct called base. It's only natural; and it's right. Perhaps you would like to praise your enemies, and abuse your friends? If that's your line, let me tell you you won't do in the noospaper business, and had better take to some other trade.' And the employer parted from his subordinate in some heat.

Mugford, indeed, feelingly spoke to me about this insubordination of Philip. 'What does the fellow mean by quarrelling with his bread and butter?' Mr. Mugford asked. 'Speak to him and show him what's what, Mr. P., or we shall come to a quarrel, mind you—and I don't want that, for the sake of his little wife, poor little delicate thing. Whatever is to happen to them if we don't stand by them?'

What was to happen to them, indeed? Any one who knew Philip's temper as we did, was aware how little advice or remonstrance was likely to affect that gentleman. 'Good heavens!' he said to me, when I endeavoured to make him adopt a conciliatory tone towards his employer, 'do you want to make me Mugford's galley-slave? I shall have him standing over me and swearing at me as he does at the printers. He looks into my room at times when he is in a passion, and glares at me as if he would like to seize me by the throat; and after a word or two he goes off, and I hear him curse the boys in the passage. One day it will be on me that he will turn, I feel sure of that. I tell you the slavery is beginning to be awful I wake of a night and groan and chafe, and poor Char, too, wakes and asks, "What is it, Philip?" I say it is rheumatism. Rheumatism!' Of course to Philip's malady his friends tried to apply the commonplace anodynes and consolations. He must be gentle in his bearing. He must remember that his employer had not been bred a gentleman, and that, though rough and coarse in language, Mugford had a kind heart. 'There is no need to tell me he is not a gentleman, I know that,' says poor Phil. 'He *is* kind to Char and the child, that is the truth, and so is his wife. I am a slave for all that. He is my driver. He feeds me. He hasn't beat me yet. When I was away at Paris I did not feel the chain so much. But it is scarcely tolerable now, when I have to see my gaoler four or five times a week. My poor little Char, why did I drag you into this slavery?'

'Because you wanted a consoler, I suppose,' remarks one of Philip's comforters. 'And do you suppose Charlotte would be happier if she were away from you? Though you live up two pair of stairs, is any home happier than yours, Philip? You often own as much, when you are in happier moods. Who has not his work to do, and his burden to bear? You say sometimes that you are imperious and hot-tempered. Perhaps your slavery, as you call it, may be good for you.'

'I have doomed myself and her to it,' says Philip, hanging down his head.

'Does she ever repine?' asks his adviser. 'Does she not think herself the happiest little wife in the world? See here, Philip, here is a note from her yesterday in which she says as much. Do you want to know what the note is about, sir?' says the lady, with a smile. 'Well, then, she wanted a receipt for that dish which you liked so much on Friday, and she and Mrs. Brandon will make it for you.'

'And if it consisted of minced Charlotte,' says Philip's other friend, 'you know she would cheerfully chop herself up, and have herself served with a little cream-sauce and sippets of toast for your honour's dinner.'

This was undoubtedly true. Did not Job's friends make many true remarks when they visited him in his affliction? Patient as he was the patriarch groaned and lamented, and why should not poor Philip be allowed to grumble, who was not a model of patience at all? He was not broke in as yet. The mill-horse was restive and kicked at his work. He would chafe not seldom at the daily drudgery, and have his fits of revolt and despondency. Well? Have others not had to toil, to bow the proud head, and carry the daily burden? Don't you see Pegasus, who was going to win the plate, a weary, broken-knee'd, broken-down old cab-hack shivering in the rank; or a sleek gelding, mayhap, pacing under a corpulent master in Rotten Row? Philip's crust began to be scanty, and was dipped in bitter waters. I am not going to make a long story of this part of his career, or parade my friend as too hungry and poor. He is safe now, and out of all peril, Heaven be thanked I but he had to pass through hard times, and to look out very wistfully lest the wolf should enter at the door. He never laid claim to be a man of genius, nor was he a successful quack who could pass as a man of genius. When there were French prisoners in England, we know how stout old officers who had plied their sabres against Mamelouks, or Russians, or Germans, were fain to carve little gimcracks in bone with their penknives, or make baskets and boxes of chipped straw, and piteously sell them to casual visitors to their prison. Philip was poverty's prisoner. He had to make such shifts, and do such work, as he could find in his captivity. I do not think men who have undergone the struggle and served the dire task-master, like to look back and recall the grim apprenticeship. When Philip says now, 'What fools we were to marry, Char!' she looks up radiantly, with love and happiness in her eyes—looks up to Heaven, and is thankful; but grief and sadness come over her husband's face at the thought of those days of pain and gloom. She may soothe him, and he may be thankful too; but the wounds are still there which were dealt to him in the cruel battle with fortune. Men are ridden down in it. Men are poltroons and run. Men maraud, break ranks, are guilty of meanness, cowardice, shabby plunder. Men are raised to rank and honour, or drop and perish unnoticed on the field. Happy he who comes from it with his honour pure! Philip did not win crosses and epaulets. He is like you and me, my dear sir, not an heroic genius at all. And it is to be hoped that all three have behaved with an average pluck, and have been guilty of no meanness, or treachery, or desertion. Did you behave otherwise, what would wife and children say? As for Mrs. Philip, I tell you she thinks to this day that there is no man like her husband, and is ready to fall down and worship the boots in which he walks.

How do men live? How is rent paid? How does the dinner come day after day? As a rule there *is* dinner. You might live longer with less of it, but you can't go without it and live long. How did my neighbour 23 earn his carriage, and how did 24 pay for his house? As I am writing this sentence Mr. Cox, who collects the taxes in this quarter, walks in. How do you do, Mr. Cox? We are not in the least afraid of meeting one another. Time was—two, three years of time— when poor Philip was troubled at the sight of Cox; and this troublous time his biographer intends to pass over in a very few pages.

At the end of six months the Upper Ten Thousand of New York heard with modified wonder that the editor of that fashionable journal had made a retreat from the city, carrying with him the scanty contents of the till; so the contributions of Philalethes never brought our poor friend any dollars at all. But though one fish is caught and eaten, are

there not plenty more left in the sea? At this very time, when I was in a natural state of despondency about poor Philip's affairs, it struck Tregarvan, the wealthy Cornish Member of Parliament, that the Government and the House of Commons slighted his speeches and his views on foreign politics; that the wife of the Foreign Secretary had been very inattentive to Lady Tregarvan; that the designs of a certain Great Power were most menacing and dangerous, and ought to be exposed and counteracted; and that the peerage which he had long desired ought to be bestowed on him. Sir John Tregarvan applied to certain literary and political gentlemen with whom he was acquainted. He would bring out the *European Review.* He would expose the designs of that Great Power which was menacing Europe. He would show up in his proper colours a Minister who was careless of the country's honour, and forgetful of his own: a Minister whose arrogance ought no longer to be tolerated by the country gentlemen of England. Sir John, a little man in brass buttons, and a tall head, who loves to hear his own voice, came and made a speech on the above topics to the writer of the present biography; that writer's lady was in his study as Sir John expounded his views at some length. She listened to him with the greatest attention and respect. She was shocked to hear of the ingratitude of Government; astounded and terrified by his exposition of the designs of—of that Great Power whose intrigues were so menacing to European tranquillity. She was most deeply interested in the idea of establishing the *Review.* He would, of course, be himself the editor; and—and—(here the woman looked across the table at her husband with a strange triumph in her eyes)—she knew, they both knew, the very man *of all the world* who was most suited to act as sub-editor under Sir John—a gentleman, one of the truest that ever lived—a University man; a man remarkably versed in the European languages—that is, in French most certainly. And now the reader, I dare say, can guess who this individual was. 'I knew it at once,' says the lady, after Sir John had taken his leave. 'I told you that those dear children would not be forsaken.' And I would no more try and persuade her that the *European Review* was not ordained of all time to afford maintenance to Philip, than I would induce her to turn Mormon, and accept all the consequences to which ladies must submit when they make profession of that creed.

'You see, my love,' I say to the partner of my existence, 'what other things must have been ordained of all time as well as Philip's appointment to be sub-editor of the *European Review.* It must have been decreed *ab initio* that Lady Plinlimmon should give evening parties, in order that she might offend Lady Tregarvan by not asking her to those parties. It must have been ordained by fate that Lady Tregarvan should be of a jealous disposition, so that she might hate Lady Plinlimmon, and was to work upon her husband, and inspire him with anger and revolt against his chief. It must have been ruled by destiny that Tregarvan should be rather a weak and wordy personage, fancying that he had a talent for literary composition. Else he would not have thought of setting up the *Review.* Else he would never have been angry with Lord Plinlimmon for not inviting him to tea. Else he would not have engaged Philip as sub-editor. So, you see, in order to bring about this event, and put a couple of hundred a year into Philip Firmin's pocket, the Tregarvans have to be born from the earliest times; the Plinlimmons have to spring up in the remotest ages, and come down to the present day: Dr. Firmin has to be a rogue, and undergo his destiny of cheating his son of money:—all mankind up to the origin of our race are involved in your proposition; and we actually arrive at Adam and Eve, who are but fulfilling their destiny, which was to be the ancestors of Philip Firmin.'

'Even in our first parents there was doubt and scepticism and misgiving,' says the lady, with strong emphasis on the words. 'If you mean to say that there is no such thing as a Superior Power watching over us, and ordaining things for our good, you are an atheist—and such a thing as an atheist does not exist in the world, and I would not believe you if you said you were one twenty times over.'

I mention these points by the way, and as samples of ladylike logic. I acknowledge that Philip himself, as he looks back at his past career, is very much moved. 'I do not deny,' he says gravely, 'that these things happened in the natural order. I say I am grateful for what happened; and look back at the past not without awe. In great grief and danger maybe, I have had timely rescue. Under great suffering I have met with supreme consolation. When the trial has seemed almost too hard for me it has ended, and our darkness has been lightened. *Ut vivo et valeo—si valeo,* I know by Whose permission this is,—and would you forbid me to be thankful? to be thankful for my life; to be thankful for my children; to be thankful for the daily bread which has been granted to me, and the temptation from which I have been rescued? As I think of the past and its bitter trials, I bow my head in thanks and awe. I wanted succour, and I found it. I fell on evil times, and good friends pitied and helped me —good friends like yourself, your dear wife, many another I could name. In what moments of depression, old friend, have you not seen me and cheered me? Do you know in the moments of our grief the inexpressible value of your sympathy? Your good Samaritan takes out only twopence maybe for the wayfarer whom he has rescued, but the little timely supply saves a life. You remember dear old Ned St. George—dead in the West Indies years ago? Before he got his place Ned was hanging on in London, so utterly poor and ruined, that he had not often a shilling to buy a dinner. He used often to come to us, and my wife and our children loved him; and I used to leave a heap of shillings on my study-table, so that he might take two or three as he wanted them. Of course you remember him. You were at the dinner which we gave him on his getting his place. I forget the cost of that dinner; but I remember my share amounted to the exact number of shillings which poor Ned had taken off my table. He gave me the money then and there at the tavern at Blackwall. He said it seemed providential. But for those shillings, and the constant welcome at our poor little table, he said he thought he should have made away with his life. I am not bragging of the twopence which I gave, but thanking God for sending me there to give it. *Benedicto benedictus.* I wonder sometimes am I the I of twenty years ago? before our heads were bald, friend, and when the little ones reached up to our knees? Before dinner you saw me in the library reading in that old *European Review* which your friend Tregarvan established. I came upon an article of my own, and a very dull one, on a subject which I knew nothing about. "Persian politics, and the intrigues at the Court of Teheran." It was done to order. Tregarvan had some special interest about Persia, or wanted to vex Sir Thomas Nobbles, who was Minister there. I breakfasted with Tregarvan in the Albany, the facts (we will call them facts) and papers were supplied to me, and I went home to point out the delinquencies of Sir Thomas, and the atrocious intrigues of the Russian Court. Well, sir, Nobbles, Tregarvan, Teheran, all disappeared as I looked at the text in the old volume of the *Review.* I saw a deal table in a little room, and a reading-lamp, and a young fellow writing at it, with a sad heart, and a dreadful apprehension torturing him. One of our children was ill in the adjoining room, and I have before me the figure of my wife coming in from time to time to my room and saying, "She is asleep now, and the fever is much lower."'

Here our conversation was interrupted by the entrance of a tall young lady, who says, 'Papa, the coffee is quite cold: and the carriage will be here very soon, and both mamma and my godmother say they are growing very angry. Do you know you have been talking here for two hours?'

Had two hours actually slipped away as we sat prattling about old times? As I narrate them, I prefer to give Mr. Firmin's account of his adventures in his own words, where I can recall or imitate them. Both of us are graver and more reverend seigniors than we were at the time of which I am writing. Has not Firmin's girl grown up to be taller than her godmother? Veterans both, we love to prattle about the merry days when we were young—(the merry days? no, the past is never merry)—about the days when we were young; and do we grow young in talking of them, or only indulge in a senile cheerfulness and prolixity?

Tregarvan sleeps with his Cornish fathers: Europe for many years has gone on without her *Review:* but it is a certainty that the establishment of that occult organ of opinion tended very much to benefit Philip Firmin, and helped for a while to supply him and several innocent people dependent on him with their daily bread. Of course, as they were so poor, this worthy family increased and multiplied; and as they increased, and as they multiplied, my wife insists that I should point out how support was found for them. When there was a second child in Philip's nursery, he would have removed from his lodgings in Thornhaugh Street, but for the prayers and commands of the affectionate Little Sister, who insisted that there was plenty of room in the house for everybody, and who said that if Philip went away she would cut off her little godchild with a shilling. And then indeed it was discovered for the first time, that this faithful and affectionate creature had endowed Philip with all her little property. These are the rays of sunshine in the dungeon. These are the drops of water in the desert. And with a full heart our friend acknowledges how comfort came to him in his hour of need.

Though Mr. Firmin has a very grateful heart, it has been admitted that he was a loud disagreeable Firmin at times, impetuous in his talk, and violent in his behaviour: and we are now come to that period of his history, when he had a quarrel in which I am sorry to say Mr. Philip was in the wrong. Why do we consort with those whom we dislike? Why is it that men *will* try and associate between whom no love is? I think it was the ladies who tried to reconcile Philip and his master; who brought them together, and strove to make them friends; but the more they met the more they disliked each other; and now the Muse has to relate their final and irreconcilable rupture.

Of Mugford's wrath the direful tale relate, O Muse! and Philip's pitiable fate. I have shown how the men had long been inwardly envenomed one against the other. 'Because Firmin is as poor as a rat, that's no reason why he should adopt that hawhaw manner, and them high and mighty airs towards a man who gives him the bread he eats,' Mugford argued not unjustly. 'What do *I* care for his being a University man? I am as good as he is. I am better than his old scamp of a father, who was a College man too, and lived in fine company. I made my own way in the world, independent, and supported myself since I was fourteen years of age, and helped my mother and brothers too, and that's more than my sub-editor can say, who can't support himself yet. I could get fifty sub-editors as good as he is, by calling out of window into the street, I could. I say, hang Firmin! I'm a-losing all patience with him.' On the other hand, Mr. Philip was in the habit of speaking his mind with equal candour. 'What right has that person to call me Firmin?' he asked. 'I am Firmin to my equals and friends. I am this man's labourer at four guineas a week. I give him his money's worth, and on every Saturday evening we are quits. Call me Philip indeed, and strike me in the side! I choke, sir, as I think of the confounded familiarity!' 'Confound his impudence!' was the cry, and the not unjust cry, of the labourer and his employer. The men should have been kept apart: and it was a most mistaken Christian charity and female conspiracy which brought them together. 'Another invitation from Mugford. It was agreed that I was never to go again, and I won't go,' says Philip to his meek wife. 'Write and say we are engaged, Charlotte.'

'It is for the 18th of next month, and this is the 23rd,' said'poor Charlotte. 'We can't well say that we are engaged so far off.'

'It is for one of his grand ceremony parties,' urged the Little Sister.

'You can't come to no quarrelling there. He has a good heart. So have you. There's no good quarrelling with him. Oh, Philip, do forgive, and be friends!' Philip yielded to the remonstrances of the women, as we all do; and a letter was sent to Hampstead, announcing that Mr. and Mrs. P. F. would have the honour of, etc.

In his quality of newspaper proprietor, musical professors and opera singers paid much court to Mr. Mugford; and he liked to entertain them at his hospitable table; to brag about his wines, cookery, plate, garden, prosperity, and private virtue, during dinner, whilst the artists Bat respectfully listening to him; and to go to sleep and snore, or wake up and join cheerfully in a chorus, when the professional people performed in the drawing-room. Now, there was a lady who was once known at the theatre by the name of Mrs. Ravenswing, and who had been forced on to the stage by the misconduct of her husband, a certain Walker, one of the greatest scamps who ever entered a gaol. On Walker's death, this lady married a Mr. Woolsey, a wealthy tailor, who retired from his business, as he caused his wife to withdraw from hers.

Now, more worthy and honourable people do not live than Woolsey and his wife, as those know who are acquainted with their history. Mrs. Woolsey is loud. Her *h*'s are by no means where they should be; her knife at dinner is often where it should not be. She calls men aloud by their names, and without any prefix of courtesy. She is very fond of porter, and has no scruple in asking for it. She sits down to play the piano and to sing with perfect good-nature, and if you look at her hands as they wander over the keys—well, I don't wish to say anything unkind, but I am forced to own that those hands are not so white as the ivory which they thump. Woolsey sits in perfect rapture listening to his wife. Mugford presses her to take a glass of 'somethink' afterwards; and the good-natured soul says she will take 'something 'ot.' She sits and listens with infinite patience and good-humour whilst the little Mugfords go through their horrible little musical exercises; and these over, she is ready to go back to the piano again, and sing more songs, and drink more "ot.'

I do not say that this was an elegant woman, or a fitting companion for Mrs. Philip; but I know that Mrs. Woolsey was a good, clever, and kindly woman, and that Philip behaved rudely to her. He never meant to be rude to her, he said; but the truth is, he treated her, her husband, Mugford, and Mrs. Mugford, with a haughty ill-humour which utterly exasperated and perplexed them.

About this poor lady, who was modest and innocent as Susannah, Philip had heard some wicked elders at wicked clubs tell wicked stones in old times. There was that old Trail, for instance, what woman escaped from *his* sneers and slander? There were others who could be named, and whose testimony was equally untruthful. On an ordinary occasion Philip would never have cared or squabbled about a question of precedence, and would have taken any place assigned to him at any table. But when Mrs. Woolsey in crumpled satins and blowsy lace made her appearance, and was eagerly and respectfully saluted by the host and hostess, Philip remembered those early stories about the poor lady: his eyes flashed wrath, and his breast beat with an indignation which almost choked him. Ask that woman to meet my wife? he thought to himself, and looked so ferocious and desperate that the timid little wife gazed with alarm at her Philip, and crept up to him and whispered 'What is it, dear?'

Meanwhile, Mrs. Mugford and Mrs. Woolsey were in full colloquy about the weather, the nursery, and so forth—and Woolsey and Mugford giving each other the hearty grasp of friendship. Philip, then, scowling at the newly-arrived guests, turning his great hulking back upon the company, and talking to his wife, presented a not agreeable figure to his entertainer.

'Hang the fellow's pride!' thought Mugford. 'He chooses to turn his back upon my company, because Woolsey was a tradesman. An honest tailor is better than a bankrupt swindling doctor, I should think. *Woolsey* need not be ashamed to show his face, I suppose. Why did you make me ask that fellar again, Mrs. M.? Don't you see, our society ain't good enough for him?'

Philip's conduct, then, so irritated Mugford, that when dinner was announced, he stepped forward and offered his arm to Mrs. Woolsey; having intended in the first instance to confer that honour upon Charlotte. 'I'll show him,' thought Mugford, 'that an honest tradesman's lady who pays his way, and is not afraid of anybody, is better than my sub-editor's wife, the daughter of a bankrupt swell' Though the dinner was illuminated by Mugford's grandest plate, and accompanied by his very best wine, it was a gloomy and weary repast to several people present, and Philip and Charlotte, and I dare say Mugford, thought it never would be done. Mrs. Woolsey, to be sure, placidly ate her dinner, and drank her wine; whilst, remembering these wicked legends against her, Philip sat before the poor unconscious lady, silent, with glaring eyes, insolent and odious; so much so, that Mrs. Woolsey imparted to Mrs. Mugford her surmise that the tall gentleman must have got out of bed the wrong leg foremost.

Well, Mrs. Woolsey's carriage and Mr. Firmin's cab were announced at the same moment; and immediately Philip started up and beckoned his wife away. But Mrs. Woolsey's carriage and lamps of course had the precedence: and this lady Mr. Mugford accompanied to her carriage step.

He did not pay the same attention to Mrs. Firmin. Most likely he forgot. Possibly he did not think etiquette required he should show that sort of politeness to a sub-editor's wife: at any rate, he was not so rude as Philip himself had been during the evening, but he stood in the hall looking at his guests departing in their cab, when, in a sudden gust of passion, Philip stepped out of the carriage, and stalked up to his host, who stood there in his own hall confronting him, Philip declared, with a most impudent smile on his face.

'Come back to light a pipe, I suppose? Nice thing for your wife ain't it?' said Mugford, relishing his own joke.

'I am come back, sir,' said Philip, glaring at Mugford, 'to ask how you dared invite Mrs. Philip Firmin to meet that woman?'

Here, on his side, Mr. Mugford lost his temper, and from this moment *his* wrong begins. When he was in a passion, the language used by Mr. Mugford was not, it appears, choice. We have heard that when angry he was in the habit of swearing freely at his subordinates. He broke out on this occasion also with many oaths. He told Philip that he would stand his impudence no longer; that he was as good as a swindling doctor's son; that though he hadn't been to college he could buy and pay them as had; and that if Philip liked to come into the back yard for ten minutes, he'd give him one—two, and show him whether he was a man or not. Poor Char, who, indeed, fancied that her husband had gone back to light his cigar, sat awhile unconscious in her cab, and supposed that the two gentlemen were engaged on newspaper business. When Mugford began to pull his coat off, she sat wondering, but not in the least understanding the meaning of the action. Philip had described his employer as walking about his office without a coat and using energetic language.

But when, attracted by the loudness of the talk, Mrs. Mugford came forth from her neighbouring drawing-room, accompanied by such of her children as had not yet gone to roost—when seeing Mugford pulling off his dress-coat, she began to scream—when, lifting his voice over hers, Mugford poured forth oaths, and frantically shook his fists at Philip, asking how that blackguard dared insult him in his own house, and proposing to knock his head off at that moment—then poor Char, in wild alarm, sprang out of the cab, and ran to her husband, whose whole frame was throbbing, whose nostrils were snorting with passion. Then Mrs.

Mugford, springing forward, placed her ample form before her husband's, and calling Philip a great cowardly beast, asked him if he was going to attack that little old man? Then Mugford dashing his coat down to the ground, called with fresh oaths to Philip to come on. And, in fine, there was a most unpleasant row, occasioned by Mr. Philip Firmin's hot temper.

CHAPTER XXXV. RES ANGUSTA DOMI

TO reconcile these two men was impossible, after such a quarrel as that described in the last chapter. The only chance of peace was to keep the two men apart. If they met, they would fly at each other. Mugford always persisted that he could have got the better of his great hulking sub-editor, who did not know the use of his fists. In Mugford's youthful time, bruising was a fashionable art; and the old gentleman still believed in his own skill and prowess. 'Don't tell me,' he would say; 'though the fellar is as big as a life-guardsman, I would have doubled him up in two minutes.' I am very glad, for poor Charlotte's sake, and his own, that Philip did not undergo the doubling-up process. He himself felt such a wrath and surprise at his employer, as, I suppose, a lion does when a little dog attacks him. I should not like to be that little dog; nor does my modest and peaceful nature at all prompt and impel me to combat with lions.

It was mighty well Mr. Philip Firmin had shown his spirit, and quarrelled with his bread-and-butter; but when Saturday came, what philanthropist would hand four sovereigns and four shillings over to Mr. F., as Mr. Burjoyce, the publisher of the *Pall Mall Gazette,* had been accustomed to do? I will say for my friend that a still keener remorse than that which he felt about money thrown away attended him when he found that Mrs. Woolsey, towards whom he had cast a sidelong stone of persecution, was a most respectable and honourable lady. 'I should like to go, sir, and grovel before her,' Philip said, in his energetic way. 'If I see that tailor, I will request him to put his foot on my head, and trample on me with his highlows. Oh, for shame! for shame! shall I never learn charity towards my neighbours, and always go on believing in the lies which people tell me? When I meet that scoundrel Trail at the club, I must chastise him. How dared he take away the reputation of an honest woman?' Philip's friends besought him, for the sake of society and peace, not to carry this quarrel farther. 'If,' we said, 'every woman whom Trail has maligned had a champion who should box Trail's ears at the club, what a vulgar quarrelsome place that club would become! My dear Philip, did you ever know Mr. Trail say a good word of man or woman?' and by these or similar entreaties and arguments, we succeeded in keeping the Queen's peace.

Yes: but how find another *Pall Mall Gazette?* Had Philip possessed seven thousand pounds in the three per cents., his income would have been no greater than that which he drew from Mugford's faithful bank. Ah! how wonderful ways and means are! When I think how this very line, this very word, which I am writing represents money, I am lost in a respectful astonishment. A man takes his own case, as he says his own prayers, on behalf of himself and his family. I am paid, we will say, for the sake of illustration, at the rate of sixpence per line. With the words 'Ah, how wonderful,' to the words 'per line,' I can buy a loaf, a piece of butter, a jug of milk, a modicum of tea,—actually enough to make breakfast for the family; and the servants of the house; and the charwoman, *their* servant, can shake up the tea-leaves with a fresh supply of water, sop the crusts, and get a meal *tant bien que mal.* Wife, children, guests, servants, charwoman, we are all actually making a meal off Philip Firmin's bones as it were. And my next-door neighbour, whom I see marching away to chambers, umbrella in hand? And next door but one the City man? And next door but two the doctor?—I know the baker has left loaves at every one of their doors this morning, that all their chimneys are smoking, and they will all have breakfast. Ah, thank God for it! I hope, friend, you and I are not too proud to ask for our daily bread, and to be grateful for getting it? Mr. Philip had to work for his, in care and trouble, like other children of men:—to work for it, and I hope to pray for it, too. It is a thought to me awful and beautiful, that of the daily prayer, and of the myriads of fellow-men uttering it, in care and in sickness, in doubt and in poverty, in health and in wealth. *Panem nostrum da nobis hodie.* Philip whispers it by the bedside where wife and child lie sleeping, and goes to bis early labour with a stouter heart: as he creeps to his rest when the days labour is over, and the quotidian bread is earned, and breathes his hushed thanks to the bountiful Giver of the meal. All over this world what an endless chorus is singing of love, and thanks, and prayer. Day tells to day the wondrous story, and night recounts it unto night.-How do I come to think of a sunrise which I saw near twenty years ago on the Nile, when the river and sky flushed and glowed with the dawning light, and as the luminary appeared, the boatman knelt on the rosy deck, and adored Allah? So, as thy sun rises, friend, over the humble housetops round about your home, shall you wake many and many a day to duty and labour. May the task have been honestly done when the night comes; and the steward deal kindly with the labourer.

So two of Philip's cables cracked and gave way after a very brief strain, and the poor fellow held by nothing now but that wonderful *European Review* established by the mysterious Tregarvan. Actors, a people of superstitions and traditions, opine that Heaven, in some mysterious way, makes managers for their benefit. In like manner, Review proprietors are sent to provide the pabulum for us men of letters. With what complacency did my wife listen to the somewhat long-winded and pompous oratory of Tregarvan! He pompous and commonplace? Tregarvan spoke with excellent good sense. That wily woman never showed she was tired of his conversation. She praised him to Philip behind his back, and would not allow a word in his disparagement. As a doctor will punch your chest, your liver, your heart, listen at your lungs, squeeze your pulse, and what not, so this practitioner studied, shampooed, auscultated Tregarvan. Of course, he allowed himself to be operated upon. Of course, he bad no idea that the lady was flattering, wheedling, humbugging him; but thought that he was a very well-informed eloquent man, who had seen and read a great deal, and had an agreeable method of imparting his knowledge, and that the lady in question was a sensible woman, naturally eager for more information. Go, Delilah! I understand your tricks! I know many another Omphale in London, who will coax Hercules away from his club, to come and listen to her wheedling talk.

One great difficulty we had was to make Philip read Tregarvan's own articles in the *Review*. He at first said he could not, or that he could not remember them; so that there was no use in reading them.

And Philip's new master used to make artful allusions to his own writings in the course of conversation, so that our unwary friend would find himself under examination in any casual interview with Tregarvan, whose opinions on free-trade, malt-tax, income-tax, designs of Russia, or what not, might he accepted or denied, but ought at least to be known. We actually made Philip get up his owner's articles. We put questions to him, privily, regarding them—'coached' him, according to the University phrase. My wife humbugged that wretched Member of Parliament in a way which makes me shudder, when I think of what hypocrisy the sex is capable. Those arts and dissimulations with which she wheedles others, suppose she exercise them on *me*? Horrible thought! No, angel! To others thou mayest be a coaxing hypocrite; to me thou art all candour. *Other* men may have been humbugged by other women; but I am not to be taken in by that sort of thing; and thou art all candour!

We had then so much per annum as editor. We were paid, besides, for our articles. We had really a snug little pension out of this *Review,* and we prayed it might last for ever. We might write a novel. We might contribute articles to a daily paper; get a little parliamentary practice as a barrister. We actually did get Philip into a railway case or two, and my wife must be coaxing and hugging solicitors' ladies, as she had wheedled and coaxed Members of Parliament. Why, I do believe my Delilah set up a flirtation with old Bishop Crossticks, with an idea of getting her *protégé* a living; and though the lady indignantly repudiates this charge, will she be pleased to explain how the bishop's sermons were so outrageously praised in the *Review*?

Philip's roughness and frankness did not displease Tregarvan, to the wonder of us all, who trembled lest he should lose this as he had lost his former place. Tregarvan had more country-houses than one, and at these not only was the editor of the *Review* made welcome, but the editor's wife and children, whom Tregarvan's wife took into especial regard. In London, Lady Mary had assemblies where our little friend Charlotte made her appearance; and half-a-dozen times in the course of the season the wealthy Cornish gentleman feasted his retainers of the *Review*. His wine was excellent and old; his jokes were old, too; his table pompous, grave, plentiful. If Philip was to eat the bread of dependence, the loaf was here very kindly prepared for him; and he ate it humbly, and with not too much grumbling. This diet chokes some proud stomachs and disagrees with them; but Philip was very humble now, and of a nature grateful for kindness. He is one who requires the help of friends, and can accept benefits without losing independence—not all men's gifts, but some men's, whom he repays not only with coin, but with an immense affection and gratitude. How that man did laugh at my witticisms! How he worshipped the ground on which my wife walked! He elected himself our champion. He quarrelled with other people, who found fault with our characters, or would not see our perfections. There was something affecting in the way in which this big man took the humble place. We could do no wrong in his eyes; and woe betide the man who spoke disparagingly of us in his presence!

One day, at his patron's table, Philip exercised his valour and championship in our behalf by defending us against the evil speaking of that Mr. Trail, who has been mentioned before as a gentleman difficult to please, and credulous of ill regarding his neighbour. The talk happened to fall upon the character of the reader's most humble servant, and Trail, as may be imagined, spared me no more than the rest of mankind. Would you like to be liked by all people? That would be a reason why Trail should hate you. Were you an angel fresh dropped from the skies, he would espy dirt on your robe, and a black feather or two in your wing. As for me, I know I am not angelical at all; and in walking my native earth, can't help a little mud on my trousers. Well: Mr. Trail began to paint my portrait, laying on those dark shadows which that well-known master is in the habit of employing. I was a parasite of the nobility; I was a heartless sycophant, housebreaker, drunkard, murderer, returned convict, etc. etc. With a little imagination, Mrs. Candour can fill up the outline, and arrange the colours so as to suit her amiable fancy.

Philip had come late to dinner;—of *this* fault, I must confess, he is guilty only too often. The company were at table; he took the only place vacant, and this happened to be at the side of Mr. Trail. On Trail's other side was a portly individual, of a healthy and rosy countenance and voluminous white waistcoat, to whom Trail directed much of his amiable talk, and whom he addressed once or twice as Sir John. Once or twice already we have seen how Philip has quarrelled at table. He cried *mea culpa* loudly and honestly enough. He made vows of reform in this particular. He succeeded, dearly beloved brethren, not much worse or better than you and I do, who confess our faults, and go on promising to improve, and stumbling and picking ourselves up every day. The pavement of life is strewed with orange-peel; and who has not slipped on the flags?

'He is the most conceited man in London,'—Trail was going on, 'and one of the most worldly. He will throw over a colonel to dine with a general. He wouldn't throw over you two baronets—he is a great deal too shrewd a fellow for that. He wouldn't give *you* up, perhaps, to dine with a lord; but any ordinary baronet he would.'

'And why not us as well as the rest?' asks Tregarvan, who seemed amused at the speaker's chatter.

'Because you are not like common baronets at all. Because your estates are a great deal too large. Because, I suppose, you might either of you go to the Upper House any day. Because, as an author, he may be supposed to be afraid of a certain *Review,'* cries Trail, with a loud laugh.

'Trail is speaking of a friend of yours,' said the host, nodding and smiling, to the new comer.

'Very lucky for my friend,' growls Philip, and eats his soup in silence.

'By the way, that article of his on Madame de Sévigné is poor stuff. No knowledge of the period. Three gross blunders in French. A man can't write of French society unless he has lived in French society. What does Pendennis know of it? A man who makes blunders like those can't understand French. A man who can't speak French can't get on in French society. Therefore he can't write about French society. All these propositions are clear enough. Thank you. Dry champagne, if you please. He is enormously overrated, I tell you; and so is his wife. They used to put her forward as a beauty: and she is only a dowdy woman out of a nursery. She has no style about her.'

'She is only one of the best women in the world,' Mr. Firmin called out, turning very red; and hereupon entered into a defence of our characters, and pronounced a eulogium upon both and each of us, in which I hope there was some little truth. However, he spoke with great enthusiasm, and Mr. Trail found himself in a minority.

'You are right to stand up for your friends, Firmin!' cried the host. 'Let me introduce you to—'

'Let me introduce myself,' said the gentleman on the other side of Mr. Trail. 'Mr. Firmin, you and I are kinsmen,—I am Sir John Ringwood.' And Sir John reached a hand to Philip across Trail's chair. They talked a great deal together in the course of the evening: and when Mr. Trail found that the great county gentleman was friendly and familiar with Philip, and claimed a relationship with him, his manner towards Firmin altered. He pronounced afterwards a warm eulogy upon Sir John for his frankness and good-nature in recognising his unfortunate relative, and charitably said, 'Philip might not be like the Doctor, and could not help having a rogue for a father.' In former days, Trail had eaten and drunken freely at that rogue's table. But we must have truth, you know, before all things: and if your own brother has committed a sin, common justice requires that you should stone him.

In former days, and not long after Lord Ringwood's death, Philip had left his card at this kinsman's door, and Sir John's butler, driving in his master's brougham, had left a card upon Philip, who was not over well pleased by this acknowledgment of his civility, and, in fact, employed abusive epithets when he spoke of the transaction. But when the two gentlemen actually met, their intercourse was kindly and pleasant enough. Sir John listened to his relative's talk—and, it appears, Philip comported himself with his usual free and easy manner—with interest and curiosity; and owned afterwards that evil tongues had previously been busy with the young man's character, and that slander and untruth had been spoken regarding him. In this respect, if Philip is worse off than his neighbours, I can only say his neighbours are fortunate.

Two days after the meeting of the cousins, the tranquillity of Thornhaugh Street was disturbed by the appearance of a magnificent yellow chariot, with crests, hammercloths, a bewigged coachman, and a powdered footman. Betsy, the nurse, who was going to take out for a walk, encountered this giant on the threshold of Mrs. Brandon's door; and a lady within the chariot delivered three cards to the tall menial, who transferred them to Betsy. And Betsy persisted in saying that the lady in the carriage admired baby very much, and asked its age, at which baby's mamma was not in the least surprised. In due course, an invitation to dinner followed, and our friends became acquainted with their kinsfolk.

If you have a good memory for pedigrees—and in my youthful time every man *de bonne maison* studied genealogies, and had his English families in his memory— you know that this Sir John Ringwood, who succeeded to the principal portion of the estates, but not to the titles of the late Earl, was descended from a mutual ancestor, a Sir John, whose elder son was ennobled (temp. Geo. I.), whilst the second son, following the legal profession, became a judge, and had a son, who became a baronet, and who begat that present Sir John who has just been shaking hands with Philip across Trail's back.[ii] Thus the two men were cousins; and in right of the heiress, his poor mother, Philip might quarter the Ringwood arms on his carriage, whenever he drove out. These, you know, are, argent, a dexter sinople on a fesse wavy of the first—or pick out, my dear friend, any coat you like out of the whole, heraldic wardrobe, and accommodate it to our friend Firmin.

When he was a young man at college, Philip had dabbled a little in this queer science of heraldry, and used to try and believe the legends about his ancestry, which his fond mother imparted to him. He had a great book-plate made for himself, with a prodigious number of quarterings, and could recite the alliances by which such and such a quartering came into his shield. His father rather confirmed these histories, and spoke of them and of his wife's noble family with much respect: and Philip, artlessly whispering to a vulgar boy at school that he was descended from King John, was thrashed very unkindly by the vulgar upper boy, and nicknamed King John for many a long day after. I dare say many other gentlemen who profess to trace their descent from ancient kings have no better or worse authority for their pedigree than friend Philip.

When our friend paid his second visit to Sir John Ringwood, he was introduced to his kinsman's library; a great family tree hung over the mantelpiece, surrounded by a whole gallery of defunct Ringwoods, of whom the Baronet was now the representative. He quoted to Philip the hackneyed old Ovidian lines (some score of years ago a great deal of that old coin was current in conversation). As for family, he said, and ancestors, and what we have not done ourselves, these things we can hardly call ours. Sir John gave Philip to understand that he was a staunch Liberal.

Sir John was for going with the age. Sir John had fired a shot from the Paris barricades. Sir John was for the rights of man everywhere all over the world. He had pictures of Franklin, Lafayette, Washington, and the First Consul Buonaparte, on his walls along with his ancestors. He had lithograph copies of Magna Charta, the Declaration of American Independence, and the Signatures to the Death of Charles I. He did not scruple to own his preference for republican institutions. He wished to know what right had any man—the late Lord Ringwood, for example— to sit in an hereditary House of Peers and legislate over him? That lord had had a son, Cinqbars, who died many years before, a victim of his own follies and debaucheries. Had Lord Cinqbars survived his father, he would now be sitting an Earl in the House of Peers—the most ignorant young man, the most unprincipled young man, reckless, dissolute, of the feeblest intellect and the worst life. Well, had he lived and inherited the Ringwood property, that creature would have been an earl: whereas he, Sir John, his superior in morals, in character, in intellect, his equal in point of birth (for had they not both a common ancestor?) was Sir John still. The inequalities in men's chances in life were monstrous and ridiculous. He was determined, henceforth, to look at a man for himself alone, and not esteem him for any of the absurd caprices of fortune.

As the republican was talking to his relative, a servant came into the room and whispered to his master that the plumber had come with his bill as by appointment; upon which Sir John rose up in a fury, asked the servant how he dared to disturb him, and bade him tell the plumber to go to the lowest depths of Tartarus. Nothing could equal the insolence and rapacity of tradesmen, he said, except the insolence and idleness of servants; and he called this one back, and asked him how he dared to leave the fire in that state?—stormed and raged at him with a volubility which astonished his new acquaintance; and, the man being gone, resumed his previous subject of conversation, viz., natural equality and the outrageous injustice of the present social system. After talking for half-an-hour, during which Philip found that he himself could hardly find an opportunity of uttering a word, Sir John took out his watch, and got up from his chair; at which hint Philip too rose, not sorry to bring the interview to an end. And herewith Sir John accompanied his kinsman into the hall, and to the street-door, before which the Baronet's groom was riding, leading his master's horse. And Philip heard the Baronet using violent language to the groom, as he had done to the servant within doors. Why, the army in Flanders did not swear more terribly than this admirer of republican institutions and advocate of the rights of man.

Philip was not allowed to go away without appointing a day when he and his wife would partake of their kinsman's hospitality. On this occasion, Mrs. Philip comported herself with so much grace and simplicity, that Sir John and Lady Ringwood pronounced her to be a very pleasing and ladylike person; and I dare say wondered how a person in her rank of life could have acquired manners that were so refined and agreeable. Lady Ringwood asked after the child which she had seen, praised its beauty; of course, won the mother's heart, and thereby caused her to speak with perhaps more freedom than she would otherwise have felt at a first interview. Mrs. Philip has a dainty touch on the piano, and a sweet singing voice that is charmingly true and neat. She performed after dinner some of the songs of her little *répertoire,* and pleased her audience. Lady Ringwood loved good music, and was herself a fine performer of the ancient school, when she played Haydn and Mozart under the tuition of good old Sir George Thrum. The tall and handsome beneficed clergyman who acted as major-domo of Sir John's establishment, placed a parcel in the carriage when Mr. and Mrs. Philip took their leave, and announced with much respectful deference that the cab was paid. Our friends no doubt would have preferred to dispense with this ceremony j but it is ill looking even a gift cab-horse in the mouth, and so Philip was a gainer of some two shillings by his kinsman's liberality.

When Charlotte came to open the parcel which major-domo, with his lady's compliments, had placed in the cab, I fear she did not exhibit that elation which we ought to feel for the favours of our friends. A couple of little frocks, of the cut of George IV., some little red shoes of the same period, some crumpled sashes, and other small articles of wearing-apparel, by her Ladyship's order by her Ladyship's lady's-maid; and Lady Ringwood kissing Charlotte at her departure, told her that she had caused this little packet to be put away for her. 'H'm,' says Philip, only half pleased. 'Suppose Sir John had told his butler to put up one of his blue coats and brass buttons for me, as well as pay the cab?'

'If it was meant in kindness, Philip, we must not be angry,' pleaded Philip's wife; —'and I am sure if you had heard her and the Miss Ringwoods speak of baby, you would like them, as I intend to do.'

But Mrs. Philip never put those mouldy old red shoes upon baby; and as for the little frocks, children's frocks are made so much fuller now that Lady Ringwood's presents did not answer at all. Charlotte managed to furbish up a sash, and a pair of epaulets for her child—epaulets are they called? Shoulder-knots—what you will, ladies; and with these ornaments Miss Firmin was presented to Lady Ringwood and some of her family.

The goodwill of these new-found relatives of Philip's was laborious, was evident, and yet I must say was not altogether agreeable. At the first period of their intercourse—for this, too, I am sorry to say, came to an end, or presently suffered interruption—tokens of affection in the shape of farm produce, country butter and poultry, and actual butcher's meat, came from Berkeley Square to Thornhaugh Street. The Duke of Double-glo'ster I know is much richer than you are; but if he were to offer to make you a present of half-a-crown, I doubt whether you would be quite pleased. And so with Philip and his relatives. A hamper brought in the brougham, containing hot-house grapes and country butter, is very well, but a leg of mutton I own was a gift that was rather tough to swallow. It *was* tough. That point we ascertained and established amidst roars of laughter one day when we dined with our friends. Did Lady Ringwood send a sack of turnips in the brougham too? In a word, we ate Sir John's mutton, and we laughed at him, and be sure many a man has done the same by you and me. Last Friday, for instance, as Jones and Brown go away after dining with your humble servant: 'Did you ever see such profusion and extravagance?' asks Brown. 'Profusion and extravagance!' cries Jones, that well-known epicure. 'I never saw anything so shabby in my life. What does the fellow mean by asking *me* to such a dinner?' 'True,' says the other, 'it *was* an abominable dinner, Jones, as you justly say; but it was very profuse in him to give it. Don't you see?' and so both our good friends are agreed.

Ere many days were over the great yellow chariot and its powdered attendants again made their appearance before Mrs. Brandon's modest door in Thornhaugh Street, and Lady Ringwood and two daughters descended from the carriage and made their way to Mr. Philip's apartments on the second floor, just as that worthy gentleman was sitting down to dinner with his wife. Lady Ringwood, bent upon being gracious, was in ecstasies with everything she saw—a clean house—a nice little maid—pretty picturesque rooms—odd rooms—and what charming pictures! Several of these were the work of the fond pencil; of poor J. J., who, as has been told, had painted Philip's beard and Charlotte's eyebrow, and Charlotte's baby a thousand and a thousand times. 'May we come in? Are we disturbing you? What dear little bits of china! What a beautiful mug, Mr. Firmin!' This was poor J. J.'s present to his god-daughter. 'How nice the luncheon looks! Dinner, is it? How pleasant to dine at this hour!' The ladies were determined to be charmed with everything round about them.

'We are dining on your poultry. May we offer some to you and Miss Ringwood?' says the master of the house.

'Why don't you dine in the dining-room? Why do you dine in a bedroom?' asks Franklin Ringwood, the interesting young son of the Baronet of Ringwood.

'Somebody else lives in the parlour,' says Mrs. Philip. On which the boy remarks, 'We have two dining-rooms in Berkeley Square. I mean for us, besides papa's study, which I mustn't go into. And the servants have two dining-rooms and—'

'Hush!' here cries mamma, with the usual remark regarding the beauty of silence in little boys.

But Franklin persists in spite of the ' Hushes!' 'And so we have at Ringwood; and at Whipham there's ever so many dining-rooms— ever so many—and I like Whipham a great deal better than Ringwood, because my pony is at Whipham. *You* have not got a pony. You are too poor.'

'Franklin!'

'You said he was too poor; and you would not have had chickens if we had not given them to you. Mamma, you know you said they were very poor, and would like them.'

And here mamma looked red, and I dare say Philip's cheeks and ears tingled, and for once Mrs. Philip was thankful at hearing her baby cry, for it gave her a pretext for leaving the room and flying to the nursery, whither the other two ladies accompanied her.

Meanwhile Master Franklin went on with his artless conversation. 'Mr. Philip, why do they say you are wicked? You do not look wicked; and I am sure Mrs. Philip does not look wicked—she looks very good.'

'Who says I am wicked?' asks Mr. Firmin of his candid young relative.

'Oh, ever so many! Cousin Ringwood says so; and Blanche says so; and Woolcomb says so; only I don't like him, he's so very brown. And when they heard you had been to dinner, "Has that beast been here?" Ringwood says. And I don't like him a bit. But I like you, at least I think I do. You only have oranges for dessert. We always have lots of things for dessert at home. *You* don't, I suppose, because you've got no money—only a very little.'

'Well: I have got only a very little,' says Philip.

'I have some—ever so much. And I'll buy something for your wife; and I shall like to have you better at home than Blanche, and Ringwood, and that Woolcomb; and they never give me anything. You can't, you know; because you are so very poor— you are; but we'll often send you things, I dare say. And I'll have an orange, please, thank you. And there's a chap at our school, and his name is Suckling, and he ate eighteen oranges, and wouldn't give one away to anybody. Wasn't he a greedy pig? And I have wine with my oranges—I do: a glass of wine—thank you. That's jolly. But you don't have it often, I suppose, because you 're so very poor.'

I am glad Philip's infant could not understand, being yet of too tender age, the compliments which Lady Ringwood and her daughter passed upon her. As it was, the compliments charmed the mother, for whom indeed they were intended, and did not inflame the unconscious baby's vanity.

What would the polite mamma and sister have said, if they had heard that unlucky Franklin's prattle? The boy's simplicity amused his tall cousin. 'Yes,' says Philip, 'we are very poor, but we are very happy, and don't mind—that's the truth.'

'Mademoiselle, that's the German governess, said she wondered how you could live at all; and I don't think you could if you ate as much as she did. You should see her eat: she is such a *oner* at eating. Fred, my brother, that's the one who is at college, one day tried to see how much Mademoiselle Wallfisch could eat, and she had twice of soup, and then she said *sivoplay*; and then twice of fish, and she said *sivo-play* for more; and then she had roast-mutton—no, I think, roast-beef it was; and she eats the peas with her knife; and then she had raspberry-jam pudding, and ever so much beer, and then—' But what came then we never shall know; because while young Franklin was choking with laughter (accompanied with a large piece of orange) at the ridiculous recollection of Miss Wallfisch's appetite, his mamma and sister came downstairs from Charlotte's nursery, and brought the dear boy's conversation to an end. The ladies chose to go home, delighted with Philip, baby, Charlotte. Everything was *so* proper. Everything was so nice. Mrs. Firmin was so ladylike. The fine ladies watched her, and her behaviour, with that curiosity which the Brobdingnag ladies displayed when they held up little Gulliver on their palms, and saw him bow, smile, dance, draw his sword, and take off his hat, just like a man.

CHAPTER XXXVI. IN WHICH THE DRAWING-ROOMS ARE NOT FURNISHED AFTER ALL

WE cannot expect to be loved by a relative whom we have knocked into an illuminated pond, and whose coat-tails, pantaloons, nether limbs, and best feelings we have lacerated with ill-treatment and broken glass. A man whom you have so treated behind his back will not be sparing of his punishment behind yours. Of course all the Twysdens, male and female, and Woolcomb, the dusky husband of Philip's former love, hated and feared, and maligned him; and were in the habit of speaking of him as a truculent and reckless savage and monster, coarse and brutal in his language and behaviour, ragged, dirty, and reckless in his personal appearance; reeking with smoke, perpetually reeling in drink, indulging in oaths, actions, laughter which rendered him intolerable in civilised society. The Twysdens, during Philip's absence abroad, had been very respectful and assiduous in courting the new head of the Ringwood family. They had flattered Sir John, and paid court to my lady. They had been welcomed at Sir John's houses in town and country. They had adopted his politics in a great measure, as they had adopted the politics of the deceased peer. They had never lost an opportunity of abusing poor Philip and of ingratiating themselves. They had never refused any invitation from Sir John in town or country, and had ended by utterly boring him and Lady Ringwood and the Ringwood family in general. Lady Ringwood learned somewhere how pitilessly Mrs. Woolcomb had jilted her cousin when a richer suitor appeared in the person of the West Indian. Then news came how Philip had administered a beating to Woolcomb, to young Twysden, to a dozen who set on him. The early prejudices began to pass away. A friend or two of Philip's told Ringwood how he was mistaken in the young man, and painted a portrait of him in colours much more favourable than those which his kinsfolk employed. Indeed, dear relations, if the public wants to know our little faults and errors, I think I know who will not grudge the requisite information. Dear Aunt Candour, are you not still alive, and don't you know what we had for dinner yesterday, and the amount (monstrous extravagance!) of the washerwoman's bill?

Well, the Twysden family so bespattered poor Philip with abuse, and represented him as a monster of such hideous mien, that no wonder the Ringwoods avoided him. Then they began to grow utterly sick and tired of his detractors. And then Sir John, happening to talk with his brother Member of Parliament, Tregarvan, in the House of Commons, heard quite a different story regarding our friend to that with which the Twysdens had regaled him, and, with no little surprise on Sir John's part, was told by Tregarvan how honest, rough, worthy, affectionate, and gentle this poor maligned fellow was, how he had been sinned against by his wretch of a father, whom he had forgiven and actually helped out of his wretched means, and how he was making a brave battle against poverty, and had a sweet little loving wife and child, whom every kind heart would willingly strive to help. Because people are rich they are not of necessity ogres. Because they are born gentlemen and ladies of good degree, are in easy circumstances, and have a generous education, it does not follow that they are heartless and will turn their back on a friend. *Moi qui vous parle*—I have been in a great strait of sickness near to death, and the friends who came to help me with every comfort, succour, sympathy were actually gentlemen, who lived in good houses, and had a good education. They didn't turn away because I was sick, or fly from me because they thought I was poor; on the contrary, hand, purse, succour, sympathy were ready, and praise be to Heaven. And so too did Philip find help when he needed it, and succour when he was in poverty. Tregarvan, we will own, was a pompous little man, his House of Commons speeches were dull, and his written documents awfully slow; but he had a kind heart: he was touched by that picture which Laura drew of the young man's poverty, and honesty, and simple hopefulness in the midst of hard times: and we have seen how the *European Review* was thus entrusted to Mr. Philip's management. Then some artful friends of Philip's determined that he should be reconciled to his relations, who were well to do in the world, and might serve him. And I wish, dear reader, that your respectable relatives and mine would bear this little paragraph in mind and leave us both handsome legacies. Then Tregarvan spoke to Sir John Ringwood, and that meeting was brought about, where, for once at least, Mr. Philip quarrelled with nobody.

And now came another little piece of good luck, which, I suppose, must be attributed to the same kind friend who had been scheming for Philip's benefit, and who is never so happy as when her little plots for her friends' benefit can be made to succeed. Yes: when that arch-jobber—don't tell me;—I never knew a woman worth a pin who wasn't—when that arch-jobber, I say, has achieved a job by which some friend is made happy, her eyes and cheeks brighten with triumph. Whether she has put a sick man into a hospital, or got a poor woman a family's washing, or made a sinner repent and return to wife, husband, or what not, that woman goes off and pays her thanks, where thanks are due, with such fervour, with such lightsomeness, with such happiness, that I assure you she is a sight to behold. Hush! When one sinner is saved, who are glad? Some of us know a woman or two pure as angels—know, and are thankful.

When the person about whom I have been prattling has one of her benevolent jobs in hand, or has completed it, there is a sort of triumph and mischief in her manner, which I don't know otherwise how to describe. She does not understand my best jokes at this period, or answers them at random, or laughs very absurdly and vacantly. She embraces her children wildly, and at the most absurd moments, is utterly unmindful when they are saying their lessons, prattling their little questions, and so forth. I recall all these symptoms (and put this and that together, as the saying is) as happening on one especial day, at the commencement of Easter Term, eighteen hundred and never mind what—as happening on one especial morning when this lady had been astoundingly *distraite* and curiously excited. I now remember, how during her children's dinner-time, she sat looking into the square out of our window, and scarcely attending to the little innocent cries for mutton which the children were offering up.

At last there was a rapid clank over the pavement, a tall figure passed the parlour windows, which our kind friends know look into Queen Square, and then came a loud ring at the bell, and I thought the mistress of the house gave an ah—a sigh— as though her heart was relieved.

The street door was presently opened, and then the dining-room door and Philip walks in with his hat on, his blue eyes staring before him,' his hair flaming about, and 'La, Uncle Philip!' cry the children. 'What have you done to yourself? You have shaved off your moustache.' And so he had, I declare 1

'I say, Pen, look here! This has been left at chambers; and Cassidy has sent it on by his clerk,' our friend said. I forget whether it has been stated that Philip's name still remained on the door of those chambers in Parchment Buildings, where we once heard his song of 'Doctor Luther,' and were present at his call-supper.

The document which Philip produced was actually a brief. The papers were superscribed, 'In Parliament, Polwheedle and Tredyddlum Railway. To support bill, Mr. Firmin; retainer, five guineas; brief, fifty guineas; consultation, five guineas. With you, Mr. Armstrong, Sir J. Whitworth, Mr. Pinkerton.' Here was a wonder of wonders! A shower of gold was poured out on my friend. A light dawned upon me. The proposed bill was for a Cornish line. Our friend Tregarvan was concerned in it, the line passing through his property, and my wife had canvassed him privately, and by her wheedling and blandishments had persuaded Tregarvan to use his interest with the agents and get Philip this welcome aid.

Philip eyed the paper with a queer expression. He handled it as some men handle a baby. He looked as if he did not know what to do with it, and as if he should like to drop it. I believe I made some satirical remark to this effect as I looked at our friend with his paper.

'He holds a child beautifully,' said my wife with much enthusiasm; 'much better than some people who laugh at him.'

'And he will hold this no doubt much to his credit. May this be the father of many briefs. May you have bags full of them!' Philip had all our good wishes. They did not cost much, or avail much, but they were sincere. I know men who can't for the lives of them give even that cheap coin of goodwill, but hate their neighbours' prosperity, and are angry with them when they cease to be dependent and poor.

We have said how. Cassidy's astonished clerk had brought the brief from chambers to Firmin at his lodgings, at Mrs. Brandon's in Thornhaugh Street. Had a bailiff served him with a writ, Philip could not have been more surprised, or in a greater tremor. A brief? Grands Dieux! What was he to do with a brief? He thought of going to bed, and being ill, or flying from home, country, family. Brief? Charlotte, of course, seeing her husband alarmed, began to quake too. Indeed, if his worship's finger aches, does not her who e body suffer? But Charlotte's and Philip's constant friend, the Little Sister, felt no such fear. 'Now there's this opening, you must take it, my dear,' she said. 'Suppose you don't know much about law—' 'Much! nothing,' interposed Philip. 'You might ask me to play the piano; but as I never happened to have learned—'

'La—don't tell me! You mustn't show a faint heart. Take the business, and do it as best you can. You'll do it better next time, and next. The Bar's a gentleman's business. Don't I attend a judge's lady, which I remember her with her first in a little bit of a house in Bernard Street, Russell Square; and now haven't I been to her in Eaton Square, with a butler and two footmen, and carriages ever so many1? You may work on at your newspapers, and get a crust, and when you 're old, and if you quarrel—and you have a knack of quarrelling—he has, Mrs. Firmin. I knew him before you did. Quarrelsome he is, and he will be, though you think him an angel, to be sure.— Suppose you quarrel with your newspaper masters, and your reviews, and that, you lose your place. A gentleman like Mr. Philip oughtn't to have a master. I couldn't bear to think of your going down of a Saturday to the publishing office to get your wages like a workman.'

'But *I am* a workman,' interposes Philip.

'La! But do you mean to remain one for ever? I would rise, if I was a man!' said the intrepid little woman; 'I would rise, or I'd know the reason why. Who knows how many in family you're going to be? I'd have more spirit than to live in a second floor—I would!'

And the Little Sister said this, though she clung round Philip's child with a rapture of fondness which she tried in vain to conceal; though she felt that to part from it would be to part from her life's chief happiness; though she loved Philip as her own son: and Charlotte—well, Charlotte for Philip's sake—as women love other women.

Charlotte came to her friends in Queen Square, and told us of the resolute Little Sister's advice and conversation. She knew that Mrs. Brandon only loved her as something belonging to Philip. She admired this Little Sister; and trusted her; and could afford to bear that little somewhat scornful domination which Brandon exercised. 'She does not love me, because Philip does,' Charlotte said. 'Do you think I could like her, or any woman, if I thought Philip loved them? I could kill them, Laura, that I could!' And at this sentiment I imagine daggers shooting out of a pair of eyes that were ordinarily very gentle and bright.

Not having been engaged in the case in which Philip had the honour of first appearing, I cannot enter into particulars regarding it, but am sure that case must have been uncommonly strong in itself which could survive such an advocate. He passed a frightful night of torture before appearing in committee-room. During that night, he says, his hair grew grey. His old college friend and comrade Pinkerton, who was with him in the case, 'coached' him on the day previous; and indeed it must be owned that,the work which he had to perform was not of a nature to impair the inside or the outside of his skull. A great man was his leader; his friend Pinkerton followed; and all Mr. Philip's business was to examine a half-dozen witnesses by questions previously arranged between them and the agents.

When you hear that, as a reward of his services in this case, Mr. Firmin received a sum of money sufficient to pay his modest family expenses for some four months, I am sure, dear and respected literary friends, that you will wish the lot of a parliamentary barrister had been yours, or that your immortal works could be paid with such a liberality as rewards the labours of these lawyers. '*Nimmer erscheinen die Götter allein.*' After one agent had employed Philip, another came and secured his valuable services: him two or three others followed, and our friend positively had money in bank. Not only were apprehensions of poverty removed for the present, but we had every reason to hope that Firmin's prosperity would increase and continue. And when a little son and heir was born, which blessing was conferred upon Mr. Philip about a year after his daughter, our godchild, saw the fight, we should have thought it shame to have any misgivings about the future, so cheerful did Philip's prospects appear. 'Did I not tell you,' said my wife, with her usual kindling romance, 'that comfort and succour would be found for these in the hour of their need?' Amen. We were grateful that comfort and succour should come. No one, I am sure, was more humbly thankful than Philip himself for the fortunate chances which befell him.

He was alarmed rather than elated by his sudden prosperity. 'It can't last,' he said. 'Don't tell me. The attorneys must find me out before long. They cannot continue to give their business to such an ignoramus: and I really think I must remonstrate with them.' You should have seen the Little Sister's indignation when Philip uttered this sentiment in her presence. 'Give up your business? Yes, do!' she cried, tossing up Philip's youngest born. 'Fling this baby out of window, why not indeed, which Heaven has sent it you! You ought to go down on your knees and ask pardon for having thought anything so wicked.' Philip's heir, by the way, immediately on his entrance into the world, had become the prime favourite of this unreasoning woman, The little daughter was passed over as a little person of no account, and so began to entertain the passion of jealousy at almost the very earliest age at which even the female breast is capable of enjoying it.

And though this Little Sister loved all these people with an almost ferocious passion of love, and lay awake, I believe, hearing their infantine cries, or crept on stealthy feet in darkness to their mothers chamber-door, behind which they lay sleeping; though she had, as it were, a rage for these infants, and was wretched out of their sight, yet, when a third and a fourth brief came to Philip, and he was enabled to put a little money aside, nothing would content Mrs. Brandon but that he should go into a house of his own. 'A gentleman,' she said, 'ought not to live in a two-pair lodging; he ought to have a house of his own. So, you see, she hastened on the preparations for her own execution. She trudged to the brokers' shops and made wonderful bargains or furniture. She cut chintzes, and covered sofas, and sewed, and patched, and fitted. She found a house and took it—Milman Street, Guilford Street, opposite the Fondling (as the dear little soul called it), a most genteel quiet little street, 'and quite near for me to come,' she said, 'to see my dears.' Did she speak with dry eyes? Mine moisten sometimes when I think of the faith, of the generosity, of the sacrifice, of that devoted loving creature.

I am very fond of Charlotte. Her sweetness and simplicity won all our hearts at home. No wife or mother ever was more attached and affectionate; but I own there was a time when I hated her, though of course that highly principled woman, the wife of the author of the present memoirs, says that the statement I am making here is stuff and nonsense, not to say immoral and irreligious. Well, then, I hated Charlotte for the horrible eagerness which she showed in getting away from this Little Sister, who clung round those children, whose first cries she had heard. I hated Charlotte for a cruel happiness which she felt as she hugged the children to her heart: her own children in their own room, whom she would dress, and watch, and wash, and tend; and for whom she wanted no aid. No aid, *entendez-vous*? Oh, it was a shame, a shame! In the new house, in the pleasant little trim new nursery (fitted up by whose fond hands we will not say), is the mother glaring over the cot, where the little soft round cheeks are pillowed; and yonder in the rooms in Thornhaugh Street, where she has tended them for two years, the Little Sister sits lonely, as the moonlight streams in. God help thee, little suffering faithful heart! Never but once in her life before had she known so exquisite a pain.

Of course, we had an entertainment in the new house; and Philip's friends, old and new, came to the house-warming. The family coach of the Ringwoods blocked up that astonished little street. The powder on their footmen's heads nearly brushed the ceiling, as the monsters rose when the guests passed in and out of the hall. The Little Sister merely took charge of the tea-room. Philip's 'library' was that usual little cupboard beyond the dining-room. The little drawing-room was dreadfully crowded by an ex-nursery piano, which the Ringwoods bestowed upon their friends; and somebody was in duty bound to play upon it on the evening of this *soirée*: though the Little Sister chafed downstairs at the music. In fact her very words were 'Rat that piano!' She 'ratted' the instrument, because the music would wake her little dears upstairs. And that music *did* wake them; and they howled melodiously, and the Little Sister, who was about to serve Lady Jane Tregarvan with some tea, dashed upstairs to the nursery: and Charlotte had reached the room already: and she looked angry when the Little Sister came in: and she said, 'I am sure, Mrs. Brandon, the people downstairs will be wanting their tea'; and she spoke with some asperity. And Mrs. Brandon went downstairs without one word; and, happening to be on the landing, conversing with a friend, and a little out of the way of the duet which the Miss Ringwoods were performing—riding their great old horse, as it were, and putting it through its paces in Mrs. Firmin's little paddock;—happening, I say, to be on the landing when Caroline passed, I took a hand as cold as stone, and never saw a look of grief more tragic than that worn by her poor little face as it passed. 'My children cried,' she said, 'and I went up to the nursery. But she don't want me there now.' Poor Little Sister. She humbled herself and grovelled before Charlotte. You could not help trampling upon her then, madam; and I hated you—and a great number of other women. Ridley and I went down to her tea-room, where Caroline resumed her place. She looked very nice, and pretty, with her pale sweet face, and her neat cap and blue ribbon. Tortures I know she was suffering. Charlotte had been stabbing her. Women will use the edge sometimes, and drive the steel in. Charlotte said to me, some time afterwards, 'I *was* jealous of her, and you were right; and a dearer more faithful creature never lived.' But who told Charlotte I said she was jealous? *O tripla bestia*! I told Ridley, and Mr. Ridley told Mrs. Firmin.

If Charlotte stabbed Caroline, Caroline could not help coming back again and again to the knife. On Sundays, when she was free, there was always a place for her at Philip's modest table; and when Mrs. Philip went to church, Caroline was allowed to reign in the nursery. Sometimes Charlotte was generous enough to give Mrs. Brandon this chance. When Philip took a house—a whole house to himself—Philip's mother-in-law proposed to come and stay with him, and said that, wishing to be beholden to no one, she would pay for her board and lodging. But Philip declined this treat, representing, justly, that his present house was no bigger than his former lodgings. 'My poor love is dying to have me,' Mrs. Baynes remarked on this. 'But her husband is so cruel to her, and keeps her under such terror, that she dares not call her life her own.' Cruel to her! Charlotte was the happiest of the happy in her little house. In consequence of his parliamentary success, Philip went regularly to chambers now, in the fond hope that more briefs might come. At chambers he likewise conducted the chief business of his *Review;* and, at the accustomed hour of his return, that usual little procession of mother and child and nurse would be seen on the watch for him; and the young woman—the happiest young woman in Christendom—would walk back clinging on her husband's arm.

All this while letters came from Philip's dear father at New York, where, it appeared, he was engaged not only in his profession, but in various speculations, with which he was always about to make his fortune. One day Philip got a newspaper advertising a new insurance company, and saw, to his astonishment, the announcement of 'Counsel in London, Philip Firmin, Esq., Parchment Buildings, Temple.' A paternal letter promised Philip great fees out of this insurance company, but I never heard that poor Philip was any the richer. In fact his friends advised him to have nothing to do with this insurance company, and to make no allusion to it in his letters. 'They feared the Danai, and the gifts they brought,' as old Firmin would have said. They had to impress upon Philip an abiding mistrust of that wily old Greek, his father. Firmin senior always wrote hopefully and magnificently, and persisted in believing or declaring that ere very long he should have to announce to Philip that his fortune was made. He speculated in Wall Street, I don't know in what shares, inventions, mines, railways. One day, some few months after his migration to Milman Street, Philip, blushing and hanging down his head, had to tell me that his father had drawn upon him again. Had he not paid up his shares in a certain mine, they would have been forfeited, and he and *his son after him* would have lost a certain fortune, old Danaus said. I fear an artful, a long-bow-pulling Danaus. What, shall a man have birth, wealth, friends, high position, and end so that we dare not leave him alone in the room with our spoons? 'And you have paid this bill which the old man drew?' we asked. Yes, Philip had paid the bill. He vowed he would pay no more. But it was not difficult to see that the Doctor would draw more bills upon this accommodating banker. 'I dread the letters which begin with a flourish about the fortune which he is just going to make,' Philip said. He knew that the old parent prefaced his demands for money in that way.

Mention has been made of a great medical discovery which he had announced to his correspondent, Mrs. Brandon, and by which the Doctor declared as usual that he was about to make a fortune. In New York and Boston he had tried experiments which had been attended with the most astonishing success. A remedy was discovered, the mere sale of which in Europe and America must bring an immense revenue to the fortunate inventors. For the ladies whom Mrs. Brandon attended, the remedy was of priceless value. He would send her some. His friend, Captain Morgan, of the Southampton packet-ship, would bring her some of this astonishing medicine. Let her try it. Let her show the accompanying cases to Dr. Goodenough —to any of his brother physicians in London. Though himself an exile from his country, he loved it, and was proud in being able to confer upon it one of the greatest blessings with which science had endowed mankind.

Goodenough, I am sorry to say, had such a mistrust of his *confrère* that he chose to disbelieve any statement Firmin made. 'I don't believe, my good Brandon, the fellow has *nous* enough to light upon any scientific discovery more useful than a new sauce for cutlets. He invent anything but fibs, never!' You see this Goodenough is an obstinate old heathen; and when he has once found reason to mistrust a man, he for ever after declines to believe him.

However, the Doctor is a man for ever on the look-out for more knowledge of his profession, and for more remedies to benefit mankind: he hummed and ha'd over the pamphlet, as the Little Sister sat watching him in his study. He clapped it down after a while and slapped his hands on his little legs as his wont is. 'Brandon,'he says, 'I think there is a great deal in it, and I think so the more because it turns out that Firmin has nothing to do with the discovery, which has been made at Boston.' In fact, Dr. Firmin, late of London, had only been present in the Boston hospital, where the experiments were made with the new remedy. He had cried 'halves,' and proposed to sell it as a secret remedy, and the bottle which he forwarded to oar friend the little Sister was labelled 'Firmin's Anodyne,' What Firmin did, indeed, was what he had been in the habit of doing. He had taken another man's property, and was endeavouring to make a flourish with it. The little Sister returned home, then, with her bottle of Chloroform—for this was what Dr. Firmin chose to call his discovery, and he had sent home a specimen of it; as he sent home a cask of petroleum from Virginia; as he sent proposals for new railways upon which he promised Philip a munificent commission, if his son could bat place the shares amongst his friends.

And with regard to these valuables, the sanguine Doctor got to believe that he really was endowing his son with large sums of money. 'My boy has set up a house, and has a wife and two children, the young jackanapes!' he would say to people in New York; 'as if he had not been extravagant enough in former days! When I married, I had private means, and married a nobleman's niece with a large fortune. Neither of these two young folks has a penny. Well, well, the old father must help them as well as he can!' And I am told there were ladies who dropped the tear of sensibility, and said, 'What a fond father this Doctor is! How he sacrifices himself for that scapegrace of a son! Think of the dear Doctor at his age, toiling cheerfully for that young man, who helped to ruin him!' And Firmin sighed; and passed a beautiful white handkerchief over his eyes with a beautiful white hand; and, I believe, really cried; and thought himself quite a good, affectionate, injured man. He held the plate at church; he looked very handsome and tall, and bowed with a charming melancholy grace to the ladies as they put in their contributions. The dear man! His plate was fuller than other people's—so a traveller told us who saw him in New York; and described a very choice dinner which the Doctor gave to a few friends, at one of the smartest hotels just then opened.

With all the Little Sister's good management Mr. and Mrs. Philip were only able to instal themselves in their new house at a considerable expense, and beyond that great Ringwood piano which swaggered in Philip's little drawing-room, I am constrained to say that there was scarce any furniture at all. One of the railway accounts was not paid as yet, and poor Philip could not feed upon mere paper promises to pay. Nor was he inclined to accept the offers of private friends, who were willing enough to be his bankers. 'One in a family is enough for that kind of business,' he said gloomily; and it came out that again and again the interesting exile at New York, who was deploring his son's extravagance and foolish marriage, had drawn bills upon Philip which our friend accepted and paid—bills, who knows to what amount? He has never told; and the engaging parent who robbed him—must I use a word so unpolite?—will never now tell to what extent he helped himself to Philip's small means. This I know, that when autumn came—when September was past—we in our cosy little retreat at the sea-side received a letter from the Little Sister, in her dear little bad spelling (about which there used to be somehow a pathos which the very finest writing does not possess); there came, I say, a letter from the Little Sister in which she told us, with many dashes, that dear Mrs. Philip and the children were pining and sick in London, and 'that Philip, he had too much pride and sperit to take money from any one; that Mr. Tregarvan was away travelling on the Continent, and that wretch—that monster, *you know who*—have drawn upon Philip again for money, and again he have paid, and the dear dear children can't have fresh air.'

'Did she tell you,' said Philip, brushing his hands across his eyes when a friend came to remonstrate with him: 'did she tell you that she brought me money herself, but we would not use it? Look! I have her little marriage gift yonder in my desk, and pray God I shall be able to leave it to my children. The fact is, the Doctor has drawn upon me, as usual; he is going to make a fortune next week. I have paid another bill of his. The parliamentary agents are out of town, at their moors in Scotland, I suppose. The air of Russell Square is uncommonly wholesome, and when the babies have had enough of that, why, they must change it for Brunswick Square. Talk about the country what country can be more quiet than Guilford Street in September? I stretch out of a morning, and breathe the mountain air on Ludgate Hill.' And with these dismal pleasantries and jokes our friend chose to put a good face upon bad fortune. The kinsmen of Ringwood offered hospitality kindly enough, but how was poor Philip to pay railway expenses for servants, babies, and wife? In this strait Tregarvan from abroad, having found out some monstrous design of Russ—of the Great Power of which he stood in daily terror, and which, as we are in strict amity with that Power, no other Power shall induce me to name —Tregarvan wrote to his editor, and communicated to him in confidence a most prodigious and nefarious plot against the liberties of all the rest of Europe, in which the Power in question was engaged, and in a postscript added, 'By the way, the Michaelmas quarter is due, and I send you a cheque,' etc. etc. O precious postscript!

'Didn't I tell you it would be so?' said my wife, with a self-satisfied air. 'Was I not certain that succour would come?'

And succour did come, sure enough; and a very happy little party went down to Brighton in a second-class carriage, and got an extraordinary cheap lodging, and the roses came back to the little pale cheeks, and mamma was wonderfully invigorated and refreshed, as all her friends could have seen when the little family came back to town, only there was such a thick dun fog that it was impossible to see complexions at all.

When the shooting season was come to an end, the parliamentary agents who had employed Philip came back to London; and, I am happy to say, gave him a cheque for his little account. My wife cried, 'Did I not tell you so?' more than ever. 'Is not everything for the best? I knew dear Philip would prosper! *

Everything was for the best, was it? Philip was sure to prosper, was he? What do you think of the next news which the poor fellow brought to us? One night in December he came to us, and I saw by his face that some event of importance had befallen him.

'I am almost heart-broken,' he said, thumping on the table when the young ones had retreated from it. 'I don't know what to do. I have not told you all. I have paid four bills for him already, and now he has—he has signed my name.'

'Who has?'

'He at New York. *You* know,' said poor Philip. 'I tell you he has put my name on a bill, and without my authority.'

'Gracious heavens! You mean your father has for—' I could not say the word.

'Yes,' groaned Philip. 'Here is a letter from him;' and he handed a letter across the table in the Doctor's well-known handwriting.

'Dearest Philip,' the father wrote, 'a sad misfortune has befallen me, which I had hoped to conceal, or, at any rate, to avert from my dear son. For you, Philip, are a participator in that misfortune through the imprudence—must I say it?—of your father. Would I had struck off the hand which has done the deed, ere it had been done! But the fault has taken wings and flown out of my reach. *Immeritus,* dear boy, you have to suffer for the *delicta majorum.* Ah, that a father should have to own his fault; to kneel and ask pardon of his son!

'I am engaged in many speculations. Some have succeeded beyond my wildest hopes: some have taken in the most rational, the most prudent, the least sanguine of our capitalists in Wall Street, and promising the greatest results have ended in the most extreme failure! To meet a call in an undertaking which seemed to offer the most certain prospects of success, which seemed to promise a fortune for me and my boy, and your dear children, I put in amongst other securities which I had to realise on a sudden, a bill, on which I used your name. I dated it as drawn six months back by me at New York, on you at Parchment Buildings, Temple; and I wrote your acceptance, as though the signature were yours. I give myself up to you. I tell you what I have done. Make the matter public. Give my confession to the world, as here I write, and sign it, and your father is branded for ever to the world as a- Spare me the word!

'As I live, as I hope for your forgiveness, long ere that bill became due—it is at five months' date, for £386, 4s. 3d. value received, and dated from the Temple, on the 4th of July—I passed it to one who promised to keep it until I myself should redeem it! The commission which he charged me was *enormous, rascally;* and not content with the immense interest which he extorted from me, the scoundrel has passed the bill away, and it is in Europe, in the hands of an enemy.

'You remember Tufton Hunt? Yes. You *most justly* chastised him. The wretch lately made his detested appearance in this city, associated with *the lowest of the base,* and endeavoured to resume his old practice of *threats, cajoleries,* and extortions! In *a fatal hour* the villain heard of the bill of which I have warned you. He purchased it from the gambler to whom it had been passed. As New York was speedily too hot to hold him *(for the unhappy man has even left me to pay his hotel score)* he has fled—and fled to Europe—taking with him that fatal bill, which he says he knows you will pay. Ah! dear Philip, if that bill were but once out of the wretch's hands, what sleepless hours of agony Bhould I be spared! I pray you, I implore you, make every sacrifice to meet it! You will not disown it? No. As you have children of your own—as you love them—you would not willingly let them leave a dishonoured   Father.

'I have a share in a *great medical discovery,* regarding which I have written to our friend, Mrs. Brandon, and which is sure to realise an immense profit, as introduced into England by a physician so well known—may I not say, professionally, *respected as myself?* The very first profits resulting from that discovery I promise, on my honour, to devote to you. They will very soon *far more* than repay the loss which my imprudence has brought on my dear boy. Farewell! Love to your wife and little ones.—   G. B. F.'

CHAPTER XXXVII. NEC PLENA CRUORIS HIRUDO

THE reading of this precious letter filled Philip's friend with an inward indignation which it was very hard to control or disguise. It is no pleasant task to tell a gentleman that his father is a rogue. Old Firmin would have been hanged a few years earlier, for practices like these. As you talk with a very great scoundrel, or with a madman, has not the respected reader sometimes reflected, with a grim self-humiliation, how the fellow is of our own kind; and *homo est*? Let us, dearly beloved, who are outside—I mean outside the hulks or the asylum—be thankful that we have to pay a barber for snipping our hair, and are entrusted with the choice of the cut of our own jerkins. As poor Philip read his father's letter, my thought was: 'And I can remember the soft white hand of that scoundrel, which has just been forging his own son's name, putting sovereigns into my own palm, when I was a schoolboy.' I always liked that man:—but the story is not *de me*—it regards Philip.

'You won't pay this bill?' Philip's friend indignantly said, then.

'What can I do?' says poor Phil, shaking a sad head.

'You are not worth five hundred pounds in the world,' remarks the friend.

'Who ever said I was? I am worth this bill, or my credit is,' answers the victim.

'If you pay this, he will draw more.'

'I dare say he will:' that Firmin admits.

'And he will continue to draw as long as there is a drop of blood to be had out of you.'

'Yes,' owns poor Philip, putting a finger to his lip. He thought I might be about to speak. His artless wife and mine were conversing at that moment upon the respective merits of some sweet chintzes which they had seen at Shoolbred's, in Tottenham Court Road, and which were so cheap and pleasant, and lively to look at! Really those drawing-room curtains would cost scarcely anything! Our Regulus, you see, before stepping into his torture-tub, was smiling on his friends, and talking upholstery with a cheerful smirking countenance. On chintz, or some other household errand, the ladies went prattling off: but there was no care, save for husband and children, in Charlotte's poor little innocent heart just then.

'Nice to hear her talking about sweet drawing-room chintzes, isn't it?' says Philip. 'Shall we try Shoolbred's or the other shop?' And then he laughs. It was not a very lively laugh.

'You mean that you are determined, then, on—'

'On acknowledging *my signature*? Of course,' says Philip, 'if ever it is presented to me, I would own it.' And having formed and announced this resolution, I knew my stubborn friend too well to think that he ever would shirk it.

The most exasperating part of the matter was, that however generously Philip's friends might be disposed towards him, they could not in this case give him a helping hand. The Doctor would draw more bills, and more. As sure as Philip supplied, the parent would ask; and that devouring dragon of a Doctor had stomach enough for the blood of all of us, were we inclined to give it. In fact, Philip saw as much, and owned everything with his usual candour. 'I see what is going on in your mind, old boy,' the poor fellow said, 'as well as if you spoke. You mean that I am helpless and irreclaimable, and doomed to hopeless ruin. So it would seem. A man can't escape his fate, friend, and my father has made mine for me. If I manage to struggle through the payment of this bill, of course he will draw another. My only chance of escape is, that he should succeed in some of his speculations. As he is always gambling, there may be some luck for him one day or another. He won't benefit me, then. That is not his way. If he makes a *coup,* he will keep the money, or spend it. He won't give me any. But he will not draw upon me as he does now, or send forth fancy imitations of the filial autograph. It is a blessing to have such a father, isn't it? I say, Pen, as I think from whom I am descended, and look at your spoons, I am astonished I have not put any of them in my pocket. You leave me in the room with 'em quite unprotected. I say, it is quite affecting the way in which you and your dear wife have confidence in me.' And with a bitter execration at his fate, the poor fellow pauses for a moment in his lament.

His father was his fate, he seemed to think, and there were no means of averting it. 'You remember that picture of Abraham and Isaac in the Doctor's Study in Old Parr Street?' he would say. 'My patriarch has tied me up, and had the knife in me repeatedly. He does not sacrifice me at one operation; but there will be a final one some day, and I shall bleed no more. It's gay and amusing, isn't it? Especially when one has a wife and children.' I, for my part, felt so indignant, that I was minded to advertise in the papers that all acceptances drawn in Philip's name were forgeries; and let his father take the consequences of his own act. But the consequences would have been life imprisonment for the old man, and almost as much disgrace and ruin for the young one, as were actually impending. He pointed out this clearly enough; nor could we altogether gainsay his dismal logic. It was better, at any rate, to meet this bill, and give the Doctor warning for the future. Well: perhaps it was; only suppose the Doctor should take the warning in good part, accept the rebuke with perfect meekness, and at an early opportunity commit another forgery? To this Philip replied that no man could resist his fate: that he had always expected his own doom through his father: that when the elder went to America he thought possibly the charm was broken; 'but you see it is not,' groaned Philip, 'and my father's emissaries reach me, and I am still under the spell.' The bearer of the *bowstring,* we know, was on his way, and would deliver his grim message ere long.

Having frequently succeeded in extorting money from Dr. Firmin, Mr. Tufton Hunt thought he could not do better than follow his banker across the Atlantic; and we need not describe the annoyance and rage of the Doctor on finding this black care still behind his back. He had not much to give; indeed the sum which he took away with him, and of which he robbed his son and his other creditors, was but small j but Hunt was bent upon having a portion of this; and, of course, hinted that, if the Doctor refused, he would carry to the New York press the particulars of Firmin's early career and latest defalcations. Mr. Hunt had been under the gallery of the House of Commons half-a-dozen times, and knew our public men by sight. In the course of a pretty long and disreputable career he had learned anecdotes regarding members of the aristocracy, turf-men, and the like; and he offered to sell this precious knowledge of his to more than one American paper, as other amiable exiles from our country have done. But Hunt was too old, and his stories too stale for the New York public. They dated from George IV., and the boxing and coaching times. He found but little market for his wares; and the tipsy parson reeled from tavern to bar, only the object of scorn to younger reprobates who despised his old-fashioned stories, and could top them with blackguardism of a much more modern date.

After some two years' sojourn in the United States, this worthy felt the passionate longing to revisit his native country which generous hearts often experience, and made his way from Liverpool to London; and when in London, directed his steps to the house of the Little Sister, of which he expected to find Philip still an inmate. Although Hunt had been once kicked out of the premises, he felt little shame now about re-entering them He had that in his pocket which would ensure him respectful behaviour from Philip. What were the circumstances under which that forged bill was obtained? Was it a speculation between Hunt and Philip's father? Did Hunt suggest that, to screen the elder Firmin from disgrace and ruin, Philip would assuredly take the bill up? That a forged signature was, in fact, a better document than a genuine acceptance? We shall never know the truth regarding this transaction now. We have but the statements of the two parties concerned; and as both of them, I grieve to say, are entirely unworthy of credit, we must remain in ignorance regarding this matter. Perhaps Hunt forged Philip's acceptance: perhaps his unhappy father wrote it: perhaps the Doctor's story that the paper was extorted from him was true, perhaps false. What matters? Both the men have passed away from amongst us, and will write and speak no more lies.

Caroline was absent from home, when Hunt paid his first visit after his return from America. Her servant described the man, and his appearance. Mrs. Brandon felt sure that Hunt was her visitor, and foreboded no good to Philip from the parson's arrival. In former days we have seen how the Little Sister had found favour in the eyes of this man. The besotted creature, shunned of men, stained with crime, drink, debt, had still no little vanity in his composition, and gave himself airs in the tavern parlours which he frequented. Because he had been at the University thirty years ago, his idea was that he was superior to ordinary men who had not had the benefit of an education at Oxford or Cambridge; and that the 'snobs,' as he called them, respected him. He would assume grandiose airs in talking to a tradesman ever so wealthy; speak to such a man by his surname; and deem that he honoured him by his patronage and conversation. The Little Sister's grammar, I have told you, was not good; her poor little *h's* were sadly irregular. A letter was a painful task to her. She knew how ill she performed it, and that she was for ever making blunders.

She would invent a thousand funny little pleas and excuses for her faults of writing. With all the blunders of spelling, her little letters had a pathos which somehow brought tears into the eyes. The Rev. Mr. Hunt believed himself to be this woman's superior. He thought his University education gave him a claim upon her respect, and draped himself and swaggered before her and others in his dingy college gown. He had paraded his Master of Arts degree in many thousand tavern parlours, where his Greek and learning had got him a kind of respect. He patronised landlords, and strutted by hostesses' bars with a vinous leer or a tipsy solemnity. He must have been very far gone and debased indeed when he could atill think that he was any living man's better:—he, who ought to have waited on the waiters, and blacked Boots's own shoes. When he had reached a certain stage of liquor he commonly began to brag about the University, and recite the titles of his friends of early days. Never was kicking more righteously administered than that which Philip once bestowed on this miscreant. The fellow took to the gutter as naturally as to his bed, Firmin used to say; and vowed that the washing there was a novelty which did him good.

Mrs. Brandon soon found that her surmises were correct regarding her nameless visitor. Next day, as she was watering some little flowers in her window, she looked from it into the street, where she saw the shambling parson leering up at her. When she saw him he took off his greasy hat, and made her a bow. At the moment she saw him, she felt that he was come upon some errand hostile to Philip. She knew he meant mischief as he looked up with that sodden face, those bloodshot eyes, those unshorn grinning lips.

She might have been inclined to faint, or disposed to scream, or to hide herself from the man, the sight of whom she loathed. She did not faint, or hide herself, or cry out: but she instantly nodded her head and smiled in the most engaging manner on that unwelcome dingy stranger. She went to her door; she opened it (though her heart beat so that you might have heard it, as she told her friend afterwards). She stood there a moment archly smiling at him, and she beckoned him into her house with a little gesture of welcome. 'Law bless us' (these, I have reason to believe, were her very words)—'Law bless us, Mr. Hunt, where ever have you been this ever so long?' And a smiling face looked at him resolutely from under a neat cap and fresh ribbon. Why, I know some women can smile and look at ease when they sit down in a dentist's chair.

'Law bless me, Mr. Hunt,' then says the artless creature, ' who ever would have thought of seeing *you,* I do declare!' And she makes a nice cheery little curtsey, and looks quite gay, pleased, and pretty; and so did Judith look gay, no doubt, and smile and prattle before Holofernes; and then of course she said, 'Won't you step in?' And then Hunt swaggered up the steps of the house, and entered the little parlour, into which the kind reader has often been conducted, with its neat little ornaments, its pictures, its glistening corner cupboard, and its well-scrubbed shining furniture.

'How is the Captain?' asks the man (alone in the company of this Little Sister, the fellow's own heart began to beat, and his bloodshot eyes to glisten).

He had not heard about poor pa? 'That shows how long you have been away!' Mrs. Brandon remarks, and mentions the date of her father's fatal illness. Yes: she was alone now, and had to care for herself; and straightway, I have no doubt, Mrs. Brandon asked Mr. Hunt whether he would 'take' anything. Indeed, that good little woman was for ever pressing her friends to 'take' something, and would have thought the laws of hospitality violated unless she had made this offer.

Hunt was never known to refuse a proposal of this sort. He *would* take a taste of something—of something warm. He had had fever and ague at New York, and the malady hung about him. Mrs. Brandon was straightway very much interested to hear about Mr. Hunt's complaint, and knew that a comfortable glass was very efficacious in removing threatening fever. Her nimble neat little hands mixed him a cup. He could not but see what a trim little housekeeper she was. 'Ah, Mrs. Brandon, if I had had such a kind friend watching over me, I should not be such a wreck as I am!' he sighed. He must have advanced to a second, nay, a third glass, when he sighed and became sentimental regarding his own unhappy condition; and Brandon owned to her friends afterwards that she made those glasses very strong.

Having 'taken something,' in considerable quantities, then, Hunt condescended to ask how his hostess was getting on, and how were her lodgers? How she was getting on? Brandon drew the most cheerful picture of herself and her circumstances. The apartments let well, and were never empty. Thanks to good Dr. Goodenough and other friends, she had as much professional occupation as she could desire. Since *you know who* has left the country, she said, her mind had been ever so much easier. As long as he was near, she never felt secure. But he was gone, and bad luck go with him! said this vindictive Little Sister. 'Was his son still lodging upstairs?' asked Mr. Hunt. On this, what does Mrs. Brandon do but begin a most angry attack upon Philip and his family. *He* lodge there? No, thank goodness! She had had enough of him and his wife, with her airs and graces, and the children crying all night, and the furniture spoiled, and the bills not even paid! 'I wanted him to think that me and Philip was friends no longer; and Heaven forgive me for telling stories! I know this fellow means no good to Philip; and before long I will know *what* he means, that I will,' she vowed.

For, on the very day when Mr. Hunt paid her a visit, Mrs. Brandon came to see Philip's friends, and acquaint them with Hunt's arrival. We could not be sure that he was the bearer of the forged bill with which poor Philip was threatened. As yet Hunt had made no allusion to it. But, though we are far from sanctioning deceit or hypocrisy, we own that we were not *very* angry with the Little Sister for employing dissimulation in the present instance, and inducing Hunt to believe that she was by no means an accomplice of Philip. If Philip's wife pardoned her, ought his friends to be less forgiving? To do right, you know you must not do wrong; though I own this was one of the cases in which I am inclined not to deal very hardly with the well-meaning little criminal.

Now, Charlotte had to pardon (and for this fault, if not for some others, Charlotte did most heartily pardon) our little friend, for this reason, that Brandon most wantonly maligned her. When Hunt asked what sort of wife Philip had married, Mrs. Brandon declared that Mrs. Philip was a pert odious little thing; that she gave herself airs, neglected her children, bullied her husband, and what not; and, finally, Brandon vowed that she disliked Charlotte, and was very glad to get her out of the house; and that Philip was not the same Philip since he married her, and that *he* gave himself airs, and was rude, and in all things led by his wife; and to get rid of them was a good riddance.

Hunt gracefully suggested that quarrels between landladies and tenants were not unusual; that lodgers sometimes did not pay their rent punctually; that others were unreasonably anxious about the consumption of their groceries, liquors, and so forth; and little Brandon, who, rather than steal a pennyworth from her Philip, would have cut her hand off, laughed at her guest's joke, and pretended to be amused with his knowing hints that she was a rogue. There was not a word he said but she received it with a gracious acquiescence: she might shudder inwardly at the leering familiarity of the odious tipsy wretch, but she gave no outward sign of disgust or fear. She allowed him to talk as much as he would, in hopes that he would come to a subject which deeply interested her. She asked about the Doctor, and what he was doing, and whether it was likely that he would ever be able to pay back any of that money which he had taken from his son? And she spoke with an indifferent tone, pretending to be very busy over some work at which she was stitching.

'Oh, you are still hankering after him,' says the chaplain, winking a bloodshot eye.

'Hankering after that old man! What should I care for him? As if he haven't done me harm enough already!' cries poor Caroline.

'Yes. But women don't dislike a man the worse for a little ill-usage,' suggests Hunt. No doubt the fellow had made his own experiments on woman's fidelity.

'Well, I suppose,' says Brandon, with a toss of her head, 'women may get tired as well as men, mayn't they? I found out that man, and wearied of him years and years ago. Another little drop out of the green bottle, Mr. Hunt! It's very good for ague-fever, and keeps the cold fit off wonderful!'

And Hunt drank, and he talked a little more—much more: and he gave his opinion of the elder Firmin, and spoke of his chances of success, and of his rage for speculations, and doubted whether he would ever be able to lift his head again—though he might, he might still. He was in the country where, if ever a man could retrieve himself, he had a chance. And Philip was giving himself airs, was he? He was always an arrogant chap, that Mr. Philip. And he had left her house? and was gone ever so long? and where did he live now?

Then I am sorry to say Mrs. Brandon asked, how should *she* know where Philip lived now? She believed it was near Gray's Inn, or Lincoln's Inn, or somewhere; and she was for turning the conversation away from this subject altogether; and sought to do so by many lively remarks and ingenious little artifices which I can imagine, but which she only in part acknowledged to me, for you must know that as soon as her visitor took leave—to turn into the 'Admiral Byng' public-house, and renew acquaintance with the worthies assembled in the parlour of that tavern— Mrs. Brandon ran away to a cab, drove in it to Philip's house in Milman Street, where only Mrs. Philip was at home, and after a *banale* conversation with her, which puzzled Charlotte not a little, for Brandon would not say on what errand she came, and never mentioned Hunt's arrival and visit to her, the Little Sister made her way to another cab, and presently made her appearance at the house of Philip's friends in Queen Square. And here she informed me how Hunt had arrived, and how she was sure he meant no good to Philip, and how she had told certain— certain stories which were not founded in fact—to Mr. Hunt; for the telling of which fibs I am not about to endeavour to excuse her.

Though the interesting clergyman had not said one word regarding that bill of which Philip's father had warned him, we believed that the document was in Hunt's possession, and that it would be produced in due season. We happened to know where Philip dined, and sent him word to come to us.

'What can he mean?' the people asked at the table—a bachelors' table at the Temple (for Philip's good wife actually encouraged him to go abroad from time to time, and make merry with his friends). 'What can this mean?' and they read out the scrap of paper which he had cast down as he was summoned away.

Philip's correspondent wrote:—

'DEAR PHILIP,—I believe the BEARER OF THE BOWSTRING has arrived; and has been with the L. S. this very day.'

The L. S.? the bearer of the bowstring? Not one of the bachelors dining in Parchment Buildings could read the riddle. Only after receiving the scrap of paper

Philip had jumped up and left the room: and a friend of ours, a sly wag and Don Juan of Pump Court, offered to take odds that there was a lady in the case.

At the hasty little council which was convened at our house on the receipt of the news, the Little Sister, whose instinct had not betrayed her, was made acquainted with the precise nature of the danger which menaced Philip; and exhibited a fine hearty wrath when she heard how he proposed to meet the enemy. He had a certain sum in hand. He would borrow more of his friends, who knew that he was an honest man. This bill he would meet, whatever might come; and avert at least this disgrace from his father.

What? Give in to those rogues? Leave his children to starve, and his poor wife to turn drudge and house-servant, who was not fit for anything but a fine lady? (There was no love lost, you see, between these two ladies, who both loved Mr. Philip.) It was a sin and a shame! Mrs. Brandon averred, and declared she thought Philip had been a man of more spirit. Philip's friend has before stated his own private sentiments regarding the calamity which menaced Firmin. To pay this bill was to bring a dozen more down upon him. Philip might as well resist now as at a later day. Such, in fact, was the opinion given by the reader's very humble servant at command.

My wife, on the other hand, took Philip's side. She was very much moved at his announcement that he would forgive his father this once at least, and endeavour to cover his sin.

'As you hope to be forgiven yourself, dear Philip, I am sure you are doing right,' Laura said; 'I am sure Charlotte will think so.'

'Oh, Charlotte, Charlotte!' interposes the Little Sister, rather peevishly; 'of course, Mrs. Philip thinks whatever her husband tells her!'

'In his own time of trial Philip has been met with wonderful succour and kindness,' Laura urged. 'See how one thing after another has contributed to help him! When he wanted, there were friends always at his need. If he wants again, I am sure my husband and I will share with him.' (I may have made a wry face at this; for with the best feelings towards a man, and that land of thing, you know it is not always convenient to be lending him five or six hundred pounds without security.) 'My dear husband and I will share with him,' goes on Mrs. Laura; 'won't we, Arthur? Yes, Brandon, that we will. Be sure, Charlotte and the children shall not want because Philip covers his father's wrong, and hides it from the world! God bless you, dear friend!' and what does this woman do next, and before her husband's face? Actually she goes up to Philip; she takes his hand—and—

Well, what took place before my own eyes, I do not choose to write down.

'She's encouraging him to ruin the children for the sake of that—that wicked old brute!' cries Mrs. Brandon. 'It's enough to provoke a saint, it is!' And she seizes up her bonnet from the table, and claps it on her head, and walks out of our room in a little tempest of wrath.

My wife, clasping her hands, whispers a few words, which say: 'Forgive us our trespasses, as we forgive them who trespass against us.'

'Yes,' says Philip, very much moved. 'It is the Divine order. You are right, dear Laura. I have had a weary time; and a terrible gloom of doubt and sadness over my mind whilst I have been debating this matter, and before I had determined to do as you would have me. But a great weight is off my heart since I have been enabled to see what my conduct should be. What hundreds of struggling men as well as myself have met with losses, and faced them! I will pay this bill, and I will warn the drawer to—to spare me for the future.'

Now that the Little Sister had gone away in her fit of indignation, you see I was left in a minority in the council of war, and the opposition was quite too strong for me. I began to be of the majority's opinion.

I dare say I am not the only gentleman who has been led round by a woman. We men of great strength of mind very frequently are. Yes: my wife convinced me with passages from her text-book, admitting of no contradiction according to her judgment, that Philip's duty was to forgive his father.

'And how lucky it was we did not buy the chintzes that day!' says Laura, with a laugh. 'Do you know there were two which were so pretty that Charlotte could not make up her mind which of the two she would take?'

Philip roared out one of his laughs, which made the windows shake. He was in great spirits. For a man who was going to ruin himself, he was in the most enviable good-humour. Did Charlotte know about this—this claim which was impending over him? No. It might make her anxious,—poor little thing! Philip had not told her. He had thought of concealing the matter from her. What need was there to disturb her rest, poor innocent child? You see, we all treated Mrs. Charlotte more or less like a child. Philip played with her. J. J., the painter, coaxed and dandled her, so to speak. The Little Sister loved her, but certainly with a love that was not respectful; and Charlotte took everybody's goodwill with a pleasant meekness and sweet smiling content. It was not for Laura to give advice to man and wife (as if the woman was not always giving lectures to Philip and his young wife!); but in the present instance she thought Mrs. Philip certainly ought to know what Philip's real situation was; what danger was menacing; 'and how admirable and right, and Christian—and you will have your reward for it, dear Philip!' interjects the enthusiastic lady—'your conduct has been!'

When we came, as we straightway did in a cab, to Charlotte's house, to expound the matter to her, goodness bless us! she was not shocked, or anxious, or frightened at all. Mrs. Brandon had just been with her, and told her of what was happening, and she had said, 'Of course, Philip ought to help his father; and Brandon had gone away quite in a tantrum of anger, and had really been quite rude; and she should not pardon her, only she knew how dearly the Little Sister loved Philip; and of course they must help Dr. Firmin; and what dreadful dreadful distress he must have been in to do as he did! But he had warned Philip, you know,' and so forth. ' And as for the chintzes, Laura, why I suppose we must go on with the old shabby covers. You know they will do very well till next year.' This was the way in which Mrs. Charlotte received the news which Philip had concealed from her, lest it should terrify her. As if a loving woman was ever very much frightened at being called upon to share her husband's misfortune!

As for the little case of forgery, I don't believe the young person could ever be got to see the heinous nature of Dr. Firmin's offence. The desperate little logician seemed rather to pity the father than the son in the business. 'How dreadfully pressed he must have been when he did it, poor man!' she said. 'To be sure, he ought not to have done it at all; but think of his necessity! That is what I said to Brandon. Now, there's little Philip's cake in the cupboard which you brought him. Now suppose papa was very hungry, and went and took some without asking Philly, he wouldn't be so very wrong, I think, would he? A child is glad enough to give for his father, isn't he? And when I said this to Brandon, she was so rude and violent, I really have no patience with her! And she forgets that I am a lady, and' etc., etc. So it appeared the Little Sister had made a desperate attempt to bring over Charlotte to her side, was still minded to rescue Philip in spite of himself, and had gone off in wrath at her defeat.

We looked to the Doctor's .letters, and ascertained the date of the bill. It had crossed the water and would be at Philip's door in a very few days. Had Hunt brought it? The rascal would have it presented through some regular channel, no doubt; and Philip and all of us totted up ways and means, and strove to make the Blender figures look as big as possible, as the thrifty housewife puts a patch here and a darn there, and cuts a little slice out of this old garment, so as to make the poor little frock serve for winter wear. We had so much at the banker's. A friend might help with a little advance. We would fairly ask a loan from the *Review*. We were in a scrape, but we would meet it. And so with resolute hearts, we would prepare to receive the Bearer of the Bowstring.

CHAPTER XXXVIII. THE BEARER OF THE BOWSTRING

THE poor Little Sister trudged away from Milman Street exasperated with Philip, with Philip's wife, and with the determination of the pair to accept the hopeless ruin impending over them. 'Three hundred and eighty-six pounds four and threepence,' she thought, 'to pay for that wicked old villain! It is more than poor Philip is worth, with all his savings and his little sticks of furniture. I know what he will do: he will borrow of the money-lenders, and give those bills, and renew them, and end by ruin. When he have paid this bill, that old villain will forge another, and that precious wife of his will tell him to pay that, I suppose; and those little darlings will be begging for bread, unless they come and eat mine, to which—God bless them!—they are always welcome.' She calculated—it was a sum not difficult to reckon—the amount of her own little store of saved ready money. To pay four hundred pounds out of such an income as Philip's, she felt, was an attempt vain and impossible. 'And he mustn't have my poor little stocking now,' she argued; 'they will want that presently when their pride is broken down, as it will be, and my darlings are hungering for their dinner!' Revolving this dismal matter in her mind, and scarce knowing where to go for comfort and counsel, she made her way to her good friend, Dr. Goodenough, and found that worthy man, who had always a welcome for his Little Sister.

She found Goodenough alone in his great dining-room, taking a very slender meal, after visiting his hospital and his fifty patients, among whom I think there were more poor than rich: and the good sleepy Doctor woke up with a vengeance, when he heard his little nurse's news, and fired off a volley of angry language against Philip and his scoundrel of a father; 'which it was a comfort to hear him,' little Brandon told us afterwards. Then Goodenough trotted out of the dining-room into the adjoining library and consulting-room, whither his old friend followed him. Then he pulled out a bunch of keys and opened a secretaire, from which he took a parchment-covered volume, on which *F. Goodenough, Esq., M.D.,* was written in a fine legible hand—and which, in fact, was a banker's book. The inspection of the MS. volume in question must have pleased the worthy physician; for a grin came over his venerable features, and he straightway drew out of the desk a slim volume of grey paper, on each page of which were inscribed the highly respectable names of Messrs. Stumpy and Rowdy and Co., of Lombard Street, Bankers. On a slip of grey paper the Doctor wrote a prescription for a draught, *statim sumendus*—(a *draught* —mark my pleasantry)—which he handed over to his little friend.

'There, you little fool!' said he. 'The father is a rascal, but the boy is a fine fellow; and you, you little silly thing, I must help in this business myself, or you will go and ruin yourself, I know you will! Offer this to the fellow for his bill. Or stay!

How much money is there in the house? Perhaps the sight of notes and gold will tempt him more than a cheque.' And the Doctor emptied his pockets of all the fees which happened to be therein—I don't know how many fees of shining shillings and sovereigns, neatly wrapped up in paper; and he emptied a drawer in which there was more silver and gold: and he trotted up to his bedroom, and came panting, presently, downstairs with a fat little pocket-book containing a bundle of notes, and with one thing or another, he made up a sum of—I won't mention what; but this sum of money, I say, he thrust into the little Sister's hand, and said, 'Try the fellow with this, Little Sister, and see if you can get the bill from him. Don't say it's my money, or the scoundrel will be for having twenty shillings in the pound. Say it's yours, and there's no more where that came from; and coax him, and wheedle him, and tell him plenty of lies, my dear. It won't break your heart to do that. What an immortal scoundrel Brummell Firmin is, to be sure! Though, by the way, in two more cases at the hospital I have tried that—' And here the Doctor went off into a professional conversation with his favourite nurse, which I could not presume to repeat to any nonmedical men.

The Little Sister bade God bless Doctor Goodenough, and wiped her glistening eyes with her handkerchief, and put away the notes and gold with a trembling little hand, and trudged off with a lightsome step and a happy heart. Arrived at Tottenham Court Road, she thought, shall I go home, or shall I go to poor Mrs. Philip and take her this money? No. Their talk that day had not been very pleasant: words, very like high words, had passed between them, and our Little Sister had to own to herself that she had been rather rude in her late colloquy with Charlotte. And she was a proud Little Sister: at least she did not care for to own that she had been hasty or disrespectful in her conduct to *that* young woman. She had too much spirit for that. Have we ever said that our little friend was exempt from the prejudices and vanities of this wicked world? Well, to rescue Philip, to secure the fatal bill, to go with it to Charlotte, and say, 'There, Mrs. Philip, there's your husband's liberty.' It would be a rare triumph, that it would! And Philip would promise, on his honour, that this should be the last and only bill he should pay for that wretched old father. With these happy thoughts swelling in her little heart, Mrs. Brandon made her way to the familiar house in Thornhaugh Street, and would have a little bit of supper, so she would. And laid her own little cloth; and set forth her little forks and spoons, which were as bright as rubbing could make them; and I am authorised to state that her repast consisted of two nice little lamb chops, which she purchased from her neighbour, Mr. Chump, in Tottenham Court Road, after a pleasant little conversation with that gentleman and his good lady. And, with her bit of supper, after a day's work, our little friend would sometimes indulge in a glass—a little glass—of something comfortable. The case-bottle was in the cupboard, out of which her poor pa had been wont to mix his tumblers for many a long day. So, having prepared it with her own hands, down she sat to her little meal, tired and happy; and as she thought of the occurrences of the day, and of the rescue which had come so opportunely to her beloved Philip and his children, I am sure she said a grace before her meat.

Her candles being lighted and her blind up, any one in the street could see that her chamber was occupied; and at about ten o'clock at night there came a heavy step clinking along the pavement, the sound of which, I have no doubt, made the Little Sister start a little. The heavy foot paused before her window, and presently clattered up the steps of her door. Then, as her bell rang—I consider it is most probable that her cheek flushed a little—she went to her hall-door and opened it herself. 'Lor', is it you, Mr. Hunt? Well, I never! that is, I thought you might come. Really, now'—and with the moonlight behind him, the dingy Hunt swaggered in.

'How comfortable you looked at your little table!' says Hunt, with his hat over his eye.

'Won't you step in and sit down to it, and take something?' asks the smiling hostess.

Of course, Hunt would take something. And the greasy hat is taken off his head with a flourish, and he struts into the poor Little Sister's little room, pulling a wisp of grizzling hair, and endeavouring to assume a careless fashionable look. The dingy hand had seized the case-bottle in a moment. 'What! you do a little in this way, do you?' he says, and winks amiably at Mrs. Brandon and the bottle. She takes ever so little, she owns; and reminds him of days which he must remember, when she had a wine-glass out of poor pa's tumbler. A bright little kettle is singing on the fire,—will not Mr. Hunt mix a glass for himself? She takes a bright beaker from the corner cupboard, which is near her, with her keys hanging from it.

'Oh—ho! that's where we keep the ginnums, is it?' says the graceful Hunt, with a laugh.

'My papa always kept it there,' says Caroline meekly. And whilst her back is turned to fetch a canister from the cupboard, she knows that the astute Mr. Hunt has taken the opportunity to fill a good large measure from the square bottle. 'Make yourself welcome,' says the Little Sister, in her gay artless way; ' there's more where that came from!' And Hunt drinks his hostess's health; and she bows to him, and smiles, and sips a little from her own glass; and the little lady looks quite pretty, and rosy, and bright. Her cheeks are like apples, her figure is trim and graceful, and always attired in the neatest-fitting gown. By the comfortable light of the candles on her sparkling tables, you scarce see the silver lines in her light hair, or the marks which time has made round her eyes. Hunt gazes on her with admiration.

'Why,' says he, 'I vow you look younger and prettier than when— when I saw you first.'

'Ah, Mr. Hunt!' cries Mrs. Brandon, with a flush on her cheek which becomes it, 'don't recall that time, or that—that wretch who served me so cruel!'

'He was a scoundrel, Caroline, to treat as he did such a woman as you! The fellow has no principle; he was a bad one from the beginning. Why, he ruined me as well as you: got me to play; run me into debt by introducing me to his fine companions. I was a simple young fellow then, and thought it was a fine thing to live with fellow-commoners and noblemen who drove their tandems and gave their grand dinners. It was he that led me astray, I tell you. I might have been Fellow of my college—had a living—married a good wife—risen to be a bishop, by George!— for I had great talents, Caroline; only I was so confounded idle, and fond of the cards and the bones.'

'The bones?' cries Caroline, with a bewildered look.

'The dice, my dear! "Seven's the main" was my ruin. "Seven's the main," and eleven's the nick to seven. That used to be the little game!' And he made a graceful gesture with his empty wine-glass, as though he were tossing a pair of dice on the table. 'The man next to me in lecture is a bishop now, and I could knock his head off in Greek iambics and Latin hexameters too. In my second year I got the Latin declamation prize, I tell you—'

'Brandon always said you were one of the cleverest men at the college. He always said *that,* I remember,' remarks the lady, very respectfully.

'Did he? He *did* say a good word for me then? Brummell Firmin wasn't a clever man; he wasn't a reading man. Whereas I would back myself for a Sapphic ode against any man in my college—against any man! Thank you. You *do* mix it so uncommon hot and well, there's no saying no; indeed, there ain't! Though I have had enough—upon my honour, I have.'

'Lor'! I thought you men could drink anything! And Mr. Brandon—Mr. Firmin you said—?'

'Well, I said Brummell Firmin was a swell somehow. He had a sort of grand manner with him—'

'Yes, he had,' sighed Caroline, And I dare say her thoughts wandered back to a time long long ago, when this grand gentleman had captivated her.

'And it was trying to keep up with him that ruined me! I quarrelled with my poor old governor about money, of course; grew idle, and lost my fellowship. Then the bills came down upon me. I tell you, there are some of my college ticks ain't paid now.'

'College lacks? Law!' ejaculates the lady. 'And—'

'Tailors' ticks, tavern ticks, livery-stable ticks—for there were famous hacks in our days, and I used to hunt with the tip-top men. I wasn't bad across country, I wasn't. But we can't keep the pace with those rich fellows. We try, and they go ahead— they ride us down. Do you think, if I hadn't been very hard up, I would have done what I did to you, Caroline? You poor little innocent suffering thing. It was a shame. It was a shame!'

'Yes, a shame it was,' cries Caroline. 'And that I never gainsay. You did deal hard with a poor girl, both of you.'

'It was rascally. But Firmin was the worst. He had me in his power. It was he led me wrong. It was he drove me into debt, and then abroad, and then into qu—into gaol, perhaps: and then into this kind of thing.' ('This kind of thing' has before been explained elegantly to signify a tumbler of hot grog.) 'And my father wouldn't Bee me on his death-bed; and my brothers and sisters broke with me; and I owe it all to Brummell Firmin—all. Do you think, after ruining me, he oughtn't to pay me?' and again he thumps a dusky hand upon the table. It made dingy marks on the poor Little Sister's spotless tablecloth. It rubbed its owner's forehead, and lank grizzling hair.

'And me, Mr. Hunt? What do he owe me?' asks Hunt's hostess.

'Caroline!' cries Hunt, 'I have made Brummell Firmin pay me a good bit back already, but I'll have more;' and he thumped his breast, and thrust his hand into his breast-pocket as he spoke, and clutched at something within.

'It is there!' thought Caroline. She might turn pale; but he did not remark her pallor. He was all intent on drink, on vanity, on revenge.

'I have him, I say. He owes me a good bit; and he has paid me a good bit; and he shall pay me a good bit more. Do you think I am a fellow who will be ruined and insulted, and won't revenge myself? You should have seen his face when I turned up at New York at the Astor House, and said, "Brummell, old fellow, here I am," I said: and he turned as white—as white as this tablecloth. "*I'll* never leave you, my boy," I said. "Other fellows may go from you, but old Tom Hunt will stick to you. Let's go into the bar and have a drink!" and he was obliged to come. And I have him now in my power, I tell you. And when I say to him, "Brummell, have a drink," drink he must. His bald old head must go into the pail!' And Mr. Hunt laughed a laugh which I dare say was not agreeable.

After a pause he went on: 'Caroline! Do you hate him, I say? or do you like a fellow who deserted you and treated you like a scoundrel? Some women do. I could tell of women who do. I could tell you of other fellows, perhaps, but I won't. Do you hate Brummell Firmin, that bald-headed Brum—hypocrite, and that—that insolent rascal who laid his hand on a clergyman, and an old man, by George, and hit me— and hit me in that street? Do you hate him, I say? Hoo! hoo! hick! I've got 'em both!—here, in my pocket—both!'

'You have got—what?' gasped Caroline.

'I have got their—hallo! stop, what's that to you what I've got?' And he sinks back in his chair, and winks, and leers, and triumphantly tosses, his glass.

'Well, it ain't much to me; I—I never got any good out of either of 'em yet,' says poor Caroline, with a sinking heart. 'Let's talk about somebody else than them two plagues. Because you were a little merry one night—and I don't mind what a gentleman says when he has had a glass—for a great big strong man to hit an old one—'

'To strike a clergyman!' yells Hunt.

'It was a shame—a cowardly shame! And I gave it him for it, I promise you!' cries Mrs. Brandon.

'On your honour, now, do you hate 'em?' cries Hunt, starting up, and clenching his fist, and dropping again into his chair.

'Have I any reason to love 'em, Mr. Hunt? Do sit down and have a little—'

'No: you have no reason to like 'em. You hate 'em—I hate 'em. Look here. Promise —'pon your honour, now, Caroline—I've got 'em both, I tell you. Strike a clergyman, will he? What do you say to that?'

And starting from his chair once more, and supporting himself against the wall (where hung one of J. J.'s pictures of Philip), Hunt pulls out the greasy pocket-book once more, and fumbles amongst the greasy contents: and as the papers flutter on to the floor and the table, he pounces down on one with a dingy hand, and yells a laugh, and says, 'I've cotched you! That's it. What do you say to that?—"London, July 4th.—Five months after date, I promise to pay to—" No, you don't.'

'La! Mr. Hunt, won't you let me look at it?' cries the hostess. 'Whatever is it? A bill? My pa had plenty of 'em.'

'What? with candles in the room? No, you don't, I say.'

'What is it! Won't you tell me?'

'It's the young one's acceptance of the old man's draft,' says Hunt, hissing and laughing.

'For how much?'

'Three hundred and eighty-six four three—that's all; and I guess I can get more where that came from?' says Hunt, laughing more and more cheerfully.

'What will you take for it? I'll buy it of you,'cries the Little Sister. 'I—I've seen plenty of my pa's bills; and I'll—I'll discount this, if you like.'

'What! are you a little discounter? Is that the way you make your money, and the silver spoons, and the nice supper, and everything delightful about you? A little discountess, are you—you little rogue? Little discountess, by George! How much will you give, little discountess?' And the reverend gentleman laughs and winks, and drinks and laughs, and tears twinkle out of his tipsy old eyes, as he wipes them with one hand, and again says, 'How much will you give, little discountess?'

When poor Caroline went to her cupboard, and from it took the notes and the gold which she had had we know from whom, and added to these out of a cunning box a little heap of her own private savings, and with trembling hands poured the notes, and the sovereigns, and the shillings into a dish on the table, I never heard accurately how much she laid down. But she must have spread out everything she had in the world; for she felt her pockets and emptied them; and, tapping her head, she again applied to the cupboard, and took from thence a little store of spoons and forks, and then a brooch, and then a watch; and she piled these all up in a dish, and she said, 'Now, Mr. Hunt, I will give you all these for that bill.' And she looked up at Philip's picture, which hung over the parson's bloodshot satyr face. 'Take these,' she said, 'and give me that! There's two hundred pound, I know; and there's thirty-four, and two eighteen, thirty-six eighteen, and there's the plate and watch, and I want that bill.'

'What! have you got all this, you little dear?' cried Hunt, dropping back into his chair again. 'Why, you're a little fortune, by Jove—a pretty little fortune, a little discountess, a little wife, a little fortune. I say, I'm a University man; I could write alcaics once, as well as any man. I'm a gentleman. I say, how much *have* you got? Count it over again, my dear.'

And again she told him the amount of the gold, and the notes, and the silver, and the number of the poor little spoons.

A thought came across the fellow's boozy brain: 'If you offer so much,' says he, 'and you're a little discountess, the bill's worth more; that fellow must be making his fortune! Or do you know about it? I say, do you know about it? No. I'll have my bond. I'll have my bond!' And he gave a tipsy imitation of Shylock, and lurched back into his chair, and laughed.

'Let's have a little more, and talk about things,' said the poor Little Sister; and she daintily heaped her little treasures and arranged them in her dish, and smiled upon the parson laughing in his chair.,

'Caroline,' says he, after a pause, 'you are still fond of that old bald-headed scoundrel! That's it! Just like you women—just like, but I won't tell. No, no, I won't tell! You are fond of that old swindler still, I say! Wherever did you get that lot of money? Look here now—with that and this little bill in my pocket, there's enough to carry us on for ever so long. And when this money's gone, I tell you I know who'll give us more, and who can't refuse us, I tell you. Look here, Caroline, dear Caroline! I'm an old fellow, I know; but I'm a good fellow: I'm a classical scholar: and I'm a gentleman.'

The classical scholar and gentleman bleared over his words as he uttered them, and with his vinous eyes and sordid face gave a leer, which must have frightened the poor little lady to whom he proffered himself as a suitor, for she started back with a pallid face, and an aspect of such dislike and terror, that even her guest remarked it.

'I said I was a scholar and gentleman,' he shrieked again. 'Do you doubt it? I am as good a man as Brummell Firmin, I say. I ain't so tall. But I'll do a copy of Latin alcaics or Greek iambics against him or any man of my weight. Do you mean to insult me? Don't I know who you are? Are you better than a Master of Arts and a clergyman? He went out in medicine, Firmin did. Do you mean when a Master of Arts and classical scholar offers you his hand and fortune, that you 're above him and refuse him, by George?'

The Little Sister was growing bewildered and frightened by the man's energy and horrid looks. 'Oh, Mr. Hunt!' she cried, 'see here, take this! See—there are two hundred and thirty—thirty-six pounds and all these things! Take them, and give me that paper.'

'Sovereigns, and notes, and spoons, and a watch, and what I have in my pocket—and that ain't much—and Firmin's bill! Three hundred and eighty-six four three. It's a fortune, my dear, with economy! I won't have you going on being a nurse and that kind of thing. I'm a scholar and a gentleman—I am—and that place ain't fit for Mrs. Hunt. We'll first spend your money. No: we'll first spend my money-three hundred and eighty-six and—and hang the change—and when that's gone, we'll have another bill from that bald-headed old scoundrel: and his son who struck a poor cler— We *will*, I say, Caroline—we—'

The wretch was suiting actions to his words, and rose once more, advancing towards his hostess, who shrank back, laughing half-hysterically, and retreating as the other neared her. Behind her was that cupboard which had contained her poor little treasure and other stores, and appended to the lock of which her keys were still hanging. As the brute approached her, she flung back the cupboard-door smartly upon him. The keys struck him on the head; and bleeding, and with a curse and a cry, he fell back on his chair.

In the cupboard was that bottle which she had received from America not long since; and about which she had talked with Good-enough on that very day. It had been used twice or thrice by his direction, by hospital surgeons, and under her eye. She suddenly seized this bottle. As the ruffian before her uttered his imprecations of wrath, she poured out a quantity of the contents of the bottle on her handkerchief. She said, 'Oh! Mr. Hunt, have I hurt you? I didn't mean it. But you shouldn't—you shouldn't frighten a lonely woman so! Here, let me bathe you! Smell this! It will—it will do you—good—it will—it will, indeed.' The handkerchief was over his face. Bewildered by drink before, the fumes of the liquor which he was absorbing served almost instantly to overcome him. He struggled for a moment or two. 'Stop—stop! you'll be better in a moment,' she whispered. 'Oh, yes! better, quite better!' She squeezed more of the liquor from the bottle on to the handkerchief. In a minute Hunt was quite inanimate.

Then the little pale woman leant over him, and took the pocket-book out of his pocket, and from it the bill which bore Philip's name. As Hunt lay in stupor before her, she now squeezed more of the liquor over his head; and then thrust the bill into the fire, and saw it burn to ashes. Then she put back the pocket-book into Hunt's breast. She said afterwards that she never should have thought about that Chloroform, but for her brief conversation with Dr. Goodenough that evening, regarding a case in which she had employed the new remedy under his orders.

How long did Hunt lie in that stupor? It seemed a whole long night to Caroline. She said afterwards that the thought of that act that night made her hair grow grey. Poor little head! Indeed, she would have laid it down for Philip.

Hunt, I suppose, came to himself when the handkerchief was withdrawn, and the fumes of the potent liquor ceased to work on his brain. He was very much frightened and bewildered. 'What was it? Where am I?' he asked, in a husky voice.

'It was the keys struck you in the cupboard-door when you—you ran against it,' said pale Caroline. 'Look! you are all bleeding on the head. Let me dry it.'

'No; keep off!' cried the terrified man.

'Will you have a cab to go home? The poor gentleman hit himself against the cupboard-door, Mary. You remember him here before, don't you, one night?' And Caroline, with a shrug, pointed out to her maid, whom she had summoned, the great square bottle of spirits still on the table, and indicated that there lay the cause of Hunt's bewilderment.

'Are you better now? Will you—will you—take a little more refreshment?' asked Caroline.

'No!' he cried with an oath, and with glaring bloodshot eyes he lurched towards his hat.

'Lor', mum! whatever is it? And this smell in the room, and all this here heap of money and things on the table?'

Caroline flung open her window. 'It's medicine, which Dr. Goodenough has ordered for one of his patients. I must go and see her to-night,' she said. And at midnight, looking as pale as death, the Little Sister went to the Doctor's house, and roused him from his bed, and told him the story here narrated. 'I offered him all you gave me,' she said, ' and all I had in the world besides, and he wouldn't— and—' Here she broke out into a fit of hysterics. The doctor had to ring up his servants; to administer remedies to his little nurse; to put her to bed in his own house.

'By the immortal Jove,' he said afterwards, 'I had a great mind to beg her never to leave it! But that my housekeeper would tear Caroline's eyes out, Mrs. Brandon should be welcome to stay for ever. Except her *h*'s, that woman has every virtue: constancy, gentleness, generosity, cheerfulness, and the courage of a lioness! To think of that fool, that dandified idiot, that triple ass, Firmin'—(there were few men in the world for whom Goodenough entertained a greater scorn than for his late *confrère,* Firmin of Old Parr Street)—'think of the villain having possessed such a treasure—let alone his having deceived and deserted her—of his having possessed such a treasure, and flung it away! Sir, I always admired Mrs. Brandon; but I think ten thousand times more highly of her, since her glorious crime, and most righteous robbery. If the villain had died, dropped dead in the street—the drunken miscreant, forger, housebreaker, assassin—so that no punishment could have fallen upon poor Brandon, I think I should have respected her only the more!'

At an early hour Dr. Goodenough had thought proper to send off messengers to Philip and myself, and to make us acquainted with the strange adventure of the previous night. We both hastened to him. I myself was summoned, no doubt, in consequence of my profound legal knowledge, which might be of use in poor little Caroline's present trouble. And Philip came because she longed to see him. By some instinct she knew when he arrived. She crept down from the chamber where the Doctor's housekeeper had laid her on a bed. She knocked at the Doctor's study, where we were all in consultation. She came in quite pale, and tottered towards Philip, and flung herself into his arms, with a burst of tears that greatly relieved her excitement and fever. Firmin was scarcely less moved.

'You'll pardon me for what I have done, Philip?' she sobbed. 'If they—if they take me up, you won't forsake me?'

'Forsake you? Pardon you? Come and live with us, and never leave us!' cried Philip.

'I don't think Mrs. Philip would like that, dear,' said the little woman sobbing on his arm: 'but ever since the Greyfriars school, when you was so ill, you have been like a son to me, and somehow I couldn't help doing that last night to that villain—I couldn't.'

'Serve the scoundrel right. Never deserved to come to life again, my dear,' said Dr. Goodenough. 'Don't you be exciting yourself, little Brandon! I must have you sent back to lie down on your bed. Take her up, Philip, to the little room next mine; and order her to lie down and be as quiet as a mouse. You are not to move till I give you leave, Brandon—mind that; and come back to us, Firmin, or we shall have the patients coming.'

So Philip led away this poor Little Sister; and trembling, and clinging to his arm, she returned to the room assigned to her.

'She wants to be alone with him,' the Doctor said; and he spoke a brief word or two of that strange delusion under which the little woman laboured, that this was her dead child come back to her.

'I know that is in her mind,' Goodenough said; 'she never got over that brain fever in which I found her. If I were to swear her on the book, and say, "Brandon, don't you believe he is your son alive again?" she would not dare to say no. She will leave him everything she has got. I only gave her so much less than that scoundrel's bill yesterday, because I knew she would like to contribute her own share. It would have offended her mortally to have been left out of the subscription. They like to sacrifice themselves. Why, there are women in India who, if not allowed to roast with their dead husbands, would die of vexation.' And by this time Mr. Philip came striding back into the room again, rubbing a pair of very red eyes.

'Long ere this, no doubt, that drunken ruffian is sobered, and knows that the bill is gone. He is likely enough to accuse her of the robbery,' says the Doctor.

'Suppose,' says Philip's other friend, 'I had put a pistol to your head, and was going to shoot you, and the Doctor took the pistol out of my hand, and flung it into the sea, would you help me to prosecute the Doctor for robbing me of the pistol?'

'You don't suppose it will be a pleasure to me to pay that bill?' said Philip. 'I said, if a certain bill were presented to me, purporting to be accepted by Philip Firmin, I would pay it. But if that scoundrel, Hunt, only *says* that he had such a bill, and has lost it; I will cheerfully take my oath that I have never signed any bill at all—and they can't find Brandon guilty of stealing a thing which never existed.'

'Let us hope, then, that the bill was not in duplicate!'

And to this wish all three gentlemen heartily said Amen!

And now the Doctor's door-bell began to be agitated by arriving patients. His dining-room was already full of them The Little Sister must lie still, and the discussion of her affairs must be deferred to a more convenient hour; and Philip and his friend agreed to reconnoitre the house in Thornhaugh Street, and see if anything had happened since its mistress had left it.

Yes: something had happened. Mrs. Brandon's maid, who ushered us into her mistress's little room, told us that in the early morning that horrible man who had come over night, and been so tipsy, and behaved so ill,—the very same man who had come there tipsy afore once, and whom Mr. Philip had flung into the street— had come battering at the knocker, and pulling at the bell, and swearing and cursing most dreadful, and calling for 'Mrs. Brandon! Mrs. Brandon! Mrs. Brandon!' and frightening the whole street. After he had rung, he knocked and battered ever so long. Mary looked out at him from her upper window, and told him to go along home, or she would call the police. On this the man roared out that he would call the police himself if Mary did not let him in; and as he went on calling 'Police!' and yelling from the door, Mary came downstairs, and opened the hall-door, keeping the chain fastened, and asked him what he wanted.

Hunt, from the steps without, began to swear and rage more loudly, and to demand to be let in. He must and would see Mrs. Brandon.

Mary, from behind her chain barricade, said that her mistress was not at home, but that she had been called out that night to a patient of Dr. Goodenough's.

Hunt, with more shrieks and curses, said it was a lie: and that she was at home; and that he would see her; and that he must go into her room; and that he had left something there; that he had lost something; and that he would have it.

'Lost something here?' cried Mary. 'Why here? when you reeled out of this house, you couldn't scarce walk, and you almost fell into the gutter, which I have seen you there before. Get away, and go home! You are not sober yet, you horrible man!'

On this, clinging on to the area-railings, and demeaning himself like a madman, Hunt continued to call out, ' Police, police! I have been robbed, I've been robbed! Police!' until astonished heads appeared at various windows in the quiet street, and a policeman actually came up.

When the policeman appeared, Hunt began to sway and pull at the door, confined by its chain: and he frantically reiterated his charge, that he had been robbed and hocussed in that house, that night, by Mrs. Brandon.

The policeman, by a familiar expression, conveyed his utter disbelief of the statement, and told the dirty disreputable man to move on, and go to bed. Mrs. Brandon was known and respected all round the neighbourhood. She had befriended numerous poor round about; and was known for a hundred charities. She attended many respectable families. In that parish there was no woman more esteemed. And by the word 'Gammon,' the policeman expressed his sense of the utter absurdity of the charge against the good lady.

Hunt still continued to yell out that he had been robbed and hocussed; and Mary from behind her door repeated to the officer (with whom she perhaps had relations not unfriendly) her statement that the beast had gone reeling away from the house the night before, and if he had lost anything, who knows where he might not have lost it?

'It was taken out of this pocket, and out of this pocket-book;' howled Hunt, clinging to the rail. 'I give her in charge. I give the house in charge! It's a den of thieves!'

During this shouting and turmoil, the sash of a window in Ridley's studio was thrown up. The painter was going to his morning work. He had appointed an early model. The sun could not rise too soon for Ridley; and, as soon as ever it gave its light, found him happy at his labour. He had heard from his bedroom the brawl going on about the door.

'Mr. Ridley!' says the policeman, touching the glazed hat with much respect—(in fact, and out of uniform, Z 25 has figured in more than one of J. J.'s pictures) —'Here's a fellow disturbing the whole street, and shouting out that Mrs. Brandon have robbed and hocussed him!'

Ridley ran downstairs in a high state of indignation. He is nervous, like men of his tribe: quick to feel, to pity, to love, to be angry. He undid the chain, and ran into the street.

'I remember that fellow drunk here before.' said the painter; 'and lying in that very gutter.'

'Drunk and disorderly! Come along!' cries Z 25; and his hand was quickly fastened on the parson's greasy collar, and under its strong grasp Hunt is forced to move on. He goes, still yelling out that he has been robbed.

'Tell that to his worship,' says the incredulous Z. And this was the news which Mrs. Brandon's friends received from her maid, when they called at her house.

CHAPTER XXXIX. IN WHICH SEVERAL PEOPLE HAVE THEIR TRIALS

IF Philip and his friend had happened to pass through High Street, Marylebone, on their way to Thornhaugh Street to reconnoitre the Little Sister's house, they would have seen the Reverend Mr. Hunt, in a very dirty, battered, crestfallen, and unsatisfactory state, marching to Marylebone from the station, where the reverend gentleman had passed the night, and under the custody of the police. A convoy of street-boys followed the prisoner and his guard, making sarcastic remarks on both. Hunt's appearance was not improved since we had the pleasure of meeting him on the previous evening. With a grizzled beard and hair, a dingy face, a dingy shirt, and a countenance mottled with dirt and drink, we may fancy the Reverend man passing in tattered raiment through the street to make his appearance before the magistrate.

You have no doubt forgotten the narrative which appeared in the morning papers two days after the Thornhaugh Street incident; but my clerk has been at the pains to hunt up and copy the police report, in which events connected with our history are briefly recorded.

'Marylebone, *Wednesday.*—Thomas Tufton Hunt, professing to be a clergyman, but wearing an appearance of extreme squalor, was brought before Mr. Beaksby at this office, charged by Z 25 with being drunk and very disorderly on Tuesday se'nnight, and endeavouring by force and threats to effect his re-entrance into a house in Thornhaugh Street, from which he had been previously ejected in a most unclerical and inebriated state.

'On being taken to the station-house, the reverend gentleman lodged a complaint on his own side, and averred that' he had been stupefied and hocussed in the house in Thornhaugh Street by means of some drug, and that, whilst in this state, he had been robbed of a bill for £386, 4s. 3d., drawn by a person in New York, and accepted by Mr. P. Firmin, barrister, of Parchment Buildings, Temple.

'Mrs. Brandon, the landlady of the house, No. — Thornhaugh Street, has been in the habit of letting lodgings for many years past, and several of her friends, including Mr. Firmin, Mr. Ridley, the Royal Academician, and other gentlemen, were in attendance to speak to her character, which is most respectable. After Z 25 had given evidence, the servant deposed that Hunt had been more than once disorderly and drunk before in that house, and had been forcibly ejected from it. On the night when the alleged robbery was said to have taken place, he had visited the house in Thornhaugh Street, had left it in an inebriated state, and returned some hours afterwards, vowing that he had been robbed of the document in question.

'Mr. P. Firmin said: "I am a barrister, and have chambers at Parchment Buildings, Temple, and know the person calling himself Hunt. I have not accepted any bill of exchange, nor is my signature affixed to any such document."

'At this stage the worthy magistrate interposed, and said that this only went to prove that the bill was not completed by Mr. F.'s acceptance, and would by no means conclude the case set up before him.. Dealing with it, however, on the merits, and looking at the way in which the charge had been preferred, and the entire absence of sufficient testimony to warrant him in deciding that even a piece of paper had been abstracted in that house, or by the person accused, and believing that if he were to commit, a conviction would be impossible, he dismissed the charge.

'The lady left the court with her friends, and the accuser, when called upon to pay a fine for drunkenness, broke out into very unclerical language, in the midst of which he was forcibly removed.'

Philip Firmin's statement, that he had given no bill of exchange, was made not without hesitation on his part, and indeed at his friends' strong entreaty. It was addressed not so much to the sitting magistrate, as to that elderly individual at New York, who was warned no more to forge his son's name. I fear a coolness ensued between Philip and his parent in consequence of the younger man's behaviour. The Doctor had thought better of his boy than to suppose that, at a *moment of necessity,* Philip would desert him. He forgave Philip, nevertheless. Perhaps since his marriage *other influences* were at work upon him, etc. The parent made further remarks in this strain. A man who takes your money is naturally offended if you remonstrate; you wound his sense of delicacy by protesting against his putting his hand in your pocket. The elegant Doctor in New York continued to speak of his unhappy son with a mournful shake of the head; he said, perhaps believed, that Philip's imprudence was in part the cause of his own exile. 'This is not the kind of entertainment to which I would have invited you at my own house in England,' he would say. 'I thought to have ended my days there, and to have left my son in comfort—nay, splendour. I am an exile in poverty: and he—but I will use no hard words.' And to his female patients he would say: 'No! my dear madam!—not a syllable of reproach shall escape these lips regarding that misguided boy! But you can feel for me; I know you can feel for me.' In the old days, a high-spirited highwayman, who took a coach-passenger's purse, thought himself injured, and the traveller a shabby fellow, if he secreted a guinea or two under the cushions. In the Doctor's now rare letters, he breathed a manly sigh here and there, to think that he had lost the confidence of his boy. I do believe that certain ladies of our acquaintance were inclined to think that the elder Firmin had been not altogether well used, however much they loved and admired the Little Sister for her lawless act in her boy's defence. But this main point we had won. The Doctor at New York took the warning, and wrote his son's signature upon no more bills of exchange. The good Goodenough's loan was carried back to him in the very coin which he had supplied. He said that his little nurse Brandon was *splendide mendax,* and that her robbery was a sublime and courageous act of war.

In so far, since his marriage, Mr. Philip had been pretty fortunate. At need, friends had come to him. In moments of peril he had had succour and relief. Though he had married without money, fate had sent him a sufficiency. His flask had never been empty, and there was always meal in his bin. But now hard trials were in store for him: hard trials which we have said were endurable, and which he has long since lived through. Any man who has played the game of life or whist, knows how for one while he will have a series of good cards dealt him, and again will get no trumps at all. After he got into his house in Milman Street, and quitted the Little Sister's kind roof, our friend's good fortune seemed to desert him. 'Perhaps it was a punishment for my pride, because I was haughty with her, and—and jealous of that dear good little creature,' poor Charlotte afterwards owned in conversation with other friends:—'but our fortune seemed to change when we were away from her, and that I must own.'

Perhaps, when she was yet under Mrs. Brandon's roof, the Little Sister's provident care had done a great deal more for Charlotte than Charlotte knew. Mrs. Philip had the most simple tastes in the world, and upon herself never spent an unnecessary shilling. Indeed, it was a wonder, considering her small expenses, how neat and nice Mrs. Philip ever looked. But she never could deny herself when the children were in question; and had them arrayed in all sorts of fine clothes; and stitched and hemmed all day and night to decorate their little persons; and in reply to the remonstrances of the matrons her friends, showed how it was impossible children *could* be dressed for less cost. If anything ailed them, quick, the doctor must be sent for. Not worthy Goodenough, who came without a fee, and pooh-poohed her alarms and anxieties; but dear Mr. Bland, who had a feeling heart, and was himself a father of children, and who supported those children by the produce of the pills, draughts, powders, visits, which he bestowed on all families into whose doors he entered. Bland's sympathy was very consolatory; but it was found to be very costly at the end of the year. 'And, what then?' says Charlotte, with kindling cheeks. 'Do you suppose we should grudge that money, which was to give health to our dearest dearest babies? No. You can't have such a bad opinion of me as that!' And accordingly Mr. Bland received a nice little annuity from our friends. Philip had a joke about his wife's housekeeping which perhaps may apply to other young women who are kept by over-watchful mothers too much *in statu pupillari.* When they were married, or about to be married, Philip asked Charlotte what she would order for dinner. She promptly said she would order leg of mutton. 'And after leg of mutton?' 'Leg of beef, to be sure!' says Mrs. Charlotte, looking very pleased and knowing. And the fact is, as this little housekeeper was obliged demurely to admit, their household bills increased *prodigiously* after they left Thornhaugh Street. 'And I can't understand, my dear, how the grocer's book should mount up so; and the butterman's, and the beer,' etc. etc. We have often seen the pretty little head bent over the dingy volumes, puzzling, puzzling: and the eldest child would hold up a warning finger to ours, and tell them to be very quiet, as mamma was at her 'atounts.'

And now, I grieve to say, money became scarce for the payment of these accounts; and though Philip fancied he hid his anxieties from his wife, be sure she loved him too much to be deceived by one of the clumsiest hypocrites in the world. Only, being a much cleverer hypocrite than her husband, she pretended to be deceived, and acted her part so well that poor Philip was mortified with her gaiety, and chose to fancy his wife was indifferent to their misfortunes. She ought not to be so smiling and happy, he thought; and, as usual, bemoaned his lot to his friends. 'I come home racked with care, and thinking of those inevitable bills; I shudder, sir, at every note that lies on the hall table, and would tremble as I dashed them open as they do on the stage. But I laugh and put on a jaunty air, and humbug Char. And I hear her singing about the house and laughing and cooing with the children, by Jove. *She's* not aware of anything. *She* does not know how dreadfully the *res domi* is squeezing me. But *before marriage* she did, I tell you. Then, if anything annoyed me, she divined it. If I felt ever so little unwell, you should have seen the alarm on her face! It was "Philip dear, how pale you are"; or, "Philip, how flushed you are"; or, "I am sure you have had a letter from your father. Why do you conceal anything from me, sir? You never should—never!" And now when the fox is gnawing at my side under my cloak, I laugh and grin so naturally that she believes I am all right, and she comes to meet me flouncing the children about in my face, and wearing an air of consummate happiness! I would not deceive her for the world, you know. But it's mortifying. Don't tell me. It *is* mortifying to be tossing awake all night, and racked with care all day, and have the wife of your bosom chattering and singing and laughing, as if there were no cares, or doubts, or duns in the world. If I had the gout and she were to laugh and sing, I should not call that sympathy. If I were arrested for debt, and she were to come grinning and laughing to the spunging-house, I should not call that consolation. Why doesn't she feel? She ought to feel. There's Betsy, our parlour-maid. There's the old fellow who comes to clean the boots and knives. *They* know how hard up I am. And my wife sings and dances whilst I am on the verge of ruin, by Jove; and giggles and laughs as if life was a pantomime!'

Then the man and woman into whose ears poor Philip roared out his confessions and griefs, hung down their blushing heads in humbled silence. They are tolerably prosperous in life, and, I fear, are pretty well satisfied with themselves and each other. A woman who scarcely ever does any wrong, and rules and governs her own house and family, as my-as the wife of the reader's humble servant most notoriously does, often becomes—must it be said?—too certain of her own virtue, and is too sure of the correctness of her own opinion. We virtuous people give advice a good deal, and set a considerable value upon that advice. We meet a certain man who has fallen among thieves, let us say. We succour him readily enough. We take him kindly to the inn, and pay his score there; but we say to the landlord, 'You must give this poor man his bed; his medicine at such a time, and his broth at such another. But, mind you, he must have that physic, and no other; that broth when we order it. *We* take his case in hand, you understand. Don't listen to him or anybody else. We know all about everything. Good-bye. Take care of him. Mind the medicine and the broth!' And Mr. Benefactor or Lady Bountiful goes away, perfectly self-satisfied.

Do you take this allegory? When Philip complained to us of his wife's friskiness and gaiety; when he bitterly contrasted her levity and carelessness with his own despondency and doubt, Charlotte's two principal friends were smitten by shame. 'Oh, Philip! dear Philip!' his female adviser said (having looked at her husband once or twice as Firmin spoke, and in vain endeavoured to keep her guilty eyes down on her work), 'Charlotte has done this, because she is humble, and because she takes the advice of friends who are not. She knows everything, and more than everything; for her dear tender heart is filled with apprehension. But we told her to show no sign of care, lest her husband should be disturbed. And she trusted in us; and she puts her trust elsewhere, Philip; and she has hidden her own anxieties, lest yours should be increased; and has met you gaily when her heart was full of dread. We think she has done wrong now; but she did so because she was so simple, and trusted in us who advised her wrongly. Now we see that there ought to have been perfect confidence always between you, and that it is her simplicity and faith in us which have misled her.'

Phil hung down his head for a moment, and hid his eyes; and we knew, during that minute when his face was concealed from us, how his grateful heart was employed.

'And you know, dear Philip—' says Laura, looking at her husband, and nodding to that person, who certainly understood the hint.

'And I say, Firmin,' breaks in the lady's husband, 'you understand, if you are at all —that is, if you—that is, if we can—'

'Hold your tongue!' shouts Firmin, with a face beaming over with happiness. 'I know what you mean. You beggar, you are going to offer me money! I see it in your face; bless you both! But we'll try and do without, please Heaven. And—and it's worth feeling a pinch of poverty to find such friends as I have had, and to share it with such a—such a—dash—dear little thing as I have at home. And I won't try and humbug Char any more. I'm bad at that sort of business. And good-night, and I'll never forget your kindness, never!' And he is off a moment afterwards, and jumping down the steps of our door, and so into the park. And though there were not five pounds in the poor little house in Milman Street, there were not two happier people in London that night than Charlotte and Philip Firmin. If he had his troubles, our friend had his immense consolations. Fortunate he, however poor, who has friends to help, and love to console him in his trials.

CHAPTER XL. IN WHICH THE LUCK GOES VERY MUCH AGAINST US

EVERY man and woman amongst us has made his voyage to Lilliput, and his tour in the kingdom of Brobdingnag. When I go to my native country town, the local paper announces our arrival; the labourers touch their hats as the pony-chaise passes, the girls and old women drop curtseys; Mr. Hicks, the grocer and hatter, comes to his door and makes a bow, and smirks and smiles. When our neighbour Sir John arrives at the Hall, he is a still greater personage; the bell-ringers greet the Hall family with a peal; the Rector walks over on an early day, and pays his visit; and the farmers at market press round for a nod of recognition. Sir John at home is in Lilliput: in Belgrave Square he is in Brobdingnag, where almost everybody we meet is ever so much taller than ourselves. 'Which do you like best: to be a giant amongst the pigmies, or a pigmy amongst the giants?' I know what sort of company I prefer myself: but that is not the point. What I would hint is, that we possibly give ourselves patronising airs before small people, as folks higher placed than ourselves give themselves airs before *us*. Patronising airs? Old Miss Mumbles, the half-pay lieutenant's daughter, who lives over the plumber's, with her maid, gives herself in her degree more airs than any duchess in Belgravia, and would leave the room if a tradesman's wife sat down in it.

Now it has been said that few men in this city of London are so simple in their manners as Philip Firmin, and that he treated the patron whose bread he ate, and the wealthy relative who condescended to visit him, with a like freedom. He is blunt, but not familiar, and is not a whit more polite to my Lord than to Jack Or Tom at the coffee-house. He resents familiarity from vulgar persons, and those who venture on it retire maimed and mortified after coming into collision with him. As for the people he loves, he grovels before them, worships their boot-tips and their gown-hems. But he submits to them, not for their wealth or rank, but for love's sake. He submitted very magnanimously, at first, to the kindness and caresses of Lady Ringwood and her daughters, being softened and won by the regard which they showed for his wife and children.

Although Sir John was for the Rights of Man everywhere, all over the world, and had pictures of Franklin, Lafayette, and Washington in his library, he likewise had portraits of his own ancestors in that apartment, and entertained a very high opinion of the present representative of the Ringwood family. The character of the late chief of the house was notorious. Lord Ringwood's life had been irregular and his morals loose. His talents were considerable, no doubt, but they had not been devoted to serious study or directed to useful ends. A wild man in early life, he had only changed his practices in later life in consequence of ill-health, and became a hermit as a Certain Person became a monk. He was a frivolous person to the end, and was not to be considered as a public man and statesman; and this light-minded man of pleasure had been advanced to the third rank of the peerage, whilst his successor, his superior in intellect and morality, remained a Baronet still. How blind the Ministry was which refused to recognise so much talent and worth! Had there been public virtue or common sense in the governors of the nation, merits like Sir John's never could have been overlooked. But Ministers were notoriously a family clique, and only helped each other. Promotion and patronage were disgracefully monopolised by the members of a very few families who were not better men of business, men of better character, men of more ancient lineage (though birth, of course, was a mere accident) than Sir John himself. In a word, until they gave him a peerage, he saw very little hope for the cabinet or the country.

In a very early page of this history mention was made of a certain Philip Ringwood, to whose protection Philip Firmin's mother confided her boy when he was first sent to school. Philip Ringwood was Firmin's senior by seven years; he came to Old Parr Street twice or thrice during his stay at school, condescended to take the 'tips,' of which the poor Doctor was liberal enough, but never deigned to take any notice of young Firmin, who looked up to his kinsman with awe and trembling. From school Philip Ringwood speedily departed to college, and then entered upon public life. He was the eldest son of Sir John Ringwood, with whom our friend has of late made acquaintance.

Mr. Ringwood was a much greater personage than the Baronet his father. Even when the latter succeeded to Lord Ringwood's estates and came to London, he could scarcely be said to equal his son in social rank; and the younger patronised his parent. What is the secret of great social success? It is not to be gained by beauty, or wealth, or birth, or wit, or valour, or eminence of any kind. It is a gift of Fortune, bestowed, like that goddess's favours, capriciously. Look, dear madam, at the most fashionable ladies at present reigning in London. Are they better bred, or more amiable, or richer, or more beautiful than yourself? See, good sir, the men who lead the fashion, and stand in the bow window at Black's: are they wiser, or wittier, or more agreeable people than you1? And yet you know what your fate would be if you were put up at that club. Sir John Ringwood never dared to be proposed there, even after his great accession of fortune on the Earl's death. His son did not encourage him. People even said that Ringwood would blackball his father if he dared to offer himself as a candidate.

I never, I say, could understand the reason of Philip Ringwood's success in life, though you must acknowledge that he is one of our most eminent dandies. He is affable to dukes. He patronises marquises. He is not witty. He is not clever. He does not give good dinners. How many baronets are there in the British empire? Look to your book, and see. I tell you there are many of these whom Philip

Ringwood would scarcely admit to wait at one of his bad dinners. By calmly asserting himself in life, this man has achieved his social eminence. We may hate him; but we acknowledge his superiority. For instance, I should as soon think of asking him to dine with me, as I should of slapping the Archbishop of Canterbury on the back.

Mr. Ringwood has a meagre little house in Mayfalr, and belongs to a public office where he patronises his *chef.* His own family bow down before him; his mother is humble in his company; his sisters are respectful; his father does not brag of his own Liberal principles, and never alludes to the Rights of Man in the son's presence. He is called 'Mr. Ringwood' in the family. The person who is least in awe of him is his younger brother, who has been known to make faces behind the elder's back. But he is a dreadfully headstrong and ignorant child, and respects nothing. Lady Ringwood, by the way, is Mr. Ringwood's stepmother. His own mother was the daughter of a noble house, and died in giving birth to this paragon.

Philip Firmin, who had not set eyes upon his kinsman since they were at school together, remembered some stories which were current about Ringwood, and by no means to that eminent dandy's credit—stories of intrigue, of play, of various libertine exploits on Mr. Ringwood's part. One day Philip and Charlotte dined with Sir John, who was talking and chirping, and laying down the law, and bragging away according to his wont, when his son entered and asked for dinner. He had accepted an invitation to dine at Garterton House. The Duke had one of his attacks of gout just before dinner. The dinner was off. If Lady Ringwood would give him a slice of mutton, he would be very much obliged to her. A place was soon found for him. 'And, Philip, this is your namesake, and our cousin, Mr. Philip Firmin,' said the Baronet, presenting his son to his kinsman.

'Your father used to give me sovereigns when I was at school. I have a faint recollection of you, too. Little white-headed boy, weren't you? How is the Doctor, and Mrs. Firmin? All right?'

'Why, don't you know his father ran away?' calls out the youngest member of the family. 'Don't kick me, Emily. He *did* run away.'

Then Mr. Ringwood remembered, and a faint blush tinged his face, 'Lapse of time. I know. Shouldn't have asked after such a lapse of time.' And he mentioned a case in which a duke, who was very forgetful, had asked a marquis about his wife who had run away with an earl, and made inquiries about the duke's son, who, as everybody knew, was not on terms with his father.

'This is Mrs. Firmin—Mrs. Philip Firmin!' cried Lady Ringwood, rather nervously; and I suppose Mrs. Philip blushed, and the blush became her; for Mr. Ringwood afterwards condescended to say to one of his sisters, that their new-found relative seemed one of your rough-and-ready sort of gentlemen, but his wife was really very well-bred, and quite a pretty young woman, and presentable anywhere—really anywhere. Charlotte was asked to sing one or two of her little songs after dinner.

Mr. Ringwood was delighted. Her voice was perfectly true. What she sang, she sang admirably. And he was good enough to hum over one of her songs (during which performance he showed that *his* voice was not exempt from little frailties), and to say he had heard Lady Philomela Shakerley sing that very song at Glenmavis, last autumn; and it was such a favourite that the Duchess asked for it every night—actually every night. When our friends were going home, Mr. Ringwood gave Philip almost the whole of one finger to shake; and while Philip was inwardly raging at his impertinence, believed that he had entirely fascinated his humble relatives, and that he had been most good-natured and friendly.

I cannot tell why this man's patronage chafed and goaded our worthy friend so as to drive him beyond the bounds of all politeness and reason. The artless remarks of the little boy, and the occasional simple speeches of the young ladies, had only tickled Philip's humour, and served to amuse him when he met his relatives. I suspect it was a certain free-and-easy manner which Mr. Ringwood chose to adopt towards Mrs. Philip, which annoyed her husband. He had said nothing at which offence could be taken: perhaps he was quite unconscious of offending; nay, thought himself eminently pleasing. Perhaps he was not more impertinent towards her than towards other women: but in talking about him, Mr. Firmin's eyes flashed very fiercely, and he spoke of his new acquaintance and relative, with his usual extreme candour, as an upstart, and an arrogant conceited puppy whose ears he would like to pull.

How do good women learn to discover men who are not good? Is it by instinct? How do they learn those stories about men? I protest I never told my wife anything good or bad regarding this Mr. Ringwood, though of course, as a man about town, I have heard—who has not? —little anecdotes regarding his career. His conduct in that affair with Miss Willowby was heartless and cruel; his behaviour to that unhappy Blanche Painter nobody can defend. My wife conveys her opinion regarding Philip Ringwood, his life, principles, and morality, by looks and silences which are more awful and killing than the bitterest words of sarcasm or reproof. Philip Firmin, who knows her ways, watches her features, and, as I have said, humbles himself at her feet, marked the lady's awful looks when he came to describe to us his meeting with his cousin, and the magnificent patronising airs which Mr. Ringwood assumed.

'What?' he said, 'you don't like him any more than I do? I thought you would not; and I am so glad.'

Philip's friend said she did not know Mr. Ringwood, and had never spoken a word to him in her life.

'Yes; but you know of him,'cries the impetuous Firmin. 'What do you know of him, with his monstrous puppyism and arrogance?' Oh, Mrs. Laura knew very little of him. She did not believe—she had much rather not believe—what the world said about Mr. Ringwood.

'Suppose we were to ask the Woolcombs their opinion of your character, Philip?' cries that gentleman's biographer, with a laugh.

'My dear!' says Laura, with a yet severer look, the severity of which glance I must explain. The differences of Woolcomb and his wife were notorious. Their unhappiness was known to all the world. Society was beginning to look with a very very cold face upon Mrs. Woolcomb. After quarrels, jealousies, battles, reconciliations, scenes of renewed violence and furious language, had come indifference, and the most reckless gaiety on the woman's part. Her home was splendid, but mean and miserable; all sorts of stories were rife regarding her husband's brutal treatment of poor Agnes, and her own imprudent behaviour. Mrs. Laura was indignant when this unhappy woman's name was ever mentioned, except when she thought how our warm true-hearted Philip had escaped from the heartless creature. 'What a blessing it was that you were ruined, Philip, and that she deserted you!' Laura would say. 'What fortune would repay you for marrying such a woman?'

'Indeed it was worth all I had to lose her,' says Philip, ' and so the Doctor and I are quits. If he had not spent my fortune, Agnes would have married me. If she had married me, I might have turned Othello, and have been hanged for smothering her. Why, if I had not been poor, I should never have been married to little Char— and fancy not being married to Char!' The worthy fellow here lapses into silence, and indulges in an inward rapture at the idea of his own excessive happiness. Then he is scared again at the thought which his own imagination has raised.

'I say! Fancy being without the kids and Char!' he cries with a blank look.

'That horrible father—that dreadful mother—pardon me, Philip; but when I think of the worldliness of those unhappy people, and how that poor unhappy woman has been bred in it, and ruined by it—I am so, so, so *enraged,* that I can't keep my temper!' cries the lady. 'Is the woman answerable, or the parents, who hardened her heart, and sold her—sold her to that—O!' Our illustrious friend Woolcomb was signified by 'that O'; and the lady once more paused, choked with wrath as she thought about that O, and that O's wife.

'I wonder he has not Othello'd her,' remarks Philip, with his hands in his pockets. 'I should, if she had been mine, and gone on as they say she is going on.'

'It is dreadful dreadful to contemplate!' continues the lady. 'To think she was sold by her own parents, poor thing, poor thing! The guilt is with them who led her wrong.'

'Nay,' says one of the three interlocutors. 'Why stop at poor Mr. and Mrs. Twysden? Why not let them off, and accuse *their* parents, who lived worldly too in their generation? Or stay: they descend from William the Conqueror. Let us absolve poor Talbot Twysden and his heartless wife, and have the Norman into court.'

'Ah, Arthur! Did not our sin begin with the beginning?' cries the lady, 'and have we not its remedy? Oh, this poor creature, this poor creature! May she know where to take refuge from it, and learn to repent in time!'

The Georgian and Circassian girls, they say, used to submit to their lot very complacently, and were quite eager to get to market at Constantinople and be sold. Mrs. Woolcomb wanted nobody to tempt her away from poor Philip. She hopped away from the old love as soon as ever the new one appeared with his bag of money. She knew quite well to whom she was selling herself, and for what. The tempter needed no skill, or artifice, or eloquence. He had none. But he showed her a purse, and three fine houses—and she came. Innocent child, forsooth! She knew quite as much about the world as papa and mamma; and the lawyers did not look to her settlement more warily, and coolly, than she herself did. Did she not live on it afterwards? I do not say she lived reputably, but most comfortably: as Paris, and Rome, and Naples, and Florence can tell you, where she is well known; where she receives a great deal of a certain kind of company; where she is scorned and flattered, and splendid, and lonely, and miserable. She is not miserable when she sees children: she does not care for other person's children, as she never did for her own, even when they were taken from her. She is of course hurt and angry, when quite common vulgar people, not in society, you understand, turn away from her, and avoid her, and won't come to her parties. She gives excellent dinners which jolly fogeys, rattling bachelors, and doubtful ladies frequent: but she is alone and unhappy—unhappy because she does not see parents, sister, or brother? *Allons, mon bon monsieur!* She never cared for parents, sister, or brother; or for baby; or for man (except once for Philip a little little bit, when her pulse would sometimes go up two beats in a minute at his appearance). But she is unhappy, because she is losing her figure, and from tight lacing her nose has become very red, and the pearl powder won't lie on it somehow. And though you may have thought Woolcomb an odious, ignorant, and underbred little wretch, you must own that at least he had red blood in his veins. Did he not spend a great part of his fortune for the possession of this cold wife? For whom did *she* ever make a sacrifice, or feel a pang? I am sure a greater misfortune than any which has befallen friend Philip might have happened to him, and so congratulate him on his escape.

Having vented his wrath upon the arrogance and impertinence of this solemn puppy of a Philip Ringwood, our friend went away somewhat soothed to his club in St James's Street. The Megatherium Club is only a very few doors from the much more aristocratic establishment of Black's. Mr. Philip Ringwood and Mr. Woolcomb were standing on the steps of Black's. Mr. Ringwood waved a graceful little kid-gloved hand to Philip, and smiled on him. Mr. Woolcomb glared at our friend out of his opal eyeballs. Philip had once proposed to kick Woolcomb into the sea. He somehow felt as if he would like to treat Ringwood to the same bath. Meanwhile, Mr. Ringwood laboured under the notion that he and his new-found acquaintance were on the very best possible terms.

At one time poor little Woolcomb loved to be seen with Philip Ringwood. He thought he acquired distinction from the companionship of that man of fashion, and would hang on Ringwood as they walked the Pall Mall pavement.

'Do you know that great hulking overbearing brute?' says Woolcomb to his companion on the steps of Black's. Perhaps somebody overheard them from the bow window. (I tell you everything is overheard in London, and a great deal more too.)

'Brute, is he?' says Ringwood: 'seems a rough overbearing sort of chap.'

'Blackguard Doctor's son. Bankrupt. Father ran away,' says the dusky man with the opal eyeballs.

'I have heard he was a rogue—the Doctor; but I like him. Remember he gave me three sovereigns when I was at school. Always like a fellow who tips you when you are at school.' And here Ringwood beckoned his brougham which was in waiting.

'Shall we see you at dinner? Where are you going?' asked Mr. Woolcomb. 'If you are going towards—'

'Towards Gray's Inn, to see my lawyer; have an appointment there; be with you at eight!' And Mr. Ringwood skipped into his little brougham and was gone.

Tom Eaves told Philip. Tom Eaves belongs to Black's Club, to Bays's, to the Megatherium, I don't know to how many clubs in St. James's Street. Tom Eaves knows everybody's business, and all the scandal of all the clubs for the last forty years. He knows who has lost money and to whom; what is the talk of the opera-box and what the scandal of the *coulisses;* who is making love to whose daughter. Whatever men and women are doing in Mayfair, is the farrago of Tom's libel. He knows so many stories, that of course he makes mistakes in names sometimes, and says that Jones is on the verge of ruin, when he is thriving and prosperous, and it is poor Brown who is in difficulties; or informs us that Mrs. Fanny is flirting with Captain Ogle when both are as innocent of a flirtation as you and I are. Tom certainly is mischievous, and often is wrong; but when he speaks of our neighbours he is amusing.

'It is as good as a play to see Ringwood and Othello together,' says Tom to Philip. 'How proud the black man is to be seen with him! Heard him abuse you to Ringwood. Ringwood stuck up for you and for your poor governor—spoke up like a man—like a man who sticks up for a fellow who is down. How the black man brags about having Ringwood to dinner! Always having him to dinner! You should have seen Ringwood shake him off! Said he was going to Gray's Inn. Heard him say Gray's Inn Lane to his man. Don't believe a word of it.'

Now I dare say you are much too fashionable to know that Milman Street is a little *cul de sac* of a street, which leads into Guilford Street, which leads into Gray's Inn

Lane. Philip went his way homewards, shaking off Tom Eaves, who, for his part, trolled off to his other clubs, telling people how he had just been talking with that bankrupt Doctor's son, and wondering how Philip should get money enough to pay his club subscription. Philip then went on his way, striding homewards at his usual manly pace.

Whose black brougham was that?—the black brougham with the chestnut horse walking up and down Guilford Street. Mr. Ringwood's crest was on the brougham. When Philip entered his drawing-room, having opened the door with his own key, there sat Mr. Ringwood, talking to Mrs. Charlotte, who was taking a cup of tea at five o'clock. She and the children liked that cup of tea. Sometimes it served Mrs. Char for dinner when Philip dined from home.

'If I had known you were coming here, you might have brought me home and saved me a long walk,' said Philip, wiping a burning forehead.

'So I might—so I might,' said the other. 'I never thought of it. I had to see my lawyer in Gray's Inn; and it was then I thought of coming on to see you, as I was telling Mrs. Firmin; and a very nice quiet place you live in!'

This was very well. But for the first and only time of his life Philip was jealous.

'Don't rub so with your feet! Don't like to ride when you jog so on the floor,' said Philip's eldest darling, who had clambered on papa's knee. 'Why do you look so? Don't squeeze my arm, papa!'

Mamma was utterly unaware that Philip had any cause for agitation. 'You have walked all the way from Westminster, and the club, and you are quite hot and tired!' she said. 'Some tea, my dear?'

Philip nearly choked with the tea. From under his hair, which fell over his forehead, he looked into his wife's face. It wore such a sweet look of innocence and wonder, that, as he regarded her, the spasm of jealousy passed off. No: there was no look of guilt in those tender eyes. Philip could only read in them the wife's tender love and anxiety for himself.

But what of Mr. Ringwood's face? When the first little blush and hesitation had passed away, Mr. Ringwood's pale countenance reassumed that calm self-satisfied smile, which it customarily wore. 'The coolness of the man maddened me,' said Philip, talking about the little occurrence afterwards, and to his usual confidant.

'Gracious Powers,' cries the other. 'If I went to see Charlotte and the children, would you be jealous of me, you bearded Turk? Are you prepared with sack and bowstring for every man who visits Mrs. Firmin? If you are to come out in this character, you will lead yourself and your wife pretty lives. Of course you quarrelled with Lovelace then and there, and threatened to throw him out of window then and there? Your custom is to strike when you are hot, witness—'

'Oh dear no!' cried Philip, interrupting me. 'I have not quarrelled with him yet.' And he ground his teeth, and gave a very fierce glare with his eyes. 'I sat him out quite civilly. I went with him to the door; and I have left directions that he is never to pass it again—that's all. But I have not quarrelled with him in the least. Two men never behaved more politely than we did. We bowed and grinned at each other quite amiably. But I own, when he held out his hand, I was obliged to keep mine behind my back, for they felt very mischievous, and inclined to— Well, never mind. Perhaps it is as you say; and he meant no sort of harm.'

Where, I say again, do women learn all the mischief they know? Why should my wife have such a mistrust and horror of this gentleman?

She took Philip's side entirely. She said she thought he was quite right in keeping that person out of his house. What did she know about that person? Did I not know myself? He was a libertine, and led a bad life. He had led young men astray, and taught them to gamble, and helped them to ruin themselves. We have all heard stories about the late Sir Philip Ringwood: that last scandal in which he was engaged, three years ago, and which brought his career to an end at Naples, I need not, of course, allude to. But fourteen or fifteen years ago, about which time this present portion of our little story is enacted, what did she know about Ringwood's misdoings?

No: Philip Firmin did not quarrel with Philip Ringwood on this occasion. But he shut his door on Mr. Ringwood. He refused all invitations to Sir John's house, which, of course, came less frequently, and which then ceased to come at all. Rich folks do not like to be so treated by the poor. Had Lady Ringwood a notion of the reason why Philip kept away from her house? I think it is more than possible. Some of Philip's friends knew her; and she seemed only pained, not surprised or angry, at a quarrel which somehow *did* take place between the two gentlemen not very long after that visit of Mr. Ringwood to his kinsman in Milman Street.

'Your friend seems very hot-headed and violent-tempered,' Lady Ringwood said, speaking of that very quarrel. 'I am sorry he keeps that kind of company. I am sure it must be too expensive for him.'

As luck would have it, Philip's old school-friend, Lord Ascot, met us a very few days after the meeting and parting of Philip and his cousin in Milman Street, and invited us to a bachelor's dinner on the river. Our wives (without whose sanction no good man would surely ever look a whitebait in the face) gave us permission to attend this entertainment, and remained at home, and partook of a tea-dinner (blessings on them!) with the dear children. Men grow young again when they meet at these parties. We talk of flogging, proctors, old cronies; we recite old school and college jokes. I hope that some of us may carry on these pleasant entertainments until we are fourscore, and that our toothless old gums will mumble the old stories, and will laugh over the old jokes with ever-renewed gusto. Does the kind reader remember the account of such a dinner at the commencement of this history? On this afternoon, Ascot, Maynard, Burroughs (several of the men formerly mentioned), reassembled. I think we actually like each other well enough to be pleased to hear of each other's successes. I know that one or two good fellows, upon whom fortune has frowned, have found other good fellows in that company to help and aid them; and that all are better for that kindly freemasonry.

Before the dinner was served, the guests met on the green of the hotel, and examined that fair landscape, which surely does not lose its charm in our eyes because it is commonly seen before a good dinner. The crested elms, the shining river, the emerald meadows, the painted parterres of flowers around, all wafting an agreeable smell of *friture,* of flowers and flounders exquisitely commingled. Who has not enjoyed these delights? May some of us, I say, live to drink the '58 claret in the year 1900! I have no doubt that the survivors of our society will still laugh at the jokes which we used to relish when the present century was still only middle-aged. Ascot was going to be married. Would he be allowed to dine next year? Frank Berry's wife would not let him come. Do you remember his tremendous fight with Biggs? Remember? who didn't? Marston was Berry's bottle-holder; poor Marston, who was killed in India. And Biggs and Berry were the closest friends in life ever after. Who would ever have thought of Brackley becoming serious, and being made an archdeacon? Do you remember his fight with Ringwood? What an infernal bully he was, and how glad we all were when Brackley thrashed him. What different fates await men! Who would ever have imagined Nosey Brackley a curate in the mining districts, and ending by wearing a rosette in his hat? Who would ever have thought of Ringwood becoming such a prodigious swell and leader of fashion? He was a very shy fellow; not at all a good-looking fellow: and what a wild fellow he had become, and what a lady-killer! Isn't he some connection of yours, Firmin? Philip said yes, but that he had scarcely met Ringwood at all. And one man after another told anecdotes of Ringwood: how he had young men to play in his house; how he had played in that very 'Star and Garter'; and how he always won. You must please to remember that our story dates back some sixteen years, when the dice-box still rattled occasionally, and the king was turned.

As this old school gossip is going on, Lord Ascot arrives, and with him this very Ringwood about whom the old schoolfellows had just been talking. He came down in Ascot's phaeton. Of course, the greatest man of the party always waits for Ringwood. 'If we had had a duke at Greyfriars,' says some grumbler, 'Ringwood would have made the duke bring him down.'

Philip's friend, when he beheld the arrival of Mr. Ringwood, seized Firmin's big arm, and whispered—'Hold your tongue. No fighting. No quarrels. Let bygones be bygones. Remember, there can be no earthly use in a scandal.' 'Leave me alone,' says Philip, 'and don't be afraid.' I thought Ringwood seemed to start back for a moment, and perhaps fancied that he looked a little pale, but he advanced with a gracious smile towards Philip, and remarked, 'It is a long time since we have seen you at my father's.'

Philip grinned and smiled too. 'It *was* a long time since he had been in Hill Street.' And Philip's smile was not at all pleasing to behold. Indeed, a worse performer of comedy than our friend does not walk the stage of this life.

On this the other gaily remarked he was glad Philip had leave to join the bachelor's party. 'Meeting of old schoolfellows very pleasant. Hadn't been to one of them for a long time: though the "Friars" was an abominable hole: that was the truth. Who was that in the shovel-hat—a bishop? what bishop?'

It was Brackley, the Archdeacon, who turned very red on seeing Ringwood. For the fact is, Brackley was talking to Pennystone, the little boy about whom the quarrel and fight had taken place at school, when Ringwood had proposed forcibly to take Pennystone's money from him. 'I think, Mr. Ringwood, that Pennystone is big enough to hold his own now, don't you?' said the Archdeacon; and with this the Venerable man turned on his heel, leaving Ringwood to face the little Pennystone of former years: now a gigantic country squire, with health ringing in his voice, and a pair of great arms and fists that would have demolished six Ringwoods in the field.

The sight of these quondam enemies rather disturbed Mr. Ringwood's tranquillity.

'I was dreadfully bullied at that school,' he said in an appealing manner to Mr. Pennystone. 'I did as others did. It was a horrible place, and I hate the name of it. I say, Ascot, don't you think that Barnaby's motion last night was very ill-timed, and that the Chancellor of the Exchequer answered him very neatly?'

This became a cant phrase amongst some of us wags afterwards. Whenever we wished to change a conversation, it was, 'I say, Ascot, don't you think Barnaby's motion was very ill-timed; and that the Chancellor of the Exchequer answered him very neatly?' You know Mr. Ringwood would scarcely have thought of coming amongst such common people as his old schoolfellows, but seeing Lord Ascot's phaeton at Black's, he condescended to drive down to Richmond with his Lordship, and I hope a great number of his friends in St. James's Street saw him in that noble company.

Windham was the chairman of the evening—elected to that post because he is very fond of making speeches to which he does not in the least expect you to listen. All men of sense are glad to hand over this office to him: and I hope, for my part, a day will soon arrive (but I own, mind you, that I do not carve well) when we shall have the speeches done by a skilled waiter at the side-table, as we now have the carving. Don't you find that you splash the gravy, that you mangle the meat, that you can't nick the joint in helping the company to a dinner-speech? I, for my part, own that I am in a state of tremor and absence of mind before the operation; in a condition of imbecility during the business; and that I am sure of a headache and indigestion the next morning. What then? Have I not seen one of the bravest men in the world, at a City dinner last year, in a state of equal panic?—I feel that I am wandering from

Philip's adventures to his biographer's, and confess I am thinking of the dismal *fiasco* I myself made on this occasion at the Richmond dinner.

You see, the order of the day at these meetings is to joke at everything—to joke at the chairman, at all the speakers, at the army and navy, at the venerable the legislature, at the bar and bench, and so forth.

If we toast a barrister, we show how admirably he would have figured in the dock: if a sailor, how lamentably sea-sick he was: if a soldier, how nimbly he ran away. For example, we drank the Venerable Archdeacon Brackley and the army. We deplored the perverseness which had led him to adopt a black coat instead of a red. War had evidently been his vocation, as he had shown by the frequent battles in which he had been engaged at school. For what was the *other* great warrior of the age famous? for that Roman feature in his face, which distinguished, which gave a name to, our Brackley—a name by which we fondly clung (cries of 'Nosey, Nosey!'). Might that feature ornament ere long the face of—of one of the chiefs of that army of which he was a distinguished field-officer! Might—Here I confess I fairly broke down, lost the thread of my joke—at which Brackley seemed to look rather severe—and finished the speech with a gobble about regard, esteem, everybody respect you, and good health, old boy—which answered quite as well as a finished oration, however the author might be discontented with it.

The Archdeacon's little sermon was very brief, as the discourses of sensible divines sometimes will be. He was glad to meet old friends—to make friends with old foes (loud cries of 'Bravo, Nosey!'). In the battle of life, every man must meet with a blow or two; and every brave one would take his facer with good-humour. Had he quarrelled with any old schoolfellow infold times? He wore peace not only on his coat, but in his heart. Peace and goodwill were the words of the day in the army to which he belonged; and he hoped that all officers in it were animated by one *esprit de corps.*

A silence ensued, during which men looked towards Mr. Ringwood, as the 'old foe' towards whom the Archdeacon had held out the hand of amity: but Ringwood, who had listened to the Archdeacon's speech with an expression of great disgust, did not rise from his chair—only remarking to his neighbour Ascot, 'Why should I get up? Hang him, I have nothing to say. I say, Ascot, why did you induce me to come into this kind of thing?'

Fearing that a collision might take place between Philip and his kinsman, I had drawn Philip away from the place in the room to which Lord Ascot beckoned him, saying, 'Never mind, Philip, about sitting by the lord,' by whose side I knew perfectly well that Mr. Ringwood would find a place. But it was our lot to be separated from his Lordship by merely the table's breadth, and some intervening vases of flowers and fruits through which we could see and hear our opposite neighbours. When Ringwood spoke of 'this kind of thing,' Philip glared across the table, and started as if he was going to speak; but his neighbour pinched him on the knee, and whispered to him, 'Silence—no scandal. Remember.' The other fell back, swallowed a glass of wine, and made me far from comfortable by performing a tattoo on my chair.

The speeches went on. If they were not more eloquent they were more noisy and lively than before. Then the aid of song was called in to enliven the banquet. The Archdeacon, who had looked a little uneasy for the last half-hour, rose up at the call for a song, and quitted the room. 'Let us go too, Philip,' said Philip's neighbour. 'You don't want to hear those dreadful old college songs over again?' But Philip sulkily said, 'You go, I should like to stay.'

Lord Ascot was seeing the last of his bachelor life. He liked those last evenings to be merry; he lingered over them, and did not wish them to end too quickly. His neighbour was long since tired of the entertainment, and sick of our company. Mr. Ringwood had lived of late in a world of such fashion that ordinary mortals were despicable to him. He had no affectionate remembrance of his early days, or of anybody belonging to them. Whilst Philip was singing his song of 'Doctor Luther,' I was glad that he could not see the face of surprise and disgust which his kinsman bore. Other vocal performances followed, including a song by Lord Ascot, which, I am bound to say, was hideously out of tune; but was received by his near neighbour complacently enough.

The noise now began to increase, the choruses were fuller, the speeches were louder and more incoherent. I don't think the company heard a speech by little Mr. Van John, whose health was drunk as representative of the British Turf, and who said that he had never known anything about the turf or about play, until their old schoolfellow, his dear friend—his swell friend, if he might be permitted the expression—Mr. Ringwood, taught him the use of cards; and once, in his own house, in Mayfair, and once in this very house, the 'Star and Garter,' showed him how to play the noble game of Blind Hookey. 'The men are drunk. Let us go away, Ascot. I didn't come for this kind of thing!' cried Ringwood, furious, by Lord Ascot's side.

This was the expression which Mr. Ringwood had used a short time before, when Philip was about to interrupt him. He had lifted his gun to fire then, but his hand had been held back. The bird passed him once more, and he could not help taking aim. 'This kind of thing is very dull, isn't it, Ringwood?' he called across the table, pulling away a flower, and glaring at the other through the little open space.

'Dull, old boy? I call it doosed good fun,' cries Lord Ascot, in the height of good-humour.

'Dull? What do you mean?' asked my Lord's neighbour.

'I mean you would prefer having a couple of packs of cards, and a little room, where you could win three or four hundred from a young fellow? It's more profitable and more quiet than "this kind of thing."'

'I say, I don't know what you mean!' cries the other.

'What! You have forgotten already? Has not Van John just told you, how you and Mr. Deuceace brought him down here, and won his money from him; and then how you gave him his revenge at your own house in—'

'Did I come here to be insulted by that fellow?' cries Mr. Ringwood, appealing to his neighbour.

'If that is an insult, you may put it in your pipe and smoke it, Mr. Ringwood!' cries Philip.

'Come away, come away, Ascot! Don't keep me here listening to this bla—'

'If you say another word,' says Philip, ' I'll send this decanter at your head!'

'Come, come—nonsense! No quarrelling! Make it up! Everybody has had too much! Get the bill, and order the omnibus round!' A crowd was on one side of the table, and the other. One of the cousins had not the least wish that the quarrel should proceed any further.

When, being in a quarrel, Philip Firmin assumes the calm and stately manner, he is perhaps in his most dangerous state. Lord Ascot's phaeton (in which Mr. Ringwood showed a great unwillingness to take a seat by the driver) was at the hotel gate, an omnibus and a private carriage or two were in readiness to take home the other guests of the feast. Ascot went into the hotel to light a final cigar, and now Philip, springing forward, caught by the arm the gentleman sitting on the front seat of the phaeton.

'Stop!' he said. 'You used a word just now—'

'What word? I don't know anything about words!' cries the other in a loud voice.

'You said "insulted,"' murmured Philip, in the gentlest tone.

'I don't know what I said,' said Ringwood peevishly.

'I said, in reply to the words which you forget, "that I would knock you down," or words to that effect. If you feel in the least aggrieved, you know where my chambers are—with Mr. Van John, whom you and your mistress inveigled to play cards when he was a boy. You are not fit to come into an honest man's house. It was only because I wished to spare a lady's feelings that I refrained from turning you out of mine. Good night, Ascot!' and with great majesty Mr. Philip returned to his companion and the hansom cab which was in waiting to convey these two gentlemen to London.

I was quite correct in my surmise that Philip's antagonist would take no further notice of the quarrel to Philip personally. Indeed, he affected to treat it as a drunken brawl, regarding which no man of sense would allow himself to be seriously disturbed. A quarrel between two men of the same family:—between

Philip and his own relative who had only wished him well?—It was absurd and impossible. What Mr. Ringwood deplored was the obstinate ill-temper and known violence of Philip, which were for ever leading him into these brawls, and estranging his family from him. A man seized by the coat, insulted, threatened with a decanter! A man of station so treated by a person whose own position was most questionable, whose father was a fugitive, and who himself was struggling for precarious subsistence! The arrogance was too great. With the best wishes for the unhappy young man, and his amiable (but empty-headed) little wife, it was impossible to take further notice of them. Let the visits cease. Let the carriage no more drive from Berkeley Square to Milman Street. Let there be no presents of game, poultry, legs of mutton, old clothes, and what not. Henceforth, therefore, the Ringwood carriage was unknown in the neighbourhood of the Foundling, and the Ringwood footmen no more scented with their powdered heads the Firmins' little hall ceiling. Sir John said to the end that he was about to procure a comfortable place for Philip, when his deplorable violence obliged Sir John to break off all relations with the most misguided young man.

Nor was the end of the mischief here. We have all read how the gods never appear alone—the gods bringing good or evil fortune. When two or three little pieces of good luck had befallen our poor friend, my wife triumphantly cried out, 'I told you so! Did I not always say that Heaven would befriend that dear innocent wife and children; that brave, generous, imprudent father?' And now when the evil days came, this monstrous logician insisted that poverty, sickness, dreadful doubt and terror, hunger and want almost, were all equally intended for Philip's advantage, and would work for good in the end. So that rain was good, and sunshine was good; so that sickness was good, and health was good; that Philip ill was to be as happy as Philip well, and as thankful for a sick house and an empty pocket as for a warm fireside and a comfortable larder. Mind, I ask no Christian philosopher to revile at his ill fortunes, or to despair. I will accept a toothache (or any evil of life) and bear it without too much grumbling. But I cannot say that to have a tooth pulled out is a blessing, or fondle the hand which wrenches at my jaw.

'They can live without their fine relations, and their donations of mutton and turnips,' cries my wife with a toss of her head. The way in which those people patronised Philip and dear Charlotte was perfectly intolerable. Lady Ringwood knows how dreadful the conduct of that Mr. Ringwood is, and—and I have no patience with her!' How, I repeat, do women know about men? How do they telegraph to each other their notices of alarm and mistrust? and fly as birds rise up with a rush and a skurry when danger appears to be near? All this was very well. But Mr. Tregarvan heard some account of the dispute between Philip and Mr. Ringwood, and applied to Sir John for further particulars; and Sir John—liberal man as he was and ever had been, and priding himself little, Heaven knew, on the privilege of rank, which was merely adventitious—was constrained to confess that this young man's conduct showed a great deal too much *laissez aller.* He had constantly, at Sir John's own house, manifested an independence which had bordered on rudeness; he was always notorious for his quarrelsome disposition, and lately had so disgraced himself in a scene with Sir John's eldest son, Mr. Ringwood—had exhibited such brutality, ingratitude, and—and inebriation, that Sir John was free to confess he had forbidden the gentleman his door.

'An insubordinate, ill-conditioned fellow, certainly!' thinks Tregarvan.

(And I do not say, though Philip is my friend, that Tregarvan and Sir John were altogether wrong regarding their *protégé.*) Twice Tregarvan had invited him to breakfast, and Philip had not appeared. More than once he had contradicted Tregarvan about the *Review.* He had said that the *Review* was not getting on, and if you asked Philip his candid opinion, it would not get on. Six numbers had appeared, and it did not meet with that attention which the public ought to pay to it. The public was careless as to the designs of that Great Power, which it was Tregarvan's aim to defy and confound. He took counsel with himself. He walked over to the publisher's, and inspected the books; and the result of that inspection was so disagreeable, that he went home straightway and wrote a letter to Philip Firmin, Esq., New Milman Street, Guilford Street, which that poor fellow brought to his usual advisers.

That letter contained a cheque for a quarter's salary, and bade adieu to Mr. Firmin. The writer would not recapitulate the causes of dissatisfaction which he felt respecting the conduct of the *Review.* He was much disappointed in its progress, and dissatisfied with its general management. He thought an opportunity was lost which never could be recovered for exposing the designs of a Power which menaced the liberty and tranquillity of Europe. Had it been directed with proper energy that *Review* might have been an ægis to that threatened liberty, a lamp to lighten the darkness of that menaced freedom. It might have pointed the way to the cultivation *bonarum literarum*; it might have fostered rising talent, it might have chastised the arrogance of so-called critics; it might have served the cause of truth. Tregarvan's hopes were disappointed: he would not say by whose remissness or fault. He had done *his* utmost in the good work, and, finally, would thank Mr. Firmin to print off the articles already purchased and paid for, and to prepare a brief notice for the next number, announcing the discontinuance of the *Review;* and Tregarvan showed my wife a cold shoulder for a considerable time afterwards, nor were we asked to his tea-parties, I forget for how many seasons.

This to us was no great loss or subject of annoyance: but to poor Philip? It was a matter of life and almost death to him. He never could save much out of his little pittance. Here were fifty pounds in his hand, it is true; but bills, taxes, rent, the hundred little obligations of a house, were due and pressing upon him; and in the midst of his anxiety, our dear little Mrs. Philip was about to present him with a third ornament to his nursery. Poor little Tertius arrived duly enough; and, such hypocrites were we, that the poor mother was absolutely thinking of calling the child Tregarvan Firmin, as a compliment to Mr. Tregarvan, who had been so kind to them, and Tregarvan Firmin would be such a pretty name, she thought. We imagined the Little Sister knew nothing about Philip's anxieties. Of course she attended Mrs. Philip through her troubles, and we vow that we never said a word to her regarding Philip's own. But Mrs. Brandon went in to Philip one day, as he was sitting very grave and sad with his two firstborn children, and she took both his hands, and said, 'You know, dear, I have saved ever so much: and I always intended it for—you know who.' And here she loosened one hand from him, and felt in her pocket for a purse, and put it into Philip's hand, and wept on his shoulder. And Philip kissed her, and thanked God for sending him such a dear friend, and gave her back her purse, though indeed he had but five pounds left in bis own when this benefactress came to him.

Yes: but there were debts owing to him. There was his wife's little portion of fifty pounds a year, which had never been paid since the second quarter after their marriage, which had happened now more than three years ago. As Philip had scarce a guinea in the world, he wrote to Mrs. Baynes, his wife's mother, to explain his extreme want, and to remind her that this money was due. Mrs. General Baynes was living at Jersey at this time in a choice society of half-pay ladies, clergymen, captains, and the like, among whom I have no doubt she moved as a great lady. She wore a large medallion of the deceased General on her neck. She wept dry tears over that interesting cameo at frequent tea-parties. She never could forgive Philip for taking away her child from her, and if any one would take away others of her girls, she would be equally unforgiving. Endowed with that wonderful logic with which women are blessed, I believe she never admitted, or has been able to admit to her own mind, that she did Philip or her daughter a wrong. In the tea-parties of her acquaintance she groaned over the extravagance of her son-in-law and his brutal treatment of her blessed child. Many good people agreed with her and shook their respectable noddles when the name of that prodigal Philip was mentioned over her muffins and Bohea. He was prayed for; his dear widowed mother-in-law was pitied, and blessed with all the comfort reverend gentlemen could supply on the spot? Upon my honour, Firmin, Emily and I were made to believe that you were a monster, sir,'—with cloven feet and a forked tail, by George!—and now I have heard your story, by Jove, I think it is you, and not Eliza Baynes, who were wronged. She has a deuce of a tongue, Eliza has: and a temper —poor Charles knew what *that* was!' In fine, when Philip, reduced to his last guinea, asked Charlotte's mother to pay her debt to her sick daughter, Mrs. General B. sent Philip a ten-pound note, open, by Captain Swang, of the Indian army, who happened to be coming to England. And that, Philip says, of all the hard knocks of fate, has been the very hardest which he has had to endure.

But the poor little wife knew nothing of this cruelty, nor, indeed, of the very poverty which was hemming round her curtain; and in the midst of his griefs, Philip Firmin was immensely consoled by the tender fidelity of the friends whom God had sent him. Their griefs were drawing to an end now. Kind readers all, may your sorrows, may mine, leave us with hearts not embittered, and humbly acquiescent to the Great Will.

CHAPTER XLI. IN WHICH WE REACH THE LAST STAGE BUT ONE OF THIS JOURNEY

ALTHOUGH poverty was knocking at Philip's humble door, little Charlotte in all her trouble never knew how menacing the L grim visitor had been. She did not quite understand that her husband in his last necessity sent to her mother for his due, and that the mother turned away and refused him. 'Ah,' thought poor Philip, groaning in his despair, 'I wonder whether the thieves who attacked the man in the parable were robbers of his own family, who knew that he carried money with him to Jerusalem, and waylaid him on the journey?' But again and again he has thanked God, with grateful heart, for the Samaritans whom he has met on life's road, and if he has not forgiven, it must be owned he has never done any wrong to those who robbed him.

Charlotte did not know that her husband was at his last guinea, and a prey to dreadful anxiety for her dear sake, for after the birth of her child a fever came upon her; in the delirium consequent upon which the poor thing was ignorant of all that happened round her. A fortnight with a wife in extremity, with crying infants, with hunger menacing at the door, passed for Philip somehow. The young man became an old man in this time. Indeed, his fair hair was streaked with white at the temples afterwards. But it must not be imagined that he had not friends during his affliction, and he always can gratefully count up the names of many persons to whom he might have applied had he been in need. He did not look or ask for these succours from his relatives. Aunt and Uncle Twysden shrieked and cried out at his extravagance, imprudence, and folly. Sir John Ringwood said he must really wash his hands of a young man who menaced the life of his own son. Grenville Woolcomb, with many oaths, in which brother-in-law Ringwood joined chorus, cursed Philip, and said he didn't care, and the beggar ought to be hung, and his father ought to be hung. But I think I know half-a-dozen good men and true who told a different tale, and who were ready with their sympathy and succour. Did not Mrs. Flanagan, the Irish laundress, in a voice broken by sobs and gin, offer to go and chare at Philip's house for nothing, and nurse the dear children? Did not Goodenough say, 'If you are in need, my dear fellow, of course you know where to come'; and did he not actually give two prescriptions, one for poor Charlotte, and one for fifty pounds to be taken immediately, which he handed to the nurse by mistake? You may be sure she did not appropriate the money, for of course you know that the nurse was Mrs. Brandon. Charlotte has one remorse in her life. She owns she was jealous of the Little Sister. And now when that gentle life is over, when Philip's poverty trials are ended, when the children go sometimes and look wistfully at the grave of their dear Caroline, friend Charlotte leans her head against her husband's shoulder, and owns humbly how good, how brave, how generous a friend Heaven sent them in that humble defender.

Have you ever felt the pinch of poverty? In many cases it is like the dentist's chair, more dreadful in the contemplation than in the actual suffering. Philip says he never was fairly beaten but on that day when, in reply to his solicitation to have his due, Mrs. Baynes's friend, Captain Swang, brought him the open ten-pound note. It was not much of a blow: the hand which dealt it made the hurt so keen. 'I remember,'says he, 'bursting out crying at school, because a big boy hit me a slight tap, and other boys said, "Oh, you coward!" It was that I knew the boy at home, and my parents had been kind to him. It seemed to me a wrong that Bumps should strike me,' said Philip; and he looked, while telling the story, as if he could cry about this injury now. I hope he has revenged himself by presenting coals of fire to his wife's relations. But to this day, when he is enjoying good health and competence, it is not safe to mention mothers-in-law in his presence. He fumes, shouts, and rages against them, as if all were like his; and his, I have been told, is a lady perfectly well satisfied with herself and her conduct in this world; and as for the next-but our story does not dare to point so far. It only interests itself about a little clique of people here below—their griefs, their trials, their weaknesses, their kindly hearts.

People there are in our history who do not seem to me to have kindly hearts at all; and yet perhaps, if a biography could be written from their point of view, some other novelist might show how Philip and *his* biographer were a pair of selfish worldlings unworthy of credit: how Uncle and Aunt Twysden were most exemplary people, and so forth. Have I not told you how many people at New York shook their heads when Philip's name was mentioned, and intimated a strong opinion that he used his father very ill? When he fell wounded and bleeding, patron Tregarvan dropped him off his horse, and Cousin Ringwood did not look behind to see how he fared. But these, again, may have had their opinion regarding our friend, who may have been misrepresented to them-1 protest as I look back at the past portions of this history, I begin to have qualms, and ask myself whether the folks of whom we have been prattling have had justice done to them: whether Agnes Twysden is not a suffering martyr justly offended by Philip's turbulent behaviour, and whether Philip deserves any particular attention or kindness at all. He is not transcendently clever; he is not gloriously beautiful. He is not about to illuminate the darkness in which the people grovel, with the flashing emanations of his truth. He sometimes owes money, which he cannot pay. He slips, stumbles, blunders, brags. Ah! he sins and repents—pray Heaven—of faults, of vanities, of pride, of a thousand shortcomings! This I say—*Ego*— as my friend's biographer. Perhaps I do not understand the other characters round about him so well, and have overlooked a number of their merits, and caricatured and exaggerated their little defects.

Among the Samaritans who came to Philip's help in these his straits, he loves to remember the name of J. J., the painter, whom he found sitting with the children one day making drawings for them, which the good painter never tired to sketch.

Now, if those children would but have kept Ridley's sketches, and waited for a good season at Christie's, I have no doubt they might have got scores of pounds for the drawings; but then, you see, they chose to improve the drawings with their own hands. They painted the soldiers yellow, the horses blue, and so forth. On the horses they put soldiers of their own construction. Ridley's landscapes were enriched with representations of 'omnibuses,' which the children saw and admired in the neighbouring New Road. I dare say, as the fever left her, and as she came to see things as they were, Charlotte's eyes dwelt fondly on the pictures of the omnibuses inserted in Mr. Ridley's sketches, and she put some aside, and showed them to her friends, and said, 'Doesn't our darling show extraordinary talent for drawing? Mr. Ridley says he does. He did a great part of this etching.'

But, besides the drawings, what do you think Master Ridley offered to draw for his friends? Besides the prescriptions of medicine, what drafts did Dr. Goodenough prescribe? When Nurse Brandon came to Mrs. Philip in her anxious time, we know what sort of payment she proposed for her services. Who says the world is all cold? There is the sun and the shadows. And the Heaven which ordains poverty and sickness, sends pity, and love, and succour.

During Charlotte's fever and illness, the Little Sister had left her but for one day, when her patient was quiet, and pronounced to be mending. It appears that Mrs. Charlotte was very ill indeed on this occasion; so ill that Dr. Goodenough thought she might have given us all the slip: so ill that, but for Brandon, she would, in all probability, have escaped out of this troublous world, and left Philip and her orphaned little ones. Charlotte mended then: could take food, and liked it, and was specially pleased with some chickens which her nurse informed her were 'from the country.' 'From Sir John Ringwood, no doubt?' said Mrs. Firmin, remembering the presents sent from Berkeley Square, and the mutton and the turnips.

'Well, eat and be thankful!' says the Little Sister, who was as gay as a little sister could be, and who had prepared a beautiful bread sauce for the fowl; and who had tossed the baby, and who showed it to its admiring brother and sister ever so many times; and who saw that Mr. Philip had his dinner comfortable; and who never took so much as a drop of porter—at home a little glass sometimes was comfortable, but on duty, never, never! No, not if Dr. Goodenough ordered it! she vowed. And the Doctor wished he could say as much, or believe as much, of all his nurses.

Milman Street is such a quiet little street that our friends had not carpeted it in the usual way; and three days after her temporary absence, as Nurse Brandon sits by her patient's bed, powdering the back of a small pink infant that makes believe to swim upon her apron, a rattle of wheels is heard in the quiet street—of four wheels, of one horse, of a jingling carriage, which stops before Philip's door. 'It's the trap,' says Nurse Brandon, delighted. 'It must be those kind Ringwoods,' says Mrs. Philip. 'But stop, Brandon. Did not they, did not we?—oh, how kind of them!' She was trying to recall the past. Past and present days had been strangely mingled in her fevered brain. 'Hush, my dear! you are to be kep' quite still,' says the nurse —and then proceeded to finish the polishing and powdering of the pink frog on her lap.

The bedroom window was open towards the sunny street: but Mrs. Philip did not hear a female voice say, "Old the 'orse's 'ead, Jim,' or she might have been agitated. The horse's head was held, and a gentleman and a lady with a great basket containing peas, butter, greens, flowers, and other rural produce, descended from the vehicle, and rang at the bell.

Philip opened it; with his little ones, as usual, trotting at his knees.

'Why, my darlings, how you air grown!' cries the lady.

'Bygones be bygones. Give us your 'and, Firmin: here's mine. My missus has brought some country butter and things for your dear good lady. And we hope you liked the chickens. And God bless you, old fellow, how are you?' The tears were rolling down the good man's cheeks as he spoke. And Mrs. Mugford was likewise exceedingly hot, and very much affected. And the children said to her, 'Mamma is better now: and we have a little brother, and he is crying now upstairs.'

'Bless you, my darlings!' Mrs. Mugford was off by this time. She put down her peace-offering of carrots, chickens, bacon, butter. She cried plentifully. 'It was Brandon came and told us,' she said; 'and when she told us how all your great people had flung you over, and you'd been quarrelling again, you naughty fellar, I says to Mugford, "Let's go and see after that dear thing, Mugford," I says. And here we are. And year's two nice cakes for your children' (after a forage in the cornucopia), 'and, lor', how they are grown!'

A little nurse from the upstairs regions here makes her appearance, holding a bundle of cashmere shawls, part of which is removed, and discloses a being pronounced to be ravishingly beautiful, and 'jest like Mrs. Mugford's Emaly!'

'I say,' says Mugford, 'the old shop's still open to you. T'other chap wouldn't do at all. He was wild when he got the drink on board. Hirish. Pitched into Bickerton, and black'd 'is eye. It was Bicker-ton who told you lies about that poor lady. Don't see 'im no more now. Borrowed some money of me; haven't seen him since. We were both wrong, and we must make it up—the missus says we must.'

'Amen!' said Philip, with a grasp of the honest fellow's hand. And next Sunday he and a trim little sister, and two children, went to an old church in Queen Square, Bloomsbury, which was fashionable in the reign of Queen Anne, when Richard Steele kept house, and did not pay rent, hard by. And when the clergyman in the Thanksgiving particularised those who desired now to 'offer up their praises and thanksgiving for late mercies vouchsafed to them,' once more Philip Firmin said 'Amen,' on his knees, and with all his heart.

CHAPTER XLII. THE REALMS OF BLISS

YOU know—all good boys and girls at Christmas know—that, before the last scene of the pantomime, when the Good Fairy ascends in a blaze of glory, and Harlequin and Columbine take hands, having danced through all their tricks and troubles and tumbles, there is a dark, brief, seemingly meaningless, penultimate scene, in which the performers appear to grope about perplexed, whilst the music of bassoons and trombones, and the like, groans tragically. As the actors, with gestures of dismay and outstretched arms, move hither and thither, the wary frequenter of pantomimes sees the illuminators of the Abode of Bliss and Hall of Prismatic Splendour nimbly moving behind the canvas, and streaking the darkness with twinkling fires—fires which shall blaze out presently in a thousand colours round the Good Fairy in the Revolving Temple of Blinding Bliss. Be happy, Harlequin! Love and be happy and dance, pretty Columbine! Children, mamma bids you put your shawls on. And Jack and Mary (who are young and love pantomimes) look lingeringly still over the ledge of the box, whilst the fairy temple yet revolves, whilst the fireworks play, and ere the Great Dark Curtain descends.

My dear young people, who have sat kindly through the scenes during which our entertainment has lasted, be it known to you that last chapter was the dark scene. Look to your cloaks, and tie up your little throats, for I tell you the great baize will soon fall down. Have I had any secrets from you all through the piece *I* I tell you the house will be empty and you will be in the cold air. When the boxes have got their nightgowns on, and you are all gone, and I have turned off the gas, and am in the empty theatre alone in the darkness, I promise you I shall not be merry. Never mind! We can make jokes though we are ever so sad. We can jump over head and heels, though I declare the pit is half emptied already, and the last orange-woman has slunk away. Encore une pirouette, Columbine! Saute, Arlequin, mon ami! Though there are but five bars more of the music, my good people, we must jump over them briskly, and then go home to supper and bed.

Philip Firmin, then, was immensely moved by this magnanimity and kindness on the part of his old employer, and has always considered Mugford's arrival and friendliness as a special interposition in his favour. He owes it all to Brandon, he says. It was she who bethought herself of his condition, represented it to Mugford, and reconciled him to his enemy. Others were most ready with their money. It was Brandon who brought him work rather than alms, and enabled him to face fortune cheerfully. His interval of poverty was so short, that he actually had not occasion to borrow. A week more, and he could not have held out, and poor Brandon's little marriage present must have gone to the cenotaph of sovereigns—the dear Little Sister's gift which Philip's family cherish to this hour.

So Philip, with a humbled heart and demeanour, clambered up on his sub-editorial stool once more at the *Pall Mall Gazette,* and again brandished the paste-pot and the scissors. I forget whether Bickerton still remained in command at the *Pall Mall Gazette,* or was more kind to Philip than before, or was afraid of him, having heard of his exploits as a fire-eater; but certain it is, the two did not come to a quarrel, giving each other a wide berth, as the saying is, and each doing his own duty. Good-bye, Monsieur Bickerton. Except, mayhap, in the final group, round the Fairy Chariot (when, I promise you, there will be such a blaze of glory that he will be invisible), we shall never see the little spiteful envious creature more. Let him pop down his appointed trap-door; and, quick fiddles! let the brisk music jig on.

Owing to the coolness which had arisen between Philip and his father on account of their different views regarding the use to be made of Philip's signature, the old gentleman drew no further bills in his son's name, and our friend was spared from the unpleasant persecution. Mr. Hunt loved Dr. Firmin so ardently that he could not bear to be separated from the Doctor long. Without the Doctor, London was a dreary wilderness to Hunt. Unfortunate remembrances of past pecuniary transactions haunted him here. We were all of us glad when he finally retired from the Covent Garden taverns and betook himself to the Bowery once more.

And now friend Philip was at work again, hardly earning a scanty meal for self, wife, servant, children. It was indeed a meagre meal, and a small wage. Charlotte's illness, and other mishaps, had swept away poor Philip's little savings. It was determined that we would let the elegantly furnished apartments on the first floor. You might have fancied the proud Mr. Firmin rather repugnant to such a measure. And so he was on the score of convenience: but of dignity, not a whit. To this day, if necessity called, Philip would turn a mangle with perfect gravity. I believe the thought of Mrs. General Baynes's horror at the idea of her son-in-law letting lodgings greatly soothed and comforted Philip. The lodgings were absolutely taken by our country acquaintance, Miss Pybus, who was coming up for the May meetings, and whom we persuaded (Heaven be good to us) that she would find a most desirable quiet residence in the house of a man with three squalling children. Miss P. came, then, with my wife, to look at the apartments; and we allured her by describing to her the delightful musical services at the Foundling hard by; and she was very much pleased with Mrs. Philip, and did not even wince at the elder children, whose pretty faces won the kind old lady's heart; and I am ashamed to say we were mum about the baby: and Pybus was going to close for the lodgings, when Philip burst out of his little room, without his coat, I believe, and objurgated a little printer's boy, who was sitting in the hall, waiting for some ' copy' regarding which he had made a blunder; and Philip used such violent language towards the little lazy boy, that Pybus said 'she never could think of taking apartments in that house,' and hurried thence in a panic. When Brandon heard of this project of letting lodgings, she was in a fury. *She* might let lodgin's, but it wasn't for Philip to do so. 'Let lodgin's, indeed! Buy a broom, and sweep a crossin'!' Brandon always thought Charlotte a poor-spirited creature, and the way she scolded Mrs. Firmin about this transaction was not a little amusing. Charlotte was not angry. She liked the scheme as little as Brandon. No other person ever asked for lodgings in Charlotte's house. May and its meetings came to an end. The old ladies went back to their country towns. The missionaries returned to Caffraria. (Ah! where are the pleasant-looking Quakeresses of our youth, with their comely faces, and pretty dove-coloured robes? They say the goodly sect is dwindling—dwindling.) The Quakeresses went out of town: then the fashionable world began to move: the Parliament went out of town. In a word, everybody who could, made away for a holiday, whilst poor Philip remained at his work, snipping and pasting his paragraphs, and doing his humble drudgery.

A sojourn on the sea-shore was prescribed by Dr. Goodenough, as absolutely necessary for Charlotte and her young ones, and when Philip pleaded certain cogent reasons why the family could not take the medicine prescribed by the Doctor, that eccentric physician had recourse to the same pocket-book which we have known him to produce on a former occasion; and took from it, for what I know, some of the very same notes which he had formerly given to the Little Sister. 'I suppose you may as well have them as that rascal Hunt,' said the Doctor, scowling very fiercely. 'Don't tell *me.* Stuff and nonsense. Pooh! Pay me when you are a rich man!' And this Samaritan had jumped into his carriage, and was gone, before Philip or Mrs. Philip could say a word of thanks. Look at him, as he is going off. See the green brougham drive away, and turn westward, and mark it well. A shoe go after thee, John Goodenough; we shall see thee no more in this story. You are not in the secret, good reader: but I, who have been living with certain people for many months past, and have a hearty liking for some of them, grow very soft when the hour for shaking bands comes, to think we are to meet no more. Go to! when this tale began, and for some months after, a pair of kind old eyes used to read these pages, which are now closed in the sleep appointed for all of us. And so page is turned after page, and behold Finis and the volume's end.

So Philip and his young folks came down to Periwinkle Bay, where we were staying, and the girls in the two families nursed the baby, and the child and mother got health and comfort from the fresh air, and Mr. Mugford—who believes himself to be the finest sub-editor in the world; and I can tell you there is a great art in sub-editing a paper—Mr. Mugford, I say, took Philip's scissors and paste-pot, whilst the latter enjoyed his holiday. And J. J. Ridley, R.A., came and joined us presently, and we had many sketching parties, and my drawings of the various points about the bay, *viz.,* Lobster Head, the Mollusc Rocks, etc. etc., are considered to be very spirited, though my little boy (who certainly has not his father's taste for art) mistook for the rock a really capital portrait of Philip, in a grey hat and paletot, sprawling on the sand.

Some twelve miles inland from the bay is the little town of Whipham Market, and Whipham skirts the park palings of that castle where Lord Ringwood had lived, and where Philip's mother was born and bred. There is a statue of the late lord in Whipham market-place. Could he have had his will, the borough would have continued to return two Members to Parliament, as in the good old times before us. In that ancient and grass-grown tittle place, where your footsteps echo as you pass through the street, where you hear distinctly the creaking of the sign of the 'Ringwood Arms' hotel and posting-house, and the opposition creaking of the 'Ram Inn' over the way—where the half-pay captain, the curate, and the medical man stand before the fly-blown window-blind of the 'Ringwood Institute' and survey the strangers—there is still a respect felt for the memory of the great lord who dwelt behind the oaks in yonder hall. He had his faults. His Lordship's life was not that of an anchorite. The company his Lordship kept, especially in his latter days, was not of that select description which a nobleman of his Lordship's rank might command. But he was a good friend to Whipham. He was a good landlord to a good tenant. If he had his will, Whipham would have kept its own. His Lordship paid half the expense after the burning of the town-hall. He was an arbitrary man, certainly, and he flogged Alderman Duffle before his own shop, but he apologised for it most handsome afterwards. Would the gentlemen like port or sherry? Claret not called for in Whipham; not at all; and no fish, because all the fish at Periwinkle Bay is bought up and goes to London. Such were the remarks made by the landlord of the Ringwood Arms to three cavaliers who entered that hostelry. And you may be sure he told us about Lord Ringwood's death in the post-chaise as he came from Turreys Regum; and how his Lordship went through them gates (pointing to a pair of gates and lodges which skirt the town), and was drove up to the castle and laid in state; and his Lordship never would take the railway, never; and he always travelled like a nobleman, and when he came to a hotel and changed horses, he always called for a bottle of wine, and only took a glass, and sometimes not even that. And the present Sir John has kept no company here as yet; and they say he is close of his money, they say he is. And this is certain, Whipham haven't seen much of it, Whipham haven't.

We went into the inn-yard, which may have been once a stirring place, and then sauntered up to the park gate, surmounted by the supporters and armorial bearings of the Ringwoods. 'I wonder whether my poor mother came out of that gate when she eloped with my father?' said Philip. 'Poor thing, poor thing!' The great gates were shut. The westering sun cast shadows over the sward where here and there the deer were browsing, and at some mile distance lay the house, with its towers and porticos and vanes flaming in the sun. The smaller gate was open, and a girl was standing by the lodge-door. Was the house to be seen?

'Yes,' says a little red-cheeked girl, with a curtsey.

'No!' calls out a harsh voice from within, and an old woman comes out from the lodge and looks at us fiercely. 'Nobody is to go to the house. The family is a-coming.'

That was provoking. Philip would have liked to behold the great house where his mother and her ancestors were born.

'Marry, good dame,' Philip's companion said to the old beldam, 'this goodly gentleman hath a right of entrance to yonder castle, which, I trow, ye wot not of. Heard ye never tell of one Philip Ringwood, slain at Busaco's glorious fi—'

'Hold your tongue, and don't chaff her, Pen,' growled Firmin.

'Nay, an she knows not Philip Ringwood's grandson,' the other wag continued, in a softened tone, 'this will convince her of our right to enter. Canst recognise this image of your Queen?'

'Well, I suppose 'ee can go up,' said the old woman, at the sight of this talisman. 'There's only two of them staying there, and they're out a-drivin'.'

Philip was bent on seeing the halls of his ancestors. Grey and huge, with towers, and vanes, and porticos, they lay before us a mile off, separated from us by a streak of glistening river. A great chestnut avenue led up to the river, and in the dappled grass the deer were browsing.

You know the house of course. There is a picture of it in Watts, bearing date 1783. A gentleman in a cocked hat and pigtail is rowing a lady in a boat on the shining river. Another nobleman in a cocked hat is angling in the glistening river from the bridge, over which a postchaise is passing.

'Yes, the place is like enough,' said Philip; 'but I miss the post-chaise going over the bridge, and the lady in the punt with the tall parasol. Don't you remember the print in our housekeeper's room in Old Parr Street? My poor mother used to tell me about the house, and I imagined it grander than the palace of Aladdin. It *is* a very handsome house,' Philip went on. '"It extends two hundred and sixty feet by seventy-five, and consists of a rustic basement and principal story, with an attic in the centre, the whole executed in stone. The grand front towards the park is adorned with a noble portico of the Corinthian order, and may with propriety be considered one of the finest elevations in the—" I tell you I am quoting out of Watts's "Seats of the Nobility and Gentry," published by John and Josiah Boydell, and lying in our drawing-room. Ah, dear me! I painted the boat and the lady and gentleman in the drawing-room copy, and my father boxed my ears, and my mother cried out, poor dear soul! And this is the river, is it? And over this the postchaise went with the club-tailed horses, and here was the pig-tailed gentleman fishing. It gives one a queer sensation,' says Philip, standing on the bridge, and stretching out his big arms. 'Yes, there are the two people in the punt by the rushes. I can see them, but you can't; and I hope, sir, you will have good sport.' And here he took off his hat to an imaginary gentleman supposed to be angling from the balustrade for ghostly gudgeon. We reached the house presently. We ring at a door in the basement under the portico. The porter demurs, and says some of the family is down, but they are out, to be sure. The same half-crown argument answers with him which persuaded the keeper at the lodge. We go through the show-rooms of the stately but somewhat faded and melancholy palace. In the cedar dining-room there hangs the grim portrait of the late Earl; and that fair-haired officer in red? that must be Philip's grandfather. And those two slim girls embracing, surely those are his mother and his aunt. Philip walks softly through the vacant rooms. He gives the porter a gold piece ere he goes out of the great hall, forty feet cube, ornamented with statues brought from Rome by John first Baron, namely, Heliogabalus, Nero's mother, a priestess of Isis, and a river god; the pictures over the doors by Pedimento; the ceiling by Leotardi, etc.; and in a window in the great hall there is a table with a visitors' book, in which Philip writes his name. As we went away, we met a carriage which drove rapidly towards the house, and which no doubt contained the members of the Ringwood family, regarding whom the porteress had spoken. After the family differences previously related, we did not care to face these kinsfolk of Philip, and passed on quickly in twilight beneath the rustling umbrage of the chestnuts. J. J. saw a hundred fine pictorial effects as we walked: the palace reflected in the water; the dappled deer under the chequered shadow of the trees. It was, 'Oh, what a jolly bit of colour!' and, 'I say, look, how well that old woman's red cloak comes in!' and so forth. Painters never seem tired of their work. At seventy they are students still, patient, docile, happy. May we too, my good sir, live for fourscore years, and never be too old to learn!

The walk, the brisk accompanying conversation, amid stately scenery around, brought us with good appetites and spirits to our inn, where we were told that dinner would be served when the omnibus arrived from the railway.

At a short distance from the Ringwood Arms, and on the opposite side of the street, is the Ram Inn, neat postchaises and farmers' ordinary; a house, of which the pretensions seemed less, though the trade was somewhat more lively. When the tooting of the horn announced the arrival of the omnibus from the railway, I should think a crowd of at least fifteen people assembled at various doors of the High Street and Market. The half-pay captain and the curate came out from the Ringwood Athenæum. The doctor's apprentice stood on the step of the surgery door, and the surgeon's lady looked out from the first floor. We shared the general curiosity. We and the waiter stood at the door of the 'Ringwood Arms'. We were mortified to see that of the five persons conveyed by the 'bus, one was a tradesman, who descended at his door (Mr. Packwood, the saddler, so the waiter informed us), three travellers were discharged at the Ram, and only one came to us.

'Mostly bagmen goes to the "Ram,"' the waiter said, with a scornful air; and these bagmen, and their bags, quitted the omnibus.

Only one passenger remained for the 'Ringwood Arms Hotel,' and he presently descended under the *porte cochère;* and the omnibus—I own, with regret, it was but a one-horse machine—drove rattling into the courtyard, where the bells of the 'Star,' the 'George,' the 'Rodney,' the 'Dolphin,' and so on, had once been wont to jingle, and the court had echoed with the noise and clatter of hoofs and ostlers, and the cries of 'First and second, turn out.'

Who was the merry-faced little gentleman in black, who got out of the omnibus, and cried, when he saw us, 'What, *you* here?' It was Mr. Bradgate, that lawyer of Lord Ringwood's with whom we made a brief acquaintance just after his Lordship's death. 'What, *you* here?' cries Bradgate, then, to Philip. 'Come down about this business, of course? Very glad that you and—and certain parties have made it up. Thought you weren't friends.'

What business? What parties? We had not heard the news. We had only come over from Periwinkle Bay by chance, in order to see the house.

'How very singular! Did you meet the—the people who were staying there?'

We said we had seen a carriage pass, but did not remark who was in it. What, however, was the news? Well. It would be known immediately, and would appear in Tuesday's *Gazette*. The news was that Sir John Ringwood was going to take a peerage, and that the seat for Whipham would be vacant. And herewith our friend produced from his travelling bag a proclamation, which he read to us, and which was addressed—

'To the Worthy and Independent Electors of the Borough of Ringwood.

'London: *Wednesday.*

'GENTLEMEN,—A gracious Sovereign having been pleased to order that the family of Ringwood should continue to be represented in the House of Peers, I take leave of my friends and constituents who have given me their kind confidence hitherto, and promise them that my regard for them will never cease, or my interest in the town and neighbourhood where my family have dwelt for many centuries. The late lamented Lord Ringwood's brother died in the service of his Sovereign in Portugal, following the same flag under which his ancestors for centuries have fought and bled. My own son serves the Crown in a civil capacity. It was natural that one of our name and family should continue the relations which so long have subsisted between us and this loyal, affectionate, but independent borough. Mr. Ringwood's onerous duties in the office which he holds are sufficient to occupy his time. A gentleman united to our family by the closest ties will offer himself as a candidate for your suffrages—'

'Why, who is it? He is not going to put in Uncle Twysden, or my sneak of a cousin?'

'No,' says Mr. Bradgate.

'Well, bless my soul! he can't mean me,' said Philip. 'Who is the dark horse he has in his stable?'

Then Mr. Bradgate laughed. 'Dark horse you may call him. The new Member is to be Grenville Woolcomb, Esq., your West India relative, and no other.'

Those who know the extreme energy of Mr. P. Firmin's language when he is excited, may imagine the explosion of Philippine wrath which ensued as our friend heard this name. 'That miscreant: that skinflint: that wealthy crossing-sweeper: that ignoramus who scarce could do more than sign his name! Oh, it was horrible, shameful! Why, the man is on such ill terms with his wife that they say he strikes her. When I see him I feel inclined to choke him, and murder him. *That* brute going into Parliament, and the republican Sir John Ringwood sending him there! It's monstrous!'

'Family arrangements. Sir John, or, I should say, my Lord Ringwood, is one of the most affectionate of parents,' Mr. Bradgate remarked. 'He has a large family by his second marriage, and his estates go to his eldest son. We must not quarrel with Lord Ringwood for wishing to provide for his young ones. I don't say that he quite acts up to the extreme Liberal principles of which he was once rather fond of boasting. But if you were offered a peerage, what would you do; what would I do? If you wanted money for your young ones, and could get it, would you not take it? Come, come, don't let us have too much of this Spartan virtue! If we were tried, my good friend, we should not be much worse or better than our neighbours. Is my fly coming, waiter?' We asked Mr. Bradgate to defer his departure, and to share our dinner. But he declined, and said he must go up to the great house, where he and his client had plenty of business to arrange, and where no doubt he would stay for the night. He bade the inn servants put his portmanteau into his carriage when it came. 'The old lord had some famous port wine,' he said; 'I hope my friends have the key of the cellar.'

The waiter was just putting our meal on the table, as we stood in the bow-window of the 'Ringwood Arms' coffee-room, engaged in this colloquy. Hence we could see the street, and the opposition inn of the 'Ram,' where presently a great placard was posted. At least a dozen street-boys, shopmen, and rustics were quickly gathered round this manifesto, and we ourselves went out to examine it. The Ram placard denounced, in terms of unmeasured wrath, the impudent attempt from the Castle to dictate to the free and independent electors of the borough. Freemen were invited not to promise their votes; to show themselves worthy of their name; to submit to no Castle dictation. A county gentleman of property, of influence, of Liberal principles—No WEST INDIAN, no CASTLE FLUNKEY, but a TRUE ENGLISH GENTLEMAN, would come forward to rescue them from the tyranny under which they laboured. On this point the electors might rely on the word of A BRITON.

'This was brought down by the clerk from Bedloe's. He and a newspaper man came down in the train with me; a Mr. —'

As he spoke, there came forth from the 'Ram,' the newspaper man of whom Mr. Bradgate spoke—an old friend and comrade of Philip, that energetic man and able reporter, Phipps of the *Daily Intelligencer,* who recognised Philip, and cordially greeting him, asked what *he* did down here, and supposed he had come to support his family.

Philip explained that we were strangers, had come from a neighbouring watering-place to see the home of Philip's ancestors, and were not even aware, until then, that an electioneering contest was pending in the place, or that Sir John Ringwood was about to be promoted to the peerage. Meanwhile, Mr. Bradgate's fly had driven out of the hotel yard of the Ringwood Arms, and the lawyer, running to the house for a bag of papers, jumped into the carriage and called to the coachman to drive to the Castle.

'Bon appétit!' says he, in a confident tone, and he was gone.

'Would Phipps dine with us?' Phipps whispered, 'I am on the other side, and the "Ram" is our house.'

We, who were on no side, entered into the 'Ringwood Arms,' and sat down to our meal—to the mutton and the catsup, cauliflower and potatoes, the copper-edged side-dishes, and the watery melted-butter, with which strangers are regaled in inns in declining towns. The town *badauds,* who had read the placard at the Ram, now came to peruse the proclamation in our window. I dare say thirty pairs of clinking boots stopped before the one window and the other, the while we ate tough mutton and drank fiery sherry. And J. J., leaving his dinner, sketched some of the figures of the townsfolk staring at the manifesto, with the old-fashioned 'Ram Inn' for a background—a picturesque gable enough.

Our meal was just over, when, somewhat to our surprise, our friend Mr. Bradgate the lawyer returned to the 'Ringwood Arms'. He wore a disturbed countenance. He asked what he could have for dinner? Mutton neither hot nor cold. Hum! That must do. So he had not been invited to dine at the Park? We rallied him with much facetiousness on this disappointment.

Little Bradgate's eyes started with wrath. 'What a churl the little black fellow is!' he cried. 'I took him his papers. I talked with him till dinner was laid in the very room where we were. French beans and neck of venison—I saw the housekeeper and his man bring them in! And Mr. Woolcomb did not so much as ask me to sit down to dinner—but told me to come again at nine o'clock! Confound this mutton—it's neither hot nor cold! The little skinflint!' The glasses of fiery sherry which Bradgate now swallowed Berved rather to choke than appease the lawyer. We laughed, and this jocularity angered him more. 'Oh,' said he, 'I am not the only person Woolcomb was rude to. He was in a dreadful ill temper. He abused his wife: and when he read somebody's name in the strangers' book, I promise you, Firmin, he abused *you.* I had a mind to say to him, "Sir, Mr. Firmin is dining at the 'Ringwood Arms,' and I will tell him what you say of him." What india-rubber mutton this is! What villainous sherry! Go back to him at nine o'clock, indeed! Be hanged to his impudence!'

'You must not abuse Woolcomb before Firmin,' said one of our party. 'Philip is so fond of his cousin's husband, that he cannot bear to hear the black man abused.'

This was not a very brilliant joke, but Philip grinned at it with much savage satisfaction.

'Hit Woolcomb as hard as you please, he has no friends here, Mr. Bradgate,' growled Philip. 'So he is rude to his lawyer, is he?'

'I tell you he is worse than the old Earl,' cried the indignant Bradgate. 'At least the old man was a peer of England, and could be a gentleman when he wished. But to be bullied by a fellow who might be a black footman, or ought to be sweeping a crossing! It's monstrous!'

'Don't speak ill of a man and a brother, Mr. Bradgate. Woolcomb can't help his complexion.'

'But he can help his confounded impudence, and shan't practise it on me!' the attorney cried.

As Bradgate called out from his box, puffing and fuming, friend J. J. was scribbling in the little sketch-book which he always carried. He smiled over his work. 'I know,' he said, 'the Black Prince well enough. I have often seen him driving his chestnut mares in the Park, with that bewildered white wife by his side. I am sure that woman is miserable, and, poor thing—'

'Serve her right! What did an English lady mean by marrying such a fellow?' cries Bradgate.

'A fellow who does not ask his lawyer to dinner!' remarks one of the company; perhaps the reader's very humble servant. 'But what an imprudent lawyer he has chosen—a lawyer who speaks his mind.'

'I have spoken my mind to his betters, and be hanged to him! Do you think I am going to be afraid of *him*?' bawls the irascible solicitor.

'*Contempsi Catilinæ gladios*—do you remember the old quotation at school, Philip?' And here there was a break in our conversation, for, chancing to look at friend J. J.'s sketch-book, we saw that he had made a wonderful little drawing, representing Woolcomb and Woolcomb's wife, grooms, phaeton, and chestnut mares, as they were to be seen any afternoon in Hyde Park, during the London season.

Admirable! Capital! Everybody at once knew the likeness of the dusky charioteer. Iracundus himself smiled and sniggered over it. 'Unless you behave yourself, Mr. Bradgate, Ridley will make a picture of *you,*' says Philip. Bradgate made a comical face, and retreated into his box, of which he pretended to draw the curtain. But the sociable little man did not long remain in his retirement; he emerged from it in a short time, his wine decanter in his hand, and joined our little party; and then we fell to talking of old times; and we all remembered a famous drawing by H. B. of the late Earl of Ringwood, in the old-fashioned swallow-tailed coat and tight trousers, on the old-fashioned horse, with the old-fashioned groom behind him, as he used to be seen pounding along Rotten Row.

'I speak my mind, do I?' says Mr. Bradgate, presently. 'I know somebody who spoke *his* mind to that old man, and who would have been better off if he had held his tongue.'

'Come, tell me, Bradgate,' cried Philip. 'It is all over and past now. Had Lord Ringwood left me something? I declare I thought at one time that he intended to do so.'

'Nay, has not your friend here been rebuking me for speaking my mind? I am going to be as mum as a mouse. Let us talk about the election.' And the provoking lawyer would say no more on a subject possessing a dismal interest for poor Phil.

'I have no more right to repine,' said that philosopher, 'than a man would have who drew number x in the lottery, when the winning ticket was number y. Let us talk, as you say, about the election. Who is to oppose Mr. Woolcomb?'

Mr. Bradgate believed a neighbouring squire, Mr. Hornblow, was to be the candidate put forward against the Ringwood nominee.

'Hornblow! what, Hornblow of Grey Friars?' cries Philip. 'A better fellow never lived. In this case he shall have our vote and interest; and I think we ought to go over and take another dinner at the "Ram".'

The new candidate actually turned out to be Philip's old school and college friend, Mr. Hornblow. After dinner we met him with a staff of canvassers on the tramp through the little town. Mr. Homblow was paying his respects to such tradesmen as had their shops yet open. Next day being market-day, he proposed to canvass the market people. 'If I meet the black man, Firmin,' said the burly squire, 'I think I can chaff him off his legs. He is a bad one at speaking, I am told.'

As if the tongue of Plato would have prevailed in Whipham and against the nominee of the great house! The hour was late to be sure, but the companions of Mr. Hornblow on his canvass augured ill of his success after half-an-hour's walk at his heels. Baker Jones would not promise nohow: that meant Jones would vote for the Castle, Mr. Hornblow's legal aide-de-camp, Mr. Batley, was forced to allow. Butcher Brown was having his tea,—his shrill-voiced wife told us, looking out from her glazed back parlour: Brown would vote for the Castle. Saddler Briggs would see about it. Grocer Adams fairly said he would vote against us—against *us*?—against Hornblow, whose part we were taking already. I fear the flattering promises of support of a great body of free and unbiassed electors, which had induced Mr. Hornblow to come forward and, etc., were but inventions of that little lawyer, Batley, who found his account in having a contest in the borough. When the polling-day came—you see, I disdain to make any mysteries in this simple and veracious story—Mr. Geenville Woolcomb, whose solicitor and agent spoke for him—Mr. Grenville Woolcomb, who could not spell or speak two sentences of decent English, and whose character for dulness, ferocity, penuriousness, jealousy, almost fatuity, was notorious to all the world—was returned by an immense majority, and the country gentlemen brought scarce a hundred votes to the poll.

We who were in nowise engaged in the contest, nevertheless found amusement from it in a quiet country place where little else was stirring. We came over once or twice from Periwinkle Bay. We mounted Hornblow's colours openly. We drove up ostentatiously to the 'Ram,' forsaking the 'Ringwood Arms,' where Mr. GRENVILLE WOOLCOMB's COMMITTEE ROOM was now established in that very coffee-room where we had dined in Mr. Bradgate's company. We warmed in the contest. We met Bradgate and his principal more than once, and our Montagus and Capulets defied each other in the public street. It was fine to see Philip's great figure and noble scowl when he met Woolcomb at the canvass. Gleams of mulatto hate quivered from the eyes of the little Captain. Darts of fire flashed from beneath Philip's eyebrows as he elbowed his way forward, and hustled Woolcomb off the pavement. Mr. Philip never disguised any sentiment of his. 'Hate the little ignorant, spiteful, vulgar, avaricious beast? Of course I hate him, and I should like to pitch him into the river.' 'Oh Philip!' Charlotte pleaded. But there was no reasoning with this savage when in wrath. I deplored, though perhaps I was amused by, his ferocity.

The local paper on our side was filled with withering epigrams against this poor Woolcomb, of which, I suspect, Philip was the author. I think I know that fierce style and tremendous invective. In the man whom he hates he can see no good: and in his friend no fault. When we met Bradgate apart from his principal, we were friendly enough. He said we had no chance in the contest. He did not conceal his dislike and contempt for his client. He amused us in later days (when he actually became Philip's man of law) by recounting anecdotes of Woolcomb, his fury, his jealousy, his avarice, his brutal behaviour. Poor Agnes had married for money, and he gave her none. Old Twysden, in giving his daughter to this man, had hoped to have the run of a fine house; to ride in Woolcomb's carriages, and feast at his table. But Woolcomb was so stingy that he grudged the meat which his wife ate, and would give none to her relations. He turned those relations out of his doors. Talbot and Ringwood Twysden, he drove them both away. He lost a child because he would not send for a physician. His wife never forgave him that meanness. Her hatred for him became open and avowed. They parted, and she led a life into which we will look no farther. She quarrelled with parents as well as husband. 'Why,' she said, 'did they sell me to that man?' Why did she sell herself? She required little persuasion from father and mother when she committed that crime. To be sure, they had educated her so well to worldliness, that when the occasion came, she was ready.

We used to see this luckless woman, with her horses and servants decked with Woolcomb's ribbons, driving about the little town, and making feeble efforts to canvass the townspeople. They all knew how she and her husband quarrelled. Reports came very quickly from the Hall to the town. Woolcomb had not been at Whipham a week when people began to hoot and jeer at him as he passed in his carriage. 'Think how weak you must be,' Bradgate said, 'when we can win with this horse! I wish he would stay away, though. We could manage much better without him. He has insulted I don't know how many free and independent electors, and infuriated others, because he will not give them beer when they come to the house. If Woolcomb would stay in the place, and we could have the election next year, I think your man might win. But, as it is, he may as well give in, and spare the expense of a poll.' Meanwhile Hornblow was very confident. We believe what we wish to believe. It is marvellous what faith an enthusiastic electioneering agent can inspire in his client. At any rate, if Hornblow did not win this time, he would at the next election. The old Ringwood domination in Whipham was gone henceforth for ever.

When the day of election arrived, you may be sure we came over from Periwinkle Bay to see the battle. By this time Philip had grown so enthusiastic in Hornblow's cause—(Philip, by the way, never would allow the possibility of a defeat)—that he had his children decked in the Hornblow ribbons, and drove from the Bay wearing a cockade as large as a pancake. He, I, and Ridley the painter, went together in a dog-cart. We were hopeful, though we knew the enemy was strong; and cheerful, though, ere we had driven five miles, the rain began to fall.

Philip was very anxious about a certain great roll of paper which we carried with us. When I asked him what it contained, he said it was a gun; which was absurd. Ridley smiled in his silent way. When the rain came, Philip cast a cloak over his artillery, and sheltered his powder. We little guessed at the time what strange game his shot would bring down.

When we reached Whipham, the polling had continued for some hours. The confounded black miscreant, as Philip called his cousin's husband, was at the head of the poll, and with every hour his majority increased. The free and independent electors did not seem to be in the least influenced by Philip's articles in the county paper, or by the placards which our side had pasted over the little town, and in which freemen were called upon to do their duty, to support a fine old English gentleman, to submit to no Castle nominee, and so forth. The pressure of the Ring-wood steward and bailiffs was too strong. However much they disliked the black man, tradesman after tradesman, and tenant after tenant, came up to vote for him. Our drums and trumpets at the 'Ram' blew loud defiance to the brass band at the 'Ringwood Arms'. From our balcony, I flatter myself, we made much finer speeches than the Ringwood people could deliver. Hornblow was a popular man in the county. When he came forward to speak, the market-place echoed with applause. The farmers and small tradesmen touched their hats to him kindly, but slunk off sadly to the polling-booth, and voted according to order. A fine, healthy, handsome, red-cheeked squire, our champion's personal appearance enlisted all the ladies in his favour.

'If the two men,' bawled Philip, from the Ram window, 'could decide the contest with their coats off before the market-house yonder, which do you think would win —the fair man or the darkey?' (Loud cries of 'Hornblow for iver!' or 'Mr. Philip we'll have *yew.'*) 'But you see, my friends, Mr. Woolcomb does not like a *fair* fight. Why doesn't he show at the "Ringwood Arms" and speak? I don't believe he can speak—not English. Are you men? Are you Englishmen? Are you white slaves to be sold to that fellow?' (Immense uproar. Mr. Finch, the Ringwood agent, in vain tries to get a hearing from the balcony of the 'Ringwood Arms'.) 'Why does not Sir John Ringwood—my Lord Ringwood now—come down amongst his tenantry, and back the man he has sent down? I suppose he is ashamed to look his tenants in the face. I should be, if I ordered them to do such a degrading job. You know, gentlemen, that I am a Ringwood myself. My grandfather lies buried—no, not buried—in yonder church. His tomb is there. His body lies on the glorious field of Busaco!' ('Hurray!') 'I am a Ringwood.' (Cries of 'Hoo—down. No Ringwoods year. We wunt have un!')

'And before George, if I had a vote, I would give it for the gallant, the good, the admirable, the excellent Hornblow. Some one holds up the state of the poll, and Woolcomb is ahead! I can only say, electors of Whipham, *the more shame for you?'* 'Hooray! Bravo!' The boys, the people, the shouting, are all on our side. The voting, I regret to say, steadily continues in favour of the enemy.

As Philip was making his speech, an immense banging of drums and blowing of trumpets arose from the balcony of the 'Ringwood Arms,' and a something resembling the song of triumph, called 'See the Conquering Hero comes,' was performed by the opposition orchestra. The lodge-gates of the park were now decorated with the Ringwood and Woolcomb flags. They were flung open, and a dark green chariot with four grey horses issued from the park. On the chariot was an earl's coronet, and the people looked rather scared as it came towards us, and said: 'Do'ee look, now, 'tis my Lard's own postchaise!' On former days Mr. Woolcomb, and his wife as his aide-de-camp, had driven through the town in an open barouche; but, to-day being rainy, preferred the shelter of the old chariot, and we saw, presently, within, Mr. Bradgate, the London agent, and by his side the darkling figure of Mr. Woolcomb. He had passed many agonising hours, we were told subsequently, in attempting to learn a speech. He cried over it. He never could get it by heart. He swore like a frantic child at his wife who endeavoured to teach him his lesson.

'Now's the time, Mr. Briggs!' Philip said to Mr. B., our lawyer's clerk, and the intelligent Briggs sprang downstairs to obey his orders. Clear the road there! make way! was heard from the crowd below us. The gates of our inn courtyard, which had been closed, were suddenly flung open, and, amidst the roar of the multitude,

there issued out a cart drawn by two donkeys, and driven by a negro, beasts and
man all wearing Woolcomb's colours. In the cart was fixed a placard, on which a
most undeniable likeness of Mr. Woolcomb was designed: who was made to say,
'VOTE FOR ME! AM I NOT A MAN AND A BRUDDER?' This cart trotted out of the yard of
the Ram, and, with a cortège of shouting boys, advanced into the market-place,
which Mr. Woolcomb's carriage was then crossing.

Before the market-house stands the statue of the late Earl, whereof mention has
been made. In his peer's robes, a hand extended, he points towards his park gates.
An inscription, not more mendacious than many other epigraphs, records his rank,
age, virtues, and the esteem in which the people of Whipham held him. The
mulatto who drove the team of donkeys was an itinerant tradesman who brought
fish from the bay to the little town: a jolly wag, a fellow of indifferent character, a
frequenter of all the alehouses in the neighbourhood, and rather celebrated for his
skill as a bruiser. He and his steeds streamed with Woolcomb ribbons. With
ironical shouts of 'Woolcomb for ever!' Yellow Jack urged his cart towards the
chariot with the white horses. He took off his hat with mock respect to the
candidate sitting within the green chariot. From the balcony of the Ram we could
see the two vehicles approaching each other; and the Yellow Jack waving his
ribboned hat, kicking his bandy legs here and there, and urging on his donkeys.
What with the roar of the people, and the banging and trumpeting of the rival
bands, we could hear but little: but I saw Woolcomb thrust his yellow head out of
his chaise window—he pointed towards that impudent donkey-cart, and urged,
seemingly, his postillions to ride it down. Plying their whips, the postboys galloped
towards Yellow Jack and his vehicle, a yelling crowd scattering from before the
horses, and rallying behind them, to utter execrations at Woolcomb. His horses
were frightened, no doubt; for just as Yellow Jack wheeled nimbly round one side
of the Ringwood statue, Woolcomb's horses were all huddled together and
plunging in confusion beside it, the fore-wheel came in abrupt collision with the
stonework of the statue railing: and then we saw the vehicle turn over altogether,
one of the wheelers down with its rider, and the leaders kicking, plunging, lashing
out right and left, wild and maddened with fear. Mr. Philip's countenance, I am
bound to say, wore a most guilty and queer expression. This accident, this
collision, this injury, perhaps death of Woolcomb and his lawyer, arose out of our
fine joke about the Man and the Brother.

We dashed down the stairs from the 'Ram'—Hornblow, Philip, and half-a-dozen
more—and made a way through the crowd towards the carriage, with its prostrate
occupants. The mob made way civilly for the popular candidate—the losing
candidate. When we reached the chaise, the traces had been cut; the horses were
free; the fallen postillion was up and rubbing his leg; and, as soon as the wheelers
were taken out of the chaise, Woolcomb emerged from it. He had said from within
(accompanying his speech with many oaths, which need not be repeated, and
showing a just sense of his danger), 'Cut the traces, hang you! And take the horses
: I can wait until they 're gone. I'm sittin' on my lawyer; I ain't going to have

my head kicked off by those wheelers.' And just as we reached the fallen postchaise he emerged from it, laughing and saying, 'Lie still, you old beggar!' to Mr. Bradgate, who was writhing underneath him. His issue from the carriage was received with shouts of laughter, which increased prodigiously when Yellow Jack, nimbly clambering up the statue railings, thrust the outstretched arm of the statue through the picture of the Man and the Brother, and left that cartoon flapping in the air over Woolcomb's head.

Then a shout arose, the like of which has seldom been heard in that quiet little town. Then Woolcomb, who had been quite good-humoured as he issued out of the broken postchaise, began to shriek, curse, and revile more shrilly than before; and was heard, in the midst of his oaths, and wrath, to say, 'He would give any man a shillin' who would bring him down that confounded thing!' Then scared, bruised, contused, confused, poor Mr. Bradgate came out of the carriage, his employer taking not the least notice of him.

Hornblow hoped Woolcomb was not hurt, on which the little gentleman turned round and said, 'Hurt? No: who are you? Is no fellah goin' to bring me down that confounded thing? I'll give a shillin', I say, to the fellah who does!'

'A shilling is offered for that picture!' shouts Philip with a red face, and wild with excitement. 'Who will take a whole shilling for that beauty?*'*

On which Woolcomb began to scream, curse, and revile more bitterly than before. 'You here? Hang you, why are you here? Don't come bullyin' me. Take that fellah away, some of you fellahs. Bradgate, come to my committee-room. I won't stay here, I say. Let's have the beast of a carriage, and—Well, what's up now?'

While he was talking, shrieking, and swearing, half-a-dozen shoulders in the crowd had raised the carriage up on its three wheels. The panel which had fallen towards the ground had split against a stone, and a great gap was seen in the side. A lad was about to thrust his hand into the orifice, when Woolcomb turned upon him.

'Hands off, you little beggar!' he cried, 'no priggin'! Drive away some of those fellahs, you postboys! Don't stand rubbin' your knee there, you great fool. What's this?' and he thrusts his own hand into the place where the boy had just been marauding.

In the old travelling carriages there used to be a well or sword-case, in which travellers used to put swords and pistols in days when such weapons of defence were needful on the road. Out of this sword-case of Lord Ringwood's old post-chariot, Woolcomb did not draw a sword, but a foolscap paper folded and tied with a red tape. And he began to read the superscription—'Will of the Right Honourable John, Earl of Ringwood. Bradgate, Smith and Burrows.'

'God bless my soul! It's the will he had back from my office, and which I thought he had destroyed. My dear fellow, I congratulate you with all my heart!' And herewith Mr. Bradgate the lawyer began to shake Philip's hand with much warmth.

'Allow me to look at that paper. Yes, this is my handwriting. Let us come into the "Ringwood Arms"—the "Ram"—anywhere, and read it to you!'

...Here we looked up to the balcony of the 'Ringwood Arms,' and beheld a great placard announcing the state of the poll at one o'clock:—

Woolcomb	216
Hornblow	92

'We are beaten,' said Mr. Hornblow, very good-naturedly. 'We may take our flag down. Mr. Woolcomb, I congratulate you.'

'I knew we should do it,' said Mr. Woolcomb, putting out a little yellow-kidded hand. 'Had all the votes beforehand—knew we should do the trick, I say. Hi! you—What-do-you-call-'im—Bradgate! What is it about, that will? It does not do any good to *that* beggar, does it?' and with laughter and shouts, and cries of 'Woolcomb for ever!' and 'Give us something to drink, your honour,' the successful candidate marched into his hotel.

And was the tawny Woolcomb the fairy who was to rescue Philip from grief, debt, and poverty? Yes. And the old post-chaise of the late Lord Ringwood was the fairy chariot. You have read in a past chapter how the old Lord, being transported with anger against Philip, desired his lawyer to bring back a will in which he had left a handsome legacy to the young man, as his mother's son. My Lord had intended to make a provision for Mrs. Firmin, when she was his dutiful niece, and yet under his roof. When she eloped with Mr. Firmin, Lord Ring-wood vowed he would give his niece nothing. But he was pleased with the independent and forgiving spirit exhibited by her son; and, being a person of much grim humour, I dare say chuckled inwardly at thinking how furious the Twysdens would be when they found Philip was the old Lord's favourite. Then Mr. Philip chose to be insubordinate, and to excite the wrath of his great-uncle, who desired to have his will back again. He put the document into his carriage, in the secret box, as he drove away on that last journey, in the midst of which death seized him. Had he survived, would he have made another will, leaving out all mention of Philip? Who shall say? My Lord made and cancelled many wills. This certainly, duly drawn and witnessed, was the last he ever signed; and by it Philip is put in possession of a sum of money which is sufficient to ensure a provision for those whom he loves. Kind readers, I know not whether the fairies be rife now, or banished from this workaday earth, but Philip's biographer wishes you some of those blessings which never forsook Philip in his trials: a dear wife and children to love you, a true friend or two to stand by you, and in health or sickness a clear conscience and a kindly heart. If you fall upon the way, may succour reach you. And may you, in your turn, have help and pity in store for the unfortunate whom you overtake on life's journey.

Would you care to know what happened to the other personages of our narrative? Old Twysden is still babbling and bragging at clubs, and though aged is not the least venerable. He has quarrelled with his son for not calling Woolcomb out, when that unhappy difference arose between the Black Prince and his wife. He says his family has been treated with cruel injustice by the late Lord Ringwood, but as soon as Philip had a little fortune left him he instantly was reconciled to his wife's nephew. There are other friends of Firmin's who were kind enough to him in his evil days, but cannot pardon his prosperity. Being in that benevolent mood which must accompany any leave-taking, we will not name these ill-wishers of Philip, but wish that all readers of his story may have like reason to make some of their acquaintances angry.

Our dear Little Sister would never live with Philip and his Charlotte, though the latter *especially* and with all her heart besought Mrs. Brandon to come to them. That pure and useful and modest life ended a few years since. She died of a fever caught from one of her patients. She would not allow Philip or Charlotte to come near her. She said she was justly punished for being so proud as to refuse to live with them. All her little store she left to Philip. He has now in his desk the five guineas which she gave him at his marriage; and J. J. has made a little picture of her, with her sad smile and her sweet face, which hangs in Philip's drawing-room, where father, mother, and children talk of the Little Sister as though she were among them still.

She was dreadfully agitated when the news came from New York of Dr. Firmin's second marriage. 'His second? His third!' she said. 'The villain, the villain!' That strange delusion which we have described as sometimes possessing her increased in intensity after this news. More than ever, she believed that Philip was her own child. She came wildly to him, and cried that his father had forsaken them. It was only when she was excited that she gave utterance to this opinion. Dr. Goodenough says that, though generally silent about it, it never left her.

Upon his marriage Dr. Firmin wrote one of his long letters to his son, announcing the event. He described the wealth of the lady (a widow from Norfolk, in Virginia) to whom he was about to be united. He would pay back, ay, with interest, every pound, every dollar, every cent he owed his son. Was the lady wealthy? We had only the poor Doctor's word.

Three months after his marriage he died of yellow fever, on his wife's estate. It was then the Little Sister came to see us in widow's mourning, very wild and flushed. She bade our servant say, 'Mrs. Firmin was at the door'; to the astonishment of the man, who knew her. She had even caused a mourning-card to be printed. Ah, there is rest now for that little fevered brain, and peace, let us pray, for that fond faithful heart.

The mothers in Philip's household and mine have already made a match between our children. We had a great gathering the other day at Roehampton, at the house of our friend, Mr. Clive Newcome (whose tall boy, my wife says, was very attentive to our Helen), and, having been educated at the same school, we sat ever so long at dessert, telling old stories, whilst the children danced to piano music on the lawn. Dance on the lawn, young folks, whilst the elders talk in the shade I What? The night is falling: we have talked enough over our wine; and it is time to go home? Good-night. Good-night, friends, old and young! The night will fall: the stories must end: and the best friends must part.

i. I am sorry to say that in later days, after Mrs. Major MacWhirter's decease, it was found that she had promised these treasures *in writing* to several members of her husband's family, and that much heart-burning arose in consequence. But our story has nothing to do with these painful disputes.

ii. Copied, by permission of P. Firmin, Esq., from the Genealogical Tree in his possession.

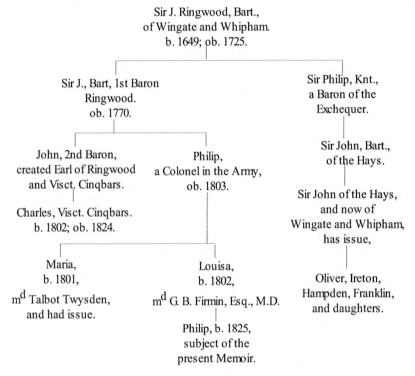

Sir J. Ringwood, Bart.,
of Wingate and Whipham.
b. 1649; ob. 1725.

Sir J., Bart, 1st Baron
Ringwood.
ob. 1770.

Sir Philip, Knt.,
a Baron of the
Exchequer.

John, 2nd Baron,
created Earl of Ringwood
and Visct. Cinqbars.

Philip,
a Colonel in the Army,
ob. 1803.

Sir John, Bart.,
of the Hays.

Charles, Visct. Cinqbars.
b. 1802; ob. 1824.

Sir John of the Hays,
and now of
Wingate and Whipham,
has issue,

Maria,
b. 1801,

m^d Talbot Twysden,
and had issue.

Louisa,
b. 1802,

m^d G. B. Firmin, Esq., M.D.

Philip, b. 1825,
subject of the
present Memoir.

Oliver, Ireton,
Hampden, Franklin,
and daughters.